THE QUEEN
WILL BETRAY YOU

THE
QUEEN
WILL BETRAY
YOU

SARAH HENNING

**TOR
TEEN**

A TOM DOHERTY ASSOCIATES BOOK
NEW YORK

THE QUEEN WILL BETRAY YOU

A Tor Teen Book
Published by Tom Doherty Associates
120 Broadway
New York, NY 10271

www.tor-forge.com

Tor® is a registered trademark of Macmillan Publishing Group, LLC.

The Library of Congress Cataloging-in-Publication Data
is available upon request.

ISBN 978-1-250-23746-0 (hardcover)
ISBN 978-1-250-23745-3 (ebook)

Our books may be purchased in bulk for promotional, educational, or
business use. Please contact your local bookseller or the Macmillan Corporate
and Premium Sales Department at 1-800-221-7945, extension 5442,
or by email at MacmillanSpecialMarkets@macmillan.com.

First Edition: July 2021

Printed in the United States of America

0 9 8 7 6 5 4 3 2 1

To my family—who walked every step of this journey with me during the year we couldn't go anywhere.

THE CONTINENT OF THE SAND AND SKY

KINGDOM OF ARDENIA

Prime Rulers: King Sendoa, the Warrior King (deceased); Queen Geneva (missing); Princess Amarande; General Koldo, regent

Sigil: Tiger

Location: Eastern coast, in mountains sandwiched between Pyrenee, to the north, and Basilica to the south.

Castle Seat: The Itspi

Prime Export: Diamonds

Attributes: The untimely death of the self-styled Warrior King Sendoa, coupled with the unwed status of the young Princess Amarande, has placed Ardenia under the regency of General Koldo and made it a tempting, jewel-filled prize for its greedy neighbors.

KINGDOM OF PYRENEE

Prime Rulers: King Louis-David (deceased); Dowager Queen Inés, regent; Crown Prince Renard (deceased); Prince Taillefer

Sigil: Mountain Lion

Location: Mountainous northeastern coast of the continent, sharing borders with both Ardenia and the Torrent. The kingdom abuts a deep strait called The Divide. The Kingdom of Eritri is on the other side of the waterway.

Castle Seat: The Bellringe, atop King's Crest

Prime Export: Gold

Attributes: Wealthy and insular, Pyrenee rules the northern tip of the continent and has a natural alliance with Ardenia as its mountainous neighbor, but the two have a frosty relationship.

KINGDOM OF BASILICA

Prime Rulers: King Domingu; Queen Nania (fifth wife); dozens of descendants: children, grandchildren, great-grandchildren

Sigil: Bear

Location: Southeastern coast; mountainous border with Ardenia and the Torrent to the north; Myrcell borders the west side; the Kingdom of Indu is across the sea to the south.

Castle Seat: The Aragonesti

Prime Export: Steel

Attributes: Rich in iron ore smelted into much coveted weapons-grade steel, Basilica enjoys a robust exports business despite King Domingu's reputation as greedy, scheming, and ambitious. The royal family tree is a sprawling one, with Domingu's descendants seeded within every Sand and Sky kingdom, making his bloodline nearly as prevalent as his famed weaponry.

KINGDOM OF MYRCELL

Prime Rulers: King Akil; Queen Sumira

Sigil: Shark

Location: Southwestern coast; mountainous border with the Torrent to the north; Basilica borders to the east; the Kingdom of Indu is across the sea to the south.

Castle Seat: Miragua

Prime Export: Pearls

Attributes: This beachfront kingdom is closely aligned with its southern kingdom neighbor, Basilica. Rich in both hemlock and pearls, it is often targeted by pirates seeking both poison and riches, who hope to take advantage of its young, inexperienced, and newly married king, Akil.

THE TORRENT / THE FALLEN KINGDOM OF TORRENCE

Prime Rulers: The Warlord; the lost crown prince, known as the Otsakumea (wolf cub)

Sigil: Leaping Flames of the Fire Pit (Warlord); Black Wolf (the overthrown Otxoa ruling family)

Location: Central portion of the continent; Basilica and Myrcell to the south; Ardenia to the east; Pyrenee to the north.

Castle Seat: Otxazulo (Destroyed)

Prime Export: None

Attributes: Under the dictatorial rule of the masked Warlord. A pro-Otxoa resistance operates underground, awaiting the return of the lost Otsakumea.

THE QUEEN
WILL BETRAY YOU

PROLOGUE

In the fevered hour after he narrowly escaped with his life, the young prince paused only to snatch up parchment and a quill.

In less than a moment, he'd written two letters.

One to a friend.

One to someone he would not call so.

Both held the same message, written in a flat, left-handed scrawl.

The tiger has fled, the mountain lion is dead, the wolf has found his head.

No signature was needed for one, nor advised for the other.

Satisfied and running out of time, he sealed the letters and sent them on their way. Then, without so much as a glance over his shoulder, he disappeared into the night.

In the captain's quarters of the pirate ship *Gatzal*, the princess watched her true love open his eyes.

From where she'd lain for the last several hours—on the wood-plank floor, her hand nestled in his—she slipped onto the edge of the bed where he slept. She was careful not to jostle him, as his chest was still raw from having been cleaved nearly in two by a prince's mad hand, and then carefully mended with a thread, needle, and stinging sagardoa.

As the boy's golden eyes focused on her face, he smiled, dimples winking. "We made it, Ama."

She kissed him then, softly, mindful of his wounds. But her love was stronger than he seemed and put gentle fingers in her auburn hair, pulling her closer, deeper. When they parted, his fingers caressed the side of her face. "Of course we did," she answered. "A wise pirate once told me love is the most powerful force on earth."

"It is indeed powerful, as it is the only reason I am still here, breathing your air. I do hope our love will readily accept the blood I've shed and call it settled, because I doubt I can take much more."

Pure joy bloomed across her face then, delight in her sea-stained eyes. "Oh, Luca, I have so much to tell you about your blood."

That was not at all what he'd expected her to say. "My . . . blood?"

She told him everything then. About what the wolfish tattoo across his heart really meant—that he was the Otsakumea, the last of the Otxoa, ruling family of the Kingdom of Torrence. About the underground movement within the Torrent to restore the kingdom, and that the black wolf she'd encountered on the plateau was a harbinger of the resistance. She told him her father had known he had a hidden prince in his care. And that the man they'd killed at the Hand knew Luca's true identity and had died trying to capture him.

"Luca, this is your birthright and the people want you to lead. They're willing to fight a ruthless tyrant to get their land back; all they need is you."

"But . . . are we sure this is true? Stableboys aren't the chosen ones."

"That tattoo is proof."

"The tattoo is simply ink."

"Not to the people who have been waiting for it." Her eyes were full and pleading, hoping that he would see. Believe. She dropped another kiss on his lips, then up the line of his jaw. Whispered in his ear. "I know this is so much. Too much. But it is your chance. . . . And our chance to be together."

To the south, the king who long ago forged his legacy in his only brother's blood sat on his balcony in the salmon-bright dawn, a contract in hand, warm salt air pushing the remains of his snow-white hair around his face.

The royal seal was peeling off the parchment, slit straight through with the dagger he preferred for a letter opener. Crumbs of wax littered his nightshirt as he read through the amended offer one last time.

The changes were not of consequence—silly, cosmetic things that did not matter. Worth much more was the fact that she either didn't or couldn't see what was actually of importance. Clearly the queen had kept her more seasoned advisors in the dark about the terms.

A smile sliding across the craggy landscape of his face, the king plucked a quill from his inkpot and, in a flourish of just a few letters, changed the entire shape of the continent. As the ink dried, the king watched the waves crash across rocks as sharp as his worst edges.

"My king, you're up early," came a small voice from within his chambers. In a moment, his fifth wife stepped into the dawn light, so young that not a line showed when she squinted from the bedroom shadows into the blinding promise of a summer day.

The king didn't roll or fold or otherwise obscure the content of the parchment. This wife wasn't the type to pry in his official business. It was a quality that until that very moment had served her well. "Let's take a walk on the beach, Nania. Just the two of us. Would you like that?"

The girl lit up like the brilliant flash of a falling star. "Oh yes, my king. I shall dress at once."

CHAPTER 1

HIGH in the mountains of Ardenia, a princess and her love stood at a crossroads.

It was time to say good-bye.

Tears hung in the corners of Princess Amarande's eyes as she summoned the strength it would take to part. Standing before her, Luca's jaw worked as she drew a shaky breath. When the words didn't come, unable to rise past her heart, she took one last look at him.

Luca stood there, clean, tall, broad shouldered, but dressed almost as if in mourning—a boy in black.

Her boy in black.

Amarande, meanwhile, was a bedraggled confection in the bloodstained tatters of her wedding dress. The lifeblood of Prince Renard of Pyrenee never had rinsed clean, the vestige of her murderous decision running the length of the entire bodice in a rusted chocolate brown. Still, Amarande wore the gown—it was evidence of the wedding she'd been forced into and then ended by taking Renard's life. If she had truly brought war to Ardenia's doorstep via regicide, she needed proof of what had actually happened.

"Come with me, Princess."

Luca pressed the back of her hand to his lips. His eyes, golden and as fierce as the summer sun above, never left her face.

Oh, and she wanted to go with him. To the Torrent, this time of his own volition—not tied to the back of a horse, blackmail to force her hand into a marriage with Renard that would've made that cruel boy king of Pyrenee. She had him back. Alive, hers, their love out in the open under the wide sky. The last thing she wanted to do was to leave him.

But to be together forever, they both knew they must part.

There was no other way. He would go west to the Torrent—the land that should by all rights be his. She would go north to the Itspi, the Ardenian castle they called home.

That was how it must be.

They'd been over it for the last few days in the close quarters of the pirate ship *Gatzal*. Running through every scenario as they charted a course from the Port of Pyrenee, through the Divide and into the East Sea, sweeping around the lip of the continent of the Sand and Sky to the Port of Ardenia.

Every facet of possibility, probability, exposed to the light and considered as they ate their fill of saltwater fish, cleaned their wounds, and lay on the deck, letting the same sun that had drained them in the Torrent recharge their spent muscles and creaking bones.

No matter how they approached it, no matter how many questions they raised, no matter how many reactions they predicted from each of the players—Ardenia, Pyrenee, Basilica, Myrcell, the Torrent— this plan always emerged the strongest.

Amarande first to Ardenia, tasked with stabilizing the throne after the death of her father and shoring up its defenses from Pyrenee's retaliation for the murder of Prince Renard. Next, she'd join Luca and the pro-Otxoa resistance in the Torrent, overthrow the Warlord, and restore peace and sovereignty to the Kingdom of Torrence. And then, finally, the Princess of Ardenia and the Otsakumea Luca, the rightful heir of Torrence, would stare down the remainder of the Sand and Sky, hand in hand.

Never to be apart again.

Her eyes met his—her best friend, her love, her future. Amarande's father, King Sendoa, whose murder had ignited all of this, always had the words for a moment such as this one—just like he always had a plan. *Survive the battle, see the war.*

The princess drew a breath, this time not so shaky. "I will come *to* you."

Luca smiled, dimples flashing. "Of that, I have no doubt."

She closed the sliver of space between them. Mindful not to apply pressure to his bandaged chest, she drew her arms around Luca's neck. His lips met hers halfway. Amarande's eyes closed as she let the rest of her senses record this moment.

The slip of his hands down the small of her back.

The beat of his heart, sure and steady to her ear.

The solid warmth of him bolstered by the spicy scent of the clove oil applied twice daily to the horror slashed across his chest. The damage Prince Taillefer created with tinctures and madness had been sewn up on the ship, but healing had only just begun.

For a moment, Amarande was back in the foyer of Pyrenee's glittering Bellringe castle, Renard staring daggers at her as she whispered a very similar good-bye. A different crossroads, that—Luca to confinement under the watch of Taillefer, Amarande to dress for a marriage to Renard she did not want.

What had come next had not gone well.

Torture. Apparent death. Revenge in the form of murder and actual, irrevocable death.

But they'd survived. They were still standing. So was their love.

And so Amarande whispered nearly the same words she'd said to Luca in that foyer, a plan crafted for success shaping their separation rather than one forged around surrender.

"I love you. Our time apart will not change that."

"I love you, too, Ama. Always, Princess."

With that, Amarande kissed Luca one last time—hard. As hard as she wished she had before he was kidnapped. As hard as she did when it was clear they'd escaped Pyrenee alive. As hard as she could—this kiss would have to hold her for days, if not weeks, or months.

"You can turn around now," she told the crew, when the kiss was finally done. Amarande met each of them with a parting nod. Ula, a pirate with a gaze as sharp as her Torrentian sword; Urtzi, the big Myrcellian brawler with a soft spot for his fellow pirate; Osana, the Basilican orphan Amarande had accidentally acquired in her escape from the Warlord—and then entrusted with her father's sword, Egia, twin to the one on her back, Maite. "Keep him safe."

At the order, Ula's gold eyes flashed. "With my life, Princess." She nodded to her companions. "And theirs, too."

Osana and Urtzi didn't object. Amarande imagined General Koldo, the current regent of Ardenia and leader of the Ardenian army—would relish immediate loyalty so unwavering. That was something that couldn't be trained into a person.

Amarande mounted her horse—one stolen from Pyrenee in their escape. She pointed the frost-coated gelding toward the Itspi. The sun was falling toward the jagged mountain horizon, but she'd make it to the castle well before full darkness. The sooner she got there, the sooner she could return to Luca's side.

Luca mounted his similarly pilfered steed and drew up alongside her—opposing directions, but still close enough to touch. Amarande's eyes met his—blue-green on his gold—and her heart lurched, desperate to go with him. Luca seemed to sense this. "As soon as we connect with the resistance, Ama, we will send word to the Itspi."

It was a promise as much as it was a plan.

Amarande reached out and touched his face—one she knew as well as her own—his skin warm and true under her fingers. "I shall see you soon, my love."

CHAPTER 2

ONCE again, Luca galloped toward the Torrent with three companions. But this time, everything was different.

First, he was conscious.

Second, he was willing—untied and on his own horse.

Third, rather than acting as bait, he was acting as the leader.

Technically, Ula and Osana led the way as they wound through a particularly steep pass through the summer-dry mountains of Ardenia, but they were less than a mile from where they said good-bye to Amarande before Luca was asked to provide direction.

"What is the plan, Luca?" shouted Urtzi from behind, where his broad shoulders protected the rear of their single-track procession.

This was not a question Luca had ever been asked.

It was true, he maintained the Itspi's royal stable, but he was nothing more than a wheel on the cart—he was not the driver. Someone who coordinated with others within the castle, most notably old Zuzen, who, beyond being the de facto educator of the palace's children, oversaw the much larger military stable on the grounds. No one, not even Amarande, had ever seriously looked to Luca for a strategy.

Luca hesitated. It wasn't meant to be a test—Urtzi wasn't the type to lay a trap. He was straightforward, steadfast, and stubbornly loyal when it came to taking orders. As usual, Urtzi was looking for guidance.

Looking to him—the Otsakumea, the wolf cub, the heir to the throne of the fallen Kingdom of Torrence. The proof was in the wolf tattoo above his heart, a symbol in ink that he was the last of the Otxoa, ruling family for a thousand years of what was now the Torrent. He could hardly believe it, and yet they'd planned it all out on the ship—a way for him to gain both his birthright and Amarande's hand by joining a pro-Otxoa resistance that had been simmering since the Warlord's Eradication of the Wolf. If all went well, soon it wouldn't be just a few friends who looked to him for guidance; it might be an entire kingdom.

Luca wet his lips, gathered his thoughts, and delegated power with his first decision as an actual leader. "The plan is to follow Ula's direction and connect with the resistance."

As he answered, Luca turned on his horse to better see the boy behind him, his eyes automatically shooting over Urtzi's shoulder for any sign of Amarande's white horse. They were too far, though, and all Luca saw was dusky sky and the silhouettes of the mountains that somewhere beyond view cradled the Itspi in its spiraling red turrets and cloud of juniper trees.

"Well, Ula?" Urtzi called when she didn't automatically respond. The big Myrcellian had made it no secret he preferred to be a follower, and he had always followed Ula, his longtime partner in the pirate life. They hadn't once mentioned their former crew leader Dunixi, whom they'd followed right up until the point they abandoned him, leaving him unconscious on the floor of the Bellringe's royal stable. "Where is the resistance?"

It was a valid question—from Ula's description, the pro-Otxoa resistance had formed in the days after the Warlord killed the royal family and burned their castle, the Otxazulo, to ash. But not once during his schoolroom lessons at the Itspi had Luca ever learned of the resistance's existence, or where those loyal to his family hid. For all he knew, they might not even be in the Torrent proper, but somewhere else, safer and away from the Warlord's deadly fire pits, which were lit nightly with the bodies of dissenters used as kindling.

"Good question. One we need to find the answer to."

"How—"

"Don't be so impatient, Urtzi; I was just going to tell you. We begin at a market."

A laugh played on Osana's lips as she caught Ula's eyes over her shoulder. "Does the resistance maintain a stall?"

Osana was new to the group, but Amarande trusted her—despite the fact that the Basilican orphan had switched sides more than once— and given the princess's natural propensity to wariness, her seal of approval was enough for the rest of them.

"Yes, they're openly selling their wares of anti-Warlord policy alongside freshly baked bread and strawberry jam," Ula replied, digging a hunk of stale bread out of her bag. She playfully lobbed it at Osana, who plucked it out of the air right before it would've dinged her between the eyes. The group laughed as Osana gnawed off a hunk and Ula turned to Luca. "Where's the nearest one?"

"Dare I ask why any market would do?" Luca was unsure—but if the ink on his chest had proved anything to him, it was that items of great consequence frequently hid in plain sight.

"A network is a series of points, Luca."

"The resistance has *that* many points?"

"They've had seventeen years of growth." Ula smirked. "These points are stars in a constellation if you know where to look."

"And if we breach any point, we have what we need to be directed to the leader?" Luca asked, before clarifying, "I assume there is a leader."

"Of course there is."

"Not to be contrary, but how do you know all this, Ula?" Urtzi asked. "I've been with you seven years, and have never once witnessed you take a secret meeting with some Torrentian rebel."

"You are forgetting the definition of *secret*, you big oaf. It is a covert operation. You aren't supposed to know." She said it kindly, but Urtzi looked to be stricken down to his marrow. "Luca, the market?"

He jerked his chin up the trail. "We'll split southeast at the next fork in the path. From there it'll be another half hour at this pace."

The market in question was the one that served the Itspi, down in the high ribbon of land that called itself a valley. It was a place Luca went at least weekly, filling the castle's tab with items for his horses—lavender oil, oats, and ointments.

When it came into view, Ula called the group to a halt at a shaded turnoff. Below, the market's colorful tents swayed, cook fires calling to the dusk. On a summer night, it would be all overfilled cups and blackened hog, song and gossip on everyone's lips. Even at this distance, its energy was tangible, licking the air with a crackle and whisper.

Ula dismounted, handed her reins to Osana, and dug through her saddlebags. "I will obtain the information." When the other pirate moved to do the same, she shook her head. "*Alone*, Urtzi."

The big Myrcellian stared daggers that would kill any other person but didn't even touch her. Ula held her stance and her gaze as he grumbled, "What if this covert person doesn't like you? Doesn't trust you?"

"They will trust me."

Urtzi ran a hand through his dark hair. The curls immediately fell right back into place. "You don't want me to come because I'm not of Torrent."

"Untrue." Ula checked her pouch again, then further dismissed his concern by changing the subject. "Do you have more coin?"

"No," Urtzi answered. "While you and Amarande were spending diamonds, Osana and I were using Renard's gold to buy that food you enjoyed so much the past few days." And the food was good—fish fried in summer herbs, and all the pickled vegetables a man could want. "And why would you have to pay the resistance?"

"I don't. But I will likely have to buy supplies as a show of good faith—they don't let just anyone enter their network for free."

Osana reached into her pocket. "Will these help? With the cost?" When her palm opened, inside were five rings, thick and gold, with a well-set stone in each.

Ula gasped. "You stole them from Dunixi?"

Osana shrugged as if she'd simply nicked loaves of bread instead of a person's most prized possessions. "When I left my post to fetch horses from the stable, I found him out cold. I thought he had bigger things to worry about."

Urtzi huffed. "His biggest problem was me."

"It was, Urtzi; it was." He was, indeed, the reason their former pirate leader had been abandoned on the floor of the Bellringe stable to begin with, having punched Dunixi straight in the temple when he forced Urtzi to decide between following him or following Ula. Now, Ula grinned at him as she dropped the rings into her pouch and cinched the cord. The market bell chimed then—seven times. "I should be back in an hour. Maybe two."

"At least take a horse," Urtzi offered. "You'll get back sooner."

"The saddle and sire are clearly of Pyrenee—King's Crest knows what's missing from its stable. It's dangerous enough that they're all we have anyway." Osana glanced away at this—her error. "No."

Urtzi sighed. "Will you ever agree with something I say?"

"I just did. About you owning our former leader. I'll be back to disagree with you more as soon as I can."

Ula made to move around him but Urtzi secured his stance, arms braced across his tree trunk of a chest. "We always do everything together. How will I know you will be fine?"

Luca nodded. "Yes, how will *we* know?"

Rather than answer his question verbally, Ula yanked down the neck of her tunic, revealing a tattoo—the looping pads of a paw print. It was much smaller than Luca's wolf but in the same general location over her heart—five distinct pieces, in an identical satiny ink and abstract style of angles creating an organic object.

"Is that what I think it is?" Osana leaned so far over the shoulders of her horse it was a wonder she could stay in her saddle.

Ula drew in a deep breath. "The sign of someone beholden to the Otxoa. There are not many of us left. Not everyone in the resistance has a tattoo like this, but as a general key to open doors, it is a good one."

Luca's mouth went dry. "*Beholden?* To the Otxoa?"

Ula's golden eyes, which Luca had always thought looked so much like his own, did not flinch. "My parents served the royal family."

CHAPTER
3

⁓⧼⧽⁓

THERE was no funeral at the Bellringe. Not yet.

The people of Pyrenee did not mourn Crown Prince Renard.

The chapel bells did not ring in the prescribed song they'd last performed four years earlier after the final, pained breath of King Louis-David.

In fact, not a letter had been sent. The rulers of the Sand and Sky had not been notified. The wedding guests were quarantined within the castle. And the servants to the grounds. The gates were closed tight, and with them, the stories of what had happened that night.

All at the order of Dowager Queen Inés.

No one questioned any of it. Which was good for them, because Inés did not have a moment's patience for anyone who would endanger her very carefully laid plans.

Her son had been murdered, the assailant and her merry band of pirates were still on the run, and she must stave off war long enough to have everything fall into place.

Rather conveniently, the only person who would bother to defy her was missing and dead to her anyway.

The Dowager Queen lit the candles within her council room. That morning as she'd received her moon cycle treatments from Medikua Aritza, clouds had rolled into the mountains from way off on the Divide, full of rain and heavy air that seeped into the walls of the Bellringe and fit her mood.

As she lit the last taper, the jewel of a room flickering with light, a procession of maids arrived from the kitchens, trays filled with thick cuts of venison, parchment-thin slices of cheese, plump grapes, and crusty bread, still warm from the hearth. Ice clinked from within frosted pitchers as they plunked the heavy crystal on the runner bisecting the long, marble-topped table.

As if hearing the dinner bell, the councilors began to trickle in.

There were ten in total—the Dowager Queen did not skimp on advice. Today, though, she planned to accept none.

"Please, fill your plates," Inés said, gesturing to the food before her. "This will likely be a long meeting. Captain Nikola, once you are ready, please give an update on the whereabouts of Princess Amarande."

Word had come as expected from the group of Bellringe guards in pursuit after the disastrous wedding: The princess was nowhere to be found. The leader of Renard's guard, Captain Nikola, was seated at this very table to formally relay these matters, as well as to discuss next steps. The captain was not much older than Inés's sons—he eschewed food to speak right away, nerves clear as he got to his feet to be better heard.

Brave boy, standing within her line of fire empty-handed.

"Most likely, the princess slipped past the lines of our soldiers at the border, and made it safely back into Ardenia," he was saying. "There is a possibility she is in the Torrent, given she'd managed to escape with her stableboy and at least two of the kidnappers who escorted him across that wasteland."

With either outcome, the Dowager Queen needed to be prepared, but it frustrated her to no end that she couldn't put a finger on the location of the princess. War was a much easier possibility to stomach with a hostage from the other side.

Councilor Laurent cleared his throat—he was the oldest of the group, bald, with milky eyes and failing teeth. "The princess and her stableboy left *with* the people who kidnapped said stableboy in the first place? What are we to make of that?"

The Dowager Queen answered quickly. "Either they inspire loyalty or the kidnappers were never truly on the opposing side."

"Don't we have one of the kidnappers?" asked Councilor Menon, who was the youngest of Inés's advisors but still a good decade older than herself. "An Eritrian was found unconscious in the stable and taken into custody. I believe he has been relegated to the dungeon, along with the others who were in Prince Renard's hired party."

The Dowager Queen had given that order, yes—that anyone who had been traveling with Renard and was not a sworn member of the guard be detained. She did not realize that a kidnapper had been one of them. "Has he been interrogated?"

"Of course, Your Highness. I questioned him personally," Nikola answered. "He had no immediately useful information. He was already unconscious and therefore not in the chapel when his companions helped the princess escape."

Inés blinked at the captain. "But surely he knows where they might have gone?"

Nikola was slow to nod but did. "The kidnapper specified that he had a ship at the Port of Pyrenee but could not produce a harbor slip. Still, we followed up by sending a party to the port. The harbormaster had no record of the ship in question."

She stared at the boy. He was a good informant, but occasionally his youth was a tremendous problem. "Did the kidnapper give you the name of the ship?"

"Yes. The *Gatzal*."

Inés toyed with the cheese she had piled on her plate—for once, she had no stomach for it. "Captain Nikola, did you and your party *bother* to interview anyone beyond the harbormaster?"

There was a pause as chairs creaked, others shifting to get a look at the young captain as his posture stiffened. Nikola smelled danger—everyone did. As well they should. "No, Your Highness. We did not think it reasonable to waste time on a lie."

Inés sighed. "While I understand that, I do not believe you've done your due diligence, Captain. You questioned a single person, an official voice that is easily bought—one pouch of gold can remove a ship from the record books and put an easy lie to a harbormaster's lips. Why did you not take the time to talk with the eyes of the harbor? The scalawags, fishermen, beggars? They have the time to be curious, many know their letters, and more than one could have likely identified the ship, if not the unusual arrival of a blood-soaked girl in *my* wedding gown."

The Dowager Queen let her rebuke hang heavy in the air. Nikola did not dare address any of it verbally. Instead, he pressed his shaking fingers into the lip of the table.

"It matters not." With a wave, Inés relieved the captain from standing, and the boy sank to his seat. "What matters now is that we prepare our retaliation for the princess's actions and plan for what Ardenia may do *if* she has returned there. They will feel the victim, though it was my dear Renard whose blood was shed."

Councilor Laurent yet again cleared his throat. For the past year, it seemed he could start a conversation no other way. "Your Highness, that begs another question. What of the matter of succession? Our hands are tied with Prince Taillefer missing. Ought we search for him—use the resources we had put into finding the princess and pivot to locating the current heir?"

The Dowager Queen raised an eyebrow as sharp as the best dagger. "You misspeak, Laurent. Taillefer is *not* the heir."

There was a very long pause.

Finally, the old man began again, labored and somewhat confused. "Forgive me, Your Highness, but with Prince Renard deceased, the second son—"

The Dowager Queen bared her teeth. "Prince Renard's loss of life is directly and unequivocally the *fault* of Taillefer, who hired the kidnapper pirates in the first place. Wherever he is, we shall no longer call him prince and he shall have no claim to this throne."

Laurent's wrinkles trembled in surprise. "You . . . you would disown him, Your Highness?"

"I already have."

"Your Highness, unfortunately, there is an official protocol for a matter such as this." A woman's voice—Colette, another ancient one.

"Make it official then," Inés snapped.

Menon waded in, brave. "I am afraid we cannot do that without solid proof."

Inés's frustration grew. "The pirate has proof."

Eyes shot to Captain Nikola, who clearly did not wish to be admonished again, but had the information the table sought. "With all due respect, Your Highness, he has a splitting headache and his word cannot be trusted."

The Dowager Queen gritted her teeth. Perhaps her circle had grown too large—a smaller group meant less disagreement. Inés drew in a swift breath and looked down her nose at the full table. "May I remind all of you that the wedding was not completed and no coronation occurred; *therefore*, I am still the Dowager Queen and regent to Pyrenee. If you will not assume Taillefer disowned and relieved of his title at this very moment, you will at least recognize that I am the only monarch in this room, and therefore, it is my word that takes precedence. Do you understand?"

A few murmurs rounded the table—though the acknowledgment was not enough for the anger that seethed beneath her silks and lace.

"*Do you understand?*" she demanded, her gaze as piercing as it was direct—no one at the table could escape it.

"Yes, Your Highness," rang out in unison.

"Good. Captain, get what you need from the pirate. Council, I demand that, once I have the necessary proof per whatever statute causes you to currently defy me, we begin the process to strip Taillefer of his title."

"Yes, Your Highness."

Inés continued without producing any expression close to approval. "I do not anticipate that process will take long; therefore, Captain Nikola, I request that you round up your best men and create a plan to put your efforts into locating Taillefer. He is to be tried for treason for his part in the regicide of his brother."

Nikola did not hesitate to answer. "Yes, Your Highness."

The Dowager Queen huffed through her nostrils. "Captain, so that we are clear on your orders: Pirate first. Then a trip to the harbor, questioning not only about the princess but also about Taillefer. Then, based on your findings, a complete, multifaceted plan of attack for retrieval of Taillefer by breakfast the day after tomorrow, not a moment later."

The young soldier accepted the order and left immediately. When he was gone and the doors creaked closed, Colette drew herself up straight. "Your Highness, while I agree with you that this is the best course of action, I would be remiss if I didn't make mention that, considering how the Basilican crown changed hands fifty years ago, Taillefer could appeal to the ruling parties of the Sand and Sky that he is the rightful heir."

This was the perfect opening, almost as if Inés had written it herself. She stood, and with a flourish, produced two scrolls, held high for all to see.

"I have news regarding my leadership and strengthening Pyrenee's position within the Sand and Sky—regardless of Ardenia's plans." She distributed the scrolls to her immediate neighbors. "This is a signed contract and an identical copy. The original was delivered this morning directly from King Domingu, confirming our intent to wed."

The table gasped. One of the men spoke—typical, given the question and the general tone of disapproval in the noise preceding it. "But the king is already married."

"He has very recently become a widower for the fifth time." The Dowager Queen let that meaning hang.

"But we should negotiate. . . ." This from her master of coin. Of course.

"The negotiation has already been completed. What you see is the final contract." Chairs scraped back from the table, some advisors getting up to read over the shoulders of those who obtained the parchment first.

After the quiet settled for a few minutes and more people read the terms, the Dowager Queen spoke again. "We leave for Basilica as soon as Captain Nikola presents a plan. Our kingdoms will be joined in a few days' time. And if Ardenia protests, it shall face the rebuke of our two armies and likely Myrcell's, as well. After what Princess Amarande did to our beloved Renard, that kingdom has no leg on which to stand."

Laurent had the stones to question her, his sour expression remaining unmoved as he spoke. "Your Highness, while I do appreciate your quick response upon the matter of our rocked throne, I would like to point out that we should deal with Ardenia first—if that kingdom is threatened, it will attack, whether the princess is within the Itspi's walls or not."

"There is more than one way to make Ardenia suffer, and this wedding is my first strike," Inés answered, with a raised brow and fork. "It will put Ardenia in the position of picking a fight against two kingdoms rather than one, all while in the headless throes of regency."

Laurent did not budge. "It is a good union and will certainly make a statement to Ardenia, but I am compelled to argue that it is perhaps unwise to become betrothed to a man who killed his own brother to win the throne and has a habit of burying his wives."

Inés speared a hunk of venison, holding it impaled on her fork—literal dead meat—before answering the old man.

"With all the respect you have not given me, Laurent, you do not understand what a woman can do within the right union. And King Domingu has never had a wife like me."

CHAPTER
4

❧❧❧

WELCOME bells did not greet the princess as she approached the Itspi.

Dusk had fully taken hold, and though Amarande knew guardsmen could likely only see clearly the ghostly white flash of her horse, she was still somewhat disappointed.

Amarande dug her boot heels into the gelding's flanks.

The entrance was sealed and manned by four guards. Sconces illuminated the touches of gold on their uniforms and the twin Ardenian tigers roaring in tandem from the gate door. Garnets and diamonds twinkled from the animals' eyes—a sight foreign to the princess. The gate had never been sealed with her on the outside.

Closing the gate and arming the exterior was what one would do at war.

"Halt! Rider, announce your intentions," a guardswoman ordered.

Amarande nearly thought it was a joke—surely they recognized her at this distance. She nosed her horse closer, hoping to catch the light. The guards drew their swords.

"I said halt!" The woman's voice carried the edge of action. Her sword did not waver. She was clearly the leader of the group.

Amarande did as instructed, the horse kicking up dust with his firm stop.

"I am Princess Amarande and my intention is to return to my home."

The guardswoman's sword faltered, but only slightly. "Your Highness?" She took a step forward, squinting across the distance. Amarande watched the guard register her face, hair, and the wedding gown, deeply stained across the golden lace at the bodice, the dark crust of blood blending with the shadows cast from the castle wall. "Is it truly you?"

"Yes, may I approach?"

The leader nodded, but all swords remained drawn. Amarande tapped the horse into motion and brought herself fully into the sconce light. All eyes went to the blood and the color drained from every face. "Your Highness, are you . . . all right? That is lifeblood, there."

This was why she'd worn the dress—there was an undeniable truth to it. Renard's face flashed in Amarande's mind—pale and stunned, just before his body fell to the dais. Her first kill, demanding to be sharp, clear, unforgotten, and always present on the backs of her eyelids. She swallowed.

"It isn't my blood."

The guard seemed to take her at her word but exchanged glances with her subordinates. "My apologies, Your Highness. It is simply that we were informed just last night that you were presumed dead."

SECOND Captain, I assure you I am not a dead woman walking," the princess reiterated as the guardswoman, Pualo, escorted her to Councilor Satordi, who had apparently been the one to announce to the castle guard and staff her presumed death.

Though the lead councilor would be tasked to make such an announcement given the current state of the Itspi, the fact that he would do so made no sense. Who would have told the Royal Council such a thing? Certainly not Renard—he'd needed her alive and would've been more likely to send word of their marriage before it actually happened than of her untrue death. And as for those remaining in Pyrenee, there would be so much more they could gain from using her as a pawn than from pretending she no longer drew breath. And where was Koldo on this? Surely the general would not agree as Ardenia's regent to such an outrageous announcement. Would she?

They passed not a soul as they marched past the red hall, into the north tower. But instead of continuing up the stairs to the council room, the guardswoman led Amarande straight through to the residential wing, which housed her father's advisors. All members of the council—Satordi, Garbine, Joseba—as well as Sendoa's other top confidants, General Koldo, Captain Xixi, and the highest-level castle guards, like Captain Serville.

At the very last door, Pualo knocked three times rapid-fire. Footsteps rang against the floorboards on the other side—juniper parquet, rather than the marble in the public spaces and royal wings. The wooden panel covering the peephole slid back, and dark eyes Amarande recognized as Satordi's flashed from within.

Immediately, the door was wrenched open. Amarande's lips parted to greet him, but instead the councilor barked at the guard, "Who saw you?"

"Only my company, sir."

"Good. Ensure their silence."

Aghast at Satordi's order, Amarande started, "Councilor—"

"Not here!" With more strength than Amarande would ever have anticipated, Satordi grabbed her arm and jerked her over the threshold before slamming the door.

She ripped herself free and wheeled on the man. "Satordi, I realize you are angry with me for my disappearance, but do not put your hands upon me without my consent. Though you've apparently announced that I am a corpse, I am still alive and still your princess. As my councilor, I expect you to treat me with respect."

Satordi stood as tall as his wiry frame allowed. "Your Highness, I apologize. Your safety outweighs formality at this moment."

"*My* safety? I was with a castle guard—I'm the safest I've been in a week. You have no idea what I've just been through other than you somehow believed I didn't survive it."

"Accept my apology or do not, Princess, we have much to discuss."

"Yes, we do." Amarande put a hand back on the door handle. "And I would prefer we get to it in the council room—call Garbine and Joseba immediately. Is Koldo here or at the front? We need her. Captains Serville and Xixi, too. As many strategic minds as we can get at this hour. Pyrenee is on my heels, bringing war to the Itspi's walls."

Satordi blocked the door. "It is best we remain here, Princess."

Amarande's frustration simmered over. Satordi never listened to her—princess, heir, alive, dead, his reaction was always the same. "Your quarters are lovely, Councilor"—she gestured to the sitting room beyond—"but this is highly—"

"*Imperative.* It is highly imperative we remain here." The voice was a woman's, regal and direct—but one the princess did not recognize.

Amarande whipped around, her retort dying on her lips. Standing in a doorway between living spaces was a woman with a cascade of dark hair, wrapped in a shade of blue that complemented her skylight eyes.

She was the most familiar stranger Amarande had ever seen.

The princess's heart faltered as she recognized her own rosebud lips, high cheekbones, and strong-but-petite frame. And the stance—shoulders back, legs firmly planted, chin tipped up—that was purely hers, too. Amarande blinked rapidly as if sand had sprayed her eyes, sure the woman would vanish.

She did not.

And so Amarande gathered every ounce of the courage her father told her she had and asked a question that broke her heart as much as it gave her a new, unexpected hope.

"Mother?"

CHAPTER
5

How many nights had Amarande dreamed of this face? Of this moment?

Her mother, Geneva—the notorious Runaway Queen—standing before her. Not a dream. Not a ruse. Not some fuzzy figure on the edge of memories she couldn't latch onto, no matter how hard she tried. Days ago, while escaping the Warlord's camp with Osana, Amarande had sure the woman in the Warlord's tent was her mother, some unnamed feeling in her gut hinting at something her memory could not confirm.

But in this moment feeling was replaced by reality.

For the first time in fifteen years, Princess Amarande of Ardenia and her mother were in the same room. The mother who had left Amarande before her first birthday, on the same night that Luca's mother had died.

Fifteen years.

Of wondering why her mother had run. Was it because she hadn't loved her father, and wanted to escape their arranged marriage?

Of wondering why she wasn't enough for her mother to stay, to fight, or to take away, too.

Of wondering if her mother was truly alive—or dead by her father's hand as the rumors whispered, not that the princess ever believed those.

And now, in Amarande's absence, her mother had returned to the Itspi. Was this simply because the princess had disappeared, or was there another reason that now, after all these years, this woman had walked out of Amarande's imagination and into her life?

The princess's reflexes were razor sharp, her body always knowing exactly what to do when facing any threat—and yet she was suddenly frozen to the spot. Her breath faltered while her heart continued to pound. As in the moment when Renard's guards had dealt her what she believed to be a death blow, Amarande felt as if she were floating outside herself. Above, in the rafters, watching as a tentative smile spread across her mother's beautiful face. Counting the steps as her mother crossed the room, flung her arms out, and embraced the still form of her sixteen-year-old daughter.

The princess lost her voice to a gasp as Geneva drew her close. This woman was real, her body warm and solid as she enveloped Amarande. She smelled of firewood and rose water, her skin soft with creams and care. As the embrace waned, mother held daughter at arm's length, brilliant eyes inspecting every inch of her girl.

"Look at you, Amarande. As beautiful as I'd expected."

Stunned, Amarande could only blink back. Gently, the Runaway Queen smoothed a lock of hair away from Amarande's brow as if she'd wanted to do such a thing every day they were apart. "My dear daughter, we have much to discuss—but first, what is this blood? Do you need a medikua? And what is this of Pyrenee on your heels?"

Amarande's suspended consciousness lurched into motion. Her breath returned, her heartbeat, her voice. "Mother . . . why are you here? Now?" It wasn't the most elegant question for this reunion, ham-fisted and too direct, but suspicion was quickly overtaking shock within Amarande as her pulse skittered and skipped. She speared Satordi with her attention—he had faded into a corner as her mother had approached. "Councilor, why did you tell the guards I was dead? What is going on here?"

Satordi glanced away, meeting her mother's eyes before her own. "I myself am very glad to see you alive, Your Highness," he said, adjusting the collar of his ivory-and-gold robes. "But you have arrived at a very awkward time."

The strangeness of that statement shook Amarande loose of her mother's palms. "Awkward? This is—"

Her voice died as another figure stepped into the candlelight. Amarande stumbled backward and the hilt of Maite, her father's sword, clanged into the stone wall behind her. The figure—a young man—came to a halt. Fully illuminated, he was the spitting image of the twenty-year-old coronation portrait hanging in the castle foyer.

This boy was King Sendoa come to life.

The princess steadied herself against the wall. "Who are you?"

Geneva tilted her head, smile suddenly not so tentative. "Come now, darling daughter; you know who he is."

Amarande's gaze didn't waver from the familiar green eyes, sunset hair, and hulking shoulders. Yes, she knew. But she wanted to hear it from the boy himself. "I addressed *him*."

The boy sank into the nearest chair. He leaned forward, elbows on his knees, failing, very much like her father had, at making himself seem small. "My name is Ferdinand." Even his voice sounded like Sendoa's. Shock ran ice cold down Amarande's spine. "From what I understand, Princess, I am your younger brother."

With the confirmation, Amarande's world shifted again. She had a brother.

Her mother had run while pregnant. And then stayed away. But . . . why? How? And did Sendoa know? More questions stacked upon the teetering pile she kept for her father's star-bound ghost. Atop it all—what was his plan? And now—was this part of it?

Three rapid knocks and General Koldo entered the room in full garnet-and-gold regalia.

"Koldo!" Amarande lunged for the woman she'd always considered a surrogate mother as much as a friend. The general was just as surprised to see the princess. Still, Koldo was as quick as ever, catching her in a natural embrace, while casting a questioning eye over Amarande.

"Princess, you're hurt. I shall call for a medikua."

This struck Amarande off guard—there wasn't *a* medikua; there was *the* medikua, Aritza. Yet her mother had used the same descriptor. How much had the castle changed in the past few days?

"No, no, it's not my blood. It is Renard's." That drew a sharp inhale from Satordi. "It can wait—please, regiments from Pyrenee may be upon our door in hours, if not this very minute."

Her mother, her brother, the general, and the councilor stilled.

"Speak first, Princess." Koldo led Amarande to a chaise across a low table from where Ferdinand sat. "The rest can come after."

The general sat next to the princess, never letting go of her arm—not that Amarande wanted her to. She needed Koldo's steadying touch, the one that had guided her through so much. Geneva chose to stand behind Ferdinand, her small hands resting against the seat back of his chair. Satordi remained standing. Amarande's world swayed.

"Fetch the princess water, Councilor," Koldo commanded, and Amarande was mildly surprised when he listened, moving to a small cupboard against the far wall. "Your Highness?"

"I left the Itspi unannounced on the night of Father's funeral because kidnappers stole away. . . ." Amarande's eyes found her mother's, and her brother's, as she grappled for a way to describe him that didn't make her feel so naked to these all-but-strangers. "Luca, my . . . my best friend . . . to push me into marriage with Prince Renard—the crown prince of Pyrenee."

"Is this the boy from the Torrent?" her mother asked. "Lygia's son?"

Amarande was surprised again by her mother's voice—and her knowledge. How long had they been at the Itspi? What did they know? Koldo nodded in answer. "Yes, a stableboy. Sendoa took a liking to him and allowed him to be a companion to the princess."

Something passed over Geneva's eyes, but Amarande pressed on. She shouldn't be surprised her mother remembered Lygia from her castle days, as they would've been a similar age—seventeen or eighteen. Luca's mother had died of a lung infection the same night Geneva had disappeared. Losing their mothers on the very same night was one of the strange coincidences that twined them so tightly. It was one thing to both not recall their mother's face; it was quite another for the person closest to you to feel the exact same thing for the exact same length of time.

"After failing to make a diplomatic peace with Renard, I felt I had no choice but to rescue Luca myself. I left immediately and covertly because I feared him to be in grave danger. After a few obstacles, I rescued Luca from the kidnappers, who had pushed deep into the Torrent. On our return, we were intercepted by Renard, his brother Taillefer, and several guards and hired hands."

"Prince Renard was intent on rescuing you." Satordi set a crystal glass before the princess. She didn't drink.

"Know that is a lie."

"I am aware."

"Rather than escorting us back to Ardenia, as I'm sure you expected he might, he insisted we turn for Pyrenee, where the two of us could be wed. I refused, of course, and when I did, he threatened to kill me and blame Luca if I did not do as he asked. Outnumbered, and surrounded in the bottom of a fire pit, I felt I had no choice but to go with him."

"He threatened to kill you *or* be married to you?" Ferdinand asked. "That is quite the gamut of choice."

Her brother had much to learn.

"The laws of succession in Pyrenee are clear. To obtain his power before his eighteenth birthday he must wed. What's more, Renard believed his mother to be making moves in a concerted effort to prevent his ascension to the throne."

"Sounds like Inés," her mother muttered and the cords in Geneva's neck tensed between heavy curtains of dark waves.

"Thus, he was eager for us to marry." The princess swallowed. "We arrived at the Bellringe in the afternoon and he demanded that we be wed before the evening meal. In the hours between, while I was being prepared for a wedding I knew the people of Ardenia did not know was occurring, I believed Luca to have died at the hands of Taillefer, who had been ordered to hold Luca hostage for my compliance. Taillefer knew that if Luca were to die then I would likely retaliate against his brother."

Just saying Luca's name seemed to thrust her heart on display—repeatedly—though she had not once admitted her true feelings to these people. "And, though I knew this to be Taillefer's aim, I still reacted in the way he wanted."

"Princess, you didn't . . ." Satordi's face had gone flat white, the weight of what she'd been trying to get across to him over the last several minutes now fully registering.

With an unsteady hand, Amarande lifted the glass to her lips and took a sip. The water tasted too warm on her tongue. Suddenly her whole face felt hot.

"They did not properly search me before the wedding." Koldo's eyes met hers and in them Amarande saw the choreography of what went down running through the general's mind. The princess had indeed done exactly as her surrogate mother would have done in the same position.

"During our vows I stabbed Renard. It is his blood on this wedding dress. I attempted to kill Taillefer as well, but failed before I fled with my life and Renard's blood on my hands. I have no doubt, though, Dowager Queen Inés wants the crown for her own; she is mounting an attack on us now and will twist what happens next to her advantage."

Amarande did not mention Luca or the pirates in her escape. The princess didn't know why, but she couldn't reveal the full story. Not to her mother, not out into the open. Not to the unsettling-yet-familiar form of her brother, deep in thought, lounging in a pose very much like that of a man whom he'd never met. Not to Satordi, who never seemed to see it her way.

She didn't trust them.

For as unsteady as Amarande was, she felt comfort in Koldo's sturdy presence and even demeanor. "Councilor Satordi, advise the rest of the Royal Council of what the princess has learned. I must warn my soldiers."

The general's hand left Amarande's as the older woman stood. She reached across the space and, to the princess's surprise, put a hand to Ferdinand's shoulder. Just one gentle touch and she was headed toward the door. The princess was floored—that was a good-bye. A wordless one, yes, but one with more emotion than she had received.

Something was not right.

"Koldo, why . . . why are you here and not the front? You'd been headed to the southern kingdoms before I left," Amarande ventured. Then she added, so that her interest didn't seem so pointed, "Did Myrcell and Basilica relent?"

The general's face was all tight angles. "No, they did not relent. They escalated."

Amarande stilled, mind racing. When battle called, Koldo was never one to be anywhere but the front lines. That had not changed with her regency.

"But why—"

"The general must go attend to what you have started, Your Highness," Satordi insisted, steering the conversation away.

"Yes, but—"

"The general is here because she is my natural mother." Ferdinand cut her off with an answer that took her breath away, his voice loud and clear and unwavering. As the weight of his admission settled between them, he looked Amarande in the eye, so much like her father she almost had to glance away.

Geneva's lips parted, and Satordi pinched the bridge of his nose. Their reactions were enough to confirm two things: that it was true, and they had decided she should not know.

Ferdinand's defiance was quiet and stiff and suddenly she saw Koldo within him.

A bastard. A half brother. A secret.

"She deserves to know all of it," Ferdinand announced in answer to the silent rebuke. "I do not want to lie to my sister. I do not care if it is stupid for me to think so, but if everyone in this room knows the truth, she should, too."

The princess's stomach plummeted so low it felt as if it might tap the knife in her boot. Amarande looked from the general to the boy, skipping over her mother in between. Heat licked at her throat as her voice found hold. "Koldo? You . . . and Father . . . ?"

Words failed her as Koldo nodded once. This was more outlandish than her original guess.

"It is as long a story as the one you've just told," the general answered, direct enough, as always, to look Amarande in the eye. "I will explain it all one day. But now, you are right—I must warn my soldiers. I am sorry, Princess. Another time."

Again, Koldo turned for the door, Satordi on her heels to alert the other councilors to Amarande's tale. When they were gone, Amarande stared at her newfound family as her insides lurched—she might never feel upon solid ground again.

Swallowing hard, the princess speared her mother with a look. "Why did you present Ferdinand as your son?"

The woman did not bat an eye. "Because he is."

Fair enough. Blood was not the only bond. "Koldo may not have had time to tell her story, but you do not have the excuse. What happened? I deserve to know."

"I would not prefer to renew our relationship this way," her mother replied, looking away, "but . . . the simple truth of the matter is this: I learned of Ferdinand's birth and stole him away in a moment of weakness."

Bile rose in the princess's throat. "You *stole* Koldo's baby?"

"He was a day old—a threat to your station and mine." Geneva's words could etch diamonds. "And after what I'd done . . . I fell in love with him. I raised him. I made him mine."

Mine.

Amarande had always pictured her mother as someone so sad that she gave up on her enchanted life. On her father. On her. Someone who had married for position and who yearned for love to the point of such desperation that she had no choice but to take action. To steal into the night and on to another adventure. But this—Amarande could barely envision the truth as her mother told it. How could she? Who would steal a baby and leave her own?

And then there was Koldo. *Did she know? All this time? How could she stand it?*

No matter which answer, something about the way the general stood in the same room with her mother and the history between them made Amarande's stomach lurch. Koldo was the strongest woman she knew, and yet the general hadn't run Geneva through with a sword the second she'd learned of this startling deception.

Was that weakness or was it strength?

Amarande stared at the Runaway Queen. "And you brought him here to claim the crown in my stead."

Her mother did not look away. "This kingdom deserves a steady-handed ruler who will not put it in danger or leave it in a precarious spot wedged between law and convenience. And though Ferdinand is not of my blood, I have no doubt he is the best choice for Ardenia."

A shiver ran across her spine. Amarande swallowed.

"He is only the best choice if I am out of the way."

"Amarande, you just committed regicide in a neighboring kingdom, bringing war to Ardenia's door. This after you shirked your duties in the name of chasing after a boy like a hen tails a rooster. Ardenia is on a precipice and you, my darling daughter, are willing to toss it over the edge."

No. It wasn't like that. Was it?

"I am your daughter. I am not a danger."

Her mother tilted her chin. "My dear, I am afraid you are both."

"And so I am to be out of the way, then." The princess shot to her feet and drew the sword at her back. She wasn't sure why—she did not plan to attack—and yet the blade was in her grip as she fought back against her mother's assertions and obvious machinations. "And so the plan is what? To lie? To tell everyone I'm dead until I reappear like you, years later and in perfect health?"

A hand clenched her neck. Squeezing precisely on the artery that supplies oxygen to the brain. An arm gripped around her middle—an arm clad in garnet-and-gold regalia.

Koldo.

Amarande's heart slowed, vision going black, limbs losing strength. She had mere seconds of consciousness left. The princess's sword fell, clanging to the marble tabletop.

"Yes, exactly that, clever girl," the Runaway Queen answered as she bent to pick up the fallen sword—Maite, it was Maite, "love" in old Torrentian. "It is not a lie if we tell them the truth eventually. After the kingdom is safe, you can return. With your stableboy, if you like. But for now, Princess Amarande of Ardenia, your presence is too much of a risk."

Just as Amarande's consciousness fled and her body went slack, the general whispered, "I am sorry, Ama."

CHAPTER 6

LUCA and his crew arrived at the next point in the resistance constellation in the black hour before dawn. It appeared to be a sheep farm, snuggled between steep grades of rock, the Torrent a hard pass and descent away.

"This is it?" Luca confirmed as they stared at the squat juniper-wood cabin. Within, candles burned with the promise of daybreak chores. Even if the sheep were for show, the chores would be real.

Ula nodded. "All of us must approach together. Follow my lead."

The pirate had indeed gotten exactly what they needed back at the market to make contact. Information on where to go next, the necessary purchases for offering, and, for Luca, a jug of antiseptic sagardon—medicinal-grade sagardoa ideal to treat his wounds and any more injuries that might come.

They stowed their horses within the farm's meager stable, then collected their saddlebags and the sack Ula had used at the market, and approached the house. Ula steadied herself and knocked five times in a certain rhythm, as she'd been instructed.

"What is your intent at this hour?" A man's voice.

Ula answered, "We come to feed the missing."

"What do they eat?" he asked.

Without skipping a beat, Ula switched into old Torrentian. "Hitz ematen dizut."

I give you my word of honor, Luca translated. His found Ardenian family of Maialen, Abene, and old Zuzen had taken pride in teaching him the ancient language, though he only ever used it with them. Until this moment he didn't know Ula knew any of it at all.

The door opened a crack and a candle shone between themselves and the darkness of the interior. Ula knew this was coming, too, and was ready—she leaned forward and pulled down the neck of her tunic, revealing her paw print.

The door opened wider, revealing the man—and a woman. Both were of Torrent, and gray with age, their skin worn from the sun and work, but their eyes brilliant and bold. Without another word, they ushered the group inside and closed the door tightly. Then they revealed tattoos of their own—more paw prints.

Luca swallowed, his heart beating fast as he read the faces of these hardy people. His people. Truly. It was all so dizzying.

"We have obtained the items requested by the resistance," Ula continued, and gestured to Urtzi, who held the sack aloft.

The man nodded. "They are in need. I shall leave at once."

Ula had explained this before their approach. This was an operation that ran on a phased set of expectations—it was as crucial as it was high risk and high reward. The basic system was simple, not efficient. If a person or persons wanted to connect with the main line of rebels based in the Torrent, they first must fulfill a list of supplies. Next, a verified rider would deliver those supplies to the last known location of the resistance—which seemed to be as nomadic as the rest of the Torrent. Then, once the supplies were accepted, the request for a meeting was either confirmed or denied. If confirmed, the rider would then return and escort the new rebels to the resistance.

Luca could barely believe the operation had remained intact so long without the Warlord's disruption. The previous outpost had been turned to ash in a raid, and thus it was easy to believe the Warlord knew of the system, yet the rebels claimed the renewed system had worked without disruption since then—two years running.

By luck or design, only the Warlord really knew.

The man immediately began donning clothing that served to protect travelers in the Torrent—hat, bandana, double-dagger belt—all in the faded fabrics that blended into the sand-scoured landscape and with the people who lived there. When he was finished, he looked exactly like any of the men Luca had seen in his travels with the pirates and Amarande.

It made him wonder exactly how to tell friend from foe.

"I will return under the cover of night—less than a day." He accepted the sack from Urtzi and a kiss from his wife.

"Before you go, we have one more crucial piece of information for you to bring them." The man and woman paused, caught on Ula's tone.

Ula nudged Luca forward, her golden eyes alight. "Come now, don't be shy."

Luca's heart began to pound again, as he looked into the faces of people who had put everything on the line each day of their lives the past seventeen years to help keep the resistance alive.

As the Otxazulo burned, his mother had escaped to Ardenia, told them her name was Lygia, and hidden him away. Surely King Sendoa knew who was hiding in his stable. Surely he had a plan to help them win it back—the Warrior King always had a plan.

Maybe the plan had died with Luca's mother. With Sendoa gone, too, he would never know.

All Luca knew was it was now up to him.

And after this, there would be no going back.

Breathing deeply, he came forward, unlashed the laces at the breast of his black tunic, and yanked down the fabric to reveal the entirety of the wolf tattoo on his chest.

Five points. Snout, ears. Unmistakable.

The woman dropped whatever was in her hand with a crash and a gasp. The man rushed forward, candle held aloft. Suddenly, Luca felt more exposed than he had ever been—his blood on the outside, rendered in thick black streaks.

"Hitz ematen dizut," Luca said. *I give you my word of honor.*

The man took a step back, lips hanging open, gaze lifting from Luca's tattoo to his face. The woman clung to her husband's elbow, her own eyes wide. They exchanged a long look and then the man addressed Luca with a voice glazed in shock.

"My Otsakumea, we have been waiting for you."

CHAPTER
7

❧⟨∾⟩❧

SEVENTEEN years they had been waiting.

Mannah and Erfu were their names, and both had been within the Otxazulo when Luca was born. They were among the few in the resistance who had personally seen him—alive and tattooed—before the Warlord's attack left the castle in ash, the royal family's heads on pikes, and the Otxoa's supporters fleeing in every direction.

Luca hadn't expected this. A lifetime of hiding out without knowing he was doing so, only to find the truth and, in short order, people like these, who'd kept memories and hope for seventeen years. Even after Ula's admission—which they still had barely discussed—it was stunning.

Luca's mind spun with all he wanted to ask them—about their hardships, the resistance, castle life. His parents, too—he'd been too young to remember what his mother had been like when she passed.

Instead, because they'd asked, he'd quickly told them where he'd been all this time—at the Itspi, raised by castle staff after his mother's death from a lung infection—and how he'd come to know of his identity. And then Erfu had to leave before the darkness lifted, and it was necessary that Mannah spent the day exactly as she would any other to throw anyone watching off the scent.

And so, the Otsakumea was left with his questions, his crew, and the weight of his name for the daylight hours. By nightfall, the cabin felt even smaller as the stars crowded in, too.

"Time to clean your wounds, Luca," Ula announced, pushing away from the table after supper. She'd made it clear he should be on a schedule—an infection in his chest from Taillefer's work or in his leg from the Harea Asp ordeal would surely put a damper on any chances of rebellion.

Luca followed without complaint, pushing away from the table too, as Osana and Urtzi remained, sipping nettle tea. Sinking to his bedroll, he discarded his tunic and began removing the dressing as Ula gathered the jug of sagardon she'd procured at the market along with a new length of linen gauze.

The sting of the process was one of a thousand bees under the skin, but the pain was minor in comparison with what he'd felt in the past week. And the wound looked only a little better, the skin bruised and raw with inflammation that ran down the whole hand-length gash in the middle of his chest, just beside his wolf tattoo. The flat black sutures were tight, straining to keep the swollen edges of flesh together. In time, his skin and muscles would heal. Just not soon enough.

Across the room, Mannah inhaled sharply. Luca's head snapped up to find her staring at him, her body frozen over her kettle, where water was boiling yet again, for another round of tea.

Mannah had not heard the story of Taillefer's torture chamber. She knew he had injuries but not what they were or how he received them. Or why.

The curse of being in love with a princess.

Actually, the old woman hadn't heard much of anything—spending the day doing chores as if she had no guests at all, as was the ruse. He'd yet to ask her the questions building within him—not wanting to burden her further.

The old woman put down the kettle and came toward Luca, fingers bent with work pressed against her gaping mouth. Her face was pale, but she did not shy away from directly examining the wound. "But what has happened to your heart, my Otsakumea?"

Luca swallowed back a shuddering breath as Ula pressed another round of sagardon to the mess of stitches. "My heart is well, thank you." And it was, though he knew that was not exactly what this woman meant. "It's a long story, but what is important is that Ula has been better than the best medikua at nursing me back to health."

The woman looked to Ula, who had applied another liberal amount of the sagardon to a scrap of linen. "You did these sutures yourself, child?"

"Yes," she answered, pressing the sagardon to Luca's snakebit leg— still flat black, but no longer swollen.

Mannah nodded. "Ula—Ulara Vidal, yes?"

Luca's breath hitched as Ula's golden eyes crept to the woman's face. Ula hadn't mentioned her parents' names or their positions at the castle, but it was clear that Mannah had been thinking back, paging through the names and faces she'd known all day. "Yes."

"I thought so when I first heard your name this morning." Something about Mannah's coloring changed, a flush flooding her cheeks. "Your mother was handy with a needle—Lygia would be proud, Ula."

Luca's heart stuttered. It almost felt as if it were on the outside of his body, beating raw and red. "Lygia?" He touched Ula's shoulder—mostly because it was what he could reach and remain relatively still. "Your mother's name was Lygia?"

"Yes . . ." she replied, unsure.

"That was my mother's name—or what she went by at the Itspi. She could not walk around as Queen Elixane, so she went by Lygia." The color drained from Ula's face, and Luca's next words rushed out under their own volition. "My mother must have adored yours to use her name."

Luca turned to Mannah, whose dark gold eyes ran between them as if reading the pages in a book. "What can you tell us about Ula's Lygia? Would she have known my mother?"

A strange expression flickered across Mannah's face. Ula, for her part, was still and silent, used linen clutched in her swordswoman's grip. Luca placed a kind hand on her wrist. "I've thought the past few days that perhaps Ula and I were destined to meet and become friends and . . . if our mothers were that way? That—two orphans could not hope for more, perhaps."

"I don't know," Urtzi deadpanned from the table, where he sat with his fourth cup of tea, "I'm an orphan who has spent a lifetime hoping for my parents."

Osana shoved him on the shoulder. "Well, stop hoping because our parents aren't coming back. But they *do* live on in memories, so shut up and let the woman talk."

Luca smiled gently at Mannah. "Please. What can you tell us? Were they friends? Lygia and Queen Elixane?"

After a long moment, the old woman answered, more guarded than before. "I was the head maid. Lygia was among my charges within the castle. I am sorry to say, my Otsakumea, but though they were acquainted, I doubt they were what you would call friends. I conversed more with Queen Elixane in a day than Lygia or any of my other girls would have in an entire year, and yet I would not say we were friends."

Luca's heart dropped. So that's how it was in the Otxazulo, then. He'd known the environment of King Sendoa's castle was unusual within the Sand and Sky—less formal, more familial. And it hit him with a sudden sadness that if everything were different and he'd grown up as a stableboy at the Otxazulo, the likelihood of befriending the princess—let alone forming an attachment that turned into love—would've been nil.

Mannah smiled softly at Ula's crestfallen face, and the disappointment in her Otsakumea's eyes. When she spoke next, it seemed as if the words had carefully arranged themselves on her tongue. "It is splendid that the two of you found each other. Here, like this—not at odds."

Ula and Luca exchanged a confused glance before the pirate drew in a breath and inquired, "Why is that, Mannah?"

The woman looked between them. "Because the last order I ever gave Lygia was to take the Otsakumea and run."

CHAPTER
8

AMARANDE awoke in yet another secret of the Itspi. A chamber that looked very much like the dungeons, buried diamond deep in the mountainside. But she was not underground—daylight streamed through two windows, higher than her eyeline. They appeared to be stained glass, but the iron bars that crisscrossed the interior of the frame made it clear they were simply a way to disguise the cell from the outside.

As she sat up, attempting to gather her bearings, the world skewed sideways. A throbbing pain pounded behind her eyes as she blinked into the weak garnet-and-cobalt-filtered illumination. She had no idea if she'd been here hours or days, only that it was daylight now.

She'd been stripped of her sword and makeshift sheath—no surprise there. Gone too was the stained wedding dress—not that Inés likely would've wanted it back anyway—replaced by a nondescript shift, itchy and coarse.

The metallic tang of Renard's blood clung to her skin despite her change in clothes. Her stays remained, and, over her heart, she could feel the prickly edges of the ransom note that had precipitated all this—her headlong pursuit of Luca and his kidnappers; their subsequent joyous reunion and heartbreaking surrender at the feet of Renard; and the wedding that ended with the crown prince's blood on her blade instead of his ring on her finger.

Marry Renard or you will never see your love again.

Its presence ensured this was not a dream, detailed how far she'd come and, it seemed, how much had changed.

She'd met her mother.

Her brother.

Stars. She had a brother. Sired by her father with a woman who was his trusted general, forever confidante, and closest friend. Raised by Amarande's own mother, after she'd stolen him away. She'd always believed the story of the Runaway Queen to be as simple as an act of love or lack thereof, but the truth was so much more complicated. Everything these days seemed to be turning out that way.

Amarande was right-side up, but her world was upside-down.

Her value diminished and path to the throne obliterated—the crown princess usurped by a prince—albeit a prince who had no legal claim. The laws were clear. The Kingdom of Ardenia fell to the male line. Ironically, it was easier to elevate a bastard than to allow a legitimate heir to rule on her own.

And then there was Luca—plowing headfirst into a deadly situation without her by his side. She'd feared war since the moment this all began and had done her best to prevent it, but now Luca was marching into a rebellion that very much could start one. They'd been together their whole lives, she could not be away from him now. Not when he needed her most.

Their plan was in shambles, but it did not matter as long as she got to Luca as quickly as possible. Amarande stood, testing her legs. The pounding behind her temples escalated to a drumbeat, but the rest of her body seemed workable.

Amarande's boot knife was a weight against her ankle. She checked to make sure—fingers brushing the hilt, disguised by her boot shaft. Still there, indeed. An oversight? Perhaps Koldo was human after all and could make mistakes.

Or perhaps it was left for a reason.

As she turned over the possibilities in her mind, the princess examined her surroundings more closely. Straw-filled mattress, chamber pot—wooden, and bolted to the floor—and shackles drilled into the wall. The rounded walls were as solid as anything else in the fortified castle of the Itspi, and the door the same heavy wood and iron with extra strips of thick steel crisscrossed over its length for reinforcement.

Yes, a cell indeed—one it was imperative that she escape. Get to Luca. Keep him safe from the Warlord. Fight for his right to rule in the Torrent and then come back and fight for Ardenia.

Prove to her mother, her brother, her councilors, and possibly Koldo that she wasn't a liability. She was an asset. And she wasn't about to spend her life hiding away, no matter the political ramifications.

The princess would not be a sacrifice.

She wasn't one when they tried to marry her off. She wasn't one when they tried to bribe her with Luca's life. She wasn't one now when they tried to hide her away.

With her boot knife, she could most definitely hack a hole in a wooden portion of the door, enough to see outside her circular room. But if a guard's oversight was more than cursory, the hole and the splintered wood would be obvious and her knife would be discovered.

She started with the window. Even on tiptoes, the bars were out of reach. Worse, they were flush with the glass, and not even the slimmest fingerhold was available that would allow her to pull herself up and afford a glimpse of the world outside.

But Amarande had a plan. Boot knife in hand, she cut a strip of cloth from the hem of her thin, colorless shift. Standing beneath the window, the princess jumped, angling the tip of the strip so that it was flush with the bars each time. After several tries, she successfully threaded it behind the first set of vertical bars and was able to pull it down just enough so that she could tie the ends into a knot. The loop was not strong enough to completely support her weight, but she just might be able to hang on long enough to quickly gauge her location within the castle.

Amarande stood on the chamber pot, balancing on either edge. In one fluid movement, she pushed off the chamber pot, her fingers caught the loop of cloth, and her arms bent just enough to lever herself above the lip of the window. For one long moment, she held herself there, arms taut and biceps screaming, boot toes digging into the solid stone wall.

The arena—she could see the lip of the arena.

Which meant she was still in the north tower, somewhere close to the council room. Just as she came to that realization, *snap*. The cloth tore and before she could lunge for another grip or pull her feet from the wall, Amarande fell with a resounding thud, the back of her head bashing into the stone floor.

Amarande lay there for a moment, stars in her eyes. Anger bloomed along with a new pain running from her tailbone to the base of her skull. Faintly, she remembered what the idiot guards at the Warlord's camp had said about her when they thought she was lying about her name: *The princess has never left Ardenia. Locked in a tower the day her mother ran away. Even the spiders crawling the Hand know that.*

Did her mother spark that lie? Or her father? Was it meant to keep her safe or make her father out to be more controlling than he was?

Amarande squeezed her eyes closed, sucked in a deep breath, and then got to her feet. This time, she grabbed her boot knife and stepped to the door. There was no knob, just a flat lock with all the meaningful parts of it on the other side—except the keyhole.

She stuck the tip of the dagger inside and jiggled it around. For one minute. Two. Five. Finally, she gave up. There was no way she could unlock it.

Frustrated, she moved back to the window and began to shear a thicker strip of cloth from the hem of her shift, enough to expose her bruised knees. As she twisted her torso around to hack it off at the back, she heard noises from the other side of the door. Amarande immediately stashed the knife beneath her bed and sat on top of it as if waiting patiently for visitors.

The door wrenched open, revealing the guardswoman who had escorted her into the castle and to Satordi's chambers. "Your Highness, you're awake."

"Second Captain, you're stuck with me, I see. You and your team from the gate in a special rotation so no one else knows of my existence, I presume?"

Without making eye contact, Pualo swallowed. Cleared her throat. "I am here to remove your boots."

"I rather like my boots and would prefer to keep them. Without them, I might get a chill. This shift is inadequate. The mountains of Ardenia grow quite cool at night, even in summer."

"My apologies, Your Highness, I will inquire about bringing you appropriate clothing from your wardrobe, but for now unadorned clothing is required." The guard's chin dipped as her gaze lifted. "As is the removal of your boots."

Amarande narrowed her eyes. "Why? If you want my boots, why did you not remove them before?"

"General Koldo's order—you have been known to carry a knife in your boot." *Ah, there it is.* "If I don't return with your boots and the knife, she will come and remove them herself."

That was exactly what Amarande wanted. And possibly what Koldo wanted, too—a reason to see Amarande that would not be suspicious.

Koldo couldn't truly be in an alliance with the woman who had stolen her child. Or against the girl whom she had personally trained to be a warrior—and loved as a surrogate daughter.

Could she?

"Let her come."

CHAPTER
9

❧❧❧

IT wasn't Koldo who came for Amarande.

No, when sound echoed through the antechamber beyond her cell door and the locking mechanism clicked free, the person who strode into the room wasn't her surrogate mother.

It was her brother.

Amarande's heart dropped. This could mean many things. That Koldo had ridden out to confront the enemy at the borders; or that her knife was truly an oversight, not a sign; or that this was what the general had intended all along.

Wearing what looked to be a garnet-and-gold uniform from her father's wardrobe, Ferdinand shut the door and presented himself with a dagger at his hip and no other visible weapon beyond his utter size. There was something absolutely stunning about him in the daylight, filtered as it was through the stained glass.

Sunset hair. Green eyes. Body of a bull ox in need of a cart.

He was in every which way a reproduction of King Sendoa, and yet not. At fifteen he had already reached his father's height, and still had room to grow. Koldo was taller than most women and some men and broad shouldered besides, therefore this was not a surprise.

But Ferdinand had not been trained by Koldo. Looks could be deceiving, and if he truly had only size as a defense he would not last long if Amarande fought to make that dagger hers.

To his credit, Ferdinand did not make pretenses. "You didn't surrender your boot knife."

In the time she'd had since the guard left, Amarande had been busy. She'd freed the chamber pot using her knife to hack away at the bolts that secured it to the wooden base and positioned it directly under the window. She'd heard him coming just as she hopped on the edges of the chamber pot to reach up and attempt to break the glass using the blade's hilt. She'd had just enough time to hide the evidence—the bolts, the knife—under the mattress and sit down upon it.

"I wanted to talk to Koldo," she answered.

"She has just returned from the Pyrenee border." Relief swept through Amarande—a return meant they were not actively at war. Though Dowager Queen Inés surely had a plan, and a delay was a strategy in itself. "The general would have come herself if I had not convinced her I could handle the chore."

Amarande had so many questions. But she simply asked, "You do not call Koldo 'Mother'?"

"I do not know her as my mother." He tilted his chin upward. "I do not know her at all."

The princess arched a brow. "I know her very well and I highly doubt she sent you alone, as *valuable* as you are. How many guards are behind that door? Two at least. Possibly four?"

He did not back down. "Sister, please take off your boots or I shall slice through the laces."

"You know me less than the woman you do not call Mother. Do not call me Sister."

A flicker of something that might have been hurt reflected in his sea-glass eyes. "*Amarande*, please take off your boots or I shall slice through the laces."

She grinned. "I'd love to see you try."

Ferdinand drew his dagger. Left-handed. *Interesting. That is something Father was not.*

As he took a step forward, the princess unlooped her arms from around her knees. "Do you know how to use that thing?"

"Of course."

"I will be the judge of that."

Ignoring her, Ferdinand advanced, and the moment he was in range Amarande's boot struck out and made jarring contact with his knee-cap. He stumbled back but did not fall. His auburn brows pulled together. "Amarande, don't make this more difficult than it has to be."

"You've already locked me away yet you plan to disarm me. What possible harm can my knife do under lock and key?"

Ferdinand glanced downward for the barest of moments. "We don't want you to hurt yourself."

"I would never." Amarande drew into herself. "And why would that worry you anyway? It would benefit you if I bled out in this room. Much easier to bury the secrets of the dead than manage the imprisonment of a living threat."

"Is that really what you think I want?" His voice lowered, thrumming with frustration. Ferdinand took a step forward, fingers tight on the dagger. "My world has opened up. I know of my father, my true mother, my sister. I want to know everything. We have just met, Amarande, but the last thing I see you as is a threat."

"That is your mistake."

When she kicked out this time, Ferdinand was ready, grabbing her boot and yanking at it, trying to wrest it off with both hands. She pulled back, but he held fast, even managing to keep the dagger in his grip. Amarande's other foot shot out and clocked his left hand. His grip faltered, he dropped his dagger, and she drove her heel hard into his knee yet again.

He swore, clutched his knee, and fell backward. Amarande pounced, scooping up the dagger. She landed in a crouch, her front foot bare, her back foot planted behind her, still shod. Ferdinand struggled up, trying to right himself as he grabbed at his battered knee. "I don't want to hurt you, Amarande; I swear it."

"Then why did you bring the dagger?"

"Your reputation precedes you. I wasn't going to use it."

"You drew it."

Ferdinand climbed to his feet, squared his shoulders, and looked directly into her eyes. "Amarande, believe me, when I found out my identity, I was far more interested in family than some title. That is precisely why I told you the truth—that Koldo is my mother, not Geneva—when we met. I do not wish to begin our relationship with a lie."

"Or you told me the truth because you believed I would not live long to shout it from the rooftops." Amarande advanced with the blade. "If you are truly interested in having me as proper family, why not march me straight out of this cell this instant?"

The boy's throat bobbed, but he did not appear panicked—his attention squarely, calmly, on the knife. He was trained. "The council believes the introduction of a royal heir who can gain access to power without marriage or an impossible law change will keep Ardenia safe and the situation will stabilize."

As she'd deduced—the introduction of a male heir, even a bastard, would be an easier pill to swallow than an unmarried woman accepting her rightful power.

The patriarchy in a nutshell.

A week ago, the princess was chattel to be bought and sold along with her kingdom—she never imagined any situation where she wouldn't be happy that scenario came to an end. And yet. "I fail to believe that is enough to halt war at every border. Pyrenee will still attack, no matter who is on our throne. Do not underestimate Inés; she has a plan."

At this, Ferdinand nodded.

"Mother has been very clear—we need to mitigate Inés. We don't know what she is waiting for, but we will be ready. In the meantime, this is what we can do to ensure no further damage."

Amarande drew in a thin breath. "When will you be introduced?"

"Sunset tomorrow. The announcement decrees have been written and are being distributed throughout the Sand and Sky, announcing my coronation."

Amarande's mouth went desert dry. "*Coronation?*"

"They are naming me king. There is no law about age here—it was rewritten for Father."

Yes. Father became king at fifteen. Two years before he wed. The laws were different from the ones Renard had navigated. Rewritten for the right ruler—yet not rewritten for her.

And just like that, her claim would be erased.

Amarande's grip strangled the knife hilt. Her voice roughened. "Ardenia is my home, my kingdom, not yours. What do you care of Ardenia? Don't answer that, you care nothing of it other than of the power it gives you."

"I don't care about power—"

"You're stealing my throne, of course you do. You don't wish to lie but I highly doubt you give a flying fig about stabilizing a land you'd never seen until days ago."

"Ardenia, my father, my true mother, you—they are fresh grains of knowledge, but it is incorrect to assume I won't do anything for them simply because they're new to me."

She took another step forward. "Such a diplomatic answer—not a lie, yet not the truth. Mother taught you well from *the Warlord's tent.*"

Amarande raised a brow and dared him to give an answer. If he really wanted to commit to a life of truth, a confirmation of what Amarande thought she saw would be vital information to relay to Luca—if she could escape this place. And armed with her brother on the defensive, she could nearly taste the fresh air of freedom.

When Ferdinand didn't respond right away she took another step toward him, and continued to press. "If you are going to lie outright, don't waste that chance here. I saw our mother in the Warlord's tent. Which means, by your own description, you were there, too."

Ferdinand leveled his gaze, so much like their father's. Though he was defenseless and backed against a wall, his words were calm and measured. Everything she was not in that moment. "You always knew who you were and what power you held. I knew nothing other than what my mother told me and even then I lived a lie."

It was true that Amarande always knew who she was, but she'd been wrong about the power she held and under what circumstances she would hold it—or have it stolen away.

"You confirm it then? Mother is the Warlord?"

He didn't answer.

A foot away from him now, Amarande gripped the knife tightly, turning over the options. Stomach. Throat. Chest—*no.*

Unbidden, the memory of Renard's death flashed before her. His storybook features screwed up in surprise before draining of color. Lifeblood blooming crimson across the white fabric at his chest before spreading black on the aubergine of his jacket.

She wouldn't kill Ferdinand, only strike him hard enough to leave her mark. The princess raised the knife. "Tell me."

Ferdinand lifted his hands in surrender. "Please, Sister."

Amarande hesitated. Words faltered on her lips. In that slight pause, he took advantage. One long arm swept up the princess's loose boot and flung it directly at her face. She blocked it with a forearm but in that second lost sight of her brother.

And that was her mistake.

When Amarande had full view of him again, she saw his hand slipping out of his own boot. The cool edge of a blade caught in the filtered light. In his hand. And then not.

It sliced through the air, quick as the strike of a Harea Asp, the knife pinning her right between the tendons that sewed her knuckles in place. Impaled, Amarande's hand flew open, dropping the dagger. The blow spun her backward and she fell. In two steps, Ferdinand retrieved Amarande's fallen knife, wrenched her uninjured arm back and clamped a shackle on her wrist—face placid and determined, looking just like Koldo.

Amarande kicked at him, going for a third strike on his damaged knee. But without leverage it was useless. Her free hand scrambled to gain purchase on something—his hair, his ear, the collar of her father's tunic he had no right to wear—but her fingers didn't seem to follow orders with a blade lodged between the tendons.

Ferdinand clamped a matching shackle to her injured hand. His warm fingers wrapped around her own. She struggled against his grip. Again, he leveled their father's eyes on her, steady and calm, though he was breathing hard.

"Please hold still as I remove the knife, Sister. I do not want to damage your hand further."

Again, she was caught off guard. If their places were switched, she would not be so kind. If she could worsen an initial strike while removing her weapon, she would. And she wouldn't use the term of endearment either. "Why are you being kind?"

"Because you could have slit my throat and escaped the second I walked in and didn't."

But . . . he still hadn't found the knife. It made no sense. Still, his demeanor was open, calm . . . honest? She stiffened as he wrapped a hand around the hilt of the dagger. He braced her wrist against the wall with the other hand and, in one smooth motion, removed the blade.

Amarande didn't cry out, even as stars swirled in her vision and blood began to pour from her hand. Ferdinand removed a handkerchief from his jacket and tied it tightly over the wound.

"I will send for a medikua." He wiped the bloodied knife on his shirt before dropping it in his own boot, the fallen dagger already sheathed at his hip. "I am sorry about that. I know you do not believe me, but I do not wish to see you hurt, especially by my hand."

Then, without hesitation, he walked over to the mattress and removed her boot knife from where she'd hidden it. As he tucked away the blade Amarande had carried since childhood, Ferdinand nodded gently. "That is where I would've hidden it, too."

Injured, unarmed, and now a threat to his very crown with her claim and knowledge of his secrets, Amarande looked away from her brother.

Ferdinand moved toward the door, boots collected, too, but then he paused and turned. "Proof of what you saw can be found on Mother's right wrist. What you find there will tell you everything you need to know."

With that, he was gone.

CHAPTER
10

❧

U<small>LA</small>, please—tell me of your parents." Luca hadn't wanted to pry, because it wasn't in his nature.

He'd known Ula was an orphan. He'd known she blamed the Warlord for it. King Sendoa, too, for his failure to halt the Eradication of the Wolf or even to mount a proper revenge.

But this? This they had to talk about, if they could.

He now knew his true mother, Queen Elixane, hadn't pretended to be someone else at the Itspi. She'd died in the Warlord's burning of the Otxazulo like his father and the rest of his family. And Ula's mother, Lygia, had saved his life—at the expense of a chance to escape with her own family.

Ula sighed but didn't speak. Luca asked again. "Please?"

"Tell him or I will," Urtzi pushed dryly, over the rind of the half wheel of sheep's cheese he'd finished with Osana in the hours of quiet between Mannah's reveal of Lygia's harrowing escape and that moment of tense, Ula-driven silence. "And we both know you don't want that because I'll get all the details wrong."

At this, Ula's lips quirked. Just a bit. "You would. On purpose—more harm than good."

"Then consider it a threat. Tell him, or I'll bungle it all so badly you'll start shouting at me and wake our host." Urtzi nodded to the rocking chair where Mannah had fallen asleep while awaiting Erfu, a blanket tight across her lap.

"Fine."

Her golden eyes glimmered in the candlelit cabin as she glanced at her hands—free now from the sagardon and gauze. They all waited—Luca on the floor near her, bandaged up; Urtzi and Osana at the table. No one said a word as Ula wet her lips and smoothed the knees of her trousers a few times.

"My father and I fled together. Across the Divide to Eritri. He was a blacksmith and found work easily, and so we got a room and just . . .

waited. Every night before I fell asleep we would pray to the stars that Mother would find us. I don't even know if he actually knew where she was or if she was alive. I just know he prayed with me."

Ula swallowed heavily, and squeezed her eyes shut as if to stave off tears. After a moment her eyes sprang open and her voice started again, even softer than before. "Then he died—an injury at the forge. I was in an orphanage by four turns of the sun."

Ula didn't add more. But then Urtzi whistled from behind. "Where you met *me*!"

Amazingly, he earned a laugh. "'Met me' means 'arrived and immediately tried to cut the supper line in front of me.'"

Now it was Luca's turn to laugh. "I am quite sure that did not go well."

"Want to see my scar?" Urtzi asked, pointing to the skin on his neck below his ear. "If you look close you can see where she stabbed me with a fork."

"So your temper started early," Osana teased.

"As if you wouldn't have stabbed him in the same situation," Ula answered. "He was a foot taller than anyone in line and not only did he try to slip in front of me, but also several smaller children."

"Okay," Osana relented, "I would've stabbed him if I knew how."

Urtzi smacked the table with both hands. "I didn't see them."

"Did you ever cut the line again?"

"No."

"And what of Dunixi?" Luca asked.

"He came when we were thirteen and fourteen turns of the sun," Ula replied. "Son of a shipping magnate that fell afoul of the Eritrian crown. Father was thrown in prison, mother was already dead, so he was sent to the orphanage as part of the sentencing. Everything wound up with the Crown—the ship, the son, those stupid rings."

She nodded to Osana here, as Urtzi made to clarify. "His father's rings." It wasn't his usual from-the-gut pronouncement; something bitter wove throughout. "He stole them off the ship as they were being taken. His father never even knew he had them."

Luca grinned. It would be like Dunixi to grab anything of worth before running—especially if it wasn't actually his. "I have a feeling he liked to show those rings to anyone with eyeballs."

"You would be correct," Ula spit.

"And yet you followed him anyway," Luca pointed out. "Why?"

Urtzi replied for the two of them. "He got us out."

That answer was enough for Osana. "That's why I followed the princess—she got me out. Though it was quite obvious she was the real deal, unlike that blowhard. Sorry, but he was."

Ula shrugged. "I don't deny it. But that blowhard came up with the plan. Knew where his father's ship had been impounded. We were old enough to know that children like us were never actually adopted, never sent into the world on our own accord. If we'd stayed, Urtzi and Dunixi would've been conscripted within a month—the Eritrian army is different than that of Ardenia. In Ardenia, anyone with smarts can rise to be an officer. In Eritri, only the children of nobility are officers; the rest are grunts. And the orphans are front line."

"Especially if they were not of Eritri," Urtzi added, that bitterness back. Urtzi did not explain why he left Myrcell for Eritri in the first place. Luca did not ask—refugees rarely had a happy reason for being displaced.

"I wouldn't have been pulled into the army," Ula clarified. "I would've been pushed onto the streets with no skills and no savings. Exactly as I came to them in the first place—"

Ula's words died out as a commotion came from outside—the goats in a ruckus.

"Erfu!" Mannah exclaimed, startling awake—she'd had years of practice in awaiting her husband's reappearance under the cover of darkness. She stood from her rocking chair, blanket dropping to the floor, and yanked open a single shutter, as she must have done so many times before.

As it yawned open, a brilliant light flared beyond the window.

Fire.

She shoved open both shutters.

The barn was completely aflame.

Luca and Ula shot up, and Osana's and Urtzi's chairs scraped back from the table—as something else came into view.

A rider.

No, more than one—three. Three men on horseback, torches in hand.

Two bent toward the split-rail fence surrounding the upper level of the property, the grazing area beyond—lighting each and every rail on fire with the methodical precision of priests lighting candles to the stars.

The third headed straight for the house.

"Out, out, everyone out!" Luca shouted. There was an audible *whoosh* as the flames touched the eaves.

This close to the Torrent, rain was sparse, especially in the summer, and the structure was made of juniper wood and dry as a bone. Within a minute or less, the whole thing would be engulfed.

Ula gathered the tinctures, thrusting them into her saddlebag, while Urtzi hauled the rest of the half-packed saddlebags and jug of sagardon. Luca hastily packed the map, unsheathed his dagger, and took Mannah's hand. She'd grabbed a fire poker as means for a weapon.

"Mannah, is there a place we can run to? Somewhere we can hide?"

"Through the rear door," the old woman directed. "We can scramble down the ravine—Erfu and I maintain a cave. Stocked with supplies."

Closest to the rear door Osana grabbed her sword and used her blade to wrench it open without touching the hot metal handle, and held it ajar. Mannah and Luca led the way, but just as they all entered the yard Ula shoved past the line and ran back into the house as the whole front smoldered.

"Ula—" Urtzi grunted, dropping everything, then headed in after her.

Smoke billowed out for a few tense seconds before they both appeared again, coughing. Ula held a wad of fabric in her hands.

"Get dressed," Ula ordered, shoving his tunic into Luca's arms.

Of course. She was right. He shrugged it on, concealing the tattoo, and surveyed the scene.

Every structure was aflame—the house, the barn, the lean-to stable, the fence surrounding the whole damned thing. The stench of burning animal flesh and hair rose to the stars. Horses screaming, a cacophony of goats, chickens, the frantic barking of the farm dogs.

The pair of riders lighting the fence were thundering their way from opposite directions, on a course to meet right in front of the rear door, and their intended targets. The man lighting the cabin rounded the side of the building and met them.

This had been intricately planned.

They'd been smoked out and now stood trapped, hemmed in by fire on all sides, their only escape path blocked by the mounted marauders who crowded before them, torches still aflame. All three wore the sand-blasted canvas and muslin popular in the Torrent, hats pulled down over their eyes, bandanas shoved over their noses.

As Luca stared them down, dagger tight in his grip, he realized this would be his first true fight without Amarande either by his side or as his pure and only motivation. He'd told the truth those moments in the meadow before everything changed.

"Of course I practice—I fight you."

No reason more, no reason less.

To the stars, Luca wanted nothing more to be on the other side of this moment. Closer to being with her again. He couldn't lose. Couldn't let her down. Couldn't leave her like this.

"I have an idea," Osana announced, eyes on the bandits as they began to advance with their torches and hard eyes. She shoved King Sendoa's sword into Luca's free hand and tagged Urtzi's arm. "I need your help."

"Wait—" Ula started, only to be cut off as Osana sprinted away, holding something she'd grabbed from their pile of saved belongings.

"Trust me!" she screamed, without so much as a backward glance.

Urtzi hesitated a moment, looking to Ula, who waved him off, and he chased after Osana, catching up in just a few long strides.

"We saw your face, girl!" the leader screamed toward Osana before she and Urtzi disappeared around the side of the cabin, toward the stable and animal pens. "You can't hide from the Warlord!"

There was no denying it then. These were the Warlord's men.

The three bandits did not change the pace of their advance or regroup—facing off against Luca with a sword and dagger, Ula and her trusty curved blade, and Mannah wielding her fire poker, fierce in defense of her hard-won home, now burning to the deadened grass.

"If that was meant to be a diversion it didn't work," Luca whispered, when not a one of them peeled off after the pair.

"It's not a diversion because they know who *you* are," Ula whispered. "Run, we'll hold them off."

"I will not."

"You can and you will," she grit out, nudging him with her shoulder.

Back toward the side of the burning cabin, where he could dart out front, find a break in the fence, and disappear into the night. Maybe.

He stepped aside. "No. I will not hide. I didn't come on this journey to hide."

As they argued, Mannah broke away, all snarl and spit. She advanced on the riders, poker out and pointed straight at the middle one, who had a mean gleam in his eyes and a bandana of Warlord blue. "What is your business here?"

"Everything you fear and everything you expect, old woman," he snarled. There was something familiar about him to Luca. Hard. Wiry. Pitiless. But perhaps all men scoured by the harsh Torrent winds and sand turned out this way—like the men whom Renard and Taillefer had hired to hunt down Amarande.

"I do not fear you!" Mannah shouted back, poker jutted forward like a spear. "Raiders! Scum! You've burned everything of value. What are you going to bring to the Warlord from this? A pile of ash?"

The leader began to laugh, as did his seconds—one scrawny, one stout, both as thorny and stubborn as shoots off a blackberry bramble. Like their leader, there was something familiar about them. "We all know what here is of value, old woman, and it is not you. That boy comes with us."

Mannah shook her poker at him. "Over my dead body he does."

The leader caught eyes with his seconds.

"If that's how you want it to be, then."

No.

Quick as a flash, Luca broke into a run, shaking off Ula's grip as she lunged for his arm. The leader leaned down from his horse and swung his torch hard—the thick wood connecting with the tip of Mannah's poker. The thin metal instrument went flying out of her grasp, leaving her defiant and defenseless. The man raised his torch once again, stabbing it toward Mannah's face.

Then Luca was there.

He thrust Mannah behind him, and met the torch with a sweeping slice from his sword. The severed head of the torch went flying. It landed beyond them, still flaming.

Luca held the sword in a high block, and pressed his dagger into Mannah's shaking hand. Together, they stared down the men. He

couldn't hear Ula, and had no idea where Urtzi and Osana were—
everything he had was poured into confronting these men and protecting Mannah.

The leader squinted down from his horse, and laughed at their
show of defiance, his teeth flashing in the twin lights of his seconds'
torches. "There's no point in putting up a fight, wolf cub. You're ours,
your friends are as good as dead, and this place is ash. Boys, take
him."

A flash of movement from Luca's right, and a dagger hurtled
toward his exposed side. Instinct and muscle memory honed during
his days in the meadow with Amarande kicked in, and Luca twisted
away.

But not fast enough.

The dagger caught the edge of Luca's tunic and slashed a shallow
gash across his side. Luca stumbled, unable to catch his balance on
his snakebit leg. His sword skitterered away as he hit the ground.
Luca rolled and tried to lunge for it, but the stout boy had already
dismounted, kicking it away.

The leader slid from his horse, drawing his own sword as his boots
hit the ground. Mannah screamed and ran at him, dagger out, and he
swatted her away as easily as a fly. She landed in a heap.

Luca willed his legs to move. Battle-hardened hands grabbed him,
a man on each side of him, yanking him up, their torches still held
in their opposite hands to give their leader light for whatever cruel
intention he had before hauling him away.

"Oh no you don't!"

Ula.

A fist-sized fireball shot over Luca's shoulder, plowing straight into
the leader's gut. Using her sword to scoop up the severed head of the
leader's torch and hurtling it back, Ula had echoed Amarande's trick
from their fight against the Harea Asps.

Even though she was not there, Luca's princess had once again
played a part in saving him.

The leader fell back, tunic and skin suddenly aflame. His bandana
slid down as he hit the dry ground behind him, his face distorted
with panic as he screamed horrifically.

The men holding Luca hesitated in shock—an opportunity he used
to wrench away from the scrawny one, planting a boot in his lean gut.

Ula's blade cut the stout one down with a blow to his wide upper back, and his grip upon Luca immediately died as he fell away.

More hoofbeats sounded behind them.

The death knell of raider reinforcements—or the sound of rescue?

Luca turned to see two riders approaching full-speed, bareback, headed straight toward the remaining bandits, stumbling away with their torches still in hand.

Urtzi and Osana.

As they got closer, Luca was able to make out Urtzi, juggling both a bucket and a thick unstoppered jug, while struggling to maintain hold of the horse's reins. Osana was similarly encumbered, clutching a bucket in both arms while steering her horse with her knees.

At the sight, Luca realized exactly what they were going to do.

"Back, back, back!" he yelled, getting fully to his feet, helped along by Ula and Mannah. Stumbling, he urgently pulled them away from the bandits as fast as they could move, toward the burning cabin.

Urtzi rode to one side, Osana the other.

"Now!" Osana screamed.

She threw her bucket at the smoldering body of the leader, writhing on the ground. The contents doused him completely and suddenly he wasn't a man, but a fireball.

WHOOSH.

Urtzi hit the other two with his own bucket and the glass jug. The instant the caustic antiseptic made contact, the torches shuddered and exploded.

WHOOSH. WHOOSH.

All three men suddenly were ablaze.

As the Warlord knew well, there was no way to survive flames like that.

CHAPTER
11

❧⟨∞⟩☙

THE Dowager Queen ruminated over the last dregs of her breakfast.
She was anxious to hear Captain Nikola's plan for locating Taillefer,
especially after successfully setting into motion his disownment. Upon
further interrogation, the imprisoned pirate had produced a contract
for hire, signed by her second son. It was proof enough of his treachery
for her councilors to do their part, but *she* needed him to stand trial for
treason so that there would be no question in anyone's mind that he
should not and could not have claim to the crown of Pyrenee.

But the captain was late, annoying her greatly because it was necessary she depart as soon as possible for Basilica. Still, his delay allowed
her time to receive one more of her daily treatments from Medikua
Aritza, something she wanted to avoid doing on the ship, as it required
swallowing a large amount of red raspberry leaf tincture—difficult
enough to keep down on solid land, much less a seafaring vessel. The
royal ship was already brimming with cargo and passengers—all it
needed was her.

After the treatment, as the medikua packed up her many tinctures,
Inés brought her to a momentary halt. "Medikua Aritza? Do you have
anything within your collection that might provide a . . . *boost* for my
betrothed? Some sort of male equivalent to the service you are providing me?"

Domingu was more than double the Dowager Queen's age and had
sired no children with his recently departed wife—a woman more
than a decade Inés's junior.

A wry smile crossed the medikua's thin lips. "Nothing I haven't
provided him before, Your Highness, if he'll take it."

"I will see to it that he does." There was a knock on the door—*ah,
finally.* "Ensure that your items are prepared for travel at ten strikes of
the bell, medikua. You shall ride to the port in my carriage."

"Yes, Your Highness."

As the medikua scuttled away, the Dowager Queen turned her

attention to her next visitor. "Come in, Captain. Tell me, I hope you have a clever plan for a clever mark?"

Nikola entered, looking ghostly pale underneath the not-yet-faded sunburn from his excursion into the Torrent with Renard's search party to "rescue" Princess Amarande. His voice was raspy and dry with lack of sleep. "We have more pressing concerns, Your Highness."

He offered a scroll. The Dowager Queen's attention snagged on the broken seal. "Captain, you know all official correspondence addressed to the Crown is to be opened by my hand only."

The boy blanched further at her tone. "It was addressed to 'The People of Pyrenee,'" he stammered. "Not to the Crown. Delivered not by rider but by *bird*. Please, read it, Your Highness."

Most unusual, indeed. Purse-lipped, Inés stood and plucked the parchment from him. She did not break eye contact with Nikola, whose desperation did not excuse his insolence. "Of course I will read it, though I am angry you took it upon yourself to do so first."

"Punish me later, Your Highness. Read it now. Immediately. Please."

In spite of his youth, Nikola did not often appear rattled—as he did now. That, in itself, was cause for concern.

Inés unfurled the parchment, revealing the painstaking penmanship of a court scribe. The Dowager Queen read the lines in silence. Her face flushed, fingers shaking as she swallowed down the lump that had formed in her throat by the conclusion.

The parchment fluttered to her breakfast table, coming to rest atop her butter dish. The Dowager Queen stared at the letter as if it couldn't be real. But there it was, the parchment immediately stained translucent with butterfat.

Ardenia had struck first. Despite all her scheming and preparation, they had made the first cut. A deep one. Nothing superficial about it. Slashing through the fraying fabric holding together the continent.

According to this document, Pyrenee now stood accused of *murdering* Princess Amarande in retaliation for Prince Renard's death, which occurred during an *illegal* wedding.

Right there on the page was the accusation that the Warrior King's daughter was kidnapped by Renard and forced into vows without the consent or knowledge of the Royal Council of Ardenia, or the kingdom's regent ruler, General Koldo. No mention was made of the signed contract the Pyrenee party witnessed Renard deliver in the council room of the Itspi.

Even more shocking, it seemed Ardenia had done its own scheming and preparation: The kingdom had crowned a new and surprising *king*—Ferdinand, Princess Amarande's brother, younger by a scant year.

Inés reread the letter. She did not care how long the captain waited in silence.

At the bottom of the parchment—beneath the stacked signatures of the new king, his suddenly reappearing mother, and each of Ardenia's Royal Council members—was a footnote specifying that copies of the letter were sent to the other standing kingdoms of the union of the Sand and Sky.

Domingu had promised to send word of the wedding on the heels of the finished contract. A short delay meant to give Inés time to inform her council and prepare to travel for the nuptials.

Those announcements would arrive tomorrow to Ardenia, Myrcell, and the nobility worth filling a court. Which meant this letter was sent without knowledge of the impending wedding.

A gutsy first strike, indeed.

A statement made because Ardenia had expected *her* to retaliate for Renard's murder right away. It also allowed for the convenient coronation of this so-called son of Sendoa. No one had heard from Geneva in fifteen years—therefore, it was tough to fathom, let alone believe, that a new, unknown male heir could just *appear* at the Itspi.

But of course Geneva would do something like this.

Of course.

The woman always found a way around an inconvenience. And this baby king was her pawn and ticket in one.

And yet Inés found small comfort in this knowledge. If it was true that Sendoa had a son, that would explain why the king had continuously rebuffed her. And, perhaps, why he had never rewritten the laws in Amarande's favor. Something that clearly frustrated both the princess and the councilors who worked so hard to marry her off.

It also meant that Amarande or one of her surrogates—the stableboy, the hired pirates, or the single hired hand in Renard's party who was unaccounted for—had delivered the story of the disastrous wedding within the Bellringe's walls straight to Ardenia itself.

The Dowager Queen's quarantine of guests meant it could be no one else . . . well, except the one other person who was missing.

Taillefer.

Inés closed her eyes and pinched the bridge of her nose. Yes, disownment would not be enough. That boy would most certainly be the death of her if she didn't kill him first.

She should have sent Taillefer away as Louis-David's illness progressed and the boy took an interest in the natural arts. She much preferred her second son torturing cadavers somewhere across the sea than in the Sand and Sky where he could wreak havoc aimed at her ambition.

Again, she went over the information about the wedding.

Yes, reading between the lines made it all so clear.

Ardenia did not have possession of the princess. "Murdered" was not a term or accusation used lightly. And they had turned the full scope of the word's power on Pyrenee as leverage to draw the other kingdoms in their favor.

The figures on the board had been set up—Tiger, Mountain Lion, Shark, Bear. And now Inés had to see to it that they all fell her way. The best way to do that besides completing the marriage as planned was to expose their lie.

"Your Highness?" The captain finally found his voice as he watched the Dowager Queen's eyes fly open and her posture reset—shoulders set back at a regal pitch, elbows planted on the table, fingers tented together. Morning light crept up her back from her open balcony, and she knew from his vantage it might appear that she was aflame along with the blazing sky.

"As you are aware, Ardenia has a new king, a reappearing queen, and what they say is a dead princess. This turn of events is too tidy, and for the good of our reputation we must prove them wrong. Captain, it is imperative that you leave immediately to find the princess."

"Is she my priority over Taillefer?"

It was an astute clarification on Nikola's part—essentially, Ardenia first or Pyrenee?

With no right of blood, the Dowager Queen's own claim to Pyrenee was weak. Inés knew it and the rest of the Sand and Sky would, too. The best move she had was to project, deflect, and bury any accusation or person in her way.

She had wanted to bury Ardenia with the threat of war, but if this was her choice she would take a strong claim and an army as her first priority. If Ardenia had used Pyrenee to sell a pack of lies fashioned to install a king with a shaky claim, the combined armies of Pyrenee and Basilica could propel Ardenia into chaos just as easily as a living, breathing princess.

"Taillefer first, Amarande second. Both if the stars align." Orders accepted, Nikola pivoted toward the door, but she held up a hand. "Captain, you do not want to return to me empty-handed. And should you run, your punishment will be even worse than death. Succeed or you will suffer."

CHAPTER
12

STINKING of smoke and urgency, Luca and his crew pushed into the rising sun of the Torrent. It was almost as if there were a second dawn here, in the flat-bowl bottoms astride the mountains. They'd already spent hours and yet gained back time.

And they would need it.

They'd left immediately, following the path into the Torrent that Mannah knew Erfu rode most often. The hope was that they would intercept him on the way back to the farm, and make the journey to the resistance's location that way. A little tardy, but under the cover of dark, and ahead of the Warlord's men who would surely be after them when the bandits did not appear with the Otsakumea in hand.

But with dawn that hope died away—along with the chances Erfu was still alive.

They were a target, plain and simple. One in search of a needle in a massive, hostile haystack. No guide, no direction, no way to locate a group that had spent seventeen years working very hard not to be found.

In moments after the narrow mountain passes opened into the cracked bottoms of the Torrent, Luca was protected on all sides, cushioned from the elements, as they rode in formation as fast as their horses would carry them. Ula out front, Urtzi behind, Osana on Luca's weak side. Ula had grumbled about leaving his dagger side open, but the numbers wouldn't allow for it. They hadn't had enough horses or people—Mannah was insistent that she should stay at the farm to redirect Erfu to them when he made it. If he made it.

And so the four of them went onward. Into the Torrent. To the resistance. Then, with any luck, to a destiny with Amarande at Luca's side.

Yet as the russet dust of the Otxoa homeland swirled about their small procession, Luca's stomach wouldn't settle. All his senses were on alert for a new threat.

The conspicuous: a band of warriors; the Warlord's caravan crushing down. The furtive: sleeping darts like the one that caught Amarande in the neck and landed her in the Warlord's captivity; a sudden dagger piercing the most vulnerable target.

The dangers were real and directed at Luca. The ink above his heart all the proof anyone needed—severed heads in bags were for kings; flayed tattoos were for long-lost heirs.

Luca's horse shifted its gait—Ula's arm thrown up in a signal. *Hold*.

Ahead there was a gap in the long line of plateaus—marked on the map as the River of Stone—the sheer faces of the rock formations shifting into nothing but swirling, open wasteland, cinnamon red, and pulsing with waves of heat lifting from the ground up into the cloudless blue of the sky. Luca combed the vertical crags for a sign, fingers already at the lip of his boot, dagger a breath away.

Ula's arm swung down and across her body, her index and middle fingers out and pointing about a third of the way up the far rock wall astride the gap.

Luca followed the slicing angle of her fingers.

There: A body strung up like a scarecrow, his limbs jammed into crevices in the rock face to keep him in place. A man—with the exact hat and bandana Erfu had donned just before leaving the outpost. They couldn't see his face. Not from here. But it had to be him.

Luca's heart lurched with the certainty that he'd sent this man to his death.

"Urtzi," Luca called, "see if it's Erfu."

Urtzi slid from his horse and plucked a dagger from his belt, eyes scanning the rock formations for any movement. Luca drew the ancient Basilican sword at his back—a parting gift from Mannah—as Ula and Osana drew theirs.

Urtzi's long strides shortened as he carefully stepped within the narrow rock cut—a hundred feet to the top of either plateau but only ten feet or so between one wall and the other. In recounting her journey to Luca, Amarande had called this chain of plateaus the dragon's spine, and this proved it was more a spine than a stone river—Urtzi wedged himself between one vertebra and another, back pressed to the wall, carefully checking every inch of rock for hidden ambush points.

Luca did not exhale until Urtzi stepped away from the southernmost part of the wall and turned to face the body. Using the heel of his dagger, he tipped the man's head up, revealing Erfu's dark and bloated face to those watching below. "Dart in his neck and an assassin's smile. Slowed him down and then sliced him open. His tunic is torn, too—they checked his tattoo. Carved an X through it."

What had Ula said? There weren't many of those with paw prints left—too easy to identify.

Osana, who'd been sold to the Warlord and held with Amarande, blinked and looked away. "That's the Warlord for you. Stars only know how long he's been like that."

"He's stiff as a board," Urtzi answered. "Probably nabbed him half a day ago, no later."

"Wait." Ula squinted at him. "How do you know that?"

Urtzi's jaw worked. "You may be surprised, but I do listen when you talk."

"Anything else?" Luca asked. "Footprints? Horse tracks?"

Urtzi spun in a circle, testing the air. He shook his head. "The wind's running north–south, it's been roaring through the cut all morning at least. I don't even see my own footprints anymore. Sand's covered them."

Silence descended as Urtzi picked his way back down to the trail.

"Was he left there as a message to us?" Luca asked, bile churning in the back of his windpipe. What would he tell Mannah? That his mere presence had destroyed not only her home but also the man she loved? How does one atone for that? Luca coughed, swallowing. "Or to the resistance in general?"

"Both. Hurts us, hurts them, hurts *anyone* who happens to see him," Osana answered, her voice low and strained. "The Warlord is all about equal-opportunity fear—the cruelty of the symbolism is the point. 'If you want to live, don't be this bastard.'"

Osana wasn't wrong. That was exactly the Warlord's game. And exactly the hold they were trying to break on the people of the Torrent. Fear was the price paid for the supposed freedom the Warlord allowed them.

Urtzi swung himself back atop his horse. "Now what?"

Luca rattled his brain for the answer. No tracks, no clues, their guide dead—

"Now you come with us."

Luca spun his horse around to face the new threat, sword at the ready. His companions took up position around him, weapons drawn. The voice had come from his dagger side—his open side. When his eyes found the speaker, crouched still as stone and watching from several feet away, Luca's heart stuttered.

A ghost. The man was a ghost. One sent to the stars by Luca's own hand and a knife, in the shadow of the Hand with Amarande fighting by his side.

Yet here he was, climbing awkwardly to his feet, one side of his body dragging as if partially paralyzed. The man took a halting step toward the mounted group.

At that, Luca found his voice, hoarse as it was. "You're dead."

The man accepted Luca's accusation with a smile. "If the knife had gone an inch either way, I would be."

The man took another painful step forward, his whole left side immobile. Luca remembered the looseness of this man's body as he fell at the campsite as he fought himself and Amarande. Just collapsed, a puppet with his strings cut—Luca's dagger protruding from his back.

The ghost turned and whistled. "It's him."

Four men materialized out of the rock face. Along with a black wolf.

Luca blinked, unbelieving as the famed sigil of the Otxoa struck out ahead of the rest. Its snout was drawn into something of a confident grin, its golden eyes still and pinned upon him.

Like him, it should've been extinct.

And yet, it looked him right in the face, let loose a low growl.

Ula stowed her sword and dismounted as the wolf trotted back to the oldest man in the group, settling down on its haunches beside him. "Hitz ematen dizut," she said, baring her paw print tattoo and offering her word of honor.

The old man smiled, lips stretched across his dark-stubbled face, his bearing proud and upright in spite of his age. His presentation was simply another sign, along with the wolf's heel, that this man was plainly the leader.

He nodded at Luca and gestured at the wolf. "Hitz ematen dizut, my Otsakumea. Beltza recognizes you. As do I. Follow us now. Quickly."

Osana and Ula stowed their weapons, as Urtzi gaped as if he'd witnessed a magic trick. "I—I checked everywhere. How did I not see you?"

The ghost answered. "We live only because we cannot be seen." The four men and the wolf—Beltza—turned. Ula remounted and kicked her horse into gear, still in the lead, but Luca did not budge. "But what of Erfu? We cannot leave him here—like this."

The leader nodded. "After dark, we will remove him and bring him to his wife. He was a good man and to ensure his sacrifice was not in vain, it is imperative that we go. Now."

"But his farm is destroyed. The Warlord's men found us and burned it. His wife is displaced and—"

"My Otsakumea, I assure you, we will see to it that all debts are paid," the leader replied, calm but firm. "Come, please. Now."

Distrust was not a natural emotion to Luca, but now that he'd been made aware of its presence, he could not shut off the sour churn of it in his gut. These people had stayed near Erfu's body. Clearly waiting for an encounter like this. A face like his. And this ghost man provided the identification—Luca had yet to show his own tattoo.

And yet, he still did not move.

"Your Otsakumea has one final question. Please." Luca addressed the man from the Hand. "You are part of the resistance?"

The man turned on his good leg, very nearly toppling over. In answer, he bared his own paw print, as did the others. The wolf simply sat and waited patiently, gold eyes brilliant and unblinking. As the ghost's tunic slipped back into place, Luca tried in vain to picture the man as a friend, failing. The man at the Hand had come to take him captive. He was sure of it. Amarande was sure of it. And he'd initiated the fight that, until this very moment, Luca thought had led to this man's death.

When he hesitated, his entire group did, too, eyes moving from Luca to the ghost and back. Finally, Luca said, "You threw a knife at me."

The same crooked smile spread across the man's face. "I aimed to miss and distract your captor."

"Not here," the leader said, some of the calm in his voice sheeting away. "The longer we stay in the open, the more danger we are in." He tipped his head toward Erfu. "We've already lost one today; let us not lose anyone else."

All eyes found Luca—but he looked to the wolf. This creature who saw him for what he was, as impossible as they both were. In that moment, the wolf stood and approached the cleavage of the space between vertebrae in the stone spine. Once there, she looked back over her shoulder, as if saying, *Follow me.*

As his eyes met Beltza's golden ones, the last Otxoa nodded. He nudged his horse forward into the gap, and the others followed.

CHAPTER
13

THE crowd anticipated a wedding announcement. What it got was a coronation.

The princess was missing and presumed dead at the hands of Pyrenee. The king was introduced, explained away, and crowned. The former Runaway Queen lauded for keeping her son safe and protected.

Because of this turn of events, Ardenia was stable and deadly—Pyrenee would be lucky to avoid a swift rebuke from the superior Ardenian army.

That was the message, anyway.

And General Koldo, in her best garnet-and-gold regalia—watching the commoners exit, first from the arena, and then from the castle grounds—hoped the people of Ardenia would accept it at face value as the gates were sealed at their backs.

Guards watched the crowds from atop the parapets. They'd already heard of unease about the closed gates—Sendoa had always left the Itspi open to the people of Ardenia. It wasn't his castle as much as it was theirs, he'd said, citing the blood, sweat, and tears conscripts gave to the army, and workers to the diamond mines. Ferdinand would see it his father's way eventually, Koldo was sure of it. But as of now he didn't protest the closed gates—the threat of war was too great as the sands on the continent settled. No chance could be taken.

And so the doors were sealed. For safety. For security.

The general's gaze skipped to the stained glass atop the north tower. *"I am sorry, Ama."*

A shadow skimmed by her as the royal party passed—Geneva, now called Queen Mother—deep in conversation with Satordi as they disappeared into the red bowels of the castle. Ferdinand paused outside the entrance.

"Koldo, a word, if you would, please. In the library."

"Yes, my king." The general's voice was stoic and professional—the exact tone she would've used to address a similar request from

Sendoa. She'd had decades of practice in hiding her real feelings in public. It would be no different with her son. That was her price to pay in all of this. A small cost in the scheme of all she'd already paid, and lost.

The pair walked silently in to the Itspi and up the stairs. Even with the hidden brace, the king had an obvious limp from his tussle with Amarande. They turned into the great library—a roomy, brightly lit space full of stacks and stacks of manuscripts ranging from poetry to treatises to maps of every known surface of the earth. Like everything else at the Itspi, and in Ardenia for that matter, its holdings had swelled under Sendoa's watch.

Koldo followed her son to the bank of windows that looked upon the training yard, and they sat beneath a giant tapestry of Sendoa's grandfather, pictured as a child, mounted regally atop a similarly regal orange-and-black tiger, holding a book. Though his great-grandfather was depicted with butter-blond hair, the resemblance to Ferdinand was striking. He sat under the whimsical portrait and stared at the general with Sendoa's eyes.

"I cannot mention this to the council or to Geneva," Ferdinand said, "but I—I was under the impression that we were *only* to say that Amarande was *missing*. To *tell* the people she is dead, when we—and a handful of guards, I might add—know that she is alive and breathing, is too far for me. Why tell a lie that we cannot take back?"

For once, Ferdinand sounded uncertain—more like a boy his age than the ruthless leader Geneva clearly hoped he would become.

The general did not break eye contact, nor did she hesitate. "It must be done."

It was clear from Ferdinand's narrowed eyes that her answer did not sit well with him. "Surely there is a way to amend this. I am not one to lie."

"A lie got you here."

He grimaced. "But it didn't have to. We could have told the crowd I am illegitimate—that I am your son—and had been made legitimate in light of recent events."

Koldo's heart leapt at the thought. She ignored it. What was done was done.

"The easiest way to lead peacefully is not to invite questions. All the caveats you list allow for too many—ones that we don't have the time or latitude to answer."

Ferdinand's voice dropped to a furious whisper. "She is my sister. You are my mother." He took her hands in his. Koldo's breath caught. "I don't like that we're hiding her away. I don't like that I have just found you and now I must act as if you are nothing to me."

Koldo slipped her hands from his grip and immediately regretted it. When would she be able to hold her son again? Then, as she must, she swallowed her feelings and became the stoic general once more.

"Your Highness, there is much to being king that you will not like, but you will do because it is the best route to keeping your people safe."

"I have learned that lesson from Geneva." Of this Koldo had no doubt, given what she'd long known. "I just thought in this position it would be different."

After a moment, Koldo answered, "I can tell you that it is good that you feel this way."

He glanced up, surprised. "Good?"

Koldo wove her fingers together so that she would not grab his hands or touch his shoulder or do anything else she craved. Instead, she smiled tightly. "Your Highness, tough decisions never get easier. Even for those with the best of intentions, because no decision is perfect. And those with the worst intentions do not care."

CHAPTER
14

Luca had ventured underground into the diamond mines of Ardenia only a few times. Dark and claustrophic, they weren't a place to play, but, as always, if Amarande wanted to go, he had followed.

The pro-Otxoa resistance lived underground, but the world Luca and the others entered under the cover of new dark was nothing like those mines. In fact, instead of a tight, dangerous burrow, these tunnels almost felt like the halls of a castle. The ceilings weren't as high, the walls were made of smoothed bedrock instead of stacked stones, but they were brightly lit with torches every few strides in a way that mirrored walking through the Itspi at night.

Tala, the leader, gestured Luca in first, followed by Ula, Urtzi close on her heels as usual, with Osana bringing up the rear. In front of him, perhaps a quarter mile down, loomed the glow of a much wider space—and with it, the low whisper of faraway voices.

His people.

In that moment, Luca hesitated, and the black wolf, Beltza, skirted past him. She paused, too, realizing he'd stopped moving, and turned his way, her yellow eyes bright, intelligent, and encouraging.

Luca's fingers flexed, wishing to touch her coat—this extinct symbol who shouldn't exist but did, just like him.

The black wolf closed the space between them, backtracking, until she was by his side. She nuzzled the top of her head against his palm, waiting.

Luca smoothed her fur, squared his shoulders, and set his attention to those who had been waiting for him all this time.

With each step, an audible thrum of energy welled up from the walls, growing until it was more than a hum, a buzz, an ache. The promise of what they'd come for, the swell of it vibrant, an energy and presence.

The wolf walked with him, perceptive eyes glancing up at him so often that he finally smiled and bent to her with a whisper. "Do not worry, Beltza. I haven't changed my mind—I want this."

And then, when the noise and sound and movement from beyond were so great they made Luca's ears ring, the wolf again halted and sunk to her haunches, waiting silently with her snout tossed over her shoulder, watching Luca advance.

Luca closed his eyes and thought of Amarande.

In the meadow devouring their lunch after swordplay, eyes alight over lemon cake.

In the slim shadows after their escape, kissing him for that first time.

In the firelight at the Hand, sharing her heart.

And, now, back at the Itspi, repairing the damage the Pyrenee wedding had done, awaiting the messenger with word that he had connected with the resistance.

Soon they would be together. Forever this time. And nothing would stand in their way.

I want this.

One final step and Luca, the Otsakumea, beheld the vast, open cavern filled with hundreds—no, thousands—of people.

Yes, his people.

The black wolf tipped her face to the ceiling and howled.

All movement ceased. All eyes fell upon Luca, standing above and before them.

For the first time in seventeen years, the people of the Otxoa beheld their Otsakumea.

Luca stared back, not sure what to say. This was something he should've prepared for. He should've been ready; he should have—

Tala took a commanding step forward and yanked the neck of Luca's tunic aside, exposing the wolf on his chest.

At once—silence.

Then an explosion of noise that nearly tipped him back—the crowd, loud and speaking as one.

"My Otsakumea, we have been waiting for you."

As the sound filled the space, the black wolf howled again, joining her voice to theirs.

And then every one of those thousands of people began to clap. It was completely overwhelming—in that moment, and then even more so as Luca, the black wolf, and the crew picked their way along the switchback ramp that guided them the rest of the way down.

Luca, Tala, and Beltza hit the ground level to a crush of people and hands and repeated exclamations of "My Otsakumea!" that echoed across the cavern.

Luca's reaction was to do what he'd seen Amarande do nearly every day of their life together. He clasped every hand. Repeated every name. Eye contact, eye contact, eye contact.

"My Otsakumea! You are the very vision of King Lotyoa!"

"My Otsakumea, your timing could not be better!"

"Oh, how I have prayed to the stars for this day, my Otsakumea! Seventeen years! I daresay I was beginning to believe the stars had grown tired of my requests!"

Finally, after almost everyone had had a chance to greet Luca, Tala clapped his hands for attention, addressing the throng.

"For seventeen years, we have had the people, the placement, the plan." Tala turned to Luca. "All we needed was you, my Otsakumea."

It was meant to be a compliment. This was his destiny, his duty. Luca looked out into the crowd and into the faces of those who had hope in him long before he knew who he was meant to be.

"I am yours. The wait is over and the Warlord will be defeated!"

Again, Tala clapped his hands. "Let stage one commence!"

The great room cleared as everyone spun into action, hundreds of people streaming down several high-arched passageways that radiated from the main cavern. Everyone knew exactly what those words meant and their role. Everyone but the piece that set it all into motion.

Tala shepherded the group into a smaller room hidden behind a pillar just off the main entry. Some sort of receiving room—a place fitted with bowls of water and linens to wash away the marks of a hard day spent in the Torrent.

Luca was uninterested in such luxuries. "Tala, forgive my questions, but I have many."

"Me too. First, I would like to know why Guille did not announce his intentions before attacking Luca," Ula said, referring to the ghost—the man he and Amarande had encountered at the Hand. "He threw a knife at Luca, and I don't want Luca anywhere near him."

"I don't remember a knife fight with Guille," Urtzi ventured, perplexed.

"That's because you didn't have one," Luca explained. "He came upon our camp after Amarande rescued me from *you* and, knowing that my three kidnappers were two pirate boys and a girl he called a 'savant with a sword,' he believed the girl had killed her partners to keep me for herself."

Ula's mouth dropped open. "He what now?"

"It was a reasonable guess," Luca continued, "given Amarande's nature."

The look in Ula's golden eyes could etch glass. "Men always think so little of women. I do not like him."

From across the room, Osana chuckled—she was the only one of the crew taking a chance to freshen up. "He called you a 'savant' . . . I mean, that's a compliment."

"Not as given."

"Guille is a watcher—the Warlord watches us; we watch her," Tala explained. "Among other things, we watch for prisoners she has special interest in. So, when the Warlord sent men to intercept a prisoner at the Hand—we did not know it was you at the time, my Otsakumea—we sent Guille. And though his injuries from that fight have ended his watch, it was lucky he recognized you. By identifying the Otsakumea the way he did, all of you avoided sleeping darts to the neck."

Ula squinted at him, still unmoving. "Like the dart on Erfu's body?"

"Yes, it's part of our protocol. We use similar methods as the Warlord does—imitation is part of our survival. Though Erfu was the Warlord's work, the technique is almost indistinguishable." The old man put a decisive hand on Luca's shoulder. "Now, shall I give you the tour? Show you how we grow our food and store it? Our drying room is quite spectacular."

A pang of frustration dropped in Luca's empty stomach.

He was the last piece—what they were waiting for, yes, but he was a piece.

"I am sure it is, Tala, but the first and most pressing question I have cannot wait." Luca faced him. They were nearly the same height, this man was once as tall as Luca, before age stooped the line of his shoulders. He was as stubborn and spindly as the trees in the forest where Amarande rescued him. Likely harboring venom as deadly as the asp's, too. Tala's eyes were as golden as his own, but hooded and lined—they did not glance away. "What *is* the plan?"

TALA ushered Luca, Ula, Urtzi, and Osana down yet another tunnel, into the strategy room. Torches in sconces lit the space, and moonlight peeked through at the crest of the vaulted ceiling, yet another man-made glimpse into the world above. The floor was a patchwork of stitched-together pelts. Large reams of parchment were rolled upright in canisters along the walls, and books—bound in careful leather binding—lined narrow wooden shelves drilled into the bedrock.

A spread of wooden platters sat in a constellation at the center of the rug, the heady scent of rosemary and thyme wafting as steam escaped from under domed lids. Clay cups marked each place setting, brimming with cool water.

"Please eat, my Otsakumea. You and your companions must be famished."

All eyes swung to Luca. His stomach grumbled, but Luca held up a hand. "Thank you for this meal. Please do not wait for us to finish before detailing the plan. The lines of communication have collapsed and the Warlord could be on the move this very moment."

"I assure you, we know exactly where the Warlord is headed and it is not here."

Another pang of frustration clawed at Luca. "That is a relief, as I have spent all day expecting assassination. Where is the Warlord headed if not here, guided by watchers? And what is the plan?"

Tala stood and pivoted toward the canisters along the wall. "Please fill your plates, and I will set the stage."

Luca gestured to the others to serve themselves first. Beneath the domed lids was a feast indeed—goat stew, roasted carrots, potatoes smothered in butter and a patchwork of herbs. Large rounds of unleavened bread lay stacked under a warm blanket of muslin, weeping more butter and begging to be dipped in the stew.

When all their plates were full—and Urtzi was unsurprisingly already on his second round—they cleared the serving dishes, allowing the middle of their circle to be bare. Tala unrolled a large parchment map so that all could see. "The plan is simple. We lay a trap before the Warlord does."

Luca and the others bent over the map—one solely of Torrent and rife with detail. While Mannah did her farm chores, Luca had spent several hours with a map like this one. All the major landmarks were marked, as were the locations of each of the Warlord's fire pits, dotting the landscape like pox. They stood where former cities did, a testament to the Warlord's power. A former civilization destroyed, and from its ashes more pain as the Warlord lit one pit a night with flames spawned by human kindling.

But there was more, too—lines marking tunnels like the one where they currently sat spidered off in arteries and veins from certain locations. The tunnels weren't completely connected, but they were extensive. Years in the making. Some were marked through with ink—damaged, dangerous, or discovered.

Tala gestured to a fire pit to the north and east of the spindle-treed forest that had sheltered Webster's and the pirates the night Amarande had rescued him. "The Warlord is here, and moving west. Tomorrow, all caravans will convene at the Hand."

Luca followed Tala's fingers, his mind picturing Koldo's stern face frowning over similar maps in the Itspi library as she tutored Amarande in military strategy. "If we are laying a trap, do we arrive before the Warlord does? Be in position and ready?"

Luca thought of Amarande—how long would it take to get word to her? How long would it take her to get here with or without her army? Surely more than a day.

Tala shook his head. "That *was* the plan, but this is exactly where your timing has proved to be excellent, my Otsakumea, and our plans have shifted with another advantage. There is a new Warlord—it is a passing title, and we believe it changed hands recently."

The sentence hung for barely a blink before the first stunned question came.

"How new?" This from Osana.

"As of a few days ago. In our position, it is difficult to be precise with timing."

Luca's mind raced. It was almost too much of a coincidence to believe that Amarande's mother was installed as the Warlord on the night she and Osana were prisoners in the Warlord's camp. Yet, Amarande was sure the woman in the tent was Geneva. Perhaps her mother wasn't installed, but on her way out—and if she were leaving why then and where was she going? Of course, it might not have been that night that the title changed hands. Or, her mother might not have been there at all—Amarande's sighting of her a figment of the princess's feverish escape.

"This new Warlord has ordered all other caravans within the Torrent to join hers—within two days, no exceptions." Tala pointed to the Hand. "Those who don't report will be hunted down and pay the price—in the fire pits."

Osana sighed. "This new Warlord is looking for protection—"

"In the form of innocents," Ula muttered.

Tala did not assuage their horror. "Burning all dissenters in the fire pits is a punishment the second Warlord instituted. The first Warlord created the caravans as a means of control—never letting the people settle down, keeping them forever on the move and starved. A hungry people can raise no rebellion. When that didn't work and some rebelled, the second punished them in the most horrifying way. The third demanded an added penance for autonomy. The fourth, it seems, does not believe penance to be enough to prove loyalty."

That was a terrible sign—it was no secret what those with royal blood would do to maintain a tenuous hold upon power in the Sand and Sky; it was something else entirely to navigate the right to rule on someone else's stolen power. Luca licked his lips. "One who will likely try to make a big statement for perceived legitimacy."

"Or one who knows we will attack and is preparing," Ula charged. She exchanged a long look with Luca before turning to Tala. "How do we know which it is?"

The old man did not so much as blink before answering, "We don't. Though the reasoning does not matter as long as we stop it. And use it to our advantage."

Luca nodded. "Hundreds, maybe thousands, are required to enter camp at once—and we enter with them."

Tala nodded. "Yes." He pointed to a location about twenty miles from the Hand. It was drawn as a tight web of tunnels just south of the forest where Amarande rescued Luca from the pirates when they were all on opposite sides. "Get in position here. Infiltrate with a small reconnaissance group to verify the watchers' reports, and then, after midnight the second night, we attack."

Luca nodded. "Stage one is to head to the secure location?"

"Yes—the staging area." Tala tapped the spot. "Everything is currently being packed and prepared for movement. Stage two is to infiltrate; stage three is report; stage four is attack."

Luca's heartbeat quickened. He'd thought perhaps it would take weeks or months to raise what was needed to strike. And somehow it was here. Immediately.

"How is that for a plan, my Otsakumea?"

It was decisive, made use of previous planning and unique circumstances, and it wiped away the present threat brought by the dead raiders and the Warlord's obvious knowledge of them.

The only thing the plan did not do was give Luca ample time to warn Amarande. If she made it back to his side in time, it would be by the greatest luck. Still, he'd promised to send word. Luca drew in a breath so deep his stitches pulled. "Tala, before we leave, I do have a request."

"Anything, my Otsakumea."

Luca felt a twinge of guilt that he'd decided to take advantage of his newfound title. "I promised Princess Amarande I would send a message as soon as I connected with the movement. She plans to fortify our fight with her power and her soldiers."

Tala's sun-worn face drew tight. "I am hesitant about this, my Otsakumea."

"Why, Tala?" Then he added, "Be direct. Please."

The old leader scraped a hand through his graying hair, gone white at the temples. "For the people of Torrence, there is much distrust of Ardenia."

Luca's first conversation with Ula about the underground movement whispered from the recesses of his memory. Lifelong loyalty to the Ardenian Crown tugged across Luca's gut. "Because King Sendoa did not turn his army on the Warlord."

Tala's lips twisted. "Yes."

"But"—Luca's brows knit together—"there's more. Isn't there?"

Tala answered, his voice low and forceful, his dark eyes piercing.

"We learned very early on after the fall of Torrence that Ardenia didn't just ignore our plight—it created it."

CHAPTER
15

THE sounds of Ferdinand's coronation were loud enough Amarande was somewhat glad she hadn't gotten the chance to break the stained glass.

Of course she wanted to hear happy sounds from her citizenry. Of course she wanted them to feel stable, secure, safe. But it was tricky to be pleased when it cost her the balance of her freedom. This cell was not that much different from the prison she would have enjoyed in the Bellringe while trapped into a marriage with Renard.

Not really, not where it mattered.

Though the food might have been better in Pyrenee's gilded cage. As the outdoor hum thinned and darkness descended through the barred windows of her cell, her single meal of the day arrived. Porridge, delivered in a wooden mug that was barely watertight.

Amarande was driving the mug into the stone floor repeatedly, aiming to make a shiv—though the wood was too wet, and therefore bending rather than splitting—when a whisper of sound came from beyond her door.

She immediately dumped the mug's misshapen carcass onto the floor beside her. There was no use in hiding it. She had no shiv, and tomorrow the guard would watch her eat, just as she had the first day. Perhaps, if she caused too much trouble, they'd free her. Or simply kill her. It was a toss-up.

Pualo entered and collected the mangled mug without a word. As she exited, another guest stepped forward, momentarily blocked by the retreating guard. Amarande had hoped for Koldo but expected the medikua, given Ferdinand's promises. Instead, her visitor was another surprise.

Her mother.

Geneva wore a dress that the princess was sure was her own. Garnet lace through the bodice and sleeves, overlaid with gold touches woven into stripes that swept on the diagonal to a point, a tiger's head broach gathering them at the shoulder. The skirts were gold and shimmered in the low light. In one hand she carried a small woven basket but she did not appear to be armed.

"I have come to tend to your wound." Geneva set the basket on the floor and sank to her knees. "Medikua Aritza is unavailable."

Unavailable? That was strange—Amarande could never remember a time when the medikua had been absent from the castle. "Where is she?"

"Wherever the coin is, I suppose," she answered, fussing with the contents of the basket. "Your father paid her well to make her residence within the Itspi. A dead benefactor cannot pay—she left right after the funeral, I'm told."

Amarande was suddenly very thankful she hadn't relied on a quick return to the castle to heal Luca from his poisonous asp encounter. Without the medikua and her potions, he would've been dead had she made that choice.

Geneva cocked a brow at her daughter. "Don't look at me like that; I know what I am doing with these tinctures—I am more capable than this gown suggests."

"It's not that I don't believe you are capable." Amarande swallowed. "Do you not have some big feast to attend to celebrate your new king? Hands to shake? Speeches to give? Groveling to accept?"

Geneva sighed and a tight smile hardened across her face. "Given the instability of Ardenia's *present situation*, we thought it best to postpone our coronation gala." She shoved the basket toward Amarande, setting the contents rattling. "Go on, investigate. I will only use the bottles you select."

She sat back on her heels, waiting. After a few moments, Amarande bent forward over the basket, her uninjured hand skimming over the pouches of herbs, the bottles of tinctures, and small pots of paste. Clove oil. Basil oil. Sagardon. Turmeric paste. Honey. Garlic bulbs piled into a small-but-sturdy mortar and pestle.

Amarande's fingers paused for the barest of moments atop the handle of the pestle. It was marble, club shaped, and just the right size to effectively remove an eye with one good thrust. With a hard enough blow to the temple it could render the victim unconscious, if not kill them outright.

"Before you act on your impulse to kill me, know that everything I ever did for you was out of love."

Amarande froze, the pestle cool against the tips of her fingers. Her eyes flashed up to her mother's, her mouth set in a sour line. "I find that hard to believe while chained to a wall."

"Trust is something you do not give easily, I see."

"Would you? In my position?"

"I didn't, when I found myself figuratively cuffed to the wall. No." She let that hang between them without explanation. Amarande recognized the bait and did not take it. Geneva continued. "I hope you've made your decision. It's been more than a day since your injury and infection has likely already set in. Let's hope you know your antiseptics. Well, what will it be?"

Amarande slowly let go of the pestle and plucked out two bottles—sagardon to kill the infection, and clove oil to add more antiseptic powers while sealing the wound. Clove wasn't necessarily better than basil, but it reminded her a little of Luca and that was no small thing.

Her mother accepted the bottles and moved the basket out of the princess's reach. But Amarande estimated that at the chains' full length, she could reach it with her foot if she stretched far enough. Heel strike to the jaw to send Geneva sprawling, then an easy loop of outstretched toes. Bottles tossed and smashed as both offense and distraction, then thrust the incapacitating blow with the pestle. Even with her right hand damaged, she had options.

And yet the princess didn't move.

Her mother drew closer, taking Amarande's injured appendage in hers, and inspected the wound. Ferdinand's handkerchief had helped, yet blood plated in a thick crust over the vertical wound, perfectly situated between the tendons that ran across the top of Amarande's hand.

The princess had examined it much in the long hours since Ferdinand's visit. A smidgen to the right or left and she could have lost the use of her hand. And yet he'd purposely kept her tendons intact, and her hand functional. He was younger than her by a year, but her brother was clearly coolheaded enough, mature enough—or merciful enough—to avoid inflicting permanent damage in the heat of battle.

Amarande didn't know if she should be impressed, relieved, cynical, or all of the above.

Geneva seemed to admire her son's handiwork as she applied the sagardon. Tears flooded Amarande's eyes as the liquid burned through any infection under her skin, but she didn't say a word. Her mother applied another round of antiseptic and Amarande tried to ignore how much the woman's hands looked like her own.

"Ferdinand said you asked to speak with General Koldo. Is that true?"

Amarande didn't move. Her mother lifted a brow and corked the sagardon. The clove oil was next. "I understand why you want to speak with Koldo—you feel betrayed. I know. But don't expect her to come and comfort you—or to apologize. You know soldiers, always compartmentalizing their emotions. Assuming Koldo has any to speak of."

Her mother laughed a little at this. Amarande did not join her, and when Geneva was through, her lips stayed quirked at the corners. Her eyes flashed up to meet her daughter's. "She is not here, but I am. Isn't there something you want to ask me?"

Once, Amarande would have. She would have asked all the questions that had plagued her ever since she was old enough to remember missing her mother.

The questions that had run through her head in that first breathless moment when Geneva revealed herself in Satordi's chambers. Questions that waned the moment Ferdinand stepped into the room. Questions that died altogether when she'd learned what her mother had done.

Now every question was but ashes upon her tongue. This woman had already proved herself not to be an ally to Amarande, no matter her reasons for leaving long ago. Therefore, her answers were unimportant. Now all that mattered was getting free and reuniting with Luca. Her true family.

Amarande stubbornly returned Geneva's gaze, holding her face still as stone, not speaking a word. As the silence stretched between them and no questions came, the expectant look in her mother's eyes faded away and walled over.

Geneva secured a roll of gauze and pulled out a length—purposefully making it short enough that Amarande wouldn't be able to use it as a weapon. She took her daughter's fingers in her own and tied up the gauze with a knot cinched against Amarande's outer wristbone. "Your hands are so much like mine. See?"

Something like delight flickering in her blue eyes, the first crinkles of crow's-feet accenting her long eyelashes as she held up a hand—small but dexterous, knuckles prominent in ode to their surprising strength. Amarande couldn't disagree—she'd already tried to ignore yet another physical similarity between them.

Amarande reached for Geneva's hand, as if to press her palm into her mother's in comparison—but didn't. In a swift movement, she changed course and pinched the elegant fabric at her mother's wrist, hauling down the sleeve.

And there, in satiny black ink not much different from Luca's own—flames leaping toward the sky. A fire pit.

"It's true. You are the Warlord."

Her mother did not flinch, did not move to conceal the ink or deny its meaning. "Ferdinand told you."

He hadn't, but he'd given her the lead. *Proof of what you saw can be found on Mother's right wrist. What you find there will tell you everything you need to know.* But she would never admit it to Geneva. For some reason Amarande felt protective of that.

"No. I *saw* you." She raised her eyes to her mother's. "I was a prisoner in the Warlord's camp, you know. *Your* camp. I told your guards my name."

If Geneva truly wanted a relationship with the daughter she'd abandoned fifteen years ago, then returned to, only to imprison her in a tower—truth was the only way forward. In watching her mother ponder her choices—would she lie, or confess?—Amarande wasn't sure which she preferred. She knew the truth; what was more?

Geneva made her choice. "Four people in all the world carry this tattoo. Each of us has been the Warlord. I was not the first and I will not be the last."

Four. All the timeline questions Amarande could never justify were swept away in this single revelation.

"The Warlord's power lies in the name and reputation. As long as both are intact, so is the Warlord's power; it does not matter who wears the mask, per se."

Amarande wasn't sure how she felt about being correct, or that her mother had chosen truth. A new question rose where the others had once been. "You are no longer the Warlord?"

"I have retired. I was the third Warlord and the longest serving—ten years."

Ten years. Amarande's mind reached back for her father's face. The scar on his cheek—a gift from the Warlord. At least, that was the story he'd told. She couldn't remember when he'd gotten it exactly. Had it been within the last decade? Most likely. Which meant . . .

"Did Father know?"

"Yes."

All the air left Amarande's lungs in a slow leak. It was true, then. The Warlord was able to run amok unchecked because the greatest warrior in the Sand and Sky refused to attack.

The princess bared her teeth. "And so what? The Torrent wasn't enough for you? You decided to use Ferdinand as your puppet in Ardenia? To kill another kingdom?"

Her mother's hand struck out, quick as a Harea Asp, crushing Amarande's injured hand in an iron grip. The princess cried out, her wound screeching with pain as bones and ligaments pressed in on the oozing gash.

"I do admire your spirit, Amarande—I will admit that when I learned of your plea for consent, a voice, a choice, I found it inspiring. You told all of the Sand and Sky what you wanted literally over your father's dead body." Her mother's voice was but a whisper of hot breath against Amarande's cheek. Suddenly, that moment on the dais at her father's funeral, where she informed her people she wanted a say in who became her husband and their king, felt almost a lifetime ago. "So dramatic in execution—and brave. And yet it was not effective in the way you'd dreamed. You shot for the heartstrings of your people, but enraged the decision-makers, did you not?"

The princess clenched her teeth to muffle her scream, looking her mother straight in the eye, breathing hard. Geneva's grip intensified. Amarande could no longer hold back an agonized sob. "Mother . . ."

"Do you think you are the only person seeking freedom of choice, Amarande?" Ferocity gathered in Geneva's tone as her words built. "You, my darling daughter, were born into a leadership that has ruled this kingdom for a thousand years. Your people are conscripted into the army—men, women, everyone—without choice or thought. If they survive that, they're sent into the mines to produce diamonds from which they will never profit. Their lives are mapped out for them just like their fathers' and mothers' before them and their fathers' and mothers' before that for the past millennium."

Geneva's thumb, so small and strong, pressed into the precise spot where Amarande's flesh gaped beneath the gauze. She cried out, tears rolling out of the corners of her eyes.

"I committed the worst acts of my life, stars save me, when I left you to protect your legacy." Geneva squeezed Amarande's hand so hard now she thought the bones might crack. "In the years since that horrific night I learned that legacy is not worth saving. Especially as a woman."

Amarande struggled to keep her eyes open, trying to read her mother's face through the unrelenting pain. Geneva's voice was dark and direct and full of the weight of a lifetime of regret. Or, perhaps, disgust.

"Up until tonight, you were the most powerful woman in Ardenia and possibly the most powerful on the continent of the Sand and Sky. And yet, even with all that power, you couldn't even rule in your own right. Love in your own right. *Be* in your own right. Could you?"

As blood soaked through the fresh gauze, snaking down their joined hands, and the pain tore at the edges of any coherent thought, Amarande's mind flashed back to another powerful woman's words. The Dowager Queen Inés, snapping back at Amarande's assertion that the Crown of Pyrenee was not hers. *Yet you have the right blood, and your claim is still worthless without you attaching yourself to another like a parasite.*

A parasite, begging for her own kingdom. These women had been through it before. They knew how to rule even if their blood and rights created a different burden for them than they had for Amarande.

Geneva squeezed even harder. Amarande's bones stretched and cracked as the wound folded upon itself, pain kissing every edge, injured or whole. "I want an answer—*could you?*"

Amarande wet her lips, her teeth suddenly chattering. "No."

The Runaway Queen dropped her daughter's hand. "And that is why we must end it. Your brother's reign is the first step."

Amarande cradled her hand against her chest, as safe a distance as she could get. She swallowed, stars at the recesses of her vision. "How is that better? Another man on a stolen throne? How is that more acceptable than my simple request to rule alone? Ferdinand may be a promising ruler, but elevating him does not solve the problem of the patriarchy. Inés is as power hungry as they come, but even she offered me a more diplomatic solution that did not call for erasing my claim by locking me in a tower."

Amarande expected another outburst—more painful retaliation. Instead, her mother found a new target. "Inés did, eh?"

"Yes, before the wedding."

"And you believed her?" Geneva cocked a brow. "I knew Inés well once—as peers do. She is much smarter than anyone gives her credit for, as distracted as they are by her face and bosom. Do not dismiss for a second the fact that she knew exactly what she was doing, appealing to your motivations in the moments before that bloodbath."

"She said that if I ran from Renard and let her do her work, we could upend the patriarchy with the right number of votes. Invoke a majority that would rewrite the laws and let me rule outright."

Again, her mother laughed. "If your father was unable to produce such a result, I can guarantee Inés would not have been able to do so. It is called a patriarchy for a reason. The Inés I knew was always one to work within it, and she indeed has done well for herself. But I plan to break it. In my own way. In my own time."

It was a threat and a promise—Ferdinand was indeed a puppet. The woman who had hidden behind a title for a decade, pulling strings, now taking her show to a new place, a new people, this time hidden behind the spitting image of a young Warrior King. Koldo had to know this, and yet she'd let it happen over not only Amarande's claim but also her own regency. Why?

Geneva neatly packed her basket of tinctures and stood, turning to the door. She was finished, but the princess was not. Amarande sucked in a steadying breath.

"Did you poison Father? Or give the order? To *end* it? Was that really the first step?"

"No."

That was it. No explanation. Just a trite reply, and another step toward the door. Amarande wasn't sure what to believe. Was she telling the truth?

The princess looked away, not wanting to give her mother the satisfaction of a closely watched exit. That was when Geneva paused.

"Lygia's boy, Luca. Where is he? You risked all for him and yet he is not here with you?"

Amarande's chest tightened, the worn edges of the ransom note caressing the skin over her heart. Silent, she watched the woman's profile. The sweep of her neck, elegant even on her petite frame. Geneva's most recent title of the Warlord may have been passed along to another, but the weight of its power still anchored her proud shoulders.

"Your silence gives me a theory." Geneva turned back to fully face her daughter. "I am no longer the Warlord, but I have a great interest in the Torrent. I knew Lygia, and I'm observant enough to know that Luca was not her child, but her charge. The tattoo on his chest was something she often tried to obscure, but I did not miss the shock on the faces of my Torrentian maids the first time they saw it."

Abene and Maialen. Amarande swallowed, willing her face to stay blank, even as panic rose within her—a wildfire.

"Darling daughter, hear me now and know what I say to be true." Geneva crossed the short distance and tipped up Amarande's chin so that she could look nowhere but into her mother's eyes—blue and aflame. "If this boy and his wolf tattoo is out to unseat the Warlord, I will personally see to it that he fails."

CHAPTER
16

CREATED it?" Luca's words tasted like ashes in his mouth. "Tala, please, spare no detail." He glanced at Ula, who looked as if she were a million miles away. She already blamed Ardenia for doing nothing to help the Torrent but this suggestion . . . it was a path that was dark indeed. "I know King Sendoa did not do enough to unseat the Warlord. How did that inaction lead to the creation of the Torrent?"

The man drew in a deep and weary breath. Suddenly Tala appeared so much older, the weight of the years and fight slumping his shoulders as he found the words to explain what had led to the resistance he had built.

"My Otsakumea, your father, King Lotyoa, was a longtime friend of King Sendoa. Our king was ten years older, and regarded King Sendoa as a brash younger brother. Their connection was much stronger than with the other rulers. King Domingu was too old to be a peer. King Akil's father, King Alladan, was dead, and the Dowager Queen Tiya was not interested in making friends. King Louis-David was a peer but was even more disinterested in such things than Dowager Queen Tiya. And so all that is to say, Lotyoa and Sendoa were friends on a continent where that is rare."

Friends. The Warrior King was friendly among those who knew him well, yes. But he considered himself protector of the Sand and Sky—a role he took on not out of friendship but as a strategy to insulate Ardenia.

Perception and perspective—did they drive everything, even at the top?

"Forgive me, Tala, but from what I know of Amarande's life, not a single person of royal blood seems to trust one another. It seems to bear no consequence if they appear to be friendly with one another." Luca gestured to where gauze peeked out from the top of his tunic, marking his wound. "I have personally experienced what a brother would do to remove his own blood from the line of succession. That blood and appearance of loyalty didn't matter; why would friendship?"

He nodded, grave. "What matters is that it didn't."

"That doesn't make sense," Urtzi grunted, gnawing on a hunk of bread.

"I was there; it does make sense if you understand the situation," Tala said. "Though they had been friends, that relationship became closer as they became older, then faced the same milestones in a sort of delayed succession—the loss of a father, elevation to the throne, marriage. They were as close as could be. And yet, right after King Sendoa married Queen Geneva, something about his relationship with King Lotyoa changed."

It hit Luca that though he knew Amarande was not like the rest, perhaps it wasn't possible to say the same about her father.

"Immediately after the wedding, King Sendoa called upon King Lotyoa. Twice, I heard raised voices from the royal chambers. Years later we discovered that within a week of that final visit, King Sendoa's soldiers moved into the Kingdom of Torrence and took the first steps toward the Eradication of the Wolf."

A chill paced Luca's spine. "Steps. What were they? How?"

"These soldiers found the first Warlord, a man by the name of Jericho Talmage." This was not a name Luca had yet heard. Looking around, it appeared, no one else had either. "They stoked his anger against the Otxoa, solidified his support, shored up his supplies, and strategized what would become, a short time later, a coup."

Luca squeezed his eyes shut. "They created it by *installing* the Warlord."

"Yes, my Otsakumea."

Luca drew in a deep breath and opened his eyes. "Why?"

"I do not know. All I know is though King Sendoa did not lift a finger in the killing of the Otxoa, he gave the order."

Luca stared at the Otxoa's most trusted advisor. The ghost of the father figure Luca had known his whole life sat heavily on his shoulders—this man who had opened his home, given him a job, ensured he was educated, could he have done such a thing? Been so generous with one hand and so cruel with the other? He attempted and failed to swallow as he read Tala's burnished face. The older man did not break eye contact, his dark pupils unwavering. "This is not secondhand information?"

"No. It is my information and it is the truth. I survived it." Tala did not raise his voice, but his words were as knife thrusts, one after another, all aimed at the memory of Sendoa so vivid in Luca's mind.

There had to be a reason. This could not be true.

Tala seemed to read Luca's thoughts. He continued. "And if you do not believe me, ask yourself why a man who styled himself as the great protector of the Sand and Sky let the continent's heart be burned down and destroyed with a shrug and a glance the other way."

Luca swallowed. "You know the name Jericho Talmage. Do you know the identity of the others?"

"No. He is the only one we have confirmed." Tala's eyes narrowed. "What are you getting at, my Otsakumea?"

Luca drew in a deep breath. "My princess believes the current Warlord—or, if your intelligence is correct and there is a new Warlord, the previous one—was her mother. You said the title did not seem to pass hands for a long time. Is it possible King Sendoa did not attack because he knew the Runaway Queen was the Warlord?"

Tala thought on this awhile, as it seemed to be news to him. After a long moment, he said, "Or that could have been what he wanted all along. Control of the Torrent. Perhaps he had it through her. And with his death, unwittingly relinquished control."

Which could mean Amarande's mother was forced out. Or dead. Days after Amarande was sure she had laid eyes on her. Maybe.

How many times had he sat in the meadow with Amarande on the anniversary of the loss of their mothers—hers to disappearance, his to illness—listening to her wander through her thoughts about her father's heartbreak over Queen Geneva's flight? How King Sendoa wouldn't marry again with his heart in pieces. How Amarande was grateful he had Koldo's friendship to bolster the broken parts of him.

Luca was not Amarande, and though he had daily access to the king, he wasn't a surrogate son. But over the course of his childhood at the castle, he'd seen enough to know what Amarande said about her father's broken heart was true. But what if it wasn't broken by Queen Geneva?

Luca tried again to swallow, his throat parched.

The room was quiet. Tala continued, tone somber and low. "King Lotyoa was known for his kindness. He was more trusting than what was prudent in his position. Of everyone and anyone, and I believe this is what was the end of him."

That weight pressing on Luca's chest tightened, squeezing his lungs until he couldn't breathe.

I am told I am kind and trusting—like my father.

I will make the same choices.

And if I make the same mistakes, I will die.

When Luca drew in a breath to speak, his voice shook. The blood in his veins was one thing, his life experience another.

"Your doubt of Ardenia is well founded. Though these actions are not in line with the King Sendoa I knew, I respect what you're telling us. But you must also understand that I trust Princess Amarande with everything I have."

The leader didn't respond.

"Tala, look at me," Luca said, placing a hand on the man's shoulder. "I would like you to trust me—be it as the Otsakumea or simply as Luca—when I say that Amarande is not her father. If she is with me, she is with you."

Luca settled back. His companions nodded, unified. Tala drew a thin breath. "You must contact her, my Otsakumea?"

"Sending a message to Amarande is a promise and I am required to keep it."

"My Otsakumea, Princess Amarande should not require anything of you. You are not her stableboy anymore."

"*I* require it, not she. If I make a promise, I keep it. Most especially to those I love."

Tala's expression did not change. He did not approve. "It is imperative that the princess comes alone, not with her army. I do not trust her that far."

"The princess will come alone." Luca needed Amarande more than any army she could bring to defeat the Warlord. He had seen the determination of his people in that cavern, felt it in their grips as they'd taken his hand and looked him in the eye. Every one of them prepared to fight. And win.

At Luca's word, Ula immediately got to her feet. "I will go to the princess."

This was not a surprise. Ula knew by virtue of her paw print she was someone equally trusted by the resistance and Amarande. The perfect bridge. Tala nodded at the girl, lips turned wryly at their craggy-faced corners. "Of course you will, Ula. You are just as brave, as loyal as your mother—willing to do what is needed without even being asked."

Of course this man knew Lygia, too. It made sense and yet her lips dropped open, her golden eyes round in surprise. A flush bloomed across Ula's face and throat, her thick fall of dark hair not enough to hide it. "Thank you."

Osana stood and steadied the scabbard that held Sendoa's sword across her back. "Luca needs your medical talents. I will go," she announced. "I know the quickest way to the Itspi and the princess gave me instructions on what I am to say to the guards."

Osana had the same compliant attitude she'd had since joining their crew at the Bellringe, but something about the way Luca read it had changed in the past day. Luca always believed the best in people, but King Sendoa's death and everything after it had added a sour note to that optimism. Still, it was a solid argument and he did not want to appear combative before Tala.

"I would feel better if someone goes with you—Urtzi, would you indulge me and join Osana? I'm sure the kitchens would be happy to fill your saddlebags before you head out."

Mid-bite, Urtzi backed off the bread in his fist and exchanged a heavy glance with Ula. "I travel with Ula."

Suddenly Luca realized his request had been much more than simple. Had they been apart since she'd literally left her mark on him as children?

"Doesn't mean you can't travel with me," Osana replied, her voice light before adding, in a heavier tone, "Especially if it's the Otsakumea's fancy."

This last bit was clearly for the benefit of Tala, who watched the exchange with his arms wound over his lean chest. He didn't like the assignment, he didn't like the resistance of orders, he didn't like any of it. Ula understood this as well as Osana, as well as Luca. And she would find a way to make Urtzi see it, too.

"Go on, you big oaf," Ula said, permission clear. "Maybe you'll appreciate my finer qualities a little more if you see what else is out there."

Urtzi hesitated a moment, but then stood. "I will go."

Relieved, Luca nodded.

Tala forced them both to confirm they would retrieve *only* the princess before heading toward the resistance's underground staging area near the Hand. "If you make it to the area before us, wait for the resistance to emerge. Whatever you do, do not seek the tunnel entrance. We must keep our location secure. From *everyone*."

"Amarande can be trusted," Luca reiterated, keeping his voice as flat as possible.

Tala held up a hand. "But those who may be watching cannot."

Luca nodded to his messengers. "Be careful." Then to Tala: "What is my role?"

"You will wait for word at the secure location as the watchers infiltrate and report back."

Luca shook his head. If he had learned anything from King Sendoa, Koldo, and Amarande, it was that leaders did not hide and wait.

"No, I will infiltrate with the watchers. I did not come here to hide, wait, or otherwise be set upon a pedestal and watch the others work." His eyes flashed upon the older man. "Tell me what to do."

CHAPTER
17

❧

IN the hours after her mother's visit, sleep did not come easily to the imprisoned princess.

Amarande's damaged hand throbbed, far worse than when it was first injured. The only thing that dulled that acute and terrible pain was the growing stiffness in her muscles from the restriction of the shackles that kept her against the circular cell's curved stone wall, a whole room away from the relative comfort of her straw mattress. There was only enough slack to allow her to slouch against the unpolished stone, not completely lie down, and even then the metal cuffs at her wrists dug into her skin if she did more than prop herself against the wall like a doll.

But it wasn't the physical pain that kept her awake.

It was the mental anguish.

Over her own decisions that led to this very moment—chained in a tower at her ancestral home, obscured in both person and title.

Over the raw horror of who her mother had become, a flesh-and-blood monster.

Over the searing combination of the two, which left Luca vulnerable in a manner she could not counteract, and for which she was solely responsible.

If this boy and his wolf tattoo is out to unseat the Warlord, I will personally see to it that he fails.

There was no nuance in that threat. Her mother was no longer the Warlord, but if she did not get out from under lock and key and get to Luca, his head would soon be on a pike just like his father's had been. His tattoo flayed and visible, too, proof as much as a threat, exposed to all in the Torrent—the caravans that followed the Warlord, and the resistance that waited for the Otsakumea. A rebellion broken, the Warlord's supreme power enhanced.

Come with me, Princess.

If only she had.

The pain in her hand would be replaced by the warmth of his gentle embrace. Her bones would be weary from fighting with him, for him. And, when the time was right they would have faced her monstrous mother's ambitions together, sparing both her throne and his from Geneva's machinations.

Instead, when sleep did come in some black hour, Amarande did not dream of what they could do together, but of what she had done. Of the look in Renard's eyes, of the color draining from his face as bright red blood gouted from the upward thrust of her strike, staining her knife hilt, hand, wedding dress.

It was the dark vision of a memory she could not escape.

Her first kill—done not for honor, or fighting for her people—but for vengeance. A life for a life. Believing that Renard, in a way, had killed Luca, her love.

It matched one of her father's tenets—*If not an eye for an eye, a lash for a lash.* And yet it was her biggest regret.

The sound of shattering glass jolted the princess upright and to full wakefulness.

With another crinkling crash, more glass shattered, salting the stones in shimmering flecks of cobalt and crimson. Hesitant to move, Amarande craned her neck as much as she could, trying to make out who or what was outside her window. Only a few jags of stained glass clung to the window frame now, leaving the steel bars in stark relief against the night.

"Luca," Amarande whispered, a reflexive prayer built on immediate, impossible hope. That their love was so strong he could feel how much she needed him, and rode to her rescue, just as she had ridden to his.

Then she heard a cork pop with a loud sizzle and hiss, and acrid-smelling smoke filled the air. Before her very eyes the bars framing the window melted away. The hilt of a dagger nudged the mangled strips of metal out of the way, creating space enough for a lithe body.

Something about the sequence caused a drop of unease to settle within her. The princess shot to her feet, her training and strategy flipping from defense to offense. She pressed herself against the wall and gathered the minimal slack of her heavy chains in a loop gripped with her uninjured hand.

Through the window a boot appeared, black and shiny. Then another. Plain breeches and the tip of a long sword followed, as a male torso snaked sideways through the space left between the disintegrating bars. Amarande's heart stuttered.

It was not Luca.

"They certainly took no chances in disappearing you away, did they?" The young man dropped gracefully to the floor. "High-up tower, under lock and key, chained to a wall while clothed in nothing but a glorified sheet. Your cage is certainly not a gilded one, Princess."

Amarande squinted across the dim light at this boy who was not Luca. He was dressed in the garnet-and-ivory of the Itspi castle guard, but a guard he was not.

Short blond hair, parted neatly. Blue eyes, the color of a fractured glacier. Jawline as regal as any artist could imagine.

Fox-like smile.

"Taillefer?"

She blinked at Renard's younger brother, not sure if she was actually awake or if she'd entered yet another dark corner of her blood-soaked nightmare.

"Princess Amarande, your eyes do not deceive you." The second son of Pyrenee bowed low, sweeping the garnet cape before his body with a flourish. "You are a damsel in distress and I am here to rescue you."

He was not incorrect, she was a damsel in distress, but *he* should not be her rescuer.

Not in a million years.

The last time she'd seen him, he was on the other end of her blade as she tried in vain to plunge it into his heart. She hadn't killed him, but that did not mean he did not intend to repay the attempt now.

The princess set her feet, legs bent at the knees—ready for action. She bunched the chain in her grip. "You're here for revenge. I am not a fool."

Taillefer took a step closer. His dagger and sword remained stowed at either hip.

"I see you are surprised." He raised his hands, palms out, as if he were approaching in surrender—as if he were the one who was unarmed. "I never thought you a fool and I do not underestimate what you can do even while chained."

"Flattery will get you nowhere."

"All I have is that and my reason. If you will not listen to flattery perhaps you will listen to reason."

Amarande tipped her chin toward his belt. "You also have your sword and your dagger."

"Fair enough." Taillefer unsheathed both and dropped them into the space between them with a clatter of steel on stone. "Take one or both—whatever you find to be enough collateral that you will accept it when I say I did not come here to murder you."

The princess dropped the chain and swept up both weapons. Amarande did not trust Taillefer, but whatever his play in disarming himself, she was certain it could not best her abilities, even while chained and injured. She held both the dagger and sword in a high guard stance, the pain in her injured hand all but muted by the deadly Basilican steel suddenly in her grip.

"Do not come an inch closer. Why are you here?"

He cocked a blond brow, and smiled in that deceptively charming way of his that might fool anyone who didn't know him into thinking he wasn't completely deranged. "Why did I travel a hundred miles, steal onto the grounds of a highly fortified castle, pilfer an ugly Ardenian uniform, shimmy up a tower, break a window, and melt cell bars all the while balancing on a two-inch-thick decorative ledge for the opportunity to arm an angry, well-trained warrior with my own weapons?"

"Yes, that."

"Because we are each other's only hope."

The princess nearly laughed but instead tightened her grip on her weapons. "I've heard this song before and we both know how that ended up for Renard."

Amarande expected to see him wince, or flush with color, or show some sort of emotion that matched the guilt that was a constant drip in her gut. Taillefer had provoked her into murder and that was something he could not dispute. Instead, he simply answered, "Precisely."

"For the love of all the stars, state your case plainly, Taillefer."

The boy straightened, the fox-like grin slipping from his face. "My mother wants your blood. Caught dead or alive, there is a bounty on your head for the regicide of Crown Prince Renard. The same for the heads of your stableboy and the pirates for aiding and abetting Renard's murder and your escape."

"None of this is surprising. Why should I believe you are here for any reason other than to shuttle me from my current prison to certain death in the Bellringe?"

"Because if I show my face at King's Crest, I will be murdered on the spot."

The prince gazed forthrightly into Amarande's eyes. "I have the same price upon my head. Think of it: Two birds, one stone. Execute a traitor and the only person standing in the way of the throne."

Taillefer had a point, but he also had royal lineage his mother did not. "She may murder you in secret, but her claim to the throne would be more powerful if she tried and executed you for treason."

"You're right; it would be more dramatic. She'd prefer that to efficiency, I suppose. A trial and public hanging. Yes—makes for a good, sorrowful song. But she doesn't need a legitimate claim; she has already moved the pawns into position for her power play."

"Taillefer, again with the riddles, can we not—"

"She is to wed Domingu—it has already been arranged."

Amarande's eyes narrowed. "But he's already married to Nania—"

"Very recently drowned, Queen Nania. So young, so unfortunate, so *unexpected*."

Stars. The Basilican king was nearly eighty now, but a man who had stabbed his own brother in the back for a crown would have no compunctions in murdering a mere wife. Especially his fifth. And especially if it meant the chance to create a joint kingdom and produce an heir to go with it—Renard's fears were coming true.

Taillefer continued. "Within days, my mother will marry Domingu. They do not need Ardenia's approval to make it so—they already have the agreement of King Akil of Myrcell. Three heads of state in agreement do not need a fourth for a majority." He paused for the barest of seconds. "That leaves Ardenia, with its new and inexperienced ruler both isolated and ripe for conquest by a new, powerful joint kingdom. It is not such a leap to believe that if Ardenia falls, so, too, will the entire continent."

Amarande's mind turned over the possibilities of what Domingu could achieve with the whole of the Sand and Sky under his thumb. Is this what her father had feared? And what of Ferdinand—and

Geneva? Would they fight? Would they bow? Domingu was Geneva's grandfather after all—was survival worth the evils of the imperial patriarchy?

Taillefer watched Amarande process this. "Do you see it, Princess?"

She did. Though she believed Taillefer was incorrect in claiming that they were each other's only hope. Each of them was an obstacle in this plan cooked up by Domingu and Inés, and together they combined to be a bigger target.

Yet Taillefer was here, offering a way out. To Luca. Amarande chewed her lip. If she were to go with Taillefer, they might not make it to dawn without blood. Even if his aims of allyship were true, his torture of Luca was not something she could ever dismiss. "Why should I trust you?"

"Why should *I* trust *you*?" Taillefer dropped his hands. "Believe me, Princess, it's a surprise to myself as well that I am even here. You tried to stab me in the chest the last time we had the pleasure of being in the same room."

Again, it sounded to her ears as if he was telling the truth.

"Why not run on your own? Why do you need me?"

"Because I don't want to run. I want to fight. And I suspect you do, too." His eyes flicked across her double-bladed stance. "Which is exactly why Geneva and Koldo took every precaution and hid you away, while handing the crown to your brother."

It was clear he understood the nuances of it, whether from the spiders or birds. Just like he knew she would need him to escape.

He continued, his voice calm and devoid of any hint of the mocking tone that he so often used. "I watched the ceremony, you know. Watched as that lead councilor of yours announced to the people of Ardenia that you were *dead* by my mother's hand. It was quite the somber moment—a massive blow to your people—before the sudden, *extremely convenient* introduction of an heir no one knew existed. Oh, the joy on those surprised faces, Princess. It was something. Quite fortunate for his stunning resemblance to Sendoa—makes for fewer questions and more blind, relieved acceptance."

Taillefer gestured at their surroundings.

"This is a death sentence, Amarande." For the first time in her memory of him, Taillefer appeared to be absolutely serious. "You still breathe, yes, but do you live? Is living being hidden in a tower? Being chained away? Being deemed a threat in your own home? It is a betrayal as much as it is the end of your life."

He took a step closer. "And you know this won't last. They may keep you a few days, a week, maybe even a month, as collateral. But once your usefulness dries up, you will disappear—for good."

It was the truth. She'd known it since the moment she'd awakened in this bare cell—in her own home—imprisoned by people she had known her entire life at the behest of the only family she had left.

Amarande sucked in a deep breath. She would accept Taillefer's help. At the moment, he was her only chance of escape. She had yet to press him on his plan—how he intended to fight for his birthright, and how he thought she could help him—but it didn't matter. With him or without him, she would push into the Torrent to reunite with Luca. Then she would reevaluate.

Luca first, everything else later.

In one smooth motion, Amarande brought Taillefer's sword down upon the manacle of her opposite arm. Once, twice, three times. The metal cracked in a hairline pattern. She shrugged out of the shackles and repeated the attack on the other side.

Free of the manacles, she faced Taillefer.

"The weapons stay with me. I lead—here and outside of this castle. Let's go."

CHAPTER
18

⟶❦⟵

THE very first steps Amarande and Taillefer took were in opposite directions. She moved toward the window through which he'd come. He pivoted to the locked door of her cell.

"Princess," Taillefer called over his shoulder, "while I can assure you that the top of this tower has a delightful view, we would break our necks on the way down. Let's make this more simple and less painful."

Amarande didn't budge. "If you're looking to unlock it, the dagger won't work. I've tried."

"I don't need a dagger." The prince slipped a gloved hand into the pocket of his stolen uniform. "I have more tincture."

Amarande inspected the bars at the window, misshapen and melted as they were, then gaped at the vial in his hand. "What *is* that?"

"Impressive, what it can do, isn't it?" He held up the bottle, oh so carefully. "A concentration of the sap of giant hogweed. I call it 'fire swamp.'" His eyes flickered to her face for a reaction. He didn't get one. "Stand back, would you? It is extremely potent."

She stepped back.

"A drop or two should do it." Taillefer angled the tip of the bottle toward the lock. The liquid was a bright mossy green, like a meadow shot through with spring sun. Or a fire swamp, whatever that was—Amarande had never heard the term before. Perhaps it was for the marshy color and its ability to melt metal. Either way, Taillefer, as usual, clearly thought he was being clever. A single fat drop rolled off the rim of the bottle and into the keyhole. Immediately, the metal began to smoke, the keyhole expanding.

Impressive, yes. But also completely terrifying—Amarande had never seen anything like it. "Does it only react to metal? Or will it dissolve stone and the like?"

"Oh, I suppose if we had enough of it, we could burn our way through the floor, but that would be quite the waste. I'd rather use it a drop at a time to unlock cell doors and disarm guards." Carefully, he replaced the cork snugly back in the neck of the bottle. "I can't let you have all the fun."

Amarande felt sick. "You would purposefully use that on a human?"

Taillefer's lips quirked as he regarded her aghast face. "You clearly did not discuss your stableboy's near death with him in great detail, did you?"

Bile licked at her throat and her hands clenched. "He didn't want to discuss it."

And now Amarande knew why. She hadn't pushed Luca to share the details of his encounter with Taillefer in the dungeons of the Bellringe, thrilled as she was that he was alive and hers and they were together. But if Taillefer was telling the truth and had used that *fire swamp* on Luca, if he wasn't lying just to throw her off balance . . . she would follow her father's tenet—*If not an eye for an eye, a lash for a lash*—in Luca's honor. No matter how long she was with the prince, whether it be five minutes or five days, she would disarm him of this fire swamp.

Taillefer might anticipate her vengeance. But anticipation wouldn't help him survive it.

For now, Amarande pushed down her rage and watched the tincture at work.

A hiss and a pop, sulfurous smoke, and the hardware of the lock melted away. Taillefer sighed in satisfaction, watching as his concoction faded in strength, but not before eating through a door thicker than two praying hands smashed together. "Amazing, isn't it?"

"I was thinking of another word."

"Impressive? Efficient? Groundbreaking?"

"Vile."

The thick hardwood door sagged open. Through it, Amarande could see a similarly heavy door at the far end of the antechamber that led to her cell. The guard would be on the other side.

Amarande strode to the outer door, sword at the ready, and peeked through the keyhole. A few yards away, she could make out Second Captain Pualo greeting the sentry who'd been standing guard. Low murmurs, then a moment later, the guard saluted the captain and disappeared—a shift change. Amarande sucked in a steadying breath.

"How many?" Taillefer whispered.

"One. Stay here. This will not take long."

Shooing him away from the door, Amarande tried the handle—unlocked—and counted silently. *One, two, three.*

The princess charged through the anteroom door and sprinted straight at the second captain. Pualo only seemed to register Amarande in the split second before the hilt of her sword crashed down upon the guardswoman's temple.

Pualo dropped like a stone into a crumpled heap on the floor.

Amarande checked the girl's pulse, confirmed she was still breathing, and said, "My apologies, Second Captain. Sleep well."

"You weren't kidding, Princess. That didn't take long at all—you're much quicker than my fire swamp—but not as decisive." His eyes narrowed. "Why didn't you kill her? Or all the other poor saps you encountered during your last thrilling adventure?"

"Not every battle should end in death."

Taillefer cocked a brow. "What about weddings? I daresay, I've heard they are supposed to end in a kiss and the union of families, but the last one I attended was far more *deadly* than expected."

If this was how Taillefer managed the speck of guilt he might have had over the whole sordid wedding affair, she wanted no part. "You expected every murderous second. Now shut up and come on."

"Gladly. Where are we exactly?"

Taillefer didn't know the castle as well as she did, but based on his ability to figure out where she'd been held from what little he did know from infrequent visits to the Itspi for state occasions, she thought he was bluffing. He was too clever to know so little. And this, like his most recent attempt at humor, would slow them down. She wheeled on the prince. "Taillefer, before we go any further, I need you to promise me you won't continue to pretend to be dense, because it really does not suit you."

The fox smile flashed. "I don't know what you mean."

"You do. It does not make me feel brilliant or trust you more for you to rely on my intelligence. It makes me feel quite concerned about our very tenuous partnership and we've barely made it twenty feet from the cell. If this continues, I'll have your tongue before we see daylight because I just *cannot* with you—the jokes are bad enough. Stop. That."

"As you wish." Taillefer stooped over Pualo's body. "I should arm myself—since you require my weapons."

He reached for the second captain's dagger but Amarande slapped his hand away. "And have you stab me in the back on the way out? No."

As long as they were in close quarters, she would not allow him any weapons—his fire swamp tincture and whatever other potions he had in that pouch were dangerous enough.

"My having a weapon does not diminish your possession."

"It does if your knife enters my back. Take Pualo's dagger and I will stab you with it and leave you here to bleed out."

To her surprise, he relented. "Fine. But only because dying in an Ardenian uniform would make for a highly embarrassing afterlife, given I am the current crown prince of Pyrenee."

The princess stood. "Follow me. And keep quiet. I'd rather not die escaping my ancestral home, no matter what I'm wearing."

THE Itspi was crawling with castle guards. The normal contingent was doubled, possibly tripled. This was new—very new, along with the locked castle gate. Koldo—or possibly Geneva—was being very cautious.

The guards patrolled the hallways in pairs, nearly coming upon Amarande and Taillefer numerous times. Still, they managed to avoid being caught as they moved cautiously into the main body of the castle, slinking through the shadows, coordinating their movements with the patrols' repetitive ones. As four guards on early-morning rounds of the north side of the castle passed their hiding place in a small alcove near the throne room, Amarande grabbed Taillefer's wrist and yanked him across the hall and into the library.

The double doors whispered closed, heavy wall and floor coverings absorbing the sound. Hundreds of shelves lined the double-height walls, stuffed full of military texts, histories, folktales, poetry, and other tales from across the continent and beyond—King Sendoa was many things and one of them was well-read. The oft-repeated tenets that ran through Amarande's mind were a mishmash of wisdom from the books on these shelves blended with his real-life experience.

"I spent quite a bit of time in your library during the funeral visit, and though your father's collection is impressive," Taillefer whispered, "I would highly doubt there's a book here that can solve our current dilemma—unless there's a hidden passageway out of the castle. Stars, tell me one of these bookcases leads to a hidden passageway." He paused, pointedly grabbing at the nearest fat-spined tome, then another and another. "Is this the trigger? What about this one? Or this one."

Annoyed, Amarande forcefully yanked him onward and again confronted his willful, pretend denseness. "If you knew the general location of where I was being kept, why on earth did you scale the tower rather than use your stolen guard's uniform to walk through the castle to get to me? I would be recognized, of course, but you wouldn't have been."

Taillefer blinked. "Had I known I would be breaking into the Itspi so soon after your father's funeral, I wouldn't have been so eager to leave my room and roam the grounds during my visit. I came across enough people in my reconnaissance of your location to know that eventually I would have the misfortune of running into someone who could put a face with my true name. I am not as forgettable as you assume I am. The second son of a king is still a prince."

They passed a long, ornate table stacked with leaning scrolls of parchment. Figurines—Bear, Mountain Lion, Tiger, Shark—dotted the open patches of tabletop. Items used in strategy sessions. Amarande's eyes snagged on a handful of black wolves mingled in with the current sigils. Each had a recently scratched *W* on its chest—old Torrence figures co-opted and reused for the Warlord. The prince paused as something caught his eye. He reached for one of the scrolls. "Hmm . . . what's this?"

"We don't need a map," she snapped. "I know where I'm going. It's up to you to follow."

To Luca. Always to Luca.

Taillefer sighed. "To your stableboy, yes. But where is he? Will you tell me that?"

Not until they were on the way. "Share with the defenseless boy who would sell me out at the first flash of Basilican steel before we are beyond the Itspi's grounds? No."

"Your trust is truly staggering."

"Until you've earned more than a modicum of it, I will not supply you with ammunition."

"I rescued you and I have only received a modicum? How very stingy of you."

Amarande wheeled on him. "You broke in, but I rescued myself. And even with your modicum you are still very much in the negative, trust-wise. I shall never forgive you for what you did to Luca with that abomination." She gestured to his pocket and the outline of the pouch that contained the fire swamp and whatever else he might be carrying.

A smirk unfurled on his face as the prince nodded. "Then I shall require a map. It's simply good practice when one *doesn't know where he is going*."

Taillefer's fingers, still gloved, combed through the scrolls as he squinted in the dim predawn light. Not finding what he wanted, the prince moved to the flattened pages littering the table with the figurines. Within a moment, the parchments rustled as he crowed with success. "This will do."

Amarande did not venture to see which map he picked. Instead, she was already moving in the direction she'd planned, to the center of the southern wall. There, a large banquette, upholstered in rich golden silk, was built into the wall beneath a large tapestry featuring the five sigils of the historic Sand and Sky.

The princess's eyes paused on the black wolf.

Taillefer caught up, adjusting the buttons of his guard's tunic, the pointed edges of the folded map sticking through the fabric. Amarande did not comment on the map, rather she simply pushed aside the tapestry to reveal a small square door cut into the wall approximately four feet from the floor. She released the latching mechanism that kept the door closed, revealing a chute and cart on a rope pulley.

Taillefer's lips quirked. "A dumbwaiter?"

"Yes. My father always went into battle with as much reference material, histories, and hand-drawn plans as he could reasonably carry." Amarande knew very little of King Louis-David's military exploits but highly doubted the man ever got close enough to the front to yearn for strategy tomes in his royal tent.

The prince leaned into the dumbwaiter, gleefully pulling on the rope mechanism and watching as the cart moved up and down. Amarande relieved him of the rope and yanked it hard enough to pull the cart up so that it revealed an unblocked shaft. All they would have to do was slide down two stories to the courtyard. "Get in."

Taillefer bowed in a way that made Amarande look away, reminded of his older brother's practiced politeness at her father's funeral. "Ladies first."

"Not on your life." She drew her dagger and gestured. "In."

"Okay, okay."

Amarande drove the dagger through the rope, pinning it in place. Then she held the door open. Taillefer positioned himself on the banquette so that he could sweep one leg over and then another. "I would recommend bracing yourself against the sides as much as you can so you don't break your ankles on your landing."

Legs in, he twisted to brace his boots against the shaft, which was barely much wider than his shoulders. One hand gripping hard against the doorframe, Taillefer arched a brow at her. "Have you done this before?"

"Yes. Many times."

Taillefer hesitated. "Will they know? If they trace us to the library, will it be a dead end or will they know exactly what you've done and race to the yard?"

"The only person who knows I've done it is not here."

"Ah, yes. Of course." Taillefer's brows pulled together. "You must have been much younger. There's no way that he would fit in here now, what with those shoulders, and biceps, and—"

"Just go, would you?"

For once, Taillefer did as he was told without trying to get the last word. Amarande counted to twenty—enough time that she felt confident from her previous experiences with Luca that she wouldn't land on him—and followed him into the darkness.

CHAPTER 19

AMARANDE thudded through the chute after Taillefer and landed in the treeless training yard. Immediately, the prince started up again with his teasing questions.

"Now tell me, what particular mischief were you two up to when you decided that would be the best way to leave the—"

Amarande cut him off with a palm thrust over his mouth. The princess gestured to the military housing across the grass—many of the windows were open and gaping with newly washed uniforms hung out to dry in the breeze. "Ears and eyes are everywhere here, not just within. Come on, to the stable."

Under her direction, they stuck to the shadows under the eaves of the Itspi, walking quickly, not running. At the sharp angle of yet another meandering curve, Amarande paused abruptly. Taillefer bumped into her with an audible *OOF*, nearly knocking her down. She steadied herself at his expense with a tight grip on his shoulder, yet again covering his mouth with a bruising palm. Then, when they were both settled and silent, she pointed—across the field that lay between their current location and the stable—upward to the ramparts of the main gate.

It was crawling with guards. Not simply a four-man crew like the night she arrived, but more than a dozen. And that was just what was visible.

Amarande hadn't counted on this—another protective addition, like the guards within the castle. For a few quiet moments she read the shadows, judging how long they would be exposed as they made for the stable. Tried to come up with a plan better than luck. But before she got there, Taillefer tapped her on the shoulder, then pointed behind them.

The North Tower of the Itspi was ablaze with torchlight.

The princess inhaled sharply.

"Our window of escape is about to slam on our fingers," Taillefer whispered. "What is the plan?"

Amarande's mind raced with the best possible strategy other than speed and stealth.

"If you don't have one," he announced quietly, "I'm going double or nothing on my modicum of trust."

"You will do no such thing."

But Taillefer was already unfolding from his crouch. "It will be my neck on the line, not yours. Wait here. You'll know when to move."

Before she could object further, he was strolling straight for the gatehouse at the main entrance to Itspi. Uncovered and unbothered, his chin held high, his royal face revealed and possibly recognizable from yards away.

Amarande's first impulse was to tackle him, but she checked herself. Her fingers itched, ready to pluck her dagger from its sheath and bury it into his back before he sold them out, but that would be the end of a perfectly good blade—

"Ho, up there!" Taillefer called up to the second story of the gatehouse. Two faces peered out over the parapet. Amarande sank to the ground in the shadows, attempting to cover her exposed skin, which was so pale it seemed to catch the moonlight. "Word from the north tower—the prisoner is missing."

"What prisoner?"

"The one guarded by Second Captain Pualo." Taillefer gestured as if he couldn't say the rest and had to be intentionally vague. "You know, *that* prisoner."

The guards looked at each other. And suddenly she understood the cleverness of his plan. It highlighted his observational skills—she hadn't even said the guard's name and title all together, and yet he'd managed to use Pualo's predicament to his advantage. It would be wise not to forget this particular talent of Taillefer's—everything she said or did could and would be used for his own gain.

"Told you she'd been reassigned," one crowed, smacking the other. Amarande cringed. These guards were as green as an Ardenian spring. Inexperienced, raw, and much in need of Captain Serville's guidance.

"Boys, not to upset your wager, but Pualo is injured and the prisoner is missing. We need you down here to aid in the search."

"All of us?"

"Yes, all of you. Report to the north tower for further orders. Go, go, go."

Amarande braced for them to question Taillefer on the prisoner's identity yet again, but he'd played it correctly—no one knew anything but didn't want to admit it.

Boots thundered down the steps and then whispered in a run across the flattened grass of the training yard. When the gatehouse door swung closed, the last boy lingered.

"We shouldn't leave the gate unguarded," he said, worrying his lip. "Our superiors would not approve."

Taillefer didn't flinch, answer at the ready. "I have been ordered to stand guard until the hunt has finished."

"But shouldn't we have more men up high? To get a better vantage point on the prisoner? Surely that point of view would help."

A calculating look flickered across Taillefer's face. He put a hand to the boy's shoulder. "That's why I'm up there—in case the prisoner makes it out of the castle. But if you and the others keep the prisoner in the castle, I won't have to be the last line of defense."

"That doesn't seem at all what the—" In the twitch of a moment, Taillefer's free hand seized the guard's dagger from the sheath at his belt, and sank it into the soft meat of the boy's side. Taillefer's other hand peeled off the guard's shoulder quick enough to muffle his dying cry.

That's when Amarande began to run. A straight shot, through the field, to the stable and the meadow's juniper trees beside it. In another minute, she heard footsteps closing in behind her—Taillefer, sprinting full bore, bloodied dagger now stashed in his belt.

Perhaps Taillefer wasn't just observant or a quick study but actually properly trained. She'd never considered that Renard truly knew how to use his ridiculously appointed sword, but perhaps she'd misjudged him. Or she'd surmised the dead prince's skill properly and Taillefer's talent with that dagger was an aberration, like almost everything else about this boy.

Whatever the case, Amarande wouldn't dismiss what she'd seen, her father's tenet sticking.

If you underestimate an opponent, you overestimate yourself.

Taillefer claimed not to be her opponent, but he was also not her friend—the tenet stood.

AMARANDE slowed as she neared the entrance to the stable, Taillefer on her heels. She unsheathed her sword and plastered herself to the side of the wooden structure, peering into the dim interior through cracks in the vertical boards. After making sure there was no movement within, they entered. Taillefer ran for the horse stalls, but she veered off to a door opposite the entrance.

"Where are you going?" he whispered, yanking a bridle off the wall.

"To change out of this. Ready the horses. Nothing too flashy."

Amarande entered Luca's quarters and shut the door tight behind her, ears and intuition ramping up for any sign of trouble. Because it was coming, no matter what.

Speed here was key. Amarande knew it in the forefront of her mind, but as her eyes adjusted to the dim light in the room that had been Luca's home for so long, all the adrenaline from the escape fled.

For the length of a deep breath, she found herself suspended in amber, floating, surrounded by the presence of her love.

Pallet bed, neatly made with a quilt lovingly knit by Maialen, one of his foster mothers. Books borrowed from the Itspi library, stacked neatly beside it—Luca had a taste for poems. At the foot of the bed, a juniper-wood chest, stuffed with the warm woolens necessary to combat the cold Ardenian winters. Against the wall, by the single window, stood a scarred wooden wardrobe. She threw its twin doors open wide, revealing a set of cedar shelves, lined with neatly folded clothes.

Amarande grabbed a gray tunic, black breeches, and a worn leather belt to hold them up. Off came her prisoner's shift, which she stuffed in the very back of the wardrobe. Amarande stepped into the breeches, tucked their extra length into the tall shafts of her boots—stolen from Pualo, along with a scabbard—and pulled the tunic over her head.

Closing her eyes, she couldn't help but take a quick whiff of the shirt—one of his well-worn favorites. It smelled fresh and clean, like new hay and the mellow cedar of the wardrobe, but there, too, was the dreamy scent of the lavender oil he used on the horses.

A shout went up. Her eyes shot open.

The guards.

The princess collected her sword and dagger, tightening the strap of the scabbard slung across her back and dropping the knife inside her boot. Before she could get to the door, Taillefer yanked it open, his eyes averted as if he assumed she was still indecent. "Hurry, Princess! We must be going!"

Amarande sprinted behind him to find two horses fully prepared— ones she knew well, twin chestnut geldings by the names of Bastian and Balkan. Taillefer held Bastian's reins out to her, and she heaved herself on.

"Did you fill waterskins?"

"I'm not an idiot."

"I wasn't saying you were, I wasn't sure you'd had enough time."

"I had possibly *too much*. Do you need me to demonstrate how one hitches a belt without the help of a maid?"

"Shut up and keep up."

The princess tore into the night, not bothering to look behind her as she directed the horse toward the exact same trail she'd used when she'd chased Luca's kidnappers into the Torrent mere days ago. Behind her, Balkan squealed as Taillefer kicked him into motion.

"There! Stop them!"

Hearing the guards' voices so near, Amarande gripped Bastian's bridle with white knuckles, hurtling toward the break in the trees and the mountain passes beyond the castle grounds. She dipped low on the horse's neck, urging him on until the only noises she could hear were the pounding of her heart, the whistle of wind in her hair, and the horse's hoofbeats.

Lone hoofbeats.

Stars. If Taillefer had been captured, she could only hope he'd keep his mouth shut. Though that was unlikely.

The princess hazarded a look over her shoulder, and found slight relief in seeing him in the near distance, thundering toward her, a grin on his face, and chaos in his wake.

Dozens of horses galloped freely across the open field between them and the Itspi's guards. The horses blocked and corralled, distracted and disturbed any attempt to follow the two fugitives. A clamor rose to the stars as the men shouted orders and imprecations. Taillefer's grin grew wider as he and Balkan caught up to Amarande and Bastian.

Past the Itspi's grounds, they looped down switchback after switchback in the foothills surrounding the castle. Soon they would be lost in the maze of mountain paths leading away from the Itspi and Ardenia. No effective chase would occur until sunup, and even then their tracks would be growing cold and muddled with summer travelers.

"Clever move, Prince, loosing those horses. But I wouldn't celebrate just yet. They'll come after us before long."

Taillefer did not drop his satisfied grin, nor did he hesitate to answer.

"It is always worth it to celebrate the little victories, Princess—it might be the last one you get."

CHAPTER
20

THE body should not have been unexpected. Still, it was disturbing.

General Koldo stood over the guard they'd found sprawled on his back near the gatehouse. Under the light of blazing sconces within the Itspi's morgue, the general frowned and inspected the body. The entry wound was precise—straight into the lung with an upward thrust. The kind of maneuver that would have destroyed the guard's capacity both to breathe and to call for help before the life bled out of him altogether.

Clearly the killing had been done by someone highly trained. It was exactly the sort of blow Koldo had taught both Amarande and Luca—decisive and deadly. That they would use their training to kill a guard in the castle they grew up in was disturbing.

But Koldo did not believe either to be the murderer.

Strategic mind churning, the general left the morgue and climbed the north tower stairs to the council room, puzzling over the clues left behind by Amarande's escape.

The window broken from the outside. The melted and misshapen metal bars that had once framed it. The similarly destroyed lock. A concussed Second Captain Pualo.

And then there were the reports of Amarande's escape into the Torrent.

The gatehouse guards sent to the tower on orders that were not given. The murdered guard, yes. The Itspi's own horses used as diversion. All perpetrated not by the princess, but according to witnesses, by her likely rescuer.

A young man dressed in an Itspi guard uniform. Blond hair, blue eyes, bare jaw.

Not Luca. Entering the council room, Koldo firmly shut the doors behind her and approached the great table. As always, her eyes darted first to Ferdinand. He sat uncomfortably in Sendoa's seat at the head of the table. Geneva paced furiously up and down the length of the room as Satordi, Garbine, and Joseba watched her warily.

"Everything about this is a problem." The Queen Mother's regal countenance was fraying, frustration sharply clipping each word. "It is well past daylight. And yet the guards have found nothing."

The princess they had pronounced presumed dead was now known to be alive and on the run—not just by a handful of castle denizens but by everyone on the Itspi's grounds. Word of the lie and Amarande's daring escape would seep past the gate and spread like wildfire throughout Ardenia, sowing distrust and confusion.

It likely had, already.

Worse than the wrath of their own people would be the ire of the remainder of the Sand and Sky. Not only had they lied, they had accused Pyrenee of murder. And no ruler on this continent would take such a horrific false allegation lightly.

It was a precarious position of their own making. And the Queen Mother would not let it stand. "Go after them, Koldo. You know Amarande better than anyone. You can find her. Disarm her. Bring her home for the good of Ardenia."

That was true. But the priorities here were complicated.

"I want Princess Amarande home and safe," the general answered, "but I believe what she told us to be accurate, and Pyrenee did force her hand only to lose its crown prince in the process. Which means we have much larger problems—ones I cannot address from the back of a horse in the middle of the Torrent."

That was where she'd gone, of course. Through the same maze of roads leading from the western border of Ardenia into the Torrent that she'd used little more than a week ago in pursuit of Luca and his kidnappers.

"Yes, Pyrenee will be coming—Inés is gathering her forces, I'm sure. *Still*." Geneva nodded. "Look, we have known she would be coming since Amarande first arrived in that putrid wedding gown. You have settled your men at the border. Let them handle her. Given Inés's lack of urgency thus far, I have no doubt you can retrieve Amarande and still have time for a decent meal and a bubble bath before returning to the front. Leave now—you should have left hours ago."

Koldo turned to the king. "Your Highness, may I finish my analysis before we decide on a course of action?"

Ferdinand gestured to the empty seat to his right. "Yes, please. Speak plainly about these larger problems."

The general pulled out the chair and angled herself both toward the king and the Royal Council. Geneva stayed behind, pacing resumed. "I spoke with the guards who were given false orders to arrive at the north tower. All of them confirmed that the man was not of Torrent. He was flaxen haired, with pale coloring—light skin, blue eyes."

Geneva paused. "Are you suggesting Amarande was not rescued by the stableboy?"

"*Luca*, Mother," Ferdinand corrected.

When it was clear Geneva would not deign to respond, Koldo pressed on—dwelling on Luca was dangerous, indeed. The general did not know if Geneva knew the stableboy's true identity, and it was not a risk she was willing to take knowing what she did about Geneva's past. "No, I'm suggesting the princess was *taken* by Pyrenee. In fact, from the descriptions I've gathered, I think the imposter could be Prince Taillefer himself."

Satordi cleared his throat. "Which is technically what we stated in our letter. If Pyrenee did free her, it only makes our case stronger. They possess her."

"Except that she was stolen from *us*," Ferdinand replied, "which is *not* what that letter said."

Tension thickened within the council room as the king's private frustrations over the lies at his coronation seeped into the space. The Queen Mother approached the table, and it was obvious to Koldo that she intended to smooth over this irritation of Ferdinand's as easily as she must have once smoothed a lock of hair out of his eyes.

"My king, the letter spoke truth. It's simply that the timeline is not quite accurate." Geneva spoke as if hours and days were as malleable as bread dough. "In time, no one will tie themselves in knots over these fiddly little details because they will remember the largest one and the only one that truly matters—that Pyrenee was behind Amarande's disappearance."

Discomfort sat on Ferdinand's young features. He looked to Koldo then, and she took it as an opportunity to steer the conversation back to what they could currently control. "It does not matter what is perceived as much as what can actually happen to the princess. If Pyrenee has her, she is in true danger."

The king nodded. "I agree with the general. Princess Amarande's well-being should be our priority, not what others *think*."

The Queen Mother chewed upon this rebuke. She did not move away from the table, but rather seemed to really *see* him now in the blazing morning light. He wasn't wearing his crown, but in that moment, sitting in his father's chair, Ferdinand suddenly appeared very much like the Sendoa she had married—and left.

"My king," Geneva bit out, "wars are won by what people think."

Koldo could not disagree more. Thoughts played a part, yes, but public perception did not wield a blade or bleed out into the trampled grass.

Yet she held her opinion—this bickering was only wasting time.

"In any case," Koldo pressed, "we have received no letters from the Dowager Queen nor Prince Taillefer threatening retribution for the death of Prince Renard—this is unusual." She leveled both of them with the concern that had been welling within her as each moment passed. "The royals of Pyrenee are known for their savvy—they will want to control the narrative on this. And yet I fear because they have not—it is possible that their silence means they are playing another game entirely."

Geneva gestured to a map that someone had set upon the table, labeled with figurines of each of the houses and showing the general alignment of Ardenia's divided forces.

"We shall send your troops at the Pyrenee border north, push all the way to the gates of the Bellringe if we have to," the Queen Mother said. "We will be defending the honor of our princess. No one can fault us for that, and Ferdinand's first act as king will be seen as virtuous— rescuing his sister after discovering she was not murdered."

Ferdinand was defiant but careful not to push Geneva's limits. "I do not want my sister used as a bargaining chip."

"Noble thought, my son, but not useful," Geneva replied gently, holding Ferdinand's gaze. "If we retrieve Amarande from Pyrenee's clutches and show the world what we have done—reinforcing our preferred timeline, of course—the princess gets what she wants. She won't live out her days in a tower as long as she recognizes Ferdinand as king."

Geneva's general dismissiveness of both her children frustrated Koldo, to say the least. Her next words were measured and careful, a soldier's to a superior, no hint of what simmered beneath. "With all due respect, Your Highness, that is the bare minimum of what Princess Amarande wants."

"Ah, yes, the stableboy. She runs after him so, and then he does not arrive with her at the Itspi. She did not even tell us what became of him after Taillefer made it appear he had died." Geneva examined her nails. "Curious, isn't it?"

Koldo treaded carefully here. "It is. However, if the princess's accomplice was Prince Taillefer, we must think about what *he* wants. His aims may not be the same as his mother's."

Ferdinand frowned for a brief moment before looking to Satordi. "As heir to Pyrenee, Renard needed to marry to gain his throne from his mother's regency before age eighteen—would Taillefer be eligible for the crown in the same way? If he married?"

No one could say Ferdinand lacked an eye for strategy.

"I am not as familiar with laws of succession in Pyrenee as I am with those of Ardenia," Satordi answered, "but it can be presumed that if the succession laws were rewritten for one son they would be for both."

Garbine arched a brow. "Prince Taillefer *does* realize how badly that tactic went for his brother, does he not?"

Satordi shook his head. "He likely does not care—he was the architect of Renard's death. The princess was clear on that. She drew the knife, but he planted the motivation."

"Could that preclude him from the crown?" Ferdinand asked.

"Perhaps." It was the youngest councilor who answered—Joseba. "He can be disowned, but his mother's claim would be weak at best with no blood in it."

Ferdinand spoke up again. "But what if Renard's paranoia was justified and his mother was trying to usurp his crown through marriage?"

Geneva made a dismissive noise. "Inés's chance at a joint kingdom via heir died with Sendoa. There is no one available. The boy king of Myrcell married last year. If it were advantageous to him, Domingu would've taken Inés's hand after Louis-David's last breath."

"That did not stop those same men from pursuing Amarande." Koldo gestured to the marriage contracts, now stacked in rolls on a sideboard, one step from being filed away.

Satordi pinched the bridge of his nose—the man enjoyed nothing more than appearing put out by women. "No, that was a clean way to join kingdoms. The princess has the blood; Inés does not."

"Blood is not the only way to take a kingdom," Geneva argued. "Conquest can do the job, too."

Joseba, as erudite as he was, could not leave it at that. "Of course the Warlord's Torrent is the best example of this, but one might argue King Domingu took his crown by both blood and conquest."

Ferdinand built upon Joseba's analysis. "What if Taillefer is using Amarande for both means—via conquest with her murder of Renard, and by blood, using a loophole?"

"Did the princess not say that she tried to kill Taillefer?" Garbine asked in answer to his question, having only as a guide Satordi's description of the events during Amarande's arrival.

"She did," Koldo confirmed. "But judging by Taillefer's own wits, it's still a worthy gamble."

After a long moment, the king searched the room for more answers. "If Taillefer married Amarande, could he take Ardenia, too? Would she still be elevated to queen?"

Satordi exhaled thinly and straightened under his thick ivory-and-gold robe. "Our laws did not foresee such a difficulty."

Difficulties that could become very ugly, very quickly. Geneva looked to the king. "We should draw in the troops from the borders. Fortify the castle."

"No. That will only mean a fight on our doorstep." Koldo leveled her steady gaze on Ferdinand. "And, if Amarande arrives with Pyrenee to take Ardenia, my soldiers and their loyalties will have to choose between the princess they've known, or the new king and his lies."

"The army fights with you, Koldo," Garbine argued. "Those men and women will take your orders."

"The army fights for Ardenia. My orders will only be suggestions when my best soldiers address split loyalties."

"Then we are back to the beginning, and wasting time with this conversation." Geneva rapped the polished tabletop with a small fist. "I agree—we must avoid war at all costs. If we capture Amarande and Taillefer, we own the narrative. General, you must reclaim the princess."

Koldo pointedly sought the king's opinion. Geneva was not in charge here and she would never be, no matter what she believed.

Ferdinand raised his eyes to Koldo's. "If anyone can retrieve her, it is you."

That she could. "I will leave at once."

"And if you're able to nab Taillefer, do," Geneva added. "He might come in handy if Amarande doesn't murder him first."

The general nodded in acceptance of the Queen Mother's order and stood to leave—but then the king's chair scraped back and he was standing, too. Eye to eye, he put a hand on her shoulder, a twin good-bye to the one she'd given him upon Amarande's arrival.

"Stay safe, General."

Koldo swallowed, a lump unexpectedly in her throat. "Of course, my king."

Then the general turned to leave. Geneva was right about one thing—she should've left hours ago.

CHAPTER 21

❧ ✦ ❧

IT was truly a travesty that Amarande was on this journey with Taillefer and not Luca.

By midmorning, it had become increasingly clear they were not being followed and, thus, the prince began his jovial form of narration, which in this case amounted to questions seemingly with the sole purpose of annoying her as they raced across the russet, arid landscape of the Torrent.

First: "Did your stableboy enjoy it here more than he let on?"

Then: "Did he go with that Torrentian kidnapper? The girl with the deadly blade? I must say her bloodlust is extremely enticing. Does he think so?"

Next: "Were you always planning to meet him here? Perhaps expecting to be imprisoned in your own home after your claim was stolen out from under you by your long-lost brother and then rescued and accompanied by your sworn enemy?"

By the time that last question was lobbed, they'd left behind the endless wall of semi-connected buttes she'd called the Dragon's Spine, and made a turn northwest toward the refreshment of the Cardenas Scar watering hole. The sky was a cloudless, endless blue and the heat was such that it shimmered off the ochre sands and into the atmosphere, blurring the lines between where solid land ended and the sky began.

Not for the first time, Amarande considered knocking out Taillefer, stealing his vial of nasty potion, and going it alone. But given his vices and ambitions, for the moment it seemed best to keep an eye on him. And so she finally answered. "Yes, I have visions. This is going exactly as planned. I want nothing more than to be hunted in the desert with you."

Taillefer knew sarcasm when he heard it and laughed heartily.

"Given our head start, if Ardenia truly wanted to find you, they would have by now. Which means instead they're fussing over how to contain the fact that an entire castle's worth of people now knows you are alive and well despite what the kingdom was told." The prince pointedly leaned in his stirrups toward Amarande, his brow arched. "If anything, once word gets out about the escape at the Itspi, my mother will only want us more. Indeed, her attentions are occupied with planning both a wedding and an invasion, but the woman never misses an opportunity to solidify her position."

Amarande hated that he was right. About all of it. Still, she had the Warrior King's reputation to uphold, and even though she knew Ardenia's famed army could not handle a war on multiple fronts, Taillefer did not. "No matter her position or Domingu's, an invasion will not happen. General Koldo will not allow it."

Taillefer examined his reins. "Strange, I did not see Ardenian soldiers near the Pyrenee settlements either time I crossed the border in the past week."

She had not seen them either, despite being told that regiments had been sent to every border after the threats that accompanied the funeral procession. Moreover, Koldo had *gone* to the Pyrenee border to warn her contingent there, and the general had never been one to bluff—though Ferdinand's whole existence shed a new light on Amarande's understanding of the general. "Not strange, strategic. A threat doesn't have to be visible to be deadly."

"I do not disagree, Princess."

Up ahead, a smudge on the horizon stood out from the cinnamon dust and brilliant blue—trees. Amarande dug her heels into Bastian's flanks and shot forward without a word—which, once he caught up, led to another Taillefer question, shouted over the thundering hoofbeats of the twin geldings. "Is that water?"

"Yes." And something else, too.

On approach, the sliver of trees surrounding the watering hole was quiet, and Amarande focused on her secondary task first. It was an errand she wished she'd made during her harrowing search for help in healing Luca's snakebite. If she had, everything might have turned out differently.

When it was clear none of their plausible hunters were hiding deeper within the copse of trees, Amarande dropped from her horse and made a beeline to a very specific hollow stump.

"Where are you going?" Taillefer asked upon dismounting, waterskin in hand.

"To improve our chances of success."

The princess bent to the stump and inspected the cavity within both for deadly predators—a Harea Asp or Quemado Scorpion were never out of the question—and the items she intended to regain. Satisfied, she carefully reached within the stump and retrieved the remains of her gold necklace setting, stashed away when she'd freed her diamonds as means for trade.

The prince craned to improve his view over her shoulder, but before he could load whatever pithy question he was planning she answered. "Currency."

"You . . . plan to trade a mangled necklace?"

"We need currency for food and information. Gold can be melted for medicinal purposes," she replied—something she'd learned the hard way when the healer Naiara had laughed off a diamond as payment for treating Luca. That mistake had cost them her horse. "Or into bars. Being of Pyrenee, you should know these things."

Taillefer reached into his trouser pockets and produced two small pouches, both tinkling with gold pieces. "Yes, I do. And I bring my gold fully prepared. Not half-baked."

Amarande's eyes narrowed. "What else do you have?"

Taillefer unlatched his saddlebag. "Almonds, prunes, dried meat, horse bread, an extra waterskin."

The princess's saddlebags were full of a single waterskin and air. He'd packed both and had clearly given her the empty one on purpose. She'd been so focused on moving forward, she hadn't interrogated him about it. "And you were going to tell me this when?"

"When you trusted me enough that I felt it right to share."

"Taillefer, you are the most petty individual I've ever met." She plucked his entire pouch of dried meat from the open saddlebag, tore off a heavy strip of it, and stowed the rest in her own bag. Chewing, she stomped toward the water's edge. "If you don't fill that extra waterskin, I will."

Parchment crinkled as he unfurled her father's map. "And if *you* don't want to tell me where we're going, you must suffer my guesses as to the location in this vast wasteland of your Luca as we replenish our waterskins."

Your Luca—that was the first time Taillefer had used her beloved's true name instead of "stableboy"—and it caught her broadside. Her father had always taught her never to refer to an enemy by name and it was likely Taillefer had been exposed to a similar sentiment within the viper's nest of the Bellringe, yet a drop of unease settled within her at his change in terminology. "The Warlord's Inn."

Taillefer crinkled the map pointedly. "Let's see, given our early shot straight west along the line of plateaus and then our turn west-north-west and, well, the complete dearth of marked water sources, I'd say we're currently at the Cardenas Scar, yes?" Taillefer was not truly looking for confirmation, but she grunted anyway. "Then the inn is . . . that way." He pointed to the north and west.

"Yes, and it will be a long ride during the hottest part of the day, so let's get our water and get going—"

The princess halted, smacked in the face by a sudden, putrid stench. Bastian struggled against the reins in her grip, planting his front feet and wrenching his muzzle away. Beside her, Taillefer and Balkan froze, and for once the prince's lips opened but no words came out.

The Cardenas Scar was quiet, but it was not empty.

Bodies lined the creek bank—two, three . . . no, five—and two more floated in the shallow waters. No blood stained their sun-bleached clothes, no stab wounds obvious, no wounds at all. The toe of Taillefer's right boot brushed against one of the corpses—a young woman's. She wore the undyed roughspun of the Torrent, her golden eyes blank as they gazed sightlessly into the pitiless glare of the sun, her lips forever stretched open. In her clenched hand, a waterskin.

Taillefer knelt to her, unafraid, his gloved hands gently prodding for an answer as to what had happened. And though the princess did not know the natural arts as well as the prince, her father's last moments, as described by Koldo, flashed before her mind.

A sip. A cough. Death.

"The water."

It was all Amarande needed to say. Taillefer nodded, still examining the woman. "They've been poisoned. Recently."

"How long ago? Based on . . ." She gestured to the woman's state.

Taillefer stood. "A day, maybe two? The sun hastens things, but there is more shade here than most parts of the Torrent."

The creek trickled along merrily without a definitive answer, but upon closer examination, fish floated on the surface—bloated and caught in the weeds. Snails and water snakes, even a Quemado Scorpion, too. Her preliminary guess was correct and the only question in her mind was if it was the same silent murderer that stole her father's breath.

"Would the Warlord poison his own people?" Taillefer again unfurled his map. "There are only four marked water sources on this map. What happens if they've all been tainted?"

Amarande felt ill. "Control. That is what happens—eliminate access, and regulate safe sources and who is allowed to use them. In the Torrent water is everything. Control the water, control everything."

Including rebellion.

"Let's go. We need to get to the inn as soon as possible."

Chapter

22

Ferdinand did not know what to do with himself in his new chambers—a vast maze of thick-walled rooms that had most recently belonged to the father he'd never met.

The quarters were a must after the coronation, the Queen Mother said, in the same breath that she announced she hated it all—heavily suggesting he adjust everything from the furniture to the sconces to make it *his*.

Ferdinand wasn't convinced the chambers could ever shed the presence of King Sendoa, no matter the changes—and he wasn't sure he wanted to plaster over any trace of his father anyway. He liked the small finds—a jar of candied lemon peel squirreled away in the desk, satchets of sandalwood stuffed in pockets, the blocks of juniper berry soap stacked precariously by the claw-foot tub—that told him more about who his father had been than anything, or anyone, else in this place.

Still, having been raised in the wide-open spaces of the Torrent—no walls, no rooms, no prolonged shadows—the king found he could only stand to stay within the interior of his chambers for small amounts of time while awake. After more than an hour, the walls felt too close. Too stalwart. Too suffocating.

And thus, he was sitting, thinking, on his open-air balcony when his mother burst into his chambers unannounced, the three council members trailing in a clamor of staccato footsteps.

Without preamble, Geneva located him outside and thrust a wax-sealed scroll into Ferdinand's face. "My king, read this immediately. It just arrived from Basilica."

"Basilica." Ferdinand squinted at the parchment. "Not Pyrenee?"

Pyrenee was whom they'd expected, yes? Basilica had the elderly king—Geneva's grandfather. Domingu—the man who stabbed his brother on their father's deathbed to claim his crown.

"Yes, Domingu's seal, and addressed to the Crown, not to you specifically. It must have been sent before your coronation." The Queen

Mother's agitation was clear. "No news is ever good news from that man. Well? Open it, open it!"

Ferdinand accepted the scroll and examined it. He broke the seal, surprised that his mother had not already done so. Perhaps she was trying to uphold appearances before the Royal Council. The king unfurled the parchment and began to read.

"*The sovereign Kingdom of Basilica is saddened to announce the death of Queen Nania.*"

A gasp from Garbine. "She was but a child!"

The Queen Mother shook her head, grave. "Given my grandfather's predilections, I assure you it was not a *natural* death." To Ferdinand she asked, "Is there more?"

Satordi pinched the bridge of his nose. "Likely there is the rest of his plan, Your Highness."

That there was. Ferdinand continued.

"*Though we mourn, the Kingdom is honored and delighted to announce the joyful nuptials of our esteemed King Domingu and Dowager Queen Inés, regent to the Kingdom of Pyrenee, long may they both reign. The ceremony will take place on the twelfth day of summer at the chapel on the grounds of the Aragonesti.*"

As Ferdinand's voice died into the afternoon air, silence hung for a long moment while the shadows crept in from the corners. Ferdinand's mind rang with Amarande's words from the night she returned to the Itspi, covered in Renard's blood.

Renard believed his mother to be making moves in a concerted effort to steal his ascension to the throne.

The plan was clear now:

Remove the heir—Renard.

Marry a king—Domingu.

Join two thrones—Pyrenee and Basilica—for control of two of the four standing kingdoms in the Sand and Sky.

Ferdinand's mind raced. Poison a king and destabilize a rival kingdom? Could that have been part of the plan? With the Warrior King dead and Ardenia headless unless Amarande married, Ardenia would have been easy pickings. Until he arrived.

"The twelfth day of summer . . . is tonight," Joseba confirmed, squinting across the grounds as if he could see Basilica, in the distance, though it was more than a hundred miles to the south.

Geneva drew in a long breath and began pacing across an open section of the balcony. As she passed him, Ferdinand caught the words she muttered under her breath. "Pure Domingu. And, it appears Inés has finally made her move."

Satordi reached for the letter and Ferdinand let him have it. "Is Ardenia not invited to the wedding? That is most unusual."

The king shook his head. "This isn't an invitation, it's an announcement."

"It is clear Renard was correct about his mother's ambitions—Inés and Domingu likely struck this deal within our walls as her sons dove into the Torrent after Amarande's disappearance," Satordi said, his dark eyes skimming the lines of text as if he could see what had happened between them while the whole of the Itspi was distracted.

Geneva nodded. "Her ambitions are one thing but Domingu does not do anything for love, and none of his wives have died by chance. Everything is calculated. Inés is simply his latest avenue to his lifelong aim: to unite the continent under one rule—his."

Ferdinand had heard his mother's speculations more than once—but . . . "But if Taillefer lives—and gains the crown by forcing Amarande into marriage as Renard tried to—Domingu has no claim over Pyrenee, married to Inés or not."

"Domingu will find another way—by blood or conquest. And once he claims Pyrenee, Ardenia will be next." Geneva's eyes flashed to Ferdinand. "Our first priority is keeping you safe. General Koldo did not agree to draw in our troops from the borders, but there's no time to waste. We must recall them."

It was a clear order from the Queen Mother, bypassing the king himself. Satordi did not question it, only clarified. "I agree with the Queen Mother. The moment Inés and Domingu marry, it means the end of the balance of the Sand and Sky as we know it. It is the Torrent all over again. We must prepare."

"It is likely best to draw from the border of Myrcell," Joseba added. "We should leave men at the borders of immediate concern—Basilica and Pyrenee."

"Fine. Yes. War is no longer a question. Primary or secondary target, it matters not—we are a target." At Geneva's words, Ferdinand's objections shriveled in his throat—his mother's voice was as firm as it had been in their previous life, when she ruled with an iron fist forged in fear and flame. "Fortify the the castle with a mile's worth of men and do it quickly."

With that, the other councilors turned for the door. As Geneva made to leave as well, Ferdinand caught her arm.

"Mother, wait." He gazed down into her fierce blue eyes and saw the woman who, night after night, presided over the blaze of the fire pit, never once showing mercy to those who were marched to the ashes as kindling. He would not question her order for soldiers, though he sided with Koldo's reasoning on leaving them at the border, but he could not leave his sister unaddressed. "What about Amarande? If we leave her out there, she is a pawn."

"She was always a pawn, a shield, a threat—depending on whose side you were on. I cannot change what Amarande is. And now it does not matter."

"It matters to me. I want her here. *Safe.* She is none of those things to me, she's my sister."

The fierceness in Geneva's eyes did not wane, though her expression softened in a way she only seemed to show him. She reached up and smoothed a lock of hair off his forehead and behind his ear. It wouldn't stay and she knew that—it never stayed. Yet she'd been sweeping it away since he was a boy anyway.

"What she is to those outside this room is not your decision to make, Ferdi—it is hers, as it was mine long ago." She pressed a finger to his lips. "I was all of those things once—pawn, shield, threat—and I survived it, barely older than Amarande is now. The stars shall tell if she will, too."

Twenty Years Prior to Present Day

O N the first day of spring the year she turned fourteen, Geneva was summoned to her grandfather's private wing within the onyx stronghold he called the Aragonesti. In a family that sprawled like the roots of the largest banyan tree, putting out shoots as far as the eye could see, a summons from King Domingu was a very special honor indeed.

And Geneva intended to make an impression.

For the occasion, Geneva had gone to great lengths to pick out just the right gown. After careful consideration, she approached the king's chambers in a rich chocolate satin adorned with accents of gold— showcasing the colors of Basilica. Brown did not flatter everyone, but Geneva knew it complemented her coveted Basilican coloring— lustrous dark hair contrasted with sky-blue eyes.

At the appointed time, she arrived at the king's private chambers, which were marked by a set of doors carved with a massive depiction of a roaring bear's head and encrusted with an entire mine's worth of jewels—diamonds, sapphires, garnets, emeralds, pearls.

The castle guards stationed outside allowed her to enter without so much as a question—another thrill. They knew who she was. Why she was here.

Geneva couldn't help it—a smile of satisfaction slid across her practiced, polished exterior.

Beyond the door was a voluminous sitting room and study—all glittering oynx stone with Basilican steel accents. Everything about it sharp and deadly and perfectly Domingu.

"My king?" she called, as that was the title he preferred, even from relatives.

"Out here, Geneva, my girl," Domingu answered from the wide balcony adjoining the study.

My girl.

Geneva beamed, chin held high as she stepped into the sunlight.

She blinked, the white brilliance of noon devouring her senses as she pointed herself toward his form—seated in the shade of a canopy.

Shoulders back and chin high, Geneva rushed earnestly forward . . . only to realize that her grandfather was not alone.

A girl about her age, one with golden braids the color of butter, dressed in the palest shade of lavender, regarded her with eyes of searing, icy blue. She stood demurely in front of the king, hands clasped politely. Geneva had never seen her before.

"Inés, darling, this is Geneva." As he smiled, deep wrinkles fanned across the king's bronze face. He was near sixty, yet still handsome—his eyes twinkled in a way only certain power could convey, his features as regal and dashing as any storybook hero's. "You two are cousins of a distant sort. Two strands on either end of the web, as they say."

Geneva curtseyed, and Inés nodded, politely. The king gestured Geneva forward to stand next to this girl, Inés. Geneva reluctantly approached, not wanting to share the spotlight she so coveted with this girl, but also having no choice.

When she was settled, their grandfather smiled and clasped his hands together—always ready to get down to business.

"I've called you here because I have a very important assignment for both of you." Domingu leveled his penetrating blue gaze on the girls—the confidence in it could make an entire army snap to attention and Geneva tipped her chin higher, attempting to mirror it.

"It will take time as well as certain training, planning, and luck, *but*—if this should go correctly, when your assignments are completed, you and two other very loyal, very clever girls will each have castles of your own, run by you for me." The king paused, reading their faces. And, apparently liking what he saw, he continued. "You will never want for anything, and your sacrifices will be a boon to the kingdoms of the Sand and Sky. One continent under one house—Basilica as the sun, the rest as orbiting stars."

Geneva's blood sparked with opportunity—she would be the most loyal, clever, successful. The brightest of the stars.

"And then we will rule, my king?" this cousin asked, bright eyed and hopeful.

Was she even listening? A question like that might easily lead to a fall from favor. Still, their grandfather demonstrated the benevolence he reserved for family—the girl was fortunate for that.

"In a sense, yes, but at *the king's* direction." He smiled in a way that was a closed door, not an open one. "This is a patriarchy, my girls. And though I am the most powerful man in the world, I cannot change that."

If Domingu couldn't change it, who could? And why not? Geneva didn't dare ask—questions like these would not be loyal or clever.

"But what I *can* do is make you the most powerful women in the world. All you have to do is what I say." His eyes glittered as he looked between them. "Now, shall we begin?"

CHAPTER
23

❧

THE bodies remained imprinted on the backs of Amarande's eyelids as she and Taillefer left the horror of the Cardenas Scar behind and pointed themselves toward the Warlord's Inn. Hours later, they were nearly within sight of it—its rambling silhouette should appear at the horizon in the shimmering heat of the day any minute.

And Taillefer was back to asking questions.

"Why were those people left to rot as an example? Just bad luck? Or were they an actual target? Roasting them nightly has been the play to deter dissenters for seventeen years—why do this? And why now?"

Taillefer was right to veer toward the guess that the Warlord was likely motivated by some new circumstance, but Amarande was not about to share anything with him. It would expose Luca and the resistance. The less Taillefer knew about literally everything, the better.

"Stop talking. We only have so much water left and you're wasting your saliva. Of course, you are welcome to turn for the glistening mountain waterfalls of Pyrenee, but I have to get to Luca. That is the plan."

Amarande was being as vague as possible on purpose about her intentions. And Taillefer was clever enough to know it. Of course. "No, that is the *goal*, Princess. The *plan* is how we're getting there. The goal and plan cannot be one and the same."

This was something her father would've said. The words didn't sound right in Taillefer's mocking inflection. "Fine. The plan is to find anyone who might know Luca's whereabouts."

"And someone at this inn—*named for the Warlord*—would know? I realize neither of us has slept, but even I see the holes in that. Do you expect Luca to be there? It seems rather stupid of him to go for the only lodging place marked on a map. Isn't there somewhere less well-known?"

Amarande let out an exasperated sigh. "It is the only one allowed by the Warlord; that is why it is on the map. I doubt he's there, though."

"Then why are we going?"

"For information."

Taillefer raised a brow at yet another vague reply. "And someone there will know where to find Luca?"

She had no answer. But given what she knew of the pirates' previous foray into the Torrent with Luca in tow, it was the logical place to start without much more to go on.

If they failed here, she would set out for the Hand. Like the Cardenas Scar and the Warlord's Inn, it was a likely place to gain information via query, theft, or threat. Or payment—her mangled necklace or his pouch of gold should do the trick.

They rode in blessed silence for another half hour before Taillefer tested her resolve yet again. "Remind me how is it that you two got separated in the first place? Surely Luca wouldn't know you were locked up and *not* rescue you, would he?"

She said nothing. Which, of course, meant Taillefer couldn't let it sit, sarcasm dripping in his raised voice as they raced west and north. "And how *were* you planning on getting to him from that cell without me rescuing you?"

He was trying to force a reaction—ignoring her assertion that she'd saved herself with him as the catalyst. He continued to needle her. "You are not answering my questions, Princess."

Amarande let the rushing wind and hoofbeats on cinnamon sand be her response.

She stared ahead at the Warlord's Inn, visible on the horizon at last. To the goal. To Luca, always to Luca. Nothing else mattered— not her crown, not her duties, and not the newfound family members who had appeared to sweep them both out from under her. The time to deal with them would come, yes, but not until Luca was safe.

"Princess, I grow weary of your silence and vague bon mots." Taillefer lunged for her reins. Grabbing them out of her hand, he brought both their horses to a halt, the earth belching dust around them as the twin geldings slid in the dry footing. "Answer me."

"Do not attempt to control me," Amarande growled as she dove for her reins.

Taillefer was stronger and had more leverage. Rather than plant her boot on his horse's shoulder to push off—the animal didn't deserve such a bruise—Amarande divested him of his own dagger, snatching it from the sheath at his belt. One slice and she cleaved the reins straight out of his grip.

Losing his leverage and his balance, too, Taillefer fell away, nearly sliding straight off the other side of his saddle. Bringing her horse back up to a gallop, she spit over her shoulder, "As much as I wanted to, I did not kill your brother with a blade I stole from him, but that doesn't mean I will be as kind to you."

Taillefer hauled himself into a more stable riding position. "'Kind' is not a word I would use to describe you in regard to my brother."

"You say that as if you are innocent."

"According to my mother I am not, though I did not pull the blade. That was all on you, Princess. And though you did not murder him with his own weapon, as you've so cleverly pointed out, his death will forever be part of your soul."

"Do you think I am not aware?! I cannot shut my eyes without seeing Renard's dying face. His death will mark me as long as I live." Her voice was high and taut as a string stretched thin. "And it is *your* fault."

Taillefer appeared completely unperturbed. "I am not evil. I am ambitious. There is a difference."

"You *are* evil!" Amarande stowed her dagger, mostly so she wouldn't stab out his eye right then and there. "There is no other name for what you did to Luca. I won't put anything past you. And let's be honest, you are only helping me because you had nowhere else to go."

Astonishingly, Taillefer said nothing.

Amarande continued, fury building, as she laid out everything she'd kept inside since Taillefer had appeared in her cell. "You are using me now just as you used me to kill your brother! I must live with that and Luca must live with what you did to him to garner action from me. *We* are the ones who live with the pain. You simply live with the satisfaction of pulling the strings. I have yet to see a single grain of remorse from you for anything you've done."

At this, Taillefer did not argue. He did not glance away. He simply accepted the fury in her face.

Which made her blood boil over.

"You have years to go and many lives to save before I would ever think of forgiving you for what you've done to my love! Trust and forgiveness are not the same and you won't earn either easily from me, no matter how long you cling to my side." Spit crowded the corners of her lips, precious hydration lost on him. "If you stay with me, stay out of my way. I will abandon you or kill you. Either way, you will be dead. Do not try me."

CHAPTER
24

AMARANDE kneed Bastian into a faster gallop, angling for the War-lord's Inn upon the horizon. Taillefer would follow or he wouldn't. She did not care either way.

A few moments later, Amarande heard hoofbeats behind her, ac-companied by his voice screaming something into the wind. She rode onward—the second son of Pyrenee would never learn to shut up. He pulled up beside her. "I know who he is!"

Her heart stuttered.

"Luca! I know what the ink means!"

Her heart nearly stopped altogether.

Stars, save me. Fear welled within the princess, cold and fast-moving, up her spine, her gut, past her flailing heart. Was it all so transparent? Had Luca always been the ultimate target of the kidnapping ruse? Her mother knew. The man they killed in camp at the Hand knew. Now Taillefer knew. Who else?

This time, it was Amarande who snatched Taillefer's reins and yanked. Both horses again came to a skidding halt, engulfed in a massive cloud of ochre dust. Coughing as the dirt fell away, Taille-fer plowed forward. "I know what the ink means. I know why we're here, in the Torrent. I know you told me not to play stupid—I was attempting to tease out what you knew."

Amarande sucked in as deep a breath as the settling dust allowed. "Why didn't you simply ask me?"

Taillefer's cough melted into a laugh. "Ask you if you know the boy you fought so hard for is the son of a dead king? Heir to a fallen throne? Don't you think that would've sounded highly suspect com-ing from me if you didn't actually know that information already?"

He had a point. Frustration warmed her cheeks—a much more comfortable emotion for Amarande than fear. "What else are you still playing stupid at? The poison?"

Taillefer did not hesitate to answer. "I assume the bodies at the watering hole were the Warlord's reaction to getting information on Luca. He is a tyrant, but he can't be an idiot—he has to know there's always been a current against him. And now that resistance has their champion. He's panicking and trying to exert control to avoid a rebellion that has been a long time coming."

The frustration within the princess cooled to deep, icy panic.

Taillefer knew so much more than he had let on. About Luca. The resistance. The machinations at play within the Torrent.

Amarande's pulse pounded in her ears, so loud she thought he could hear it.

Now she had no choice—she had to do everything she could to keep Taillefer with her, considering all he knew.

All he could do.

And so the princess very carefully, very purposefully did exactly what she knew would work—she stated her purpose and then gave him the option he would expect and decline.

"Taillefer, we have to reach Luca before the Warlord finds him." She nodded toward the lumbering structure in the distance. "This is where we start. Again, you—"

"Can leave. I know. You've said it so many times, I daresay you would prefer it." Squinting at the building, Taillefer sighed. "I suppose we shall get this over with."

*O*NE *at a time and your life on the line.*

Taillefer peered at the rhyming proclamation scrawled in blood across the sign that announced their arrival to the Warlord's Inn in all its rambling, wooden glory.

"Do you think this is the best course of action?" he asked, gaping wearily at the hulking compound that stretched before them. "I knew this would be suspect if the Warlord allowed it but *that* looks like certain death."

Indeed, the Warlord's Inn was a dangerous aberration—its mere existence went against every understood rule about the Torrent.

In a place where cities were burned and people were kept on the move to avoid resistance born in static congregation, this was a sprawling, stalwart, stationary thing. Large main building, massive fence flowing off it like a ship's wake, full of Warlord-sanctioned campsites—covered and away from the elements—to be purchased for the right price.

Even more stunning, the entire thing was made of wood in an almost treeless landscape of nothing but parched earth and open sky for miles around. That made it expensive, permanent, and wholly unbelievable.

And therefore, very dangerous.

Something Amarande could confirm personally.

Still, the princess slid off her horse and tied the gelding to the hitch post beside the sign. "Taillefer, my offer still stands if you'd like to leave."

"Despite the sign's whimsical warning, I'm coming with you." He dismounted and tied Balkan next to his brother. "That said, if we are not heeding the posted proclamation, I would like to request you return my dagger."

The prince fell into step beside her, approaching the main building's large portico and yawning door. Amarande answered, "I would, but weapons are not allowed."

Taillefer jogged ahead to face her as she advanced, walking backward. "Which is exactly why you have that sword strapped to your back and your boot knife thunking against your ankle. Very wise— did you wear your weapons before?"

Amarande continued her trajectory to the covered porch and sunworn structure beyond. "I am wearing my weapons precisely because of what happened before."

"I feel compelled to ask what happened before."

Taillefer caught her wrist. It was not forceful, just a way to get her attention. Maybe he was learning that she did not respond well to physical coercion, but either way she did not want him touching her. She snatched her wrist out of his grasp. He placed his hands on his hips, and glanced at the black hole of an open door and the uncertainty behind. He'd taken her joke about the weapons well, but now the droll nature of his usual expression was gone, his face serious. "Amarande, if my life will be on the line in this building, tell me the whole truth. My neck deserves at least that."

In answer, she offered him his bloodied dagger.

"There is a man inside called the Innkeeper. As you surmised, he is loyal to the Warlord, who allows him to maintain this inn, which would otherwise go against the rules prohibiting stationary congregation. It is allowed because he is paid in many ways that benefit the Warlord, but most importantly is that he is paid in information."

Taillefer palmed the dagger and brightened a bit. "Seems like my kind of fellow—bending the rules and gaining knowledge."

"You might not want to proclaim that until you meet him . . . if he is still alive."

"Princess," Taillefer chided, again stepping into her path.

Amarande pushed past him, sights set on the building. "When I was last here, the Innkeeper's guard tried to kill me and the aftermath likely injured the Innkeeper. I left before I knew if he survived."

Taillefer fell into step beside her. "So, we're entering an enclosed space, trying to extract information from someone who you may have had a hand in severely maiming or killing?"

"Yes."

"Suddenly my dagger does not seem sufficient."

Amarande rolled her eyes. "Taillefer, I witnessed you murder that guard with a single blow of that dagger."

He didn't try to deny it. "That was only because the boy was caught unawares."

The more Amarande thought about the technique he'd used on the guard, the more convinced she was that Taillefer could slay several *aware* men with that dagger and his wits. "You have that fire swamp terror. Use that."

Despite the danger they faced, he laughed softly. "I realize you called me evil not long ago, but I'm disturbed that *you* would suggest I unstopper that, toss it in someone's face, and watch their flesh melt off the bone."

She stared at him. He was exactly that person. If he would use it on Luca or to disarm a guard as he'd suggested at the Itspi, he wouldn't hesitate here. Amarande drew her sword. "Stay alert. And do not expect me to rescue you."

The wooden boards of the porch creaked under their weight as they stepped into the shade of the overhang, blinking into the open maw of the building's entrance. The doors were missing—nothing left but a black mouth with punched-out windows on either side.

In silence, the pair entered, weapons at the ready as the change in light briefly wiped out their vision. Listening hard to the kind of silence that made the hairs on the back of her neck stand on end, Amarande held herself in a strong high blocking stance, grip tight on her sword as she blinked into the dim until the haze of blindness lifted.

The fine vases and plants and specimens of wealth were gone or shattered, the whole place sacked. Where the floor had been charred by the candle during her fight with the Innkeeper's giant, the boards were splintered. Every door to the building's interior was off its hinges, the rooms behind littered with debris. Dried blood marred the once-intricate rugs, more evidence of the princess's previous visit.

"Is this the *aftermath* you mentioned?" Taillefer whispered. "If so, I believe you undersold what happened here."

"The guard was a giant. Most of the mess is not mine."

"That may be but given this nasty array, I highly doubt this Innkeeper person survived."

She nodded to the marble desk, in ruins on the floor in the back of the room. "In theory, but also last I saw him he was pinned under that slab of marble."

"Perhaps that is why I feel as if we're being watched."

The princess nodded. She felt it, too. They moved together, inching toward the back of the room. As they came upon the desk, Amarande paused, her attention caught on a brilliant sliver of daylight—in what once had looked like a solid, ornate wall. But no, on closer inspection it was actually a hidden door, its hinges and handle designed to melt into the gilded pattern and purposeful shadows of the Innkeeper's work space.

"A door," she whispered, chin tipping toward the light. "Stay behind."

Sword in high guard and ready to defend, Amarande inched toward the door, pressing her weak-side shoulder against the wall, eyes pinned to the white light beyond for any movement.

Nothing.

With a fingertip, she nudged the door open a little wider and cautiously peered into the sliver of sunlight beyond.

Still nothing.

Leading with her weapon, she pushed the door fully open. The effect was blinding, and she stood there in her trusty high guard stance, blinking into the brilliance for one moment.

One moment too long.

Amarande felt it before she saw it—a vicious downward blow that cracked her stance as her injured hand struggled to maintain a grip.

She knew what to do in any swordfight—sweep the blow aside with a turn of her blade, release the pressure, return to a guard stance. But before she could do as she'd been trained, the pressure on her sword increased as something or someone *grabbed hold* of the edge of her blade—and dragged the princess right through the door and into the light.

CHAPTER
25

⟡

THE world washed out into a blinding brightness. Amarande's other senses picked up on what her vision couldn't—the weight of other bodies surrounding her. And whatever held on to her sword was not about to release it. So the princess did the only thing she could do.

She let go.

The sword and attacker fell away and Amarande rolled into a crouch, boot knife immediately in her grip. As dark spots danced between her and the attackers facing her, a noise came from behind, then a rush of air and a battle cry.

Taillefer.

Another blink, and the picture sharpened, the edges and reality clear.

A black wolf. Her sword clasped in its jaws.

The prince barreled past and tackled the animal to the sandy ground. They rolled across the earth in a smack of bodies and a smear of black, white, and red—the garnet cloak of his pilfered Ardenian uniform caught in the wind and movement.

A woman ran after the wolf and Taillefer as they tumbled past, wailing in a sob of old Torrentian. A man was in motion behind her, running across the massive space. It was as Luca had described to her—a giant yard, free of grass, only undulating sands in shades ranging from the typical copper to flat white. Edged along the exterior fence were the inn's open-air "rooms"—small, fenced-in campsites.

That left two attackers facing Amarande.

Another man and woman—him balding, and holding a dagger tight in his right hand. Her with both hands wrapped around the hilt of a sword. All four of them were of Torrent, eyes a golden brown and hair dark.

All teeth bared and bloody, facing her with blades just as deadly as hers.

Yet they were here. With another impossible black wolf. Stationary and defiant within the Warlord's domain. Which gave her a sliver of hope that these people were actually exactly whom she needed to find.

Still crouched and armed with her dagger, Amarande slowly straightened. She held her free hand out, imploring. "Please, we seek the resistance."

The balding man burst into mocking laughter. "Says the girl last here with the Warlord's spy!"

What in the stars? She'd been here, yes, but with Osana—

A knife shot out of the man's hand, and the princess dove to the side. She rolled to her feet, dagger out and ready. His companion immediately rushed at her, sword tip aimed straight at Amarande's belly. The princess pivoted and flattened, and the woman crashed forward under the weight of her driving weapon. As she fell to the dirt, Amarande immediately smashed the blunt hilt of her dagger down upon the back of her skull, rendering her unconscious.

"Please! Listen to me!" she pleaded. "We don't want to hurt you!"

"Speak for yourself!" Taillefer gasped from somewhere across the open yard. It was a wet sound—blood or saliva marring the tone. Behind it, the clash of metal.

"Look what you did to my wife!" the balding man bellowed, rushing in a wide arc around Amarande in an attempt to retrieve his dagger, which had clattered to the dirt behind her.

"I knocked her out so that she wouldn't get hurt!" Amarande answered, scooping up the dagger he aimed to grab and flinging it straight toward the man. It caught him precisely as she'd hoped—piercing not his skin, but the extra fabric of his tunic, pinning him straight into the wooden wall of the inn's main building.

Out of the corner of her eye, the princess saw her next move.

If Amarande were someone else, she might have left Taillefer to fend for himself while she pried the resistance's location from this man's lips. She'd warned the prince not to expect a rescue, after all. But—as much as she hated Taillefer, she'd thrown in her lot with him, and, without his distraction a minute ago, she likely would've been injured or worse.

Satisfied the man was securely detained by the pinned dagger, the princess collected his wife's sword and her own dagger and raced toward the prince—who was still struggling with the wolf, the woman, and the man who'd given chase.

They were toward the center of the yard, fumbling in the dirt close to where it faded from stark ochre to sun-bleached white. As Amarande got closer, she saw the man on the ground with a stab wound to the leg, slightly apart from where the woman loomed over Taillefer with a sword an inch from his sternum, the black wolf grinning at her side.

"So much for that famed Ardenian fighting talent," the woman taunted.

Blood mottled the front of Taillefer's Itspi uniform, dripping from his mouth, purple bruises already forming against his temple and jaw. Cloak holding on by a thread and the uniform shredded by the wolf's teeth and claws, Taillefer lay warily on his back, eyes fixed on the woman and wolf. His sword had been kicked away, toward the blotch of frost-white sand.

For once, he didn't say a word.

Hoping to provide a distraction before the woman or wolf closed the distance with blade or teeth, Amarande pleaded her case yet again. "We are pro-Otxoa and looking to connect with the resistance!"

The woman didn't budge. Behind her, the injured man laughed so hard he coughed, wet and gasping. "Princess Amarande and her guard, pro-Otxoa? That is the most ludicrous thing I have ever heard."

Taillefer finally regained his voice, holding out a hand as he tried to get his feet out from under him and stand. "You are mistaken. This is not the princess. My uniform is stolen, and we hail—"

Whatever lie he'd fabricated died away as the woman spit out a command.

The black wolf leapt straight for Taillefer's throat.

Teeth bared, spittle flying, fur arched along his spine. Its paws connected with Taillefer's chest and shoved him to the ground. He struggled to push away the animal's jaws as the whole of the wolf's weight was on him now, the snarling beast holding all the leverage.

Amarande cursed and sprinted at them but she was too far away, and the woman and her blade were ready, blocking them. She had two choices—fight the woman and hope to make it to Taillefer in time, or sling her boot knife at their writhing, entwined forms and hope to hit fur instead of skin.

But then, as the woman came so close into view Amarande could see her teeth ground together, sword held high, the princess realized she had a third option.

Without the slightest hesitation, Amarande barreled at the woman full-speed, sword out. The woman's stance stiffened, her eyes squinting over her gritted jaw, bracing for impact.

Three. Two. One.

At the very last second, Amarande dodged and slid. Sword flung wide to avoid cutting the woman off at the legs, the princess let the sandy earth and her momentum do the work for her as she skidded past the waiting woman and straight at the combined mass of the prince and black wolf.

Past the reach of the woman's blade, Amarande veered into the fray, her only aim to be a human-sized blunt object. Her knees and boots connected with the animal's side body, giving Taillefer just the momentum he needed to push the wolf away. The combined thrust sent the animal flopping onto its side with a mournful yowl.

It skidded away in a plume of cinnamon dust all the way to the edge of the flat white sand.

"That . . . appeared . . . to be . . . a . . . rescue," Taillefer bit out, rolling onto all fours in a heaving attempt to right himself.

"Not over yet." Amarande coughed and stood, sword out in a single-handed grip of her uninjured hand, up as protection from the woman, who was still there with a blade and a vengeance.

Yet in that moment, the woman dropped her sword altogether and rushed forward.

Past Amarande. Past Taillefer.

The princess and prince whirled around, to see only the black wolf's snout and ears visible—the rest of it swallowed into the white sand where it had landed in the tussle. It had been swallowed in mere seconds. Slurped down as easily as sagardoa, straight into the earth.

Behind them, the injured man screamed. "NO! Rena, no!"

The princess and prince watched in amazement as the woman threw herself down to the sand in a swirl of muslin and dust. She was on her belly, thrusting desperate arms into the sludgy sand, boot heels digging into the terra-cotta earth for purchase.

Amarande gasped, remembering the Innkeeper's words from her first visit.

The compost. Fed by a hot spring. Scorching enough to boil you alive. Spit you back out, dead meat, whether by suffocation or poaching, it mattered not.

Amarande sprang into motion, sprinting toward them. The woman had somehow managed to get the wolf onto solid ground but in the process, the compost had gotten hold of her, drawing her inexorably into its maw.

The sludge belched and burbled as it pulled her entire top half into the sand. By the time Amarande and Taillefer reached her, only the woman's left boot remained above the sandy surface. The wolf whined, panting hard, caked in wet white sand.

The princess stowed her dagger and sword as she dove for the edge, the fingers of her injured hand brushing the heel of the woman's boot but no more.

"*Stars,*" Taillefer swore, dropping his sword. He ripped the cloak from his uniform and shoved one end into Amarande's hands. He met her eyes. "Don't let go."

Then Taillefer dove headfirst into the sucking sand, holding the opposite end of the cloak tight in his grasp.

The cloak stretched taut but it was too short. Amarande threw herself onto the sand, stretching, stretching—trying to maintain leverage as the weight shifted beneath the earth. She dug all her pointy pieces—elbows, knees, boot tips—into the sand, and cursed her damaged hand. Grip weak, it was all she could do to hang on. The bandage on her injured hand slipped off completely, exposing the raw, angry wound to the sun.

Amarande gritted her teeth as the seconds ticked by. A minute.

But then one gloved hand appeared.

And another.

Next the top of Taillefer's blond head appeared, hair plastered to his skull. With every muscle in her body, Amarande painfully held on to her end of the cloak as Taillefer slowly levered himself out of the sucking sludge, the woman miraculously clinging to his back.

With every straining muscle in her upper body, Amarande pulled as Taillefer gained enough leverage to swing a leg up and over and deposit both himself and the woman onto the safe red sand.

Hacking and coughing, all three lay exhausted, trying to catch their breath. The black wolf approached and nosed at the woman's face, whimpering.

When her breathing slowed, Amarande hauled herself up, checked her weapons, and extended her uninjured hand to Taillefer. He accepted it and stood, eyes narrowed and lips quirked into something like a smile—and proceeded to prove to her that she'd been wrong about him. "You see, I can be selfless and trusted with a weapon."

"I will admit I didn't expect—"

"The Warlord shall find you in the stars."

The man she'd pinned to the wall.

Taillefer's eyes widened, and Amarande dropped the prince's hand to address this man—to make her case.

Not a second later his boot connected with her twisting back.

The blow knocked the princess off-balance and she stumbled forward, her exhausted body lunging for solid ground.

Where there wasn't any.

Amarande's boot made contact with the white sand and was immediately swallowed, the rest of her body teetering toward it, stretched out, unbidden.

Stunned.

Taillefer tried to catch her arm, but missed as it flailed . . . just as the woman he'd saved swung a leg out and caught the back of his knees, sending him sprawling face-first after the princess.

And, in one tectonic belch, Amarande and Taillefer were swallowed into complete and utter darkness.

CHAPTER 26

THE kiss wasn't as awful as Inés had expected.

It wasn't Domingu's age that had made her dread it—this was a man who had been married five times before and had enjoyed the favors of countless other women. It was that she hated him so much she was not sure she could do it with a straight face. But she did. And for her determination, received much in return.

A new ring sat on her finger.

A new crown in her hair. The castle jeweler made quick work of joining her Pyrenee circlet—aubergine and emeralds—with what had been worn by previous queens of Basilica—moonstone and chocolate.

But more than all that: a new title.

Queen Inés of the joint Kingdom of Pyrenee and Basilica.

They'd signed the papers making it so. She'd brought the dowry he'd requested—all those little glass vials clinking the whole way, until they were finally carried down the gangplank and handed to Domingu's guards. She'd brought gold, too, but that was the least of it. Most important, she'd brought herself and her willingness to become Domingu's sixth wife.

It was transactional, really. And no one objected. Not about the fact that they were technically related—after all, Domingu was related to most of the noble houses of the continent. Not about the fact that ink was barely dry on the disownment of Taillefer. Not about anything.

And now they both had twice the land, twice the army, twice the power. Even better, their new joint kingdom sandwiched both Ardenia and the most populous part of the Torrent. Any rebellion against the newest kingdom could be easily suffocated.

Dowager no more, the queen's heart lifted. She had every player exactly where she wanted them.

And now Inés stood shoulder to shoulder with her new husband on a dais in the great hall of Basilica's onyx jewel of a castle, the Aragonesti. Swathed in a deep aubergine wedding dress embellished in gold and chocolate, Inés stood tall behind a great table dripping garlands of bougainvillea and stacked with summer bounty from both the sea and the land.

Scallops swimming in brown butter; fresh mangoes, fragrant and juicy; pheasants, roasted and brined; pickled pepper and red onion relish served with creamy avocados and pineapple rounds—no bananas as she did not want them browning and stinking up the spread. And, at each place, a gilded cup that had been filled with the famed white wine of the region—Traminer in all its sweet glory.

As the guests settled into the seats, Inés surveyed the scene. The kingdoms in attendance—Myrcell and the formerly separate but now joined parties of Pyrenee and Basilica—were grouped together in their previous alignments. In Domingu's case, his ten children, some of their spouses, grandchildren, great-grandchildren, all sat together beyond the king's left elbow. Her thread of the family web was sadly diminished, and few were left to invite. Guards of all three houses lined the hall—an equal number from Basilica and Pyrenee; many fewer from Myrcell.

The power in this room matched the sun above when it came to this continent. The absence of Ardenia and the Torrent did not matter, not when the majority stood together as one.

The queen's cheeks warmed. Next to her, Domingu exuded a combination of secretive glee, amused condescension, and casual arrogance—fitting for one who had gambled and won so often that defeat was no longer a viable option, or even a consideration.

A sixth bride and more power than ever.

Of course he thought he'd won.

The queen smiled.

King Akil of Myrcell stood to give a toast, as planned. "Before we begin with this succulent meal, I would like to offer a toast to the man I consider to be my second father, and to his new, beautiful bride." The young king's smile sparkled across the distance, the brightest thing in the room.

Inés raised her glass high, catching eyes with Akil as she admired his handsome face from the dais. He had never seriously accepted her advances. That was too bad. Poor man.

"I will make my comments brief," Akil continued. "Scallops are too precious to let cool before hitting our tongues."

A few titters of laughter rolled around the room at the less-than-witty banter. Royalty and the sycophants who lived within its glow never missed a cue.

"What has happened here today is nothing less than historic in the vaunted tale of our continent—the joining of the outright rulers of two of our kingdoms. Though we mourn the unfortunate events that led to this moment—rest well, Prince Renard and Queen Nania—we must still celebrate and mark this unique situation, the first of its kind to occur in the history of the union of the Sand and Sky." The young king raised his glass. "To the Kingdom of Pyrenee and Basilica! To the new Sand and Sky!"

"To the Kingdom of Pyrenee and Basilica! To the new Sand and Sky!" the crowd echoed, glasses held aloft. Royalty, noble guests, councilors, courtiers, and guards—Domingu had ensured that everyone would toast.

With a flourish, Akil finished his speech and took a long gulp of his wine. Domingu, too, drank from his preferred chalice—gilded metal in the shape of a bear paw. Ugly as sin. The king caught his latest wife's eye and lowered his glass, sweet white wine glittering on his lips. "Inés, my dear, it is bad luck not to drink."

The queen bared her teeth in a sweet smile. "I wouldn't dare tempt fate."

And, as Domingu started to respond, his queen tossed her full cup of wine directly in his face, aiming straight for his gaping mouth.

Her wine hit its mark.

The old king's eyes went wide as he sputtered and coughed, instinctively trying to expel the liquid. A roar went up as everyone in the hall struggled to make sense of what their eyes had witnessed. Queen Inés further confused the narrative by cupping Domingu's chin, smiling into his eyes, and leaning close to whisper in his ear. "Did you really believe I would be so stupid as to fulfill your request for Taillefer's effects without investigating them first? Did you really think I would drink this *poisoned wine* and die quietly? That I would let you murder me as *you killed Sendoa?*"

Just then King Akil coughed violently, choking and sputtering. The attention in the hall now turned to Akil—his handsome face blank, lips flecked with white foam—as his wife, Sumira, screamed in horror. The young king dropped like a stone, smacking his skull on the edge of the table and into his wife's lap. Blood pooled into her pale green dress as she fainted.

Domingu was next, the king's bear paw chalice falling from his fingers as his free hand clutched at his throat. Inés did not release Domingu's chin as he thrashed, words burbling up through the white foam on his lips. "No . . ."

"*Yes.*"

The queen tightened her grip. Looked him right in the eye. "You must have thought yourself safe. That I needed *you* for my plan to work—just as you needed me all those years ago. That I would have been comfortable living in fear of your older children, who waited so long to rule but never would if I gave birth to an heir to our joined throne. But I am no stranger to contingency. As it turns out, thanks to your *obvious* plot, I do not need a man for my plans or to rule."

As Inés spoke, the effects of the poisoned wine cascaded in waves around the hall—bodies falling, horrified screams, a rush toward the barred doors.

The queen released her grasp on her second husband and long-ago mentor, and his body fell limp against the banquette. She nodded to the guards in Pyrenee uniforms who stood stationed behind the set of tables where Domingu's kin were stirring in panic.

"*Now!*"

Dozens of Pyrenee soldiers spilled onto the mezzanine and poured down the stairs. Swords and daggers drawn, they descended like a storm upon the tables where Domingu's family awaited their fate—their wine, of course, not poisoned. Their blades made swift work of Domingu's direct descendants—men first, then women who tried to fight.

As blood sprayed in great arcs, the queen did not look away. This was necessary, but that did not mean she enjoyed such violence.

Inés clapped her hands together and shouted over the chaos.

"Remaining guests, you have two choices. Bend the knee to me and you shall live; otherwise, you will die." She gestured to her soldiers, whose blades now threatened all those who were still standing. "Domingu expected to rule all of the Sand and Sky before his dying breath, and yet he failed. Test me and you will join him in death."

No one moved.

"Know this: I did not poison the wine. Domingu did." The truth settled over the remaining crowd, and she nodded. *Yes, yes, he did that. With Taillefer's help.* "It is only with me that you get the chance to live."

The great dining hall of the Aragonesti went still, death or capitulation taking each soul, one by one. Those who chose death drank the poison or succumbed to their wounds, helped along by the queen's soldiers. Those who bent the knee awaited orders.

When all was silent, Queen Inés surveyed the room. A third of the guests lost to the wine, and a third to the sword. About what she'd expected. A few members of her own party had succumbed to the wine, but what was lost would be worth it for all she'd gained.

Pyrenee was hers. Basilica was hers. And, with a few strokes of ink, the remaining party of Myrcell would hand her that salty strip of southern land—and the pearl trade and the army that went with it.

For a thousand years on this continent, kingdoms had been gained through blood or conquest. Yet with cleverness of mind and steely consciousness, she would now rule three-fifths of the Sand and Sky, because she had conquest in her blood.

But it was not enough.

Three-fifths of the continent would not do, just as it would not have done for Domingu—had he succeeded in his scheme.

She wanted all of it. And she would have it. No matter Geneva's plans for Ardenia, formerly ruled by the Warrior King. No matter the Warlord's control of the pitiful patch of sand called the Torrent. No matter the unresolved matter of her son Taillefer and Princess Amarande.

In the last two minutes she had bent the entire patriarchal history of the Sand and Sky to her will, using nothing but the framework that had kept her caged for so long.

But no more.

"Those of you who have bent the knee, congratulations—arise

and join the future of your continent." It was theatrical, yes, but necessary—this was a dramatic moment, indeed. And so, Inés tipped her chin and met the weary, tentative survivors with her most benevolent grin. "Yes, stand with me. Stand! Stand with me for the new Sand and Sky. A place where the old kings are dead, and a single queen shall reign."

CHAPTER
27

OSANA halted at the cut of a switchback, staring through the cleaved meeting of two mountains, at the Itspi below, a garnet gem bathed in sunset orange. The castle wall encircled the grounds like a ruby-crusted belt, pulled tight around heavily graded summer-dry grasses shaded by stands of fragrant juniper trees.

"Stars, it looks just like that ball gown of hers," Osana said, not glancing over at Urtzi, who sat cramming strips of dried meat into his mouth. The big Myrcellian had seized every pause in their journey as an automatic opportunity to eat—so often, in fact, that she could barely believe he had anything edible remaining in his saddlebag, yet more food materialized each and every time he reached within.

"It looks like a castle." He shrugged and swallowed.

"A *beautiful* castle. The Bellringe was grand and imposing but a little frigid. This one—it sparkles like a gem yet still looks like a *home*. I envy Amarande and Luca for having grown up here."

"We are not here to ogle the castle. Get in; get the princess; get out. You can admire the architecture on your next visit."

"Fine. So, I suppose we go and . . . knock on the gate like we're calling for cake and coffee? I flash my sword and we ask for the princess . . ."

"No, we go through the . . . wait. It's closed?"

"The gate appears to be closed, yes. And manned with soldiers."

Urtzi froze, staring down at the Itspi, cataloging each section of it. As his mind overlaid the current view with the castle he had visited not even a week before, Osana plucked the last strip of dried meat from his fist and shoved it in her mouth.

When he didn't admonish her, Osana knew something was wrong.

"What?" she asked, still chewing.

Urtzi's black eyebrows threaded together. "When we arrived, the gates were open. Perhaps for the funeral, but when we took the assignment we were told it would not be difficult to gain entry. We had a story at the ready in case we needed to talk our way in, but we didn't even need it." He dipped his chin to the scene below. "The gate was wide open. And though Ardenia is famed for its soldiers, guards did not crawl the grounds like so many ants."

They did look like ants. On the ramparts. Crisscrossing the grounds. Thick at the front gate as well as every entry to the castle itself. They stood sentry at every building she could see from this angle—the chapel, the arena, the royal and military stables—their opulent garnet cloaks fluttering in the mountain breeze.

Urtzi ran a hand through his hair, the curls flattening out for a moment and then springing back into place. He pointed toward a cluster of trees, tucked down by the stable. "There's a cut through to the Torrent there. The topography, junipers, and a stream walling it off. Bet you there's a line of guards there, too."

"But . . . why the guards?"

"Pyrenee, maybe? For all the Dowager Queen seemed to hate Renard, maybe she plans to retaliate for his murder? But if that's the case, why haven't we seen any signs of it?"

"Could be. Though with Renard's death, she's one step closer to the crown, isn't she? That doesn't deserve a war as much as it does a 'thank you.'"

"One would think. But that is not how these people work."

"I didn't know you knew so much about royalty, pirate."

"I know all about greed, thief."

"So what do we do?" Osana asked. "Climb the wall? Try the soldiers at the stand of juniper? Or do we just waltz up to the gate? I could still flash the sword and ask for Captain Serville—the name Amarande gave me."

"They must know he's dead by now." Urtzi shook his head. "And if we assault their soldiers, they will likely not grin and lead us to an audience with the princess."

"Then how about this? Instead of forcing it or spinning a story, we simply walk up to the gate, introduce ourselves, and let Amarande do the rest? She knows us. They will at least *ask* her before killing us, I'd think."

"Yes, that might work. Let's get going."

"I'll take agreement as something near a compliment from you."

"You have spent too much time with Ula already."

OSANA took great pains to instruct Urtzi on how they were to appear; how she should do the talking; how Egia, the sword Amarande had entrusted her with, could serve as further identification if necessary. After all, King Sendoa's crest was stamped at the base of the blade.

Urtzi pointed out that drawing a sword could end up with them in shackles—either because they did not believe her about proving it was the king's or simply because she *could* prove it. A toss-up of last resort, really. But Osana was just as good a talker as she was a thief.

They arrived at the gate, chins high, faces as open and trustworthy as they could make them.

"Halt! Riders, announce your intentions," a guardsman ordered. Three more stood at his side, blocking the gate. Many more manned the gatehouse and crowded the ramparts of the castle. All had their eyes on the pirate and the thief.

Osana politely addressed the guard who had spoken. "Our intentions are to enter, as we have been invited."

The guard didn't blink. "The grounds of the Itspi are not currently open to guests. If you have come for the coronation, you are a day too late."

Next to her, she felt Urtzi tense with surprise—they had changed the laws and crowned the princess after all. Osana offered a friendly grin. "The princess Amarande is now queen? How fortunate, as she is the one who invited us."

The leader hesitated, eyes momentarily sliding to the guardswoman on his right. Something passed between them.

"She is not queen and she did not invite you." Ignoring their confusion, he pointed back down the road from which they came. "Now go away."

"She did. She gifted me this sword and told me to show it at the gate. Anyone trained under Captain Serville, may he rest in the stars, should recognize it for what it is. May I present it to you?"

After consulting with the guardswoman, he gave a reluctant nod. "Hand it over. I will inspect it."

"It was King Sendoa's and an heirloom; I would rather not—"

"Either hand it over to me or leave." The guards at the gatehouse punctuated his order by drawing their bows. Within a blink, six sets of arrows were pointed at the pair. It was then that Osana realized these might not actually be guards, but *soldiers*.

When Osana hesitated, knowing that the second the sword left her grasp it would not be returned to her, Urtzi's deep voice rumbled into the falling night. "Urtzi and Osana. Those are our names. Run that up to Princess Amarande and we will get this straightened out."

The soldier took a step forward. "Dismount before entering."

Urtzi slid to the ground right away, a head taller than any of the men.

Again, Osana hesitated, eyes lifted to the gatehouse and the ramparts. "Guard, can you please call off your archers? We are not a threat."

The man waved up at the gatehouse and the archers immediately withdrew their bows. Osana stowed the sword and dismounted. But the moment her feet touched the ground, she realized she'd made a grave error. The archers had withdrawn, but on the ground, a contingent of soldiers emerged from the thick juniper stands that lined the road.

In a moment, she and Urtzi were surrounded by dozens of men and women with swords.

Osana held up her hands. "The princess will be very disappointed when she sees how you have treated us."

From behind, one of the soldiers sliced straight through the leather straps of her scabbard with the tip of his sword. King Sendoa's famed weapon fell to the ground behind her in a clanging heap, and was whisked away.

"I think not," the leader said. "The princess was murdered by Pyrenee."

"No," Urtzi insisted, frustration raising the volume of his voice, his eyebrows wild. "We were there! She was not."

The soldier arched a brow. "You were there?"

"No," Osana answered, but Urtzi was already shouting, "Yes!" over her as four heavily armed men moved in to tie his hands. Two more went after Osana. Their horses were led away.

"Yes?" the man asked Urtzi, side-eyeing Osana as she scanned the ground.

"Yes. Unhand me and I will tell you all about it. The kidnapping, the wedding, Renard, Taillefer, Luca, all of it."

The leader spoke soberly. "No, you will tell us anyway. King Ferdinand and Queen Mother Geneva will want to know what happened to the princess. And whom to blame for her death."

"Who in the dragon's piss are those people?" Urtzi glanced to Osana for help, but the girl's olive skin had blanched, eyes gone glassy and distant. He began to struggle, his voice growing louder. "We last saw Amarande *alive*! If she's dead, we had nothing to do with it. You are not hearing me."

"We have heard you loud and clear. And for that, you are now under our care as prisoners of the Kingdom of Ardenia."

"No! You don't understand," Urtzi insisted, as eight soldiers surrounded him, tying his hands. They divested him of his weapons and prodded him through the just-lifted gate. "Osana! Tell them! What's wrong with you?"

Osana walked ahead, not fighting. Not saying anything at all.

CHAPTER 28

THE pirate and the thief were ushered not to the throne room, nor to the red hall, where supper was just being set. No, they were taken down five flights of stairs, straight to the dungeons that lined the bowels of the Itspi, deeper than the level of Ardenia's famed diamond mines, and locked into matching cells.

Osana sank straight to the straw-packed dirt, curling into a ball, forehead pressed to her knees. In the cell across from hers, Urtzi examined the steel bars, set so narrowly that he couldn't even snake his arm through past the wrist. "Told you they wouldn't smile and lead us to the princess. I hope they're wrong about her being dead."

Osana didn't answer. This confused Urtzi, as she'd always been very talkative, but it was no secret that women tended to confuse him no matter what. Always the follower, he decided he might try to take the lead here, and leave Osana to whatever journey of the mind she was making.

From what he could see by craning his neck at the edges of his cell, they were the dungeon's only inhabitants. He listened, and could hear nothing other than the flicker and pop of torches set in sconces along the dimly lit corridor, and the scratching of rats scuttling along the walls.

"Perhaps the fact that we're alone is a good thing. Maybe this is just an in-and-out detention. They'll ask us some questions, we'll tell them what we know, and they'll send us on our way." Urtzi figured this was a pretty optimistic view—perhaps all that time with Luca had rubbed off on him as much as Ula had rubbed off on Osana.

Still, Osana said nothing.

He blinked at her. "Or they'll just kill everyone."

No reaction.

"And they'll serve us up for dinner. Heads on a plate, swimming in olive gravy, pine needles sticking out our noses."

Nothing.

"Osana. Hellooooo, Osana. What's gotten into you? If we're going to get out of here, we're going to have to work together."

"We're not getting out of here."

Her voice was so small, he almost wasn't sure he'd heard correctly. "What—why?"

If she answered, he didn't hear it, because the doors at the end of the hall burst open. In strode a small, dark-haired woman dressed in a rich garnet gown. She walked with a terrifying amount of purpose— her shoulders thrust back and her chin so high, as if she could part the Divide with each ensuing step. Though she wore no crown, Urtzi knew immediately this must be the Queen Mother the guard had mentioned. She was so stunning that Urtzi did not immediately realize that a man—no, a tall boy—trailed in her wake.

Osana was on her feet, snapped out of her trance, face pressed to the bars.

"I didn't know who you really were," she insisted. Never blinking. Never glancing away. Her jaw was as firm as her gaze, but all the color had drained from her face. "I swear. I didn't know. Not until they said Ferdinand's name at the gate. And even then I wasn't sure until you walked in this room."

The regal lady pursed her lips.

"Here you will address him as King Ferdinand. And me as the Queen Mother. Do you understand, Osana?" The girl nodded solemnly, her blue eyes drifting over the woman's shoulder to the hulking form of the king. The boy's clear green eyes hadn't strayed from her face since he'd entered the room, something like sadness glistening in them, in contrast to his mother's obvious fury. "You did not know we'd gone because you had already *left us*."

"Osana," Urtzi ventured, joining the conversation from his cell. "I get the sense you know them."

The Queen Mother's lips quirked. "And *I* get the sense you didn't tell your new friends exactly who you are."

"Who . . . ?"

"Osana is a watcher." This from the king, who suddenly looked like he hadn't slept in a millennium. "For the Warlord. Or was. Until she escaped with my sister."

Urtzi swallowed, this new information buzzing in his ears. He tried to read Osana's face, to figure out whose side she was on now, but she looked away.

"Girl, you are lucky you have information we need," the Queen Mother announced. *And the king's interest, for what it was worth.* "Our soldiers tell us you arrived at the gate looking for Princess Amarande. Why did you believe she was here?"

Osana glanced at the king, but his mother was not having it. "Do not look to him. Answer the question."

Her throat working, Osana swallowed. Quick as a snake, the Queen Mother's right hand shot out, snagging Osana's fingers and yanking her forward until she had the girl's arm jammed between the bars at a painful angle.

Osana cried out, and the king took a step toward them, reaching out as if he could stop it. But then he abruptly retreated, his eyes pinned on a dagger that appeared in his mother's left hand. The woman twisted the arm further, revealing the blue veins at Osana's wrist.

The Queen Mother pressed the tip of the dagger to the constellation of veins until it drew blood, all the while pinning Osana with her gaze. Waiting.

The girl squeezed her eyes shut, tears snaking out the corners. Then, quickly and clearly, she gave away the entire plan. "Amarande was supposed to come here, shore up Ardenia's defenses against Pyrenee's retaliation for Renard's death, and then await a message and meet us."

"Us?" The blade pressed deeper, the blood snaking rivulets around the steel tip. "Say his name, girl."

"Us—Luca, the Otsakumea. The resistance."

The Queen Mother smiled. "You will take us to the Otsakumea. You and this pirate. And we will put an end to that ridiculous resistance once and for all."

"Wait. Mother, we're expecting *war* any day," the king argued at her back, an urgency in his features that he did not betray in his voice. "Send a message. Have a team of watchers go. It cannot be us. And we certainly can't send any of Ardenia's soldiers to do the Warlord's bidding."

"I don't see why not. We tell them we believe the resistance is tied to King Sendoa's death. Simple."

"I believe I've made it clear how I feel about lies, Mother." Here, he took a step forward, and placed a hand softly on her back, his eyes on the dagger still pressed to Osana's pulse. "That battle can wait, the one for Ardenia cannot. One battle at a time. Send the message; await news from Basilica and Pyrenee. Please."

The Queen Mother's jaw worked and she swallowed once before seeming to relent, her shoulders softening. The king's stiff posture relaxed a touch, too. And then the woman was removing her blade from Osana's wrist—but not without one final dig.

Osana yelped, and Ferdinand flinched.

The nick was deep, just missing the vein but drawing a fresh crop of thick droplets of red blood. The Queen Mother coolly released Osana's arm. "When you don't return with the princess the wolf cub will panic. We will simply wait until Luca comes running himself. Amarande ran after him; there is no indication he will not do the same in return."

The Queen Mother turned her attention then to Urtzi. He immediately withdrew his hands from the bars—this woman would take a finger without warning. It was strange, facing him, she did look so much like Amarande in size and stature it was disconcerting. "Do you have reason to believe differently, pirate? You were there for the wedding at the Bellringe, no?"

"Yes, I was at the wedding; no, I don't believe differently."

The Queen Mother examined every inch of his face, then nodded, satisfied. "Good." She stowed her dagger and turned on her heel, calling to the king, who had stepped to Osana's cell and was wrapping her wounded wrist with a clean white handkerchief. "Dinner with the Royal Council, my king. Now."

Ferdinand made to follow his mother, already stomping toward the exit, but Osana caught his fingers with her good hand. The king paused and flipped her grip so that he was holding her hand just as much as she was clutching his.

"Is Amarande truly dead?" she whispered.

"My king, we are *late*," his mother prodded, not deigning to look back. "She won't bleed out if she ties the knot herself."

The king did not answer, instead he simply shook his head a minuscule amount, squeezed Osana's fingers, and walked away.

CHAPTER
29

AMARANDE awoke where the stars could not see.

She blinked into the humid darkness, startled at the realization that death was more temperate than she'd thought it would be. It was not an assortment of chills leading to rigid stiffness, but incandescent heat. On her skin, in her chest, her muscles. Her head throbbed with it, a heartbeat behind the new, searing reality of what it was like to open her eyes.

Perhaps the stars could not see her because she was one with them, wrapped in so much light it appeared onyx dark.

She blinked again and a single light appeared. It hovered in the distance, this ball of illumination. Perhaps a neighboring star. Someone else recently gone from this world.

"Father? Is that you?"

Her voice was dry, the metallic tang of blood at the back of her throat. She tried and failed to swallow it away.

The glow came closer. And closer. Until she could nearly reach out and touch it. Her eyes were drawn to the light, clinging to it like fireflies circling a torch. A spirit, perhaps, the blaze within, as all the starborn priests evangelized.

But then the light had a voice.

"You have the hardest head I've ever seen, Princess."

Not her father.

Taillefer.

Amarande's mind churned into motion—of course *he* would be the nearest star. He'd died within a breath of her own death. Even the afterlife of the Sand and Sky was brutal.

I should be with Luca. I should be next to Luca in the eternal sky.

But then Taillefer's pale face, marred with grit and a smear of blood, loomed into her vision, along with the white light of flame. His blue eyes caught the firelight, as vivid as they were alive.

"No surprise given your stubbornness, but a blow like that would've killed most men. Yet here you are, blinking as if your brain is still intact. I have yet to see it slide out of your nose, but I still was not convinced you'd open your eyes again."

Amarande ran a hand over the back of her head, where she'd smacked it on the floor in her cell at the Itspi only days ago. The knot there had subsided under the heaviness of her hair, but now there was a new, bigger bump right above it—the size of the goose eggs Maialen so celebrated upon their arrival to the Itspi kitchens.

A gloved hand appeared in the dead shadow between herself and Taillefer's face. The light shifted. His already-tattered guard's tunic was even more shredded than before. He had cut strips of it to bandage up the wounds he had suffered at the jaws of the black wolf.

Amarande accepted his hand and sat up. The blood in her head swept forward in a rush, her eyes automatically squeezed shut as an aching tide hit her temples. Her stomach lurched and she retched—whatever water was left in her system dribbled out of her mouth, narrowly missing her trousers and boots. She dropped Taillefer's hand and rolled onto her hands and knees, clutching the soft earth until the nausea passed and nothing remained in her system.

Amarande wiped her face on her sleeve and sat back on her haunches. "How long was I out?"

"The first question *I* would've asked would've been 'Where are we?' And the answer is in an underground cavern as big as a dining hall and littered with bones. But to answer *your* question—hours. Several. I'm not sure how many." Taillefer shoved something into her palm. "Eat this. You need sustenance."

She squinted at the oblong object. "Is that . . . a potato?"

"Yes. Peel it first—scrape to the inner flesh with your nails. Raw potatoes can make you ill enough to vomit again, but the toxin that causes the problem is mostly found in the skin."

That natural arts knowledge of his, on display, giving her spinning head another rush of nausea. "I'm not going to eat it."

She tossed it at his face. Taillefer caught it and pressed it back into her palm. "You haven't eaten in at least a day and you've taken a blow to the head. You have to eat."

Amarande handed it back. "Use your torch to roast it first. Or lend me the torch and I will do it. I would very much not like to chance another round of vomit."

Taillefer blinked. Clearly he'd partaken of raw potato. "I have underestimated your shrewdness."

As the prince did as she requested, the princess pushed herself slowly, painfully to her feet. The strength in her legs was missing, limbs wobbly beneath her. That pounding behind her eyes wasn't dissipating. Her mouth was parched raw. Her injured hand throbbed. Yet all she could think was of the time they had lost.

Hours. Several.

Time she couldn't get back on her way to find Luca. All the information she needed to get to him and the resistance piling in her mind.

Her mother was in communication with the current Warlord, knew Luca's name, expected the rebels to strike.

Then there was the poisoned water at the Cardenas Scar. How many other places were affected? Would Luca and the entire resistance be poisoned as they prepared to fight the Warlord?

And now there was the accusation of the man at the Warlord's Inn—that she had last arrived there with a Warlord spy. Could he have meant Osana? If so, the implications of her traveling with Luca could be disastrous. Amarande's gut didn't want to believe it, but if blood didn't matter on the continent of the Sand and Sky, then clearly a few moments on the same side didn't matter either.

Amarande's eyes snagged on the prince's back.

As much as the thought of all the time they'd lost made fear and dread collect in the pit of her recently vacated stomach, there was something else disturbing here. She'd spent hours unconscious with Taillefer nearby, conscious, and in full possession of his faculties. Not a good thing under any circumstance.

Taking inventory, Amarande discovered, as she'd feared, that her boot knife and her sword were missing. "Taillefer, did you—"

"Relax, Princess. I *borrowed* your steel to make my bandages. And to spark the fire—there's barely any wood down here and most of it is too wet to use anyway." He turned, revealing that he held her dagger in his hand, two potatoes skewered on the blade, half-roasted over his torch, which he'd staked into the loamy earth. He cocked his head near a pile of rotten sticks he'd collected. "Your sword is over there."

Moving more quickly than was wise, Amarande limped over to her sword. The Basilican steel felt twice its normal weight in her injured hand, but Amarande gritted her teeth and stowed it away in the scabbard still slung across her back. "I will require my dagger."

"You are welcome to do the roasting, then." He gestured at the pile of small, shriveled potatoes beside him. "My blades did not make the journey into this pit of despair with me."

It was on the tip of her tongue, that this was a waste of time, but as she took a step toward him, another wave of nausea crashed over her, enough that she swooned on her feet—her knees softening, boots shuffling heavily across the soft loam beneath her soles as she steadied herself. Her empty stomach lurched and rolled, her vision blurred, and suddenly her heart was beating far too fast.

Taillefer was correct—she needed sustenance.

After a few careful steps, the princess sank down next to him, recovering her boot knife and starting the job of roasting the potatoes. He plucked the two he'd done first off the blade with what appeared to be sharp shards of pottery, and loaded the knife with two more before handing it back.

Amarande sank her teeth into her potato like it was an apple, the steam rising from its skin to her dirty cheeks. It was old and bland, but possibly the most amazing thing she'd ever tasted. The starch hit quickly, and with every bite, she felt renewed.

After her third tuber, she plucked two more from the pile, put them on the fire, and glanced at the prince. "Where did you find the potatoes?"

"In a stash of terra-cotta pots, over that way." Taillefer nodded over his shoulder. "By a pair of tunnels. One is caved in; the other appears passable, but I didn't have time to see where it led after I found the stores. I was worried about you."

A cache of food and supplies meant people. And, she hoped, the resistance—who else would leave supplies stored underground but people with something to hide? "Then I suppose that's where we start in looking for a way out."

"Not until you've eaten every potato in that pile. Don't think for a second I didn't see you nearly fall over just trying to stand. Eat. Regain your strength. Then we'll go."

CHAPTER
30

"I<small>T</small> stinks, doesn't it?" Taillefer asked Amarande once their bellies were full, their legs more sure, and they'd found another stick both dry enough and long enough that the princess could also carry a torch. "Sulfur. Feeds the spring that created the slurry that sucked us down here."

Amarande held her flame aloft and squinted through the distance, though the light was too weak to see much. This cave was at least three stories high, and the sharp spines of aragonite cave flowers bloomed across what she could see of the ceiling. "The Innkeeper told me that his 'compost' would lead to certain death. Good thing he was wrong."

"Compost? I believe 'quicksand' is the technical term," Taillefer replied, gesturing to their right. "And there are plenty of examples of certain death in that pile—dead meat but not the kind you'd like to eat."

"Are you sure the tunnels are this way? You aren't turned around?"

"They are. Just have to move beyond the sulfuric graveyard, first."

The stench increased until it made her eyes water. Bones littered the sulfuric mire, and farther on appeared to be a solid wall but was, upon further inspection, silt and slurry, stacked on top of itself all the way to the surface. A handful of skulls in various configurations peered out from the layered mass, which shook with each grinding gulp from the earth.

"We survived simply by being lucky. We came down on the very edge of that mass and were heavy enough to fall through and bounce to where we landed. I moved you to more solid ground when I realized you weren't going to wake." Taillefer paused, pointedly. "*You're welcome.* Anyhow, if we'd been dropped into the sand ten to fifteen feet in the other direction, our skin would be broiled off in that slurry."

Amarande worked the sequence through in her mind's eye. Taillefer's analysis was sound. "The people at the inn knew of the sand but not that it was not equally deadly across its entire surface."

"Yes. Quite the favor they did us."

"I suppose so." She turned away. "If only they had listened to reason."

"They are not your subjects. They are not obligated to listen to you, Princess."

That nearly made her smile. "The past week has taught me that no one will listen to me anyway because I am not a man. It's enough to drive a woman mad, and I'm the lucky one—the direct heir."

"Perhaps it's no wonder then that my mother and yours are so particularly vengeful."

The princess bit back a sorrowful laugh. Yes, queens who would hunt, jail, and possibly kill their own children were shaped into their evil, not born that way. Not for the first time, Amarande wondered what kinds of experiences had so twisted her mother—and how she could avoid the same fate.

They arrived at the fork of two tunnels. "The one to the left is where I found the potato cache. It seems to veer for a half mile, and then there is a pile of rubble partially blocking it, but given the potatoes were nearby, I believe there is likely a way through the blockage." That assumption was enough for Amarande. "If you're thinking the resistance is literally underground, I second that theory—these natural caves have most definitely been augmented with tools."

She peered within. "What direction do you think it leads?"

Tallifer had already done this calculation. "Based on where we started and where we landed after becoming compost, I'd say generally to the southeast."

"That is another clue that this might be a structure frequented by the resistance—that direction would put us close to another man I know with a black wolf."

"Wait, that was really a black wolf?" He seemed genuinely intrigued. "I thought they'd been extinct for years and that one was a cleverly bred dog."

"They aren't extinct. I met one before. Considering how brazenly pro-Otxoa the breeding of a supposedly eradicated species would be, I'm quite confident that those people back there at the inn were members of the resistance. Now we just need to find more—like the man to the east."

Taillefer cut a quick grin. "Well, if we find any, maybe they'll do something worse to us than fight us, not listen to our pleas, and then banish us to quicksand after we save them and the wolf from the same fate. Like our friends back there did."

His brand of sarcasm was as sharp as any blade. And utterly annoying. Amarande ignored this.

Bowing like the royal scion he was, Taillefer stepped aside and gestured to the tunnel on the left. "After you. Since you have both a torch and the weapons."

"I plan to keep them, too."

The tunnel was tall enough that neither of them had to stoop, though it was thin enough that it demanded they walk single file, their torches flickering wildly with each damp step. The ground was more solid than within the cavern, but the dirt was soft enough Amarande could easily follow Taillefer's footsteps from hours earlier as they picked along the path.

Before they'd even made the first turn, Taillefer was back to asking questions. "Tell me about the man with a black wolf. How did you become acquainted? Was he friend, foe, or otherwise?"

Amarande wet her lips. "At one point early in my hunt for Luca and the kidnappers, I climbed a large plateau to gain better vantage."

"Seems reasonable."

"I thought so—a few sore muscles would be worth it for a glimpse of the riders who'd stolen him away or some other clue as to their direction. What I did not expect was that hauling myself over the edge of the plateau would put me face-to-face with the snarling jaws of a black wolf."

"I'm unsure if the most unbelievable part of that story is that you were attacked by a black wolf or that this supposedly extinct animal was living atop a plateau." Taillefer laughed softly. "And, I assume, this one was trained like the one I faced?"

"You are correct. The wolf's master shot me with a sleeping dart while I fought his animal. Next thing I knew, I awoke in chains, penance to the Warlord."

The prince nodded—the Warlord's tax was something about which he already knew—and sighed. "I am beginning to suspect you could make an enemy out of virtually every encounter. You're terrible at making friends, aren't you? And the pirates don't count because their change of allegiance was entirely Luca's doing, not yours."

Amarande opened her mouth, then closed it. Was he right? It was true, growing up, she had no real friends other than Luca. But she'd always thought it was because she didn't need any. Luca was enough.

She quickened her pace, torch raised high and back stiff. "I suppose you could do better. You have *lots* of friends. Which was why when you had to flee your homeland they dropped everything and came with you—oh wait."

"Very funny, Princess." Taillefer allowed a dark laugh. "Do not take this the wrong way, but before this journey I've never argued so inanely with anyone save for my brother. We used to drive our tutors mad with our bickering when we were little."

Amarande did not take it the wrong way. In fact, it made her a little sad that she could picture Taillefer and Renard together as children. Perhaps that latest blow to the head had made her far more sympathetic than she should be to the sons of Pyrenee. "Trading barbs, disagreeing, tenuous trust supported by occasional teamwork and wrecked by constant suspicion—that was your childhood, no?"

"No." Taillefer paused for a long moment. "Yes. I did like him best when I managed to get under his skin. I am sure it's unhealthy. You have not missed anything not knowing your brother, Princess."

She held up her wounded hand. "He's already literally gotten under my skin."

Taillefer laughed. "I am proud to say you have yet to successfully stab me."

"I appreciate the 'yet.'"

After a pause, Taillefer circled back to the task at hand. "So, the plan currently is to find this man and his black wolf, hope he's out of sleeping darts and holds off on commanding the wolf to attack just long enough that we can state our case and get you to your love?"

"Precisely. I will find Luca, warn him, and then fight by his side. The rest of the continent's concerns can come later."

"While I am not denying that is romantic and undoubtedly noble, I still do not understand what we are warning Luca *about*. The Warlord obviously knows of his existence—the bodies at the Cardenas Scar are proof of the Warlord's attempt to control the opposition just as the pro-Otxoa rebels overtaking the inn are proof that change is in the air. Movement is happening. If it's obvious to us, it's likely obvious to the resistance, if they're worth their salt."

Amarande chewed the inside of her mouth as he continued.

"The point is, Luca is facing the regime, not the person. In the scheme of things, this knowledge does not matter." The mocking lilt to his tone slipped away, his next question sincere. "What are you not sharing, Princess? Something tells me you know far more than you let on."

Amarande picked her way around a bend, stacked with the terracotta pottery Taillefer had promised—the rubble must be up ahead. The princess swallowed, hoping to stave off his insistence long enough for the distraction and immediate problem of the blocked tunnel. She couldn't tell him about her mother's past. That was just too much—he could use that knowledge against her, gain Geneva's favor—

"Princess," Taillefer prodded. "I don't know what else I can—"

A hissing rattle stopped Amarande dead in her tracks. "Is that—"

In answer, the distinct body of a Quemado Scorpion scuttled out of the pile of rocks that clogged the tunnel. An arm wrapped around her midsection, hauling her back and away. Amarande shoved at Taillefer's grip. "It's just one."

But then, from within the nooks and crannies between rocks ranging in size from a melon to a pebble, came more rattling. The scorpion's warning signal before spitting or stinging—or both.

"Five . . . ten . . . no, twenty," Taillefer counted. "We must retreat."

Again, he grabbed hold of her, this time at her wrist. Amarande shook him off hard enough that she ended up scooting forward in the dirt. The frontmost scorpion's stinger engaged. The princess swallowed, her heart pounding as she glanced between the creatures, fanning out across the width of the tunnel, and the blockage.

"No." They were still pointing toward the dragon's spine and the plateau where she knew the man with the black wolf would be. "We can draw them out, use our flame, kill them—"

"*What?*" He nearly screeched at her strategy. "Are you insane? One sting and nothing can help you. Back. Up."

"We can make it."

"I know these creatures. We cannot." Amarande remembered what Luca had told her about Taillefer's workshop in the Bellringe. Brimming not only with potions like the fire swamp, but also full of specimens of all kinds. Stuffed. Jarred. Live.

Which gave her an idea. "The fire swamp. Use that!"

"No. It'll just enrage them further."

The scorpions advanced, seemingly working together, forming a line. Taillefer yanked Amarande's arm hard enough to test the socket. "Not the time for stubbornness, come on!"

Struggling against the torque of his grip might have flung her straight into the charging, deadly scorpions, and so for once Amarande did as she was told.

She ran.

CHAPTER
31

QUEEN Inés stood on the dock in the Port of Basilica, surveying all she'd gained in a single night's effort.

The sea was clean and crisp, the brine and spray permeating air thick with the swoop and call of gulls. The beaches gave way to dark rocks and mountains behind and beyond—hinting of the ore used to smelt the steel that kept Basilica's coffers ripe and ready.

Atop one of those mountains—she would either learn the name or change it—was the Aragonesti, her newest home. It was all glittering onyx, a starry night in the middle of the day. The perfect contrast to the pristine white walls of the Bellringe. Her castle homes were polar opposites in both looks and location. Miragua, the seat of Myrcell, was the same shade as the sand beyond it. Perhaps it would be a summer home.

But that was a premature thought. Restful balconies in the salt air must wait until she reached her final goal—calling every last inch of this continent hers.

At her back, the royal ships were packed with remaining vials of poison, members of her new court, and, of course, thousands of soldiers, sworn to the new queen of the joined kingdoms of Pyrenee, Basilica, and Myrcell. There had been no time to sew new uniforms, but that did not bother Inés. There were only two sides—hers and the wrong one—and if these men and women didn't fight for her they would die.

Ardenia would weed out the skittish ones for her while she marched to victory at the Itspi—the baby king wetting his pants along the way. She might offer to marry him, if he was the malleable sort. Maybe.

But she was done with needing a man to help her achieve her goals. And the baby king did not rule in Ardenia. The true power behind the throne belonged to a woman, the Queen Mother, as Geneva now styled herself.

No, control over the continent of the Sand and Sky was down to its two remaining queens. And it would be a battle, indeed.

She had once called Geneva a friend, long ago, when they were pawns in the same game. When they'd banded together and rebelled, rather than see it through. When they both received not-so-veiled threats from an enraged Domingu.

You chose to make a stand rather than make a move. A mistake.

True. But since then, both she and Geneva had made their moves. Hers within the confines of her cage. Geneva outside of it. But Inés knew her well enough to know the renewed Queen Mother was still playing from outside the house, even as she called the Itspi home each night.

And Inés would use that to her advantage en route to destroying Geneva, her baby king, and a divided and distant Ardenian army.

Next, to the Torrent. The Warlord thought he was safe from the whims of the kingdom states. But that safety dissolved the moment Sendoa had passed away. It was only his disinterest in resolving the problem of the Torrent that kept it going for so long. No one else in the Sand and Sky wanted to waste their armies on the sunburnt belly of the continent—no laws, no resources, no interest in being led.

But now she had an army three times what Sendoa had. And soon his great military would bow to her. Even the rebels circling the Warlord would have to kneel to that.

Or die trying.

"My queen?"

Inés turned at the approach of a Basilican soldier. She addressed him with a taut smile. "Second Captain Micael?"

"My queen, the ships are prepared to disembark at your command."

Inés looked to her royal ship. The three sigils had been sewn together, the flag heavy but the harbor breeze strong enough to lift it. The heads of the Bear, Shark, and Mountain Lion joined together as one. Below the flag, her remaining councilors, fresh blood from her acquired kingdoms, and Medikua Aritza lined the deck.

"Let us go. The fastest route possible."

"Yes, my queen."

Micael scuttled off and Inés turned for the gangplank leading to her ship.

Nikola had not yet arrived. Still out there somewhere with Amarande and Taillefer. That misstep was frustrating. But it didn't matter.

She had everything she needed to be successful and then some.

The paperwork. The army. The element of surprise.

As she'd calculated back in her chambers at the Bellringe, the fig-ures on the board had been set up—Tiger, Mountain Lion, Shark, Bear. Now only one and a phantom remained.

And she was ready to play.

Nine Years Prior to Present Day

IT had been said the Warlord's face reflected back the viewer's deepest fear.

That when meeting face-to-face, the tyrant shifted forms until he was only recognized by the viewer's soul, making them see the thing that kept them up at night, leaving claw marks on the darkest parts of the mind.

Sendoa, Warrior King of Ardenia, did not believe this.

It was a myth. It was, like everything else in the Torrent, smoke and mirrors designed to protect the leader. A reputation can often be stronger than a suit of armor. This was something Sendoa believed. He knew it to be true through personal experience.

He was a warrior king, and it didn't hurt to call himself one.

His army was the best in the world, and it paid to regularly make mention of it.

His kingdom was the richest in the Sand and Sky, and as long as diamonds were mined no one weighed the coffers.

And so Sendoa stood in the middle of the Warlord's camp. A fire pit large enough to swallow any ship in the Port of Ardenia roared at his back. At his side, General Koldo. They were without their swords, the famed blades left with the Ardenian contingent a mile outside of the Warlord's camp.

This meeting was not on Sendoa's terms.

Not his land, not his decision, not his advantage.

It was not ideal, but he'd worked for six years to have this meeting. And he would have it. Unarmed and alone was worth it for a chance at peace. To finally negotiate with this person who had orchestrated the murder of his royal friends. Whose very leadership led to bandits and raiders crossing into Ardenia to steal from people whose peaceful existence made them a target.

"Koldo." He nodded to his general, a lock of sunset hair falling forward, the words both a good-bye and an order. No matter what happened inside that tent, the general would keep Ardenia safe. Keep Amarande safe.

Two of the Warlord's women moved before him, an escort. He walked between them. In twenty paces, the escort split on either side of the entrance, stepping beside twin torches driven into the soft earth, and pulled open either flap of the curtain, revealing nothing but blinding light and palpable heat.

The Warrior King stepped into the tent. A figure stood so close to the fire it almost appeared to be formed of smoke. Backlit. Black. Swathed in the blue and white of the hottest flames.

The figure turned. Stepped forward.

The king's knees weakened. Something that could have been fear stabbed straight through his heart.

Real. She was real.

"Hello, Sendoa."

Under several days of ginger scruff on the Warrior King's cheeks, all color drained until only the blush of a Torrent sunburn remained atop his nose and cheekbones.

He stared at her uncovered face, cataloging features mirrored upon his own young daughter. Clear eyes, full lips, tapered chin. What's more, her frame was commanding though it was slight—his daughter would be this way, too, as she grew.

Sendoa tried to speak. His tongue shriveled in his mouth. All the moisture in his body seemed to turn to dust. He could only utter a single word.

"Why?"

The woman smiled at him, the disdain in it sharp enough to draw blood.

"You're going to have to be more specific."

She began pacing—her steps as powerful and cutting as the edges of her tone.

"Why did I leave you? Why am I here? Why in the stars would I agree to meet with you and show my true face?" She strode up to him, close enough to reach up, place her palms to his cheeks, and smile into his eyes as she'd used to. She'd always been petite, more than a foot shorter than he, and yet at that moment, Sendoa felt she'd surpassed him in stature. "Or should it be '*how*'? How did I build this? How did I do it under your nose? How did you not know?"

The Warlord felled the Otxoa eight years before. This woman, the mother of his child, the so-called Runaway Queen, Geneva of Basilica, had left little more than six years before. Voice still strangled, he spit out the question she wanted to hear. "How?"

"The Warlord is an idea, not a person. A shame you never suspected." She cocked a brow at him. "You came here to meet with the Warlord. The person who killed your regal black wolf friends and burned their castle to ash. The person who rose up on a wave of support from those sick of monarchy, sick of not having a voice. I am not that person, but I am no less beloved."

"*Beloved?*" It came out as a curse. One word and his full voice returned. The pressure retreated from his eyes. "The Warlord's rule has made the Torrent uninhabitable to anyone other than bandits, thieves, mercenaries. You are not beloved—you are *feared*."

The Warlord did not blink.

"Untrue. As you leave, look around this camp, Sendoa. Families live here. Children play and sleep tight. They are free." She bared her teeth. "I keep them safe with perception and reputation, not unlike yourself, *Warrior King*. Is your army truly the world's best, or is that reputation simply armor forged in whispers and not actual battle?"

The Warrior King did not take the bait.

"Is it true what you do to maintain your reputation?" he spit, gaining steam fed by righteousness. "Forcing your people to always move, never put down roots? Burning dissenters alive to spark your fire pits? Cultivating a culture where stealing is better than a hard day's work? You create chaos and purposeful interference—your people can't sit long enough to realize the faults in their way of life."

"'Purposeful interference'—quite the phrase." She tilted her head at him and the length of linen tossed over her shoulders—a covering for her face anywhere but this tent—went with it. "Let us go back to the beginning. You are surprised to see me, yes, but there is more than one reason you did not expect my face."

Again, Sendoa's cheeks drained of their color.

With new eyes, he tried to read this woman she'd become.

A smile cut across her beautiful face. "Oh yes, Your Highness, I know exactly who you expected to be in this tent. Jericho Talmage, bandit of the red sands, rebel rouser, enigmatic organizer. His reputation, like yours, is one of legend." Sendoa looked away. "But you know all of that. Because *you* installed him."

The Warrior King did not reply.

"Why did you need to conscript your men and women into the 'world's greatest army'? Not for some altruistic reason that allows your people to feel powerful and safe. No, because you needed bodies. Why did you need bodies? Because you were busy overthrowing a vulnerable kingdom."

Sendoa's jaw worked as the facets and angles and possibilities flashed through his mind. There was no strategy for this. He was behind the curve. Finally, the king asked, "Where is Talmage?"

The Warlord's smile twisted. "After Talmage killed your regal black wolf friends, burned their castle to ash, and christened the Torrent on the backs of the citizenry with *your* support?" He did not reply. This only sparked amusement on the Warlord's face. "Jericho Talmage needed a recess. And thus he retired."

"Retired?"

"Oh, was that not what he was supposed to do?" She punctuated her false surprise with a coquettish laugh. "Ah, yes, your handshake agreement—you would support him in felling the Otxoa, and then within a few years' time you would relieve him of the burden of leading and rescue the Torrent for yourself, bringing the headless nation into the fold to expand Ardenia's borders and influence. Yes?"

The Warrior King did not deny it.

"And this was supposed to be that meeting. You are seven years too late for Talmage. Therefore, you get me." She reached up to pat his colorless cheek. "Lucky you."

Sendoa's molars ground together as he inhaled thinly through his nose, watching this woman who was not the one he married. No, the teenage bride he'd wed had been demure, quiet, solemn—their arranged marriage always seemed to be much more of a duty to her than to him.

"Do not put this solely on me. There would be no Torrent without you, *before all this*." He gestured to the silken drape of her deep blue gown and matching scarf used to cover her face. "Or has power made you completely forget what it was like to be a teenage girl, betrothed to a man whom you'd been ordered to kill?"

Geneva inhaled deeply, her firelit eyes skipping away. There was no way she'd forgotten—no matter who she was now or how many years stood between them then.

The plan was pure Domingu. Installing his kin within the walls of each castle, awaiting instruction. He'd handpicked from his brood those who had the best potential. The right age for a possible match. The right temperament. Deep within the Aragonesti, he gave each one the right training, without the knowledge of their parents, siblings, minders.

Then he waited for the right timing.

To place one child in each castle.

Years between them, and each of their doorways into another kingdom different.

An arranged marriage—Ardenia, Pyrenee.

A governess for the dowager and her lonely son—Myrcell.

An unplanned death, and, later, another suggested match—Torrence.

And, once everyone was in place and no one was prepared: Mass, coordinated regicide. Kingdoms taken by force by a man who'd taken everything that way.

Domingu had managed to keep it from being too obvious—rather than being the father-in-law to the entire continent, he simply used the most unobtrusive means.

Sixteen-year-old Geneva had laid it all out to Sendoa on their wedding night. Crying in her chambers. Insisting it was best the king did not see her, know her, spend any time alone with her.

And so Sendoa did what he must.

He told his closest friend first—Lotyoa, whose brother was betrothed to one of Domingu's more distant kin. But Lotyoa didn't believe such a thing could happen and didn't want to, joyfully awaiting the arrival of his second child.

Dowager Queen Tiya was too lonely to listen.

And Louis-David was too smitten with his wife's bosom to care.

"I was the messenger, but you wielded the knife. You supported Talmage. You murdered the royal family."

"That was not his order. He was to disrupt—"

"You cannot give orders to those whose knees do not bend to you."

Her teeth were bared. "And no matter your regrets, that is what happened. The rebellion you sparked burned your *dear friend* and his kingdom to ash. And though Talmage went too far, you and your fearsome army did not ride in to avenge Lotyoa's murder because, *what?* The goal was still achieved? Domingu's plans of coordinated regicide passed as his fear of a similar people's rebellion crept in. And so you let the Warlord reign untouched, using that fear to keep the most dangerous person on the continent in check. Funny how little lives are worth when they pay for your success."

There was no defense. It was true.

Once death had taken the Otxoa, the strategy was to keep Domingu from striking until it was time to claim the Torrent for his own. And one day give it to the boy whom he'd hidden in his stables in the chaos. Cushioned with a new name, lies, and love from those who knew the truth.

But giving Torrence back to him would be much more difficult without the Torrent in his possession until the boy came of age. He'd never told Geneva of Luca's true identity. Not once. Not even after Amarande's birth and the connection they'd made in that. And yet she'd inserted herself in his reformed plan anyway.

And so the Warlord's lips quirked smugly. Unaware of Sendoa's end game. Not power for himself, but putting things as right as he could after as wrong as they went.

"You see," she said, confident that she held the upper hand. "You came here to execute a deal you made with a man who is no longer here. He entrusted the title of Warlord to his second-in-command—a woman, much like *your own*." Of course she knew—he'd always suspected. Still, he said nothing. "And then she entrusted it to me. He told her everything of course, and she told me. But that knowledge does not bind me to the original deal, does it?"

Sendoa took a deep breath. If he was ever going to atone for his mistake, he must get this right, despite his plan disintegrating. "What are your terms, Geneva?"

But the Warlord did not answer. Instead, she asked, "She's here, isn't she?"

Geneva didn't need to say Koldo's name. And she wouldn't; Sendoa knew that much. "Yes, of course."

"Always by your side, but not *at* your side." Geneva's eyes flashed to his hand, no band of gold to be found. "Doesn't that hurt?"

Sendoa didn't blink—she would expect him to fight back. To relent would be to invite questions he did not want to answer. "Does your heart hurt for our daughter? Or did you cut her out of your heart like you did me? You have not mentioned her once and she's the bond between us that is unbroken."

Geneva bared her teeth. "I left Amarande because I love her."

"*Love her?* You do not even know her—"

The Warlord moved like a lightning strike.

A lunging step, a glint of metal, and blood began to bloom in a slash on Sendoa's cheek.

The act left the king so stunned, Geneva was able to grip his chin with her blade-free hand, forcing him still and level, with nowhere to look but in her eyes as his cheek wept.

"Do not question my love. You have no idea what I have done for my daughter."

The Warrior King did not answer as her anger washed over him, as fierce as the bear her native kingdom had long ago adopted as a sigil.

All teeth and anger and ferocity.

Geneva tapped the knife tip against his skin, just below the cut. "That, Sendoa, is my gift to you. I could have easily slit your throat and let your whore general drag your body back home. And yet I did not. It is also my promise, that if you do not attack me, I will not attack you."

In answer, he stared back. Unblinking. Breathing hard. Restrained.

"Let me operate as I please, keep my identity off your tongue, and the Sand and Sky will not know that you made the first cut in slicing a thousand years of unity apart."

Was that truly what she wanted? With all the power he'd let her believe she had over him? That was it? It was a noble but weak combination—there had to be more behind it.

"That's your trade? Anonymity and freedom?" he asked, calm. There had to be more. He was just not sure what. And that, like the surprise of her very presence, was unsettling. It was not often that the Warrior King was left in the dark.

Expression betraying nothing, the Warlord removed the blade from his skin, releasing Sendoa enough so that he could see the dagger full on. His blood glinted in the firelight, the reflection of it in Geneva's eyes.

"You keep my secrets, Your Highness, and I shall keep yours."

CHAPTER 32

THE sky was a muted navy when the general arrived at the fire pit nearest to Ardenia.

Koldo dismounted, wrapped her horse's reins around the jutting edge of a boulder, and walked to the pit. She climbed over the lip and descended into the ash-filled crevice. She didn't need to go far—only twenty or thirty feet—before the newest ash line became clear, even in the waning light.

Yes, five or six days ago—a week at most—the Warlord's caravan was here. Burning bodies and stars knew what else when the title of Warlord passed to another. Privately, and within the Warlord's tent, in the utmost secrecy, without any fanfare. The tattoo chiseled on a wrist, perhaps a few ceremonial words, the passing of a flask. And then the emergence of someone new wearing the Warlord's clothes and title.

The rules among the Warlord kin were clear—no one within the caravan saw the Warlord's face uncovered. Security was paramount and only those trusted enough or about to die would see the Warlord's naked identity. Often it was impossible to know which you were until that very moment.

Yet those who traveled with the caravan were not blind to change. To Koldo's knowledge, Geneva had been with the caravan for most, if not all, of Ferdinand's life and had been Warlord for a great deal of that time, too. The signs of change were obvious—new orders, the consolidation of caravans, and in its most obvious indication: no Ferdinand. The Warlord's face was unseen, yes, but his face was well known and stood out. At least, that was Koldo's experience during her yearly investigative trips to the caravan—though, in truth, Ferdinand was always exactly what she was looking for whenever she visited.

Here and now, Koldo found something she was not expecting from this fire pit. Horse tracks. More than that—evidence of a fight.

The general stepped closer. She was tempted to light a torch but knew that might actually make it more difficult to see in this sort of twilight.

The large pit in the ash had all the markings of a horse briefly falling to its side before becoming upright a few feet away. Directly facing the site where the horse had regained its footing was a minefield of hoofprints. Koldo skirted around the edge of them, her keen senses at work as she took in the angles, the pressure of the marks, the positioning.

A single horseman confronted by more than a dozen opponents.

The general knew that she'd found the place where Renard and his soldiers had captured Amarande and Luca. The signs matched the timeline and confirmed the princess's story even if she had not described the encounter to Koldo in detail—not that neither she nor the others had given Amarande the opportunity to do so.

Koldo saw now how much of a mistake it was.

The soldiers stationed high in the Ardenian mountains above the valley borderland with Pyrenee had not seen Amarande or Taillefer. Neither had the new contingent of scouts integrated with the military encampments spaced strategically along the border after the death of Prince Renard. No one had news except a tidbit about a lone captain, someone named Nikola, riding alone from the Bellringe with orders to find Taillefer or Amarande.

Clearly Taillefer was not working with whoever—likely Inés—gave that order.

Which meant what?

Koldo trudged back up the pit and hoisted herself up onto solid ground. Ash clung to her boots and gloves, the wind swirling it back toward the mountains dividing Ardenia and Pyrenee.

The general sighed and shut her eyes. Picturing Amarande's face, fierce and determined, her father's daughter in every way that mattered.

Loyal. Loving. Brave.

Koldo knew that given her druthers, Amarande would always go to Luca. Always.

Yet she had gone with Taillefer. Seemingly willingly, given the evidence. Despite what he had done to Luca. Torture so unspeakable that she had killed Renard in revenge.

Though—Amarande would never have allowed herself to be taken unwillingly by anyone, let alone someone like Taillefer. It was not possible. He was clever, yes, but not enough to sneak her out of the Itspi with force.

But what if it was with persuasion?

The princess had said it herself.

Taillefer knew that if Luca were to die then I would likely retaliate against his brother. And, though I knew this to be Taillefer's aim, I still reacted in the way he wanted.

The general's eyes flew open.

"He's giving her what she wants."

And suddenly she knew exactly where to go.

Chapter 33

THE princess tailed the prince silently through the other tunnel he'd found—winding south and, it appeared, west. They'd stopped running, not just because they were in the clear of the Quemado Scorpions, but because they were too exhausted to do so without stumbling about. Though their bellies were full of food, they had no water, and their bodies were stiff and sore.

Accordingly, they moved single file at a frustratingly labored pace.

Given the direction of the tunnels, Amarande hoped they were headed toward the Hand. Not where she'd wanted to go, but it had been a step in her original plan—a natural place for congregation, and therefore answers.

Another hour or so and the hot promise of renewed total exhaustion swept into the corners of Amarande's eyes. Her throat was so parched it seemed to throb louder than any of the other warning bells dinging throughout her body—lack of true sleep, hunger for proper food, the bump on her head. All of it.

"Can we move faster?" Amarande shot the question at the prince's back as he picked through a thinning section of tunnel, careful to keep his torch from snuffing itself on damp rock. She'd lost her torch in the retreat from the scorpions and was stuck following him—a position she hated, naturally.

"We will make it to Luca in time, Princess."

Amarande was still faintly surprised that Taillefer would dignify Luca with the use of his proper name, as opposed to calling him "boy" or "stableboy." But he'd been doing this for more than a day now, which gave Amarande hope that he'd accepted Luca's true parentage—and if he had, perhaps peers of the Sand and Sky would, too.

Or perhaps Taillefer now saw Luca as a tool of another kind. One who would accept an apology for his cruelty and be shaped into an eventual ally. Amarande would never accept such a thing after what he'd done, but she knew Luca would.

That said more about Luca's kind heart than Taillefer's persuasive talents.

"*You're welcome*, you know," the prince said, "for *again* saving you, this time from your insane stubborn streak."

He was not wrong. "Thank you. And *you're welcome* for saving you from certain death at the hands of the rebels at the inn."

"I would have survived without you."

"Not likely."

He paused. "At least anyone hunting us won't find us down here."

That was true, though Amarande would risk any possible hunters if it meant they could find their way out of this accursed tunnel and back to the surface.

Another hour and their underground track began to angle uphill. A new burn settled into her calves and thighs and a new hope came with it—that perhaps they were climbing toward the surface and with it fresh air and a sense of direction.

At the crest, Taillefer paused for a moment to touch a particularly low stalactite that glistened in the weak firelight. He rubbed his gloved fingers together and then *sniffed* them.

"Taillefer, what—"

"I think it's water."

The princess immediately reached out to touch the damp rock. Her fingers came away wet and she sniffed—there wasn't a trace of the sulfuric stench from the cave. "Do you think there's more?" she asked, but Taillefer was already on the move, the torch held high, following the glistening promise of drops beading along the stone surface.

In a few lunging steps, he was jogging ahead, one hand trailing along the tunnel wall.

"More terra-cotta. There! Look. They marked it."

Indeed, ahead the tunnel widened to a round little space, a burrow set with flat-topped rocks, jugs of pottery, and—jutting from the glistening wall—a spigot.

While Taillefer went to stow the torch upright between the flat rocks, Amarande lunged at the little steel spout, turning the lever until a trickle of water spilled out. She cupped her hands beneath, barely waiting for her palms to fill with more than a sip before gulping it down. The water slid cool and lovely down her parched throat. As she shoved her palms beneath for another delicious drink, Taillefer appeared beside her, gloves removed and two terra-cotta cups in his hands.

"This is perhaps more efficient, Princess."

"Perhaps."

They drank their fill—two, three, four cups—before inspecting the site further. There was no additional food, nor any additional clues as to where they might find the resistance, other than in this spot at a time that was not the present.

"May I ask you something?"

Taillefer's voice pulled Amarande from her thoughts. "My preference in regard to answering has not stopped you from asking before."

It was the tart reply she thought he deserved, but then when she glanced up after the words slipped from her mouth, she regretted them. On the flat rock across from her, Taillefer sat, eyes reading his hands, a blush sweeping his newly cleaned face in the firelight. Sheepish—that was what someone would call it with literally any other boy. Amarande's smirk sank and she swallowed, waiting.

"It's just that . . . is Luca really your true love or just all you've known?"

Amarande stared. "Of all your ridiculous questions . . . are you really asking me this now? Amid a days-long journey to find *my true love?*"

Taillefer wet his lips and turned to her, that glimpse of shyness gone, the brilliant blue of his eyes austere. "I am really asking, yes. Because I believe it's a fair question. How many young men orbit your star, Princess?"

He helpfully picked up the torch and waved it in a little circle that framed her face—as if she were the sun and it the earth. Amarande scoffed and looked away. "There need not be any. Because I have Luca."

His lips quirked at her stubbornness, his typical sardonic delivery building with each word. "Assuming he is accepted as the true heir of Torrence—*if* the resistance somehow manages to overthrow the Warlord, that is—do you plan to marry him? What is so special about him that you would risk so much, never having spent time with other eligible suitors?"

Amarande wound her arms across her chest. "Taillefer, I realize you don't know what it is to be a princess, but you do realize that the last thing the phrase 'eligible suitors' typically amounts to is true love."

"I do not deny it," Taillefer agreed. "But I do, *respectfully*, wonder as to why your father allowed you, the future of his kingdom, to have a relationship of quite possibly amorous intentions with his stable-boy."

She looked him dead in the eye. "You know why. My father could see the ink on Luca's chest just as easily as you."

"Ah, so you do plan to marry him."

Amarande snatched the torch from his hand and began to stalk away, deeper into the tunnel the direction they had been going, her voice stubbornly tossed over her shoulder. "He is a *prince*—and one coup away from being a king. Therefore, a marriage between us would fulfill the necessary requirements as dictated by law allowing *me* to rule Ardenia. If I must marry for my power, my true love is the obvious choice. My father knew that."

The prince didn't immediately follow. Taillefer avoided fights; he lashed out with words instead—she could feel him winding up like a catapult, all tension and inert energy. He had truly been thinking on this for a long time. Amarande sped up.

"You are telling me you believe your father staked the future of his kingdom and legacy on the hope that you'd found your true love in a hidden prince. And then the two of you would beat a system designed for strategy and not love to create a marriage that joined two kingdoms, including a fallen one?" He had the gall to laugh. The sound reverberated off the walls. "I am one for long games, Princess, but that, my dear, is unfathomable."

Amarande slowed briefly. When presented that way, it did seem rather far-fetched. Luca had expressed similar doubts to her in the captain's quarters of the *Gatzal* but in a much softer presentation than Taillefer's sardonic tone.

"You did not know my father."

"Oh no, I didn't, not really. But you know very well what kind of environment raised me." Amarande recalled her meeting with Inés. The Bellringe was truly a viper's nest. It did not excuse his tendencies. "And I can tell you that even if Sendoa was playing the long game, this belief of yours makes little sense. At any moment he could've marched that vaunted army of his to the Torrent, killed the Warlord, and returned home in time for supper."

Taillefer's argument was so sound it was nothing more than infuriating. The narrow pass she'd etched through her father's actions—and particular inaction—seemed now but a trick of the light. She'd been so sure upon learning of Luca's birthright that her father had always intended this.

He had a plan. He always had a plan.

"He didn't change the law." Even to her ears now, this argument was cobweb thin.

The prince laughed darkly from behind, gaining ground. "Likely he didn't change the law because he didn't expect to be *assassinated*. He thought it wouldn't matter. By the time his reign ended, you'd be long married—maybe to your true love, or maybe in a political alliance, but either way it would not matter."

"*He had a plan.*" Her voice broke—audible, unmistakable.

Amarande trudged forward, almost jogging now, her steps lengthing as the trail tipped downward again. The tunnel on this side of the water stop was at least twice as broad as the one they'd been in for hours, and there was room enough for Taillefer to walk alongside her if he dared.

Yet there were no footsteps coming from behind now. Taillefer's progress had stopped altogether. She didn't have to look back to know he was watching her and the light race away. From him, from her insistence that this was what the Warrior King had planned, from all of it.

When he spoke again, his voice, for once, wasn't brimming with sarcasm or laced with the joy of a private joke. Instead, it was cool and straightforward, and his words stayed in her mind rather than being rejected outright.

"Amarande, you can go over and over your father's plans in your mind, but the idea that he was protecting your heart while giving you the task of overthrowing the Warlord in order to rule *your own* kingdom is wholly unlikely."

The princess halted, her frustration welling into solid, indominable sadness. She stood there, breathing hard, the underground air too warm and stale for any relief. When Taillefer reached her, she screwed her eyes closed and swallowed the sob that had settled in her throat. "It is all I have, Taillefer. It is what I have to believe."

Amazingly, the prince let that sit. And in that silence came another surprise.

The distinct rush of water.

It was distant yet unmistakable. Their eyes met for the briefest of moments, and then they were running. Full-bore, down the shaft, as fast as the weak light and terrain would allow.

They stumbled around another bend of the tunnel and found themselves in a cavern twice the size of the one underneath the quicksand that had swallowed them whole. And there, banked against the far side, was an underground stream—wider than the Cardenas Scar. The water pushed south, its current flowing into the mouth of a dark, high tunnel.

Propped against the nearest wall were a few man-made rafts, formed from the strange, spindly deciduous trees of that bizarre forest where Amarande had rescued Luca from the pirates.

If the stars could see her heart from here, perhaps one would deliver her straight to Luca and the resistance.

"A much more comfortable way to travel," Taillefer said, inspecting the raft nearest to where they'd entered. "This one should do nicely. Grab us paddles, would you?"

It took less than a minute for them to carry the raft to the water, retrieve the most viable paddles from a nearby pile, and arrange themselves and their torch in such a way that they could push off the bank. The water moved at a lazy clip, but even if they eventually became too tired to paddle, it was going to be a faster mode of transportation than walking, and yet another confirmed sign that they were on the right path to Luca and the resistance.

Perhaps it was that certainty that sparked within Amarande the need to finally repay Taillefer and his curiosity with questions of her own.

"Taillefer, why did you not simply escape into the ether? You say we're each other's greatest hope and yet you have proved thus far that you won't die in the elements without putting up somewhat of a fight. You could have very easily left me, disarmed and disoriented in that cave, and made your way out on your own. Why didn't you?"

"Come now, we both know you would've bashed my head in with a rock before I got too far."

She squinted at him, watching his eyes in the torchlight. "Why put yourself in a bind where you know you are dead if you go, and might die if you push forward? Never mind the fact that I cannot control what Luca may do to you once we finally reach the resistance—his talents with a blade rival mine and he has more than one reason to make sure you die an excruciating death."

"Ah, yes, I suppose he will save none of his storied kindness for me."

Amarande looked him in the face and lied because she loved Luca and knew that with the torture Taillefer had inflicted upon him the prince would never fear his victim, no matter how his power grew. "No, he won't, and neither will the rebels supporting him."

"Yes. Perhaps I am doomed if I stay or if I go. . . ." Taillefer turned and the torchlight caught the angles of his face, softening in a way that almost made him appear like a child. Not a sixteen-year-old boy with blood on his hands and a bounty on his head. "Princess, I chose to free you, follow you, and stay with you not because you're my greatest hope—that was a bit of a stretch, I know. Rather . . . it is because I have never been alone."

Taillefer looked away as if something resembling shame bent his neck and rounded his shoulders.

"I know I had a direct hand in Renard's death. I did horrible things to Luca because I wanted you to help me achieve the dream I'd held tightly for far too long. That the crown would be mine, and I could rule. I cannot tell you how many nights I fell asleep to plots and plans and urges to clear my brother out of the way. Perhaps not in the brash manner of Domingu, but to forge my own path to the crown I so desperately wanted."

His voice softened to near a whisper. "Those schemes fed me for so long that when they came true, I was blind to the reality of what they meant. I'd lost my other half, my constant companion, the person who was with me every day of my life. And he was . . . until he wasn't."

The weight of his words hit Amarande hard enough her breath hitched. To her astonishment, the ice blue of Taillefer's eyes shone wet in the firelight, though his voice did not betray his tears.

"Princess, have you ever wanted something so much it filled you up, every crack and crevice within you, and when it finally happens and the want falls away, all that is left is ash?"

"Yes," Amarande whispered.

Taillefer turned away. There was nothing left to say.

They paddled onward, into the winding dark.

CHAPTER 34

THEY left without word from Osana, Urtzi, or Amarande. This did not sit well with Luca. But the plan could not wait. After seventeen years, this was a window that could not be gambled.

And so he sat with Ula within the body of a carriage, meant to look the part of a Torrent-burnt caravan vehicle, watching the sliver of night splicing shadows across their space.

Their tight-knit unit was full of dedicated watchers. Tala leading—his black wolf left behind, of course—along with twenty others, all assigned for their acumen and specific skills in communication, strategy, dart making, sword fighting, and the like.

Together, they rode to join the Isilean Caravan. With the help of loyal members of the resistance who had been planted in the caravan years earlier, they planned to slip in with it as cover to enter the Warlord's camp for one final reconnaissance before the planned uprising.

Still, as the plan became closer to being a reality, Luca could not ignore the fear in his stomach that something had gone very wrong for Osana and Urtzi. Apparently, Ula was thinking about it, too.

"I should have been the one to get Amarande. Not Osana. I could've gone alone. I know the way, and I wouldn't have needed a babysitter," Ula grumbled, as they sat in silver silence, the fabric tightly drawn across the carriage's windows to protect their identity—this was the dangerous part. Five carriages did not a caravan make, and until they were with a larger group, they were extremely suspicious. Then, much more quietly: "I wouldn't have let you down. I swore my life and I meant it."

It wasn't Ula's oath that worried Luca. It was Osana. There was something about her that he couldn't quite put his finger on, and he wished he had asked more questions of Amarande about her during those few hours they had together on the *Gatzal*. Though it was just him and Ula in the carriage, he found himself lowering his voice. "Do you know how Osana came to join Renard's party?"

Ula, who had been sharpening her sword, stiffened. "Why?"

"Tell me and then I'll tell you."

Ula stared at Luca speculatively. "She was with the Pyrenee party when they came upon Dunixi, Urtzi, and myself. I remember her saying something to Renard and then we were surrounded. There weren't any other girls."

Luca nodded, working through the scene in his mind. The scorching Torrentian sun, Renard's desperation to find Amarande, and the prince's likely elation at discovering the kidnappers she'd sought, fought, and escaped. "Is it possible she was identifying you? When she was speaking to Renard?"

Ula squinted at him, trying to read his face in the shadows before answering. "I never asked, but yes, perhaps she was identifying us. When we were tasked with guarding the princess's tent at the Pyrenee camp, I was prodding Amarande about why on earth she would go with Renard, because she obviously loved you as much as you loved her. Osana chimed in—saying she'd seen *us* at the watering hole, and that she wouldn't forget the way you loudly spoke of Amarande."

Ula continued. "I do remember a girl there. It must have been Osana if she was imprisoned with Amarande at the Warlord's camp. But I never asked." A little smirk crossed her lips. "I was distracted by saving you."

Luca ignored Ula's teasing, his mind stuck on the leader's words during the attack at the resistance outpost.

"We saw your face, girl! You can't hide from the Warlord!"

They'd been stuck in his mind for days now, tumbling around with the man's sneering familiarity. All of it festering together until his uncertainty became something more tangible—and problematic.

"It's just . . ." he started. "It *was* Osana at the watering hole. I remember her now, but I didn't realize it until after the attack at the outpost. She never mentioned it to me."

"Okay," Ula answered, unsure. "But she didn't keep it a secret—she told both the princess and myself."

Yes, but. Luca drew a deep breath. "I only realized it was her when I recognized the lead bandit and his men—they were her escort."

Gazing sightlessly out the window, Ula said nothing for a moment. Finally, she asked, "Are you sure?"

"I'm sure. Her plan to burn the bandits with the sagardon was a good one, though she didn't need to fetch the horses with Urtzi for it to work—we could've just rushed them with the jug as it was. But she *did* need to get away before they recognized her and even then, she wasn't fast enough."

Ula swallowed and Luca knew she was replaying the scene in her mind. The bandits converging on them; Osana's fevered plan; the leader yelling in her wake that he'd seen her face. "I want to hear you say exactly what you think this means."

Luca did not hesitate. "I worry that Osana may be a watcher for the Warlord."

Ula froze, still as the Hand.

Luca continued, speaking quickly. "She told Amarande her father had sold her to the Warlord's men and then those men killed her father, and escorted her to the Warlord. Which was when she would've seen us at the watering hole. She did not react as one would to seeing those men again. What's more, on our journey she has made it clear she knows quite a bit about the Warlord despite being a new captive."

The pirate chewed her lip, her golden eyes in the middle distance, jaw working as her grip tightened around her sword hilt. "If you think she's a watcher for the Warlord, why did you accept her offer to go after Amarande? Is that why you sent Urtzi along?"

The carriage jostled, cutting him off as Luca was about to reply. Both of them got to their feet, angling for the drawn canvas. Ula pushed Luca back into his seat.

"Stay there," she ordered in a fierce whisper.

He did as he was told, steadying himself against the seat as the carriage jolted before coming to an abrupt stop. With careful nonchalance, Ula pulled back the canvas and peered into the black night, her sword tightly concealed in her grip. A few words of Old Torrentian floated in the breeze, too low for Luca to make out.

Ula withdrew from the window, stowed her sword, and rolled the canvas back down tight. "It's the Isilean Caravan, up ahead. We're going to merge onto its tail." In a lurch, they were moving again. "Beyond them is a light that can only be a fire pit."

Chapter 35

Eyes heavy with uninvited sleep, Amarande didn't notice the darkness fading from pitch to pewter until the raft began to stutter, scraping soft earth below, the water petering out.

The princess hauled herself to attention, willing her eyes to focus, the torchlight long blown out. They'd run aground in another stalactite-studded cave, yet the coolness of a morning in the desert whipped at Amarande's face.

Fresh air.

"Taillefer," she breathed, shoving his shoulder where he lay curled up in a ball, paddle tucked under his cheek like a pillow. "Wake up. *Daylight.*"

Whisper quiet, she edged to where cave rock met the open sky. Thin lines of smoke curled in the near distance—campfires edging on cold. The morning was still more black than blue, though true daylight came closer with every breath.

If it was the right camp, they might get information leading to Luca and the resistance. And if not, no matter who it was, they would have horses, food, and waterskins. They had nothing left to trade or barter, Taillefer's coin and her mangled necklace back in the saddlebags still on their horses at the Warlord's Inn.

"A camp?" Taillefer asked, crouching next to her and peering out. "Do we stroll up to the first person we see and ask if anyone's seen Luca?"

"You know, the wrong person might read your sarcasm as stupidity. Come on, let's get closer. *Quietly.*"

The underground river trickled out of the cave and into a dry creekbed, silt soft and narrow. There were no clues about the rebels as they abandoned the raft and exited the cave—no other rafts, no footprints, no potatoes, no pottery, or any other signs of life. It was a slight disappointment—just the ghosts of their movements. No clues, a trail gone cold.

Silently, they crested the eastern bank, pressing their bodies into the russet silt, eyes peering over the side.

The camp laid out before them was massive. It curled around the Hand, which they'd been blind to before, up and to their left, its fingers collecting the coming dawn. From there, it blanketed desert landscape far enough to the east and north that it seemed to stretch past the curve of the earth.

In the distance, before them and to the right, where Amarande had thought dawn was beginning, it wasn't just the sun lighting up the horizon. There, too, were the white flames of a massive blaze.

A fire pit in use.

Immediately, she searched the spread of tents for the large blue one she'd seen that night with Osana. Even in the low light and at a distance, she found it easily, towering against the southern edge of the camp, near the fire pit, the golden top of its center pole collecting the flame light—a blinding brass beacon.

A confirmation.

"The Warlord."

Amarande's blood sparked as the tyrant's name died on her lips. She peered back at Taillefer, surprised to find his face obviously ashen even in the low light. "What?" she asked, startled—he wasn't one to telegraph emotion. "The Warlord has no quarrel with you."

He shook his head—that wasn't it. When he explained, his whisper was as equally drained as his features. "You said at some point that the king's supporters built the Hand out of the ashes of the Otxoa castle. . . ."

Amarande nodded. "The Otxazulo. Yes. It was burned to rubble and re-formed by the rebels to create the Hand."

Taillefer tipped his chin the opposite direction of the camp, past the other bank of the creekbed. Amarande followed his gaze to where the Torrent's cracked landscape pooled into a shallow, extended indentation like a thumbprint on a slice of lemon cake.

"I think this was where the castle must have stood." He began to, very quietly and carefully, unfold his map. "I bet you that underground river fed into the castle, not only providing a water source but also possibly providing entry and exits."

This hit Amarande as a likely truth—the tunnels they'd traveled were so well formed, they'd likely been there much longer than the resistance itself.

Taillefer had the whole map unfurled now. He pointed at something on it and the wind caught the edge, the parchment crinkling in the breeze. Amarande snatched up the corner to silence it. In the process, she took her first real look at the map—and was met with surprise.

This was not just any map of the Sand and Sky. It was the old overlaid with the new—the particulars of the Kingdom of Torrence intercut with the scribbles of more modern landmarks such as the Hand, the single functioning port in the Torrent, dozens of settlements run through with thick, inky *X*s. Former settlements—now delineated as fire pits by a small notation.

"That's my father's ink work. Everything drawn like the slash of a blade."

Taillefer nodded and traced a gray line that snaked out from under an intricate depiction of a castle rendered between the gaping jaws of a howling black wolf. The water and cave entry.

Time stopped for Amarande as she pictured Luca slung to Lygia's back as she ran from the castle in the moments before it was breached and set aflame. Sloshing through the water, against the flow of the tide, eyes frantic in the dark. All gasping breath, pounding heart, sprinting and stumbling, propelled forward by adrenaline and fear.

The image was horrifying—the last-ditch effort of a woman doing everything she could to save a child.

The rest of Luca's family had been put to the sword, their heads mounted on pikes, surrounded by the gutted bodies of black wolves, the eradication of their house symbolically complete. A whole line and their sigil turned to ash.

"Yes, you're right," she whispered.

Amarande blinked hard, tears pricking at her eyes. She was exhausted, famished, and dehydrated, and yet her stomach sank with the intense assurance that she was failing Luca.

What if she'd sent him to his death in the name of power he didn't want? Via this Warlord, her mother, poison, or even Osana and her loyalties . . . wherever they might lie?

What if this time death wasn't a ruse but the truth?

Parchment rustled as Taillefer nudged Amarande, pointing at some lines of text. "If those drawings are your father's, then perhaps this is his handwriting?"

Wetness blurred her vision, and she pressed the heels of her hands to each eye. It still took her a moment to focus on what he was referencing. He tapped the right edge of the map with a gloved thumb. There, in the margin, were sloping lines of text, written in pieces—a list.

> Rebel chain needs forest link.
> Warlord vulnerable at Hand—use river? Converge there?
> Black gold sale to Indu? Fund horses?

Next to the line about the rebels was some sort of key—one filled-in dot and one empty circle. Amarande's eyes skimmed the map—they were spread all across the Torrent, and some even in Ardenia and the rest of the standing Sand and Sky kingdoms. Filled-in ones made up the majority and were in several places, while three empty circles sat at the mouth of the forest—the Oiartzun, by the name on the map—where she'd rescued Luca from the pirates and Harea Asps.

The empty circles were clearly the missing link—the filled dots worked in almost an unbroken line in the same way the constellations promised images.

Amarande's attention was drawn to the eastern quadrant, near the tail end of the Dragon's Spine—also known as the River of Stone, apparently. It was the area they'd struck out for underground before the scorpions stopped them. In that spot there was a cluster of five filled dots, and several hand-drawn lines leading out from the spine, both north and south.

Her instincts had been right. They needed to find the man with the black wolf for their best chance of locating Luca and the rebels.

"He was planning to attack," Taillefer whispered, color flooding back into his cheeks. "This map was on top of a stack. Flat, and recently used, not rolled up for storage."

That hit Amarande like a lightning bolt. The figurines littering the library table—black wolves with W carved on their sides. Her fingers scrambled for the map's corners. "Did Father write anything else?"

As quietly as possible, Taillefer reversed the map, revealing the back of it. There, written more neatly with room to work, was another list, carved into the parchment in Sendoa's knife-slash hand:

L—working with A and K
Tell A first? Or at same time?
K to T after solstice for preparation
Move before equinox
G—capture alive

Amarande read it again and again.

Her father was going to attack for Luca. With Luca.

If her father had not died, they would've spent this summer preparing for war. Her father's plan. *He always had a plan.* All of it laid out in shorthand letters.

Still, something heavy dropped in the princess's empty stomach as the letters swirled before her, the message undeniably clear. The only thing she couldn't decipher was who T was. Not Taillefer, surely. Koldo would know—there could be no other K. Not that she would tell her who the T was. Not that it mattered now. The plan was dead but within Amarande it caught flame.

This plan was as much of a directive then as it was now.

She couldn't fail Luca. Her father's words rang in her mind with exactly what she must do to ensure her love would stay safe.

Make the first mark.

She could take her blade to the Warlord's throat in the next ten minutes and change the course of everything.

Even if she didn't get out alive, Luca would survive. The Warlord's reign would fall to chaos. Her mother wouldn't be able to revive it—not with her commitment to Ardenia so public.

The call of action was hot in her blood, her pulse thundering at her wrists, her temples, her jaw. She dropped the map, not caring for the noise it made, and drew her sword.

"What do you think you're doing?" Taillefer's hand shot out, going for her wrist but missing. "They will attack anyone who enters their camp with a sword at the ready."

Amarande crested the lip of the creekbed. "I'm going to pay a visit to the Warlord."

Taillefer lunged with both hands now, going for her legs. He snatched her ankle, voice rising in intensity as he hung on. Her boots slipped in the soft silt, unable to gain purchase. She slid down until her sword tip caught the earth, stopping his progress and leaving her shoulders and head exposed to anyone awake and alert in the camp. The princess didn't care.

"You *cannot*."

"I can and I will."

"No." Taillefer cuffed her shoulders and the sword tip gave, Amarande and her weapon sliding down the embankment with him. "Princess, I understand what you're thinking. The strategy is sound—it is. It would buy Luca time and give him a reeling regime to dismantle, which would be much easier than what he's staring down now. I'll admit, that is bordering on genius, except for one thing: You will not make it out alive."

"I will."

Taillefer's stare did not waver. For a boy who did not traffic in seriousness, the stern angles of his face were unsettling. "You heard the rebels at the inn—*The Warlord shall find you in the stars.* That did not sound like wishing their enemies to have tea; it sounds like the Warlord knows you're coming."

He pointed at the map as proof, though he didn't know what she did about her mother. "Amarande, there are more than a thousand people here who would cut you down, believing you are trying to finish what your father *obviously* was about to start and was likely killed for."

Amarande shook her head clear, trying to deny the truth of the points Taillefer had connected. But she wanted them to go another way. Needed them to.

If Geneva killed her father, her mother—Koldo, too—had much more to do with the events that followed than even the boy across from her. Someone who suddenly could've actually been a pawn. She grimaced, jaw muscles firing. "That is a chance I will have to take."

"No. You won't." Taillefer switched his grip to cuff the wrist of her sword arm. His eyes caught the light, shards of ice in this vast desert. "Think of Luca. He'll die of a broken heart."

That stopped Amarande's breath dead in her lungs. "Taillefer, when on earth did you become a romantic?"

His eyes dropped. "I will only say that . . . it was very clear how much he loved you when we spent time together."

Amarande wrestled her wrist away. That sick feeling sloshed in her gut, and she had to swallow down bile lapping at her throat. "You mean when he believed he would die at your hand? When you tortured him within an inch of his beautiful life? When you paraded him out as a cadaver to force my hand?"

"Yes." To his credit, Taillefer looked up to answer her. "I know you won't believe it, but I do regret my actions. Very much."

She said nothing, but she did not move either, her sword still in her grip.

"Princess, you will win his kingdom—with him, for him. I promise." Taillefer's focus upon her was unflinching. She turned farther away. "But do not sacrifice yourself and your future at this moment for something that may not work. Please."

For a long while, silence stood between them, the light wind rustling the matted ropes of her hair, the ashen dirt kicking up around them. Amarande sheathed her sword.

She met Taillefer's relief with a tip of her chin. "Fine. We go into the camp for supplies only. Horses, food, waterskins, and, if we can manage it, new clothing for you. Your uniform is far too noticeable, even without the garnet cloak."

The smallest of his slippery smiles kicked up at the prince's lips.

"I hate to tell you this, Princess, but no matter how I am dressed, all eyes will be on you." Her lips dropped open, not sure how to answer this statement, and the realization of how it must have hit her ears crossed his face, his eyes shooting wide open. "I didn't mean that as a compliment."

Amarande turned her back on him and scrambled over the edge and onto solid ground. "Come on."

CHAPTER 36

WHEN Luca opened his eyes to the indigo of morning in the Warlord's camp, everything smelled of smoke. The Warlord letting her power linger over her people. Reminding them with every breath who held their fate in her hands.

Exhaustion deadened Luca's limbs, as did his injuries: the wound in his chest, courtesy of Taillefer; the bite from the Harea Asp that had nearly killed him. He hadn't had enough sleep in the last few days. Not enough for the healing he must do. Not for the night he would have to survive.

Yet he knew he slept—crammed into a diagonal on the carriage floor; Ula crunched onto her seat bench, blade hugged to her chest—because he'd dreamed of Amarande.

Of the night they'd fallen asleep at nearly the same site, side by side, under the stars. She'd insisted he sleep in the tent. He wouldn't, though. Not because she was a princess but because it was the right thing to do. And when her stubbornness had led them to both sleeping in the open night, they'd drifted off, hands laced together.

He'd told himself he'd never let go. Not literally, of course, but that he would fight for what they had as long as he was still standing. Today would bring not the last step, but a big step.

That morning, Amarande thought she'd awoken first. But what she didn't know was that despite his exhaustion and comfort next to her, his body ran on its usual stable schedule, his eyes fluttering open in the cold blue before dawn—just as they had this morning.

The horses had to eat, and his body knew their rhythms better than his own.

And that morning, he lay under the brightening sky, watching each ray touch her face. He never saw her off guard like that. Sweet, and silent—no one would call her that while she was awake.

In the night, Amarande had kept her hold of his hand but tossed herself from her back to her side, her cheek pressed into the mostly flat crook of one arm. She was left facing him, knees pulled up toward her stomach, boots crossed just so.

The sun illuminated the cut of her jaw, the sunburn atop her cheeks, her nose, the crest of her forehead. The fine hairs running to her hairline, auburn blazing along with the new light. Her eyelashes were as dark as her coloring would allow, and a fine spray of freckles had been raised by the Torrent's sun, something one could only see so close.

Before Amarande woke, her breathing shifted and she tossed herself back onto her spine, her knees staying twisted toward him, their twined hands dragging through the dirt as she shook herself from sleep.

Luca had closed his eyes then, embarrassed by the utter amount of time he'd watched her. This person he knew so well but had never seen like that.

On the pirate ship, she'd slept next to the bed in the captain's quarters, holding his hand from her spot on the floorboards. He would've lain there, too, if the pain weren't so great. Her stubbornness won out yet again.

When this was all over, he wanted nothing more but to fall asleep with her hand in his and wake with the horses, pausing just long enough to watch the light cross her face.

Always, Princess.

Rustling came from Ula's side, and the swordswoman sat up— braid abandoned and hair everywhere, kerchief slipping, the sword flung across her lap. "Urtzi? Did you—"

She blinked at Luca and immediately swiped at the canvas, unfastening it as much as she dared to get a good look at their surroundings. Then she cleared her throat. "We need to start a breakfast fire soon. We must look like them. If we hide in here, they will become suspicious."

Luca had meant what he said to Tala—he did not come on this journey to sit in relative safety. To hide. Yet he hesitated. He did not come on this journey to fail either.

This was reconnaissance, not the actual mission. That would come the next night. What if . . . it went wrong?

Luca had lived his life with his destiny literally written on his skin and had been safe. Now somehow, even with the wolf tattoo nestled under layers of gauze and two tunics, it seemed as if the moment he stepped out of the carriage everyone would know.

Even with the disguise, the fictitious name, the cover of hundreds of boys around the same age, some with similar coloring and height, the fear he'd been driving down deep since the night before ran roughshod under his skin. "We're one carriage of thousands."

Ula stood. "Yes, and if every single other carriage and tent has a cook fire, we will be noticed. Come. Let us try out our disguises before full light."

CHAPTER
37

❧❧❧

DESPITE the exhaustion, Amarande's blood and breath sang with her plan as she and Taillefer edged into the boundary of the War-lord's camp.

Cloak. Food. Horses. Head straight for the plateau where she'd been taken captive by the man with the black wolf. Find him, find the resistance, find Luca.

Then all would be right—together, they could survive anything.

But first she had to survive with Taillefer.

Their agreed-upon approach was this: If an easy target for clothing and supplies made itself known on the way to the horses, they would confer before taking action. They needed horses more than anything else and getting to the corral—on the extreme northeastern side of the camp, at least a mile from their starting edge—was priority number one.

And above everything: Don't get caught.

Walking as quickly as they dared, the pair wound along the outer ring of tents. Past dying fires, hushed conversations, babies crying with the new morning.

The princess made a hard right, down an offshoot that barreled closer to the center of the camp—her instincts told her it would be quieter. Fewer babies and families, tents of a smaller, more singular size. Bachelor row. Still, a few clothing lines were strung up on poles or between consenting tents, clothing being aired out after a day's travel. Taillefer's stride slowed a half step. "Cloak, north-by-northeast."

Amarande's eyes caught on the item, hanging heavily on a line— this garment wouldn't perfectly mask his tattered Itspi guard's uni-form, but it was definitely an improvement. She gave him a wordless go-ahead.

Taillefer diverted toward the clothing line, plucking off the cloak without a single hesitation or a pause in his stride. He made another right, Amarande on his heels, and shrugged it on. The garment was a rugged brown, thick with the mingled odor of campfire and leather oil. It was a little short but did the job—hiding the golden thread and ripped shoulders where Taillefer's sewn-on cloak had previously been. It also had a hood, which would come in handy.

They hooked left, realigning their path with the horse pen, which was now straight ahead, about a half mile from where they'd veered.

"Perhaps we save the food and waterskins for closer to the horses," Amarande whispered, glancing over her shoulder at some sort of commotion—two men with raised voices near where they'd nabbed the cloak.

Taillefer saw it, too. "Step faster."

No titles or names until they were past all this—that was something they'd discussed, too. With a thousand sets of ears, there were too many wrong people around to hear a clue.

"We cannot appear to be running," she whispered.

Taillefer responded by cuffing her wrist to pull her along. He was basically jogging now, his knees picking up, obscured a little by the flow of the cloak. She wrenched her arm away as they turned another corner, trying to put tent peaks between themselves and the two men. "I am with you; you don't need to—"

"OOF."

Taillefer was sprawled flat on his back before Amarande's head jerked up. A man the size of the ogre she and Osana had met at the Warlord's Inn stood there, coffee splattered down the front of his tunic and dripping down the sides of a tin mug in one of his massive hands.

Surprise wound the meaty swoops of his features. "Where's the hurry, man?" he spat, rolling his shoulder as if it'd been knocked out of its socket with the blow that had landed Taillefer on the ground. A bruise was already blooming on the prince's cheek as he blinked up at the lightening sky, trying to make sense of what had just occurred.

"We're sorry; it won't happen again," Amarande answered for Taillefer, quickly and quietly, extending a hand to him so that he might stand and they could get out of the way.

"Little Queen, is that you?"

Amarande's breath caught, as her eyes shot toward the ancient voice and a campfire a horse length away. And, there, raising herself from a stoop, was Naiara, the healer who saved Luca's life in the Isilean

Caravan. As if in confirmation, her apprentice Señe appeared at the old woman's shoulder, coffee carafe held tight. Commotion came from behind them as someone tripped and fell, almost as if they'd walked right off the edge of the precipice where the princess was very carefully standing.

Before Amarande could answer, Naiara took a step forward, angling to get a proper look at the hooded boy on the ground. "*Kidege? Luca?*"

In that moment, time seemed to stop—the giant suddenly aggressively rigid; Amarande wishing the stars would steal those two syllables back; Taillefer pushed up on one knee, not yet to standing.

Then it all crashed into motion.

"*Luca?*" The giant's voice was louder than anything Amarande had heard since the wedding that wasn't. His meaty gaze drilled into Taillefer. "This is the boy who would unseat our Warlord?"

Stars, no.

Naiara audibly gasped. For all her talents and knowledge, it appeared the wisewoman did not understand the power of Luca's name.

Taillefer got to his feet and purposely shrugged off his hood to prove he had no Torrentian blood. "No, no, this is a misunderstanding. My name is not *that*. I—"

The giant grabbed Taillefer by the front of his tunic and hoisted him into the air.

Amarande's sword was out front in a flash. "Put him down. We mean no harm."

"Your sword says otherwise, girl."

The sound of more unsheathed steel rang out. Two female guards stood at the conjunction of a pair of tent rows. Amarande didn't dare glance at Naiara or Señe—the healers would be in trouble enough for harboring knowledge of Luca. A pang of regret hit as she wished she hadn't turned her head at the first sound of the healer's voice.

"Have your friend put him down, and I shall stow my sword," Amarande said to the guards—both carried swords like Ula's, curved and deadly.

"Release him, Kerbasi."

The large man smiled wide at Taillefer, who gasped and kicked. "Gladly."

The word was barely out of his mouth when the giant flung Taillefer into the air. Sword still raised, Amarande shuffled backward, aiming to get out of the way.

But the movement she'd anticipated didn't come—the prince's body was tossed vertically, not horizontally. And, as he plummeted back toward the cracked earth, the man's leg shot out and his boot connected with Taillefer's gut.

The crunch of a shattered rib reverberated in the air, a cry escaping into the new dawn with it. Taillefer landed in a heap, blood rolling out of his mouth.

"Tai—" Amarande started only to be cut off with a warning.

"*Little Queen!*"

Naiara's fevered shout brought Amarande's attention from Taillefer's fresh blood to a blur of motion—the two guards, barreling in from either side.

"*Stars,*" she cursed under her breath.

The guard on the left was the faster of the two, sword arcing down against the princess's weak side. Amarande met her in a cross-body strike. The broad side of the princess's sword caught the thin edge of the guard's blade—with enough power and torque to flip the momentum of her slashing movement.

It was enough to put that guard off-balance. The princess struck the girl's knee with the sole of her boot as the guard rotated away, shoving her out of the picture and onto the ground.

Amarande's sword was up again and slashing on the offense as the second guard approached. This one drove her blade in toward the body in such a way that the fattest part of the curve connected with Amarande's weapon.

As steel met steel, Taillefer found his voice over her shoulder. "I could really use a blade here. Any blade!" he bellowed in her direction.

The giant drew a weapon of his own, a sword made just for him— longer than a traditional one and broader, too. Taillefer danced away from it, running out of room in the narrow confines of the tent city.

"Steal his! Mine is busy!" Amarande called back, the edge of her blade colliding with the curve of her own assailant's weapon in a high guard, her arms gaining strength from adrenaline alone, hunger still clouding her energy.

How had this gone so badly so quickly?

Taillefer huffed out a sigh, dodged a swing, and darted into the giant's body, rolling against the man's belly and driving off his heels to send an elbow straight into his nose.

Blood sprayed the sandy dirt not far from where Taillefer had marked it, a much louder, madder shout wrenching into the morning light. The giant stumbled and Taillefer caught the man's dagger from his belt. In a flash of salmon light and movement, the raised blade slashed down and into the soft curve of the man's exposed side body.

The giant's liver, spleen, stomach—one or all of them punctured.

"You are an immeasurably helpful presence in my time of need," Taillefer chided, collecting the dagger from the man's side as he thrashed. The giant nearly rolled right onto Taillefer's boots, which would've pinned him, but somehow he eluded the man's weight.

"I knew you could do it!" Amarande shouted. It was a call back to the night of the wedding—not one she'd meant.

For one blinding moment, Renard's lifeless body scraped across her eyelids as she blinked after yet another clash of steel.

Eyes open, the princess hesitated.

A mistake.

The guard managed to use the momentum of their swords crashing together to pull herself into Amarande's body. The girl's knee connected with the top of her thigh. It was enough that the princess stumbled backward, and the guard gained purchase enough to shove her to the ground, their swords caught in a cross that was slowly lowering toward the crown of Amarande's head.

The princess tried to shove back, but her injured hand was on top and the pressure of the hilt upon her wound was making it difficult to hold, even if her trained muscles could do it. Amarande locked eyes with the guard and gritted her teeth. She'd push back until she was standing again; she would—

Suddenly Amarande was blind, grains of cinnamon sand cast straight into her face.

All the torque between their two swords evaporated as the princess tried in vain to see, falling to the dirt and blinking hard. A boot heel crunched onto her injured hand—the bandage marking it as a weak spot. She yelped, the sword wedged between her grip and the earth.

"Drop it." The other guard. Her voice was full of blood and hard. She pressed all her weight onto the princess's hand.

Amarande's fingers splayed open.

Someone grabbed the sword. Someone else hauled her up to her knees.

Amarande's vision still failed her. She blinked rapidly, tears working in vain to eliminate the scratchy grains of sand from her eyes. Yet the princess had her wits about her, keeping her chin down, hoping against hope she wasn't as recognizable as Taillefer had suggested. Hoping Naiara wouldn't be questioned about the two instances in which she called this assailant Little Queen. She'd had her frustrations with the healer, but she'd saved Luca's life and Amarande would forever be in her debt.

"I have her sword and her wrists; check her boots." That was the first guard.

The princess tried to kick her legs from kneeling—she caught someone in the jaw, but the other guard used her outstretched position as she made contact to bear-hug her boot. Her weight effectively clipped Amarande's momentum—she was too heavy to shake off.

"There's a knife in here," the guard announced, her face pressed tightly against the inner line of that boot. Amarande expected her to release one hand and slip it against the outside of the ankle to snatch the dagger, but instead she simply used all that weight of hers to haul it off the princess's wriggling foot. The girl peeled off Amarande's body with the boot, and the knife skittered across the ground.

"The knife! Grab it!" she screamed toward where Taillefer should have been, using the distraction and falling momentum to wrench herself out of the other guard's grasp.

Amarande's order received no answer as she twisted to face the guard, hands at the ready to grab her sword, the guard's sword, her long hair—*anything*.

But just as soon as she turned to the girl, something thunked hard against Amarande's temple, tossing her off-balance. Her opponent used that split second to roll onto the princess, driving Amarande's face into the sandy earth as she sat atop the princess's back, pinning her in a way that left all of Amarande's fight useless.

From the corner of her eye, the princess watched through blurred vision as her own boot rolled to a stop—the heel the blunt object the guard had found to use against her.

Beyond the boot, she saw Taillefer, also splayed on the ground, two other female guards taking lengths of rope to his wrists, which, like hers, were wrenched behind his back. As her own guards gathered rope for her wrists, his captors moved on to his legs, binding them above the knees so that he could walk but not run. They followed the same procedure with Amarande. The injured giant looked on, unblinking, hand pressed hard to his bleeding side. His nose was no longer straight.

When both sets of guards were finished, they wrenched their captives to standing.

The princess was suddenly aware of how large the crowd was— what had started at a half dozen was now at least a hundred people. Men, women, children, all startled awake by the fight and blinking into the rising sun. Naiara and Seňe were nowhere to be seen. *Good.*

Amarande wondered if the guard she'd attacked when chained up was present and watching.

If he would tell them who she'd said she was. *Little Queen,* indeed.

If the new Warlord would hear of it and believe it.

Or if perhaps this Warlord had already received word of Amarande's escape into the Torrent straight from her mother. Just as Luca's very name was a flash point to the giant and the crowd.

In the end Amarande never learned how they knew. Only that they did.

"The Warlord demands your presence, Princess Amarande."

CHAPTER 38

LUCA'S heart sat in his throat as he lay with his chin to the ground, Ula covering him, their cook fire and its smoke all that shielded the pair of them from the guards as they marched Amarande and Taillefer to the Warlord's tent.

The questions in his mind were grains of sand, swirling together in a never-ending swell and spiral.

Ula's weight shifted as she disentangled herself from how she'd tackled and smothered him at the sudden close mention of his name. There was no "fitting in" with the way she'd yanked him down—no way to explain her actions other than to call it a protective measure—but all eyes had been on the princess.

Kidege? Luca?

He'd known they were sheltering in Naiara's caravan. But hearing his name on her lips? After believing she may have seen him? Or, more accurately, seeing and recognizing Amarande and hoping her hooded companion at a distance was him?

That was about as much as to be expected as seeing Amarande herself. Here. Feet from the fire they'd lit for assimilation's sake, so that Ula could burn coffee beans and toast day-old bread. So close that even before Ula tackled him he recognized Amarande was wearing his tunic—sleeves rolled up but obvious.

Fierce and beautiful and fighting alongside Taillefer.

Taillefer.

"Stay down," Ula whispered.

He could not. Luca pushed to standing, shaking off her protective hand. "We have to follow them."

"That is not brave; that is insane. If Taillefer sees you, he will out you."

"If Taillefer sees me, our disguises were not good enough and we'd be dead anyway," Luca whispered. "We're here to watch. I need to watch."

"*Miguel*, we shall have the others go." She motioned toward Tala's carriage, ten or so down the line. "I will flag down—"

"No, *Sera*." He was already on the move. Straightening the hat he wore as part of his disguise. It was dirty, the brim snakebit from the elements, and so caked with dust that it was impossible to gauge the original color. He wore Ula's sword as his own, and she had his dagger on her hip, her own hair tied in the twin braids popular in the Isilean Caravan, rather than the single one and handkerchief she usually wore. The disguises weren't much, but the subtlety was the key anyway.

"Please don't," Ula pleaded, though she obliged as she fell in step beside him. Amarande and Taillefer were up ahead, but they were plodding—the guards proud of their work, showing off. And the people gave them what they wanted.

"Everyone is watching them," he argued. "Not us. If thousands of people are gawking, no one will notice us."

Ula sighed at her own logic, tossed back in her face. "We should tell the others."

"If they are any good at their jobs, they have already observed us leaving."

"Miguel, I do not agree with any of this."

"You know it is the right thing to do. If you were alone, Sera, you would have followed them without hesitation."

Ula was silent. That was enough of a confirmation.

Heads down, they swept past the healer's carriage—Luca hoped they'd rushed away. Someone would want to trace the first murmur of his name.

Next, they slipped past the crowd, still bunching around the lane of packed earth where the fight went down. Blood spattered black against the russet dust, boot marks etched in a sweep of lunging steps and countermeasures.

"This could ruin everything," Ula whispered at his side. "Change everything."

"It already has."

They skirted along the edges of the path, gaining ground. Two guards buffered Amarande's back from the crowd. She was shorter than her captors, but with every few steps the rising sun hit just right, and the fall of her reddish hair flashed through the space between bodies.

A beacon. A flame in the dark.

It was one thing to know the direction of the final goal—to envision it on the back of one's eyelids and flesh it out in dreams. It was quite another to see the end goal right before you, in danger, being delivered to the person who had every reason to kill you on the spot.

The line of gawkers grew—word of the princess's capture making it around the camp. Luca and Ula let the newcomers—stacked a dozen deep watching the procession—provide cover as they made up enough time that they were quickly in line with Amarande.

Her chin jutted proudly forward, one guard holding her bound hands, the other leading the procession. Luca wished she would catch his eye through the distance. As she had during her father's funeral. Amarande always seemed to know where he was at all times.

Look here.

See me.

I'm here for you, Ama. Always, Princess.

Luca did not know if her sixth sense would work when she believed him miles away and not simply yards.

"Why is she with him?" Ula whispered. "Not exactly discreet in that uniform. Even with the outer cloak. He's too clever to ruin her disguise with his own—unless he *wanted* to."

"Your questions are my own. And they are important. But none of it matters if the Warlord slits her throat on sight."

The blue-and-gold spire of the Warlord's grand tent was only a few rows of campsites away. Everything this close to the fire pit lived in a plume and haze, the air stinging as it hit the lungs, even with the flames extinguished.

"For a prisoner like her it will be a spectacle. And a spectacle takes time to produce."

Luca hoped she was correct. Though the march through the camp was much more of a spectacle than the actual delivery of the prisoners. Without a public word from the Warlord, the guards simply pulled back the fabric entrance to the tent and shoved Amarande and Taillefer within. A moment later and the guards reemerged to bracket the entrance, hands firmly on the pommels of their stowed swords.

Luca's pounding heart stuttered in his chest. *No.* He had to see. He had to know what the Warlord *would* do to her. *Could* do to her.

"There." Ula knocked his cheek with her knuckles, redirecting his gaze to the back side of the tent, nestled against the body of the War-lord's carriage. Without hesitation, Ula skirted through the long shadow thrown by the dawn and sank to her stomach, sweeping herself beneath the carriage. Luca followed her lead, and they scooted and shuffled until their bodies were completely covered by the carriage, the wheels and shadows welling between the tent structures, keeping their cover.

From there, they could peer into the Warlord's tent, the edge of the blue fabric within arm's reach. The back exit was tied closed, but the wind had caused it to sag in the night. And though what they could see was slim and suspect, if they held their breath and faced their ears so they were just beside the edge of the shadow, Luca and Ula could hear every word from within the tent as clear as day.

CHAPTER 39

AMARANDE'S jaw tightened as the gilded tentpole of the Warlord's home came into view, smoke curling around it, reaching for the brightening sky.

The princess spit grit from her fight back to the earth.

Fear, blood, loyalty—not a one should be owed to a person who would poison her own and corral them in their encampment under penalty of death if noncompliant. This Warlord, this person who shared Amarande's mother's legacy, who was threatened most by Luca's every breath, was everything a leader should not be.

The Warlord was not a monarch. The people did not kneel. But they were on their knees no less, "free" as they were from the shackles of royalty.

And now that Amarande knew the Warlord and caravan knew of not only the resistance's plans but also Luca's name—there was but one way to solve that.

Her father's saying—*Survive the battle, see the war*—rang in Amarande's ears as they made their final approach, but at that very moment in time she could see nothing else other than running a blade straight through this person's heart.

Killing the Warlord *was* the war.

For the people, for Luca, for the future of the Torrent.

There was no way around it.

Their captors brought them straight into the entrance of the large blue tent, no introduction. It was not a surprise that the Warlord expected them.

Amarande and Taillefer were deposited on their knees in front of a roaring fire.

The tent seemed empty save for the silhouettes of the finer things in life, positioned around the corners that were not burned from view by the fire before them. Beneath them was a rug, finely woven, and softer than anything either of them had touched since the wedding night.

Without a word, the guards swept out back the way they came, surely within striking distance at the first sign of distress. Still, Amarande's mind was already running through ways to get free despite her arms tied behind her back and her legs lashed together at the thighs.

Head butt, shoulder strike, hip thrust—any could push this person off-balance enough to send them into the fire, where the flames could do the rest. A combination that stole consciousness before the flames hit would be best—one scream would ruin any chance she had to clear the binds at her legs that sapped the possibility of a speedy escape in the chaos that was sure to follow.

Taillefer would likely be no good to help, even if he wanted to.

Shoulders shaking in their binds next to her, he wheezed and coughed, blood in it splattering onto the fine weave of the rug. That cracked rib of his had caught the base of a lung—Amarande was sure of it. And, given his affinity for the natural arts, Taillefer likely knew it, too.

The slightest dark movement wrenched Amarande from her thoughts.

"The Warrior King's daughter, in the flesh."

The Warlord's voice stretched across the space, from somewhere beyond the flames. It was feminine—and Amarande wasn't surprised that her mother had passed along the title to another woman, too. Somehow, the voice seemed familiar, though it was not one Amarande recognized.

After a long moment of carrying the weight of a stare she could not see, Amarande blinked as the Warlord stepped out of the shadows and into view.

Though in the private confines of her tent, the Warlord's face was covered, muslin draped about her head the same shade as her flowing robes of sea blue. The secretive identity was meant to intimidate, as all masks were. But Amarande felt an immediate sense of relief that this Warlord did not share her face because it might mean they would live long enough to attack.

The Warlord's chin dipped, as she made a show of inspecting the princess. The filthy trousers and tunic, caked in a paste of blood, sweat, cinnamon dirt, quicksand, and creek water; hair a tangled and muddied mass at her shoulders; her face—obviously recognizable despite a layer of grime and wear of sleepless nights. "I'll admit, you're much smaller than I expected."

Unblinking, Amarande addressed her faceless opponent with a strike disguised as the truth. "I am told I take after my mother."

She watched the muslin, hoping this successor might stumble into an admission. But Geneva had trained her to avoid the truth much better than she'd taught Ferdinand.

"Indeed." The Warlord's voice gave no hint of understanding. "I was hoping we would meet in person, as I've only previously met the ghost of your presence, bloodying up our guards and setting the whole line of captives free—quite the performance."

Amarande said nothing.

"I'll admit I initially did not believe it could be you. But when you convinced *my sister* to abandon us, I knew it could only be this myth of a girl—the Warrior King's daughter."

A drop of recognition buzzed in the princess's throat. It could be a lie, of course, but it felt like a boast. And a confirmation. "Osana."

"As intelligent as you are violent. Of course." The way this girl said it did not seem to be a compliment. "She spied for us, of course. My men would take her out and 'capture' her every few days. Then she would sit in our pen for a day or two—eavesdropping on the girls as they rotated through. She was not my only trusted hostage, but she was the only one who took her role too seriously when she escaped with you."

That was it, then. The loyalty Amarande had worried over now out in the light, a truth. A danger. Osana was with Luca—the Warlord's spy and the Warlord's target, together—and the princess was the one who had allowed it. Encouraged it. Vouched for it.

Amarande was going to be sick. Bile rose from her gut, the stench cutting through her nostrils as she swallowed. She couldn't show weakness to this girl, not like that.

"Do not look so betrayed, Princess. Osana has always been good at telling tales, and the best tales have some truth to them, from what I understand." The Warlord swirled a hand in the air, moving on. "Anyhow, today was nicely done as well. Not nearly as successful, I'm afraid."

The Warlord gestured to their bound bodies and forced postures. Taillefer coughed, punctuated by a pained wheeze and a dribble of blood on the fine rugs. The Warlord sighed at the sight of yet another ruined carpet and set her shoulders at a haughty angle.

"And one might wonder, knowing as gifted as you are . . ." Amarande felt an eyebrow lift. "Why, after escaping the Warlord's caravan, would you come back here? With a guard in Ardenian colors, no less?" She let those questions hang, lilt mocking. "Is it pure ego? Stupidity? Or perhaps motivated by something more palatable yet still idiotic in its pure form—love?"

Though she'd braced for it, it took everything Amarande had not to look away as Luca's presence barreled into the room.

It didn't matter, though; the Warlord's voice veered from lilting to joyfully cruel. "Tell me, Princess, you wouldn't happen to know much of the pro-Otxoa rebels, would you?"

Again, Amarande said nothing. Though the first rolling drip of fear slid down her spine.

The Warlord swept closer, but not in range for a head butt, shoulder strike, or hip thrust. Her voice warmed with her guest's cold shoulder. "Come now; surely you have something to say on the matter."

Amarande glared ahead. Giving nothing. She would be stone until the end of time, or until this girl dared to come within striking distance.

"Perhaps your guard can help persuade you to answer." The Warlord drew a blade from her hip—a dagger with a slight curve. Grabbing a fistful of short blond hair, she wrenched Taillefer's head back, exposing the length of his neck. She placed the sharpest arc of the knife edge against the pulse beneath Taillefer's chin.

A move like that was meant to garner a visceral reaction.

Amarande did not flinch.

Focus unbroken, Amarande gave Taillefer the only leverage he might get in this situation, though she was not convinced it would keep him from turning on her. "That is not my guard—he is worth more to you alive than dead in the name of persuasion. This is Prince Taillefer, the heir to the throne of Pyrenee."

The Warlord did not remove her blade. "Interesting. I thought you would lie."

"I do not lie."

The tyrant laughed. "Yes you do. We all do. Even if you are un-truthful because you want to protect someone, it is still a lie."

When Amarande said nothing, the Warlord pressed harder and red slashed across the knife edge, his skin nicked. That is when the prince started to laugh, the sharp edge catching his skin more with the movement.

"Warlord, you misunderstand our relationship," Taillefer clarified. "The princess has been wishing me dead for days now. She isn't protecting me; she's simply alerting you to the fact that you do not have the leverage you think you have. Slit my throat and she won't blink an eye."

"From what I have heard about you, Princeling, I am surprised you have lived long enough to face my blade." Again, her attention turned to Amarande. "But I suppose perhaps even the Warrior King's daughter might spare the greedy prince who rescued her."

She knew of the rescue?

Amarande ground her teeth together. She would not be baited.

The Warlord removed her dagger only to use its tip to lift Amarande's chin so that the princess had no choice but to look her in the eye. The Warlord knew what she was doing. The pressure was enough that any sudden movement from the princess—even a careful attack—would drive the point into her windpipe. Amarande's pulse bucked against the cold steel, Taillefer's blood marring her skin, but she did not glance away.

"Princeling, I did not think she was protecting *you*. Rather, she is protecting her *love*—lying by omission."

Amarande's skin throbbed against the blade, blood thundering past, under pressure. "If you do not lie, Your Highness, you must tell me what you know of the resistance and their newfound leader. Luca, the lowly stableboy with an auspicious tattoo, who moved a *certain* princess to abandon her kingdom, and now is asking the foolish to die with him as he tries to build a throne of his own."

Defiant, Amarande did not look away as hot tears whispered in her eyes, first as a gleam, then enough to well.

The Warlord's face covering shifted—a definite smile.

"Yes, I know all about *Luca*, the much-awaited Otsakumea. I know of his great height, golden eyes, handsome dimples. I know of the wolf over his heart. And I know he seeks his destiny not for himself but for you. To be the prince you can marry to gain your crown, besting those inconvenient laws that stand in the way."

The blade pressed harder, forcing Amarande to arch her back along with her neck, the Warlord purposefully setting her at an impossibly uncomfortable angle. "I can only assume he expected you to join him. But you arrived home to a welcoming committee that did not appreciate the sight of your face. I know that this princeling rescued you for his own gain. And that he is too late."

"You know nothing," Taillefer answered, lips curving into his fox grin.

"Really? Princeling, I assume you know that your mother has wed?"

"Yes. To Domingu." He sounded purposefully bored, repeating what Renard had feared as if it were old news. "They plan to have an heir to displace me before I come of age."

"Not quite." The Warlord straightened, blade nicking the soft skin under Amarande's chin as it withdrew, sharp as it was. "That may have been the plan once, but it is not what happened. The doors were barred during the wedding reception, and when the hall was open again, two-thirds of the attendees were dead, including Domingu and all of his kin, and standing tall was Inés, proclaiming herself leader of Pyrenee, Basilica, and Myrcell, too—King Akil also perished."

Amarande gasped.

Domingu—the most ruthless of them all—gone? At his own wedding reception?

Taillefer coughed again—blood now dribbling down one corner of his lips—and shook his head. For once, he was not smiling. "No, that can't be. She doesn't even have rights. I am the heir to Pyrenee. She can't make claim to any of that by way of regency to my crown; she cannot—"

"She did. The councilors of Pyrenee confirmed you disowned ahead of the marriage proceedings. Power by conquest does not have to be taken with war. Sometimes all it takes are a few ink strokes and cups full of poison." The Warlord made it a point to catch eyes with Amarande. "We can only assume the same one killed your father."

The princess thought back to her only true audience with Inés, when the Dowager Queen had snuck into her chambers at the Bellringe before the wedding. She'd told Amarande then that she did not kill Sendoa. Amarande had believed her then. But now? Inés was suspect number one. Perhaps she'd also poisoned the watering hole—a warning shot to both the Warlord and the resistance.

"Being Warlord comes with extreme advantages, including aegis over a vast network of watchers, and our fleet of trained caracaras that deliver news far faster and less obtrusively than riders clad in the colors of a kingdom. So, yes. All of this is true." The Warlord took a large step back toward the fire, blade still ready, surveying the disowned prince and discarded princess before her. "Right this very moment, Inés is using her new power—legal or not—to collect her army and bore down upon Ardenia. And when blood stains the halls of the Itspi, she will turn to the last piece: the Torrent. And then the continent will be under her command."

Here, the Warlord most definitely smiled beneath the thin fabric.

"But the thing about taking power by conquest is that as long as blood is around, there will be questions. Inés, for all her charms, has just *very* recently gained two-thirds of her army. And those soldiers, dutiful creatures that they have been trained to be, are going through the motions for her, no passion in it. Assurance stokes that passion, and she can get that with the death of any question of blood." She pointed her blade at Taillefer. "And that means, she needs you, safely put away in her possession. To kill, to torture, whatever. Neutralized."

Yes, tried for treason and murdered. Out of the way, no matter the paperwork.

"And so we are to be handed to my mother? Blackmail to keep the Torrent?" He nodded to himself, not really asking questions so much as working through a problem in his mind. This boy and his strategies and games. "If you think I am valuable enough on my own to keep my mother's ambitions out of your hair, then you do not understand the depths of that woman."

Perhaps he wanted to keep them together. Thinking he could lessen his punishment with the hand that killed Renard under the same roof. But it would not work.

"No," Amarande answered, voice resigned. "I am headed to Ardenia."

Taillefer's strategic mind whirred ahead. "But Ardenia's plans to aid the resistance died with Sendoa. Geneva and Ferdinand have no reason to tussle with the Torrent, especially when they learn of what my mother has done." He straightened himself a little taller on his knees, imploring. "Handing Amarande to Inés only furthers your requests of autonomy and peace."

The Warlord spun on Amarande, her head tilted to a viciously questioning angle. "He has come all this way, and yet you have not told him, Princess?"

Amarande felt Taillefer's eyes settle on her profile. She steeled her breath, turned to him, and answered resolutely, "My mother was the previous Warlord."

Taillefer did not react except to widen his eyes—it was possible this boy had never before felt true surprise.

"I am headed to Ardenia because the Torrent and Ardenia are now aligned," she concluded. "It is an act of allyship, not barter."

The Warlord shifted on her feet. "That is *almost* it."

Amarande slowly raised her eyes to the girl—what did she miss?

At first, she did not believe the Warlord would give her a true answer. But then the girl's anger got the best of her in the way it would not an older, true leader.

"Your mother has left me to guard her interests as her proxy. We had a ceremony, made announcements—" In a flourish, she held up her wrist and pointed to a smudge of ink there. "She even pretended to brand me with the tattoo every Warlord has carried through the years. But the ceremony was for show. The power is hers. I am but a vessel. That is much different than giving me the power I deserve."

Amarande's heart slowed to a stop. Her mother wasn't just looking out for her best interests. She was still pulling the strings. From the throne room of the Itspi.

Stars.

Now Taillefer spoke out of the side of his mouth. "Princess, it certainly sounds as if this Warlord is insinuating she is acting regent and your mother *is* the actual Warlord in addition to being the Queen Mother of Ardenia."

Both girls ignored him.

"Your mother has not relinquished the title to me." The Warlord let her sleeve fall back. "You, Princess, will buy me the Torrent."

Yet again, Amarande was something to be bartered. Claimed. Won. She was so far from where she'd been in the days after her father's death. And yet here she was again. The same. This time, a pawn between two of her own repressed gender. Three, if one counted Inés. And it was clear *that* queen would not be counted out.

Three so-called queens, all jockeying for position on their little continent.

Amarande cut her chin at a defiant angle. Bared her teeth. "You can go ahead and try to buy the Torrent with my head, but you will lose it in kind. If not to my mother, who, no doubt, will not give away the title quietly, by Luca's hand. The Torrent cannot be conquered without the fall of the Warlord. My Luca will come for you."

The Warlord laughed. Amarande's face pinched in confusion as she watched the girl toss her head back. Meanwhile, Taillefer sighed and found his voice—as low and heavy as Amarande's was defiant and resolute. "No, Princess. He will come for *you*. True love is as powerful as it is predictable." A sudden jolt of tears pulled at her eyes. "She is counting on it. His people will feel betrayed, the revolution will fall apart, and she will own the Torrent."

"Exactly."

Amarande's mind raced with all that was left unsaid. The dregs of the Sand and Sky fighting it out, with Ardenia as the battlefield, war brought to her people. With herself and her love locked away or murdered. Neutralized. Same as Taillefer on his side.

"We must make haste and arrive at Ardenia's gates ahead of Queen Inés and her new army. It is not ideal to broker payment in the middle of a battle." The Warlord's hands clapped together loudly three times—a signal to the guards. The women immediately entered. Running down the line, she gave orders. "Janea, ready our fastest caracara for flight to the Itspi. Grania, Tomli, clean and feed our prisoners and place them in transport cells. Manu, ring the bell—we leave immediately."

CHAPTER
40

W**E** leave the carriage and head out on the horses. Go straight to the hideout. The rest of the team can take our carriage and follow along with the caravan. We'll go east, parallel. Cut them off."

Ula's plan flowed out of her in whispered breath as they made their way across the Warlord's camp to where their carriage, cook fire, and the other resistance members waited.

The brim of Luca's hat was pulled low over his eyes as they skirted through the narrow walkways weaving between tents and carriages, cook fire smoke and coffee scent trailing—breakfast delayed slightly by the spectacle of Amarande's capture.

"No."

Ula clutched his forearm, nails digging in, as sharp as her low tone. "*No?*"

"No. She's here. We can't leave. We're here. We stay with her."

"*Miguel,*" Ula snapped. A few people turned at her admonishment, clearly yearning for more entertainment after an exciting morning. Every other word was "Princess" or "Ardenia" slipping through the haze of smoke and chores.

Luca's dimples flashed and he hooked an elbow around her neck, leaning in to her ear as their bodies came together for what should've appeared to be a lovers' moment. "At the carriage."

Ula complied with a smile for those around them, before spitting through her teeth, "But Urtzi. With *her.* Her sister! And with you-know-who at the castle!"

Yes. His worst fears about Osana had been confirmed and heightened knowing her relationship to this Warlord in search of power. Still, he answered, "At the carriage."

Ula pasted her lips together in another forced smile and tapped his cheek as if he'd made a joke. He laughed, and they quickened their steps, silent the rest of the way. Luca's mind churned.

Amarande was alive, and here.

Her mother was alive, and at the Itspi.

And apparently, she had a brother and he was on the throne?

All the times the princess had wondered after her mother fell on top of one another in Luca's mind, intertwined and thick as a bird's feathers. As she'd grown older there were always comments about how much they looked alike, padded with theories as to where her mother had gone and what had happened. Or how the disappearance was simply a cover for what had been orchestrated by her father's hand—that theory was one at market, never within the Itspi where the king's true character was properly understood.

Until Luca'd met Ula and the resistance, he'd always thought he knew King Sendoa as well as he might have known his own father. Now he wasn't sure he'd really known him at all.

Luca drew in enough breath to fill the emptiness in his gut.

Amarande. Focus on Amarande.

Everything was spidering together, strands in a web. In the meadow on the day of King Sendoa's funeral, after Taillefer came upon them and inquired about Amarande murdering Renard for him, he'd asked her if all the royal players were all like the second son of Pyrenee. Even though neither of them knew what was to come with Taillefer, Amarande's answer was immediate.

Greedy? Backstabbing? Opportunistic? Every last one of them.

Luca now understood the web was much wider than he'd thought. Understood, too, that he would not leave this caravan until she did, preferably at his side.

His whole chest—his heart, throbbing under the strain of his wound and stitching and all the layers of protection—pounded with the truth that he could not be anywhere else knowing Amarande was here and in the Warlord's clutches. Not with the promise he'd made to her as they vanished into the dark after the wedding, alive despite it all.

Never let anyone take either of us again, promise?

Always, Princess.

On the heels of that promise had come the confirmation that she loved him. He'd loved her for so long and had found his own way to say it for years . . . and yet it seemed like an impossibility that she felt the same way until the words slipped into the air between them as they ran for their lives.

The carriage came into view, the cook fire still smoldering. Their companions sat stoking their own breakfasts, trying very hard not to appear to be watching them too closely as they approached. Luca nodded to Petri and gathered Tala's faux name. "Call Simu, would you?"

Then the two of them disappeared into their carriage, and Luca drew the entrance flap tight. The sliver of light from the window disappeared, and suddenly they were shrouded in the haze of canvas curtaining full daylight.

"No," Luca said again, louder. "We don't leave. We stay."

"You heard them!" She flung both arms out in exasperation. "They are *expecting* you to go after her. It would be against my oath to let you walk right into the trap they are laying for you."

"They expect me to come; they don't expect me to already be here. I am here. I stay here."

Ula was silent. Breathing hard. She held up a finger and squeezed her eyes shut. And, when she had calmed herself enough, she gripped the meat of her own arms as hard as she could and willed herself to look at him.

"I am aware and understand that the Warlord is changing our plans for us. Based on her own designs for power and her arrangement with Geneva, it would have changed whether Amarande came into the equation or not." Ula sucked in a shaking breath. "*But* you know how Tala feels about the princess. He is distrustful of . . . her hold over you. I worry that if we stay—even if that aligns with the original plan—it will be seen as abandoning the end goal for Amarande. They will believe your loyalties are divided, and not equally or in their favor."

Luca sucked in a deep breath. It felt like he could inhale all the air in this carriage and it wouldn't be enough. His heart took up the whole of his chest.

"No, my loyalties are tied together, closer than before." How could he explain this? Luca swallowed. "We will still do all the things you mentioned. We send riders to warn them. And then Tala takes that plan he's had working for nearly my entire lifetime and he pivots again. Whether that attack comes tonight or in Ardenia itself, we cannot change the fact that he now has two targets—this Warlord, and the actual one, pulling the strings. The road to defeating the Warlord now cuts through Ardenia—stars, *the future* of the Sand and Sky runs through Ardenia."

Luca let that thought sit, watching Ula's tightly balled fists loosen as she came to visualize, understand, and locate obstacles. "And what if they steal her away from this caravan? Straight on through to the castle, wrapped up like a bow. Before the resistance gets here? Or, worse, during the fight?"

Luca did not blink. "We rescue the princess."

"What if we get to the Itspi and the transaction has been made?"

"Then we storm the castle."

"Are you insane?"

"No, only knowledgeable of what we've done before."

This made her smile, but she chased it with a scoff. "Before we had Urtzi, who, despite the trouble I give him, accounts for a lot. And we didn't *storm* anything—we hid out and fled. There was no storming of the Bellringe."

Luca's dimples flashed. "For someone who once called herself a pirate, you are surprisingly lacking in a sense of adventure."

Ula sighed. "That night we spent in the Pyrenee camp, I was so taken with your love for the princess and her love for you that I argued with Amarande in our tent. I told her that true love is the most powerful force on earth—we just forget it because those with power here deal in fear rather than love." She drew in a shaky breath. "Prove me right, Luca. Prove me right."

Relief peeled off him in one shattering sheet. "I intend to."

A knock came—Tala. Luca drew open the entry flap. The leader wore a deep hat like his and careful attire. He stepped inside without a word and Luca drew the carriage shut again.

"You've heard."

Tala nodded. "What don't I know?"

Luca sent forth all he knew. About Amarande, Taillefer, Inés, Geneva, Ferdinand. The names swirled around them, Luca's knowledge of Sand and Sky intrigue from his meadow time with Amarande creeping into the small space. Then, when he was finished, Luca took a heavy pause and laid out the argument for what he wanted to do.

"Geneva holds the keys to the Torrent, this Warlord holds Amarande for a trade, and Inés holds designs on controlling the whole continent. We cannot change the collision course of these powerful women—the wheels and ships and lines of soldiers are already in motion. We can only do our best to prevent it. And we undercut *both*

Warlords if we save Amarande. My heart and the resistance are currently aligned"—he looked between them—"and if you can't see that then it is because you don't want to."

Breathing hard, Luca left it at that. Almost.

"Argue with me, but *I need you*. And so does Amarande. We will have a plan. We will account for everything. And in the end we will win."

Ula was still as stone. Tala scraped at his stubble.

Finally, the longtime leader of the resistance stood. "I will tell the others."

CHAPTER 41

AMARANDE was stripped of her clothes and scrubbed painfully clean. Her wounds were slathered in clove oil and sealed with honey before being wrapped in linen where appropriate. It was quite clear the Warlord had no intention of allowing any infection to linger before they arrived in Ardenia.

The Warlord did not want Amarande to suffer from dehydration or starvation either. Once the princess was deposited in a specially fortified traveling cart, she was given cool water, muddled cherries, sheepherder's bread, cheese, and spiced dried meat.

It was the best she'd eaten since that last night on the *Gatzal*, when she and Luca, Ula, Urtzi, and Osana had sat cross-legged under the stars and enjoyed roasted fish they'd caught themselves. Sprayed in lemon juice and wrapped in seaweed, it had been delicious.

So much had changed since then and her stomach ached, having difficulty digesting both this amount of food and the possibilities of what might come. She wished she knew what to do. Her father and his tenets were silent in her mind.

By midmorning the chaos that was the camp packing up ended, and the mood shifted—they would be on the road, and soon. Men and women bustled around her cart, readying, moving, doing. Amarande stood and watched from the open bars that lined the long sides of the cell. This particular cart had two sides, divided by a solid wooden wall, the same as the roof—Amarande was sure they'd gotten the wood and wagon wheels from the frequent raids conducted on neighboring kingdoms. For at least an hour the other side of the cart was empty, but then came a thud, footsteps, and the clang of the locking mechanism.

A moment later came Taillefer's voice. Nearly cheerful, though worn with exhaustion. "When were you planning to tell me your mother was the Warlord? That seems like information that would've been nice to have, oh say, when we witnessed dead bodies floating at the watering hole. Or when we stepped up onto the portico at the Warlord's Inn, or, possibly when we snuck into the Warlord's camp for supplies."

Frustration tugged at Amarande. With him. With herself. She blew out an impatient breath. "I did not know she was the *current* Warlord. And I only knew about her previous occupation because Ferdinand confirmed it for me when I guessed. He also does not prefer to lie."

Taillefer's tone was snakebitten. "What else don't I know? You have been holding back more than simply that truth. And though it is not an outright deception, a lie by omission is still a lie."

"Even the best of us are willing to lie for those we love."

As soon as it was out, she realized she'd built upon an answer the Warlord had given. Taillefer did not call her on it. Instead, he added, "The worst of us, too."

She nearly asked him who he loved enough to lie for because the prospects were slim.

His mother wanted his head on a pike.

His brother was murdered by Amarande's own hand from a series of events he orchestrated.

And sickness took his father so long ago that it seemed an impossibility that he would benefit from a lie told today.

The truth Amarande should have shouted from the mountaintops slid quietly to the tip of her tongue. All things considered, now might be the only remaining chance she'd get to speak it outside the thick walls of the Itspi.

"Ferdinand is a bastard."

The prince barked out a laugh. "You're telling me your mother had a son by another man who happened to look just like King Sendoa?"

Amarande managed a thin breath through her nose, her whole body suddenly seeming as tight as a bowstring. "He's General Koldo's child with my father. Yet my mother raised him as her own."

"Now *that* is a scandal," Taillefer crowed, breathlessly. "Why on earth didn't you escape and then drag me to the nearest market to scream at the masses? That is storm-the-castle-with-pitchforks material. Especially if you could prove your mother was the Warlord. Does she have a tattoo?"

"Yes."

"Princess, love has blinded you to this opportunity."

Amarande drew her knees tightly to her chest, balling all her tension over her tender heart. She imagined Taillefer on the other side of the wall, her diametric opposite—lying loose and unbound, no tension in his body at all. "No, I had to get to Luca first. Mother knew of him, and of the resistance's plan to attack the Warlord."

"My injuries confirm that she isn't the only one with such knowledge."

Which meant that if Luca came for Amarande before her transfer to the Itspi he was walking into a trap in more ways than one. Bile clawed at her throat, her recent meal threatening a reappearance.

Taillefer shifted, and there was a slight thud on the divider—his spine settling against the wood, all his weight in it. She pictured him, temple pressed against the partition as his head tipped to the side in that mocking way he had. "Your friend, *Little Queen*, she treated my injuries."

"No punishment?" Amarande's voice was low; she wished to cause the woman who saved Luca's life no more trouble.

"She did her work in chains at knifepoint." After a long pause, Taillefer's voice came again. "Not that you asked, but it seems I have shattered a rib—not something anything but time can repair, I'm told, but she did her best to make me as comfortable as one can be with a bone shard mosaic embedded in at least one lung."

"I am surprised you let her heal you."

"She can't heal me." Taillefer paused and Amarande realized his voice didn't sound tired but rather strained. "No one can. But . . . why?"

"You know enough of the natural arts to do great damage—surely the inverse would be true. Or have you only learned to destroy, not heal?"

Amarande expected some shade of flippant answer, lobbed at her immediately. Something that would turn into a taunt to undermine her or keep her off-balance. Something that might even hurt her—because in truth and against all odds, a trust had started to grow between them.

She'd returned his blade after stealing it and he hadn't tried to stab her.

She'd eaten food he'd provided.

She'd shared the secret of Ferdinand's blood.

Instead, there was a pause from his side, and with a loud rumble, shouts and curses from either direction and creaking of carriages, the caravan lurched into motion.

As the prison cart settled into a steady pace, Taillefer responded softly, his voice not flippant or sardonic in the least. Rather, it sounded stiff, sad. "You know why I began to dabble in the natural arts at all?"

Caught off guard by his tone, Amarande found herself replying almost in a manner she'd expect from him. "Answering a question with another question is very rude. But yes, tell me."

"My father."

Amarande settled against the wood that separated them. Her memories of King Louis-David were hazy. He'd died four years before, and she'd traveled with her father and Koldo to the Bellringe for the funeral. It was the last funeral she'd attended before her father's, and it was the last time she'd been at the Bellringe before her very recent trip and escape.

"I didn't know he was scientific."

"He wasn't. But—he *was* sick for more than two years before he passed. Most people, even Sand and Sky royalty, believe it was an infection that took him, but that was just the nail in the coffin—he'd been dying for a very long time."

The prince sucked in a deep breath. A cough rattled up. He steadied. Tried again.

"I was ten, almost eleven, when I decided I could do something about the cough that would never leave him. I devoured any book I could on herbs, tinctures, potions—even magic. I begged my mother to ship me off to train with a medikua."

Amarande rested her cheek against the wall. She'd never heard his voice sound so truly candid.

"Mother didn't, of course," he said, anger tingeing his low tones. "She didn't even send for your storied Medikua Aritza—your father was the one who brought her to our doorstep. It was a kind gesture, but far too late—she arrived after the final infection settled in. Within a week, it claimed his life for good."

It was difficult enough to process the sudden death of her father at sixteen; Amarande couldn't imagine waking every day for two years as a much younger child and not knowing if that day would be the day to say good-bye.

"Some nights, I can still hear him coughing in my sleep," Taillefer said. "The sound of it came from somewhere so deep within him it was like his soul was rattling with his bones."

There was no sarcastic turn to this admission, no caveat, no attempted stab at self-deprecation. It was raw and honest, and the pain of it took Amarande's breath away.

After everything they'd been through together, the hatred she'd borne him for what he'd done to Luca, she could not help but respond to the desolation in his voice. Taillefer had exposed his heart to her and she could only say, "I am sorry, Taillefer."

And she was.

After another long pause, he quietly continued. "I do not have much left of him now. Not at the Bellringe. And certainly not here with me now."

"You brought nothing but your potion and gold pieces?"

"Only that and my memories."

There was a rustling of parchment, and then, to Amarande's surprise, Taillefer's ungloved hand appeared around the corner formed by the wall that separated them and through her cell bars. Held tightly in his fingers: the map.

"Here. I want you to have your father's map. Take it."

Amarande didn't hesitate, though she was shocked to see it in his possession. "Didn't they search you? How did you manage to keep it?"

"Come now, I know you admire my cleverness and it was just that sensibility that allowed me to keep it. I am no less clever because we were captured—just as you are no less talented with a sword."

The princess slipped a finger between the folds, opening it just enough to reveal a snippet of her father's writing in the margins.

Warlord vulnerable at Hand—use river? Converge there?

She traced the letters there.

I did, Father. I did.

And now she was the vulnerable one.

Amarande lifted the hem of the plain tunic they'd given her—very much like what Osana had been wearing when they'd met—and tucked the folded map into the waistband of her breeches. Not as romantic as carrying Luca's ransom note over her heart, but the size of the map and the basic nature of the clothes did not allow for dramatics, only practicality.

They sat for the next several minutes in silence. The cart creaked along at a lumbering but steady pace, the caravan not slowing for even a brief rest in the heat of the sun. If Amarande pressed her face to the bars, squinting against the blistering light of an unfiltered Torrent, she could glimpse the extent of the caravan—an endless line of riders, carriages and carts pulled by small, hardy draft horses. It wouldn't be long before they reached the Itspi, and her mother.

Would she again hope Luca would come to her in the tower? Had he made it to the resistance? Did they have a plan? She was blind to him and everything they aimed to do.

As she settled back down against the wall, she remembered something.

"Taillefer?" The excitement in her voice carried his name with an energy she hadn't had since the churn of battle.

"Princess?"

"If you managed to hold on to the map, what about the vial?"

He did not answer as quickly as she would have preferred. After several moments, he said, "Yes."

She gripped the bars, the thrill of opportunity coursing through her veins, enough so her fingers began to shake. "Use it! The locking mechanism on the cell. Do yours and then pass it over and I'll do mine . . . or I'm sure the wood would react even better. We could burn a hole through the divider wall and then straight through the cart floor!"

Taillefer didn't answer. Amarande blew out an impatient breath. "Taillefer, give me the vial."

The cart lurched, men's voices shouting out loud imprecations around them. Beneath the noise, she could barely hear his response.

"I do not want to escape."

"What do you mean you don't want to escape?!" She jumped to her feet, thrusting her hand through the bars and around the corner of the divider. "You literally have our chance to escape in your pocket. Unstopper it and let's get out of here. I want to get to Luca before—"

"You do not own the monopoly on want, Princess. I am capable of wanting just as badly as you."

Amarande felt that like a knife in the gut.

For all she'd trusted he wouldn't stab her in the back, with the next words he ran her straight through.

"As much as you want to find Luca, I want Pyrenee. For my future, for the future of my people, *stars*, for the future of all the Sand and Sky," he said. "The seed of my mother's power is in what she stole from me—without trial, without blood, without the will of the people. She is no better than the Warlord, burning the Otxoa to rot."

How does someone go from being a conniving, torturing monster to empathizing over the shared loss of a parent to actually pretending to give a spit of sagardoa about anyone other than himself, much less the whole continent?

Amarande ground her teeth in frustration. "Why did you leave then? Why not confront her? Or at least blame me and do just as you did—rescue me, double-cross me as I expected you to do, and then arrive at Bellringe with me wrapped in a bow, your title on the line? Why traipse across the continent on my whims?"

"I thought there was time." His own anger came through, his words acute and sharp. "I thought the Torrent could be ours—Luca's."

"It still can be!" Her voice was raw with the sort of ache neither her effort nor the rush of the wind could conceal. There was doubt in her mind that the prince could hear it. "Give me the bottle and let me escape. Let me save Luca from this trap. The Torrent can be his and—"

"No!" Taillefer shouted. Then, realizing his volume, his voice dropped into a seething whisper. "*No*. Not with what my mother has done."

"Taillefer," Amarande started, not bothering to scrub the pleading from her tone, "come now—"

"I did not realize my mother had the means to outsmart Domingu and claim three kingdoms without a single true battle. But she has, and I *must* disrupt it. I am not sorry about that, Princess. To confront my mother in this present situation, I need you *with me* as bait or I am a dead man." A creak came from his side as Taillefer moved as far from the divider as he could. Away from her. Away from this argument. Away from any compromise at all. "I cannot let you go."

CHAPTER
42

FOR all his love of arguments, Taillefer would not be baited.

Amarande worked for hours—prodding him, provoking him, begging him for the fire swamp vial. Yet for all that effort her only accomplishments were a wilted voice, parched throat, and his extended silence.

At some point, Amarande fell asleep. The stress and the sun combined to lull her into restless slumber. When her eyes blinked open, it was under a low-hanging sun.

Mountains loomed ahead, backlit, disappearing on the edge of the bowl that was the Torrent. Not just any mountains—her mountains, the mountains of Ardenia. Dusty ivory rock, juniper clinging to the deep jags and fissures. But they still stood at a distance.

After a quick glance to make sure no one was looking, she fished out her father's map and turned herself away from the bars. As discreetly as possible, she unfurled it enough so that she could surmise where they were based on the distance to the mountains and how far she estimated they'd come from the Hand.

Yes. It was possible to make it to the border of Ardenia by the end of the day. They would have to travel even faster than before without stopping, which could not be comfortable for either the riders or the horses, but when you were the Warlord no one would stop you. The mountains would slow you, though. This many carts and bodies on those steep switchbacks? That might take them a day or more.

Which meant more time for the Warlord to dangle her as bait to Luca.

Amarande knew she would be a distraction. Taillefer was correct. The resistance's aim was in restoring the Otxoa and the Kingdom of Torrence. Nowhere did she fit into that plan. She was a wedge as much as she was a shield until they reached the Itspi.

And just as she began to hope that this Warlord was greedy enough to hazard Ardenia's mountain passes in the dead of night, the prison cart lurched.

The entire caravan began to slow.

"Stars and hell," Amarande muttered, obscuring her map and checking both sides of her cage to get a better idea of where they were stopping.

The bars to the south revealed a sliver of the River of Stone slicing through the distance—they were quite a bit north of the massive line of red plateaus, rather than alongside it as she had previously traveled.

Taking pains to covertly unfurl the map, she walked her fingers back from the ink that signified Ardenia's edge and up from the massive line of plateaus.

And there, clear as day, was one of her father's sword-cross Xs.

A former city. A fire pit.

But not just any fire pit—likely the one where she and Luca had been rounded up by Renard and his men.

Taillefer was on the opposing side then. Now, she didn't know where he stood.

There was no dismissing the fact that his refusal to help her—despite all they'd been through, despite the tenuous trust they'd built—was a betrayal.

One she would not so easily dismiss.

Amarande quickly stowed the map and crawled to the farthest forward section of her cage to look about further. The prison cart was positioned in the first third of the caravan. The rest of it curved like a scythe, the tail stretching so far that the shadows of the Torrentian bowl devoured them. She could also see, at close range, Taillefer's ungloved hands gripping the bars of his cell. She ignored him. For now. He was lucky for that.

As they came to a complete stop, shouts rose from the direction of the Warlord's carriage at the very front of the caravan. Like her tent, the vehicle was sky blue, opulent, and heavily guarded, mounted guards positioned in phalanx two or three deep on every side.

A figure emerged dressed in vibrant blue silks—the same hue but three shades darker than the color of the carriage. The Warlord, or perhaps a decoy—there were many advantages to being a leader behind a mask, none of them good for opponents and supporters alike—climbed up onto the footboard of the carriage. With great fanfare, the figure grasped the chain of a steel bell held aloft by two of her men and rang in three great chimes.

A whoop went up, followed by a surge of movement in every

direction, every step practiced and familiar as the caravan came to halt for the first time on their journey. Guards secured the camp, barking orders as lesser minions set up cooking pots and started fires and others watered the horses.

Before long, Amarande noticed two of the Warlord's guards riding straight toward the prison carriage. With barely a pause, the men addressed the guards who drove their cart. "The Warlord requests the pleasure of an audience with the prince and princess."

From beyond the divider, Taillefer clucked his tongue in a disappointed way. "If it is a request, then I refuse it. Send the Warlord my best wishes but I'm afraid all this traveling has left me quite exhaust—"

Of course it was not truly a request—Taillefer's reply was cut short as the drivers pulled the cart out of position and carefully drove it forward to the front of the caravan where the Warlord awaited them.

The princess gripped the bars, taking in what she could about the layout of the camp, searching out the tents that held stores and provisions as well as the corral where the horses were kept. Even without the fire swamp, she would find a way out—and to Luca.

The Warlord was ready and waiting for them as they arrived, standing outside her great blue tent, already erected. The cart drivers slowed the horses that pulled them in such a precise way that when they stopped, Amarande's prison bars were perfectly in line with the Warlord's slight form.

Though her face was obscured by cloth, Amarande was sure she was smiling.

"Did you enjoy that display, Princess?" the Warlord asked, a note of pride thick in her voice. "We move as one better than even what has been called the greatest army in all of the Sand and Sky, no?"

No. Unpacking was not akin to battling as one.

Amarande said nothing, gazing steadily at the masked figure but not responding in any way. The Warlord drew in an annoyed breath—yet again, she wished for a hostage who played along.

"If that did not impress you, perhaps tonight's fire pit ceremony will—I will see to it that you have a front-row seat." The Warlord turned away but paused, as if she had forgotten to mention something. "Perhaps your precious Luca will attend."

CHAPTER
43

THEY'D hammered out a plan on the long journey. It was solid. But it also meant Luca did have to hide—if only for a little while. He'd only show his face when the time was right. Ula ran point on everything. Setting up camp with the others, reluctantly stowing away the horses in the corral, and mapping the site as it stood.

From their location, they had a straight shot to the fire pit, the Warlord's tent, and the prison carts, all nicely lined up around the ashen lip. Easy kindling for the great flames.

Luca had heard the Warlord's threat with his own ears, yes. But he would not put it past a power-hungry woman like that not to abandon her own plan and toss Amarande to her death simply for the spectacle. His was a heart that always bent toward the greater good, but by necessity he had to plan for the greater evil and all its whims.

Tonight. Tomorrow. Ever after with Amarande. If all went as planned.

Under the tight panel of linen wrapping his stitched skin and back wound, his breath caught. How had Koldo done this for twenty years? The buildup, the climax and plans and actions of others one could not control? It all felt as if they'd made camp atop the Innkeeper's vaunted compost pile, grains of sands pulling them to the stars above, or destiny for the ages.

"*Miguel*, my hands are full!" Ula called from outside the carriage.

Luca undid the latch and held the entrance flap as she shouldered in with a jug of water from the Warlord's rationed supply, and two plates of stewed meat; cured olives, briny with vinegar; and a pair of small bread loaves, piping hot.

Luca took the plates and set them down as she reached within the folds of her tunic and pulled out a small map. "Petri is off with the map and instructions. Everything will be in its place." That was a relief—they weren't sure they'd be able to get a rider out while escaping notice. Ula gestured to the plate before him. "Here, eat."

Luca didn't move to feed himself. "And Ama?"

"Tiger in a cage. As gorgeous and deadly as ever."

Luca's dimples flashed. "Rub it in that I can't see her for myself, will you?"

"Had to." Ula grinned, pouring herself a cup of water as she rattled off all she'd observed. "Injured hand, no weapons, cell cart mates with Taillefer. I didn't get too close because she had a crowd."

Of course.

"They took the wheels off her carriage. The other cell carts, too. Locks and guards. Don't want any Ardenia-hating idiot tipping her into the fire if she's the ticket to an empire."

"Or they want to have enough people around to heave her in if her mother doesn't agree to the Warlord's terms."

She mock gasped. "Look at you with the dark thoughts—I never thought I'd see the day."

Optimism, which had always colored his world, had most definitely taken on a new shade of late. Luca was unsure if he'd actually changed or if the shift in perspective gained through his recent past had darkened the corners.

"It's hard to see the best in people when those jockeying for power intend to show you their worst."

"Eyes on the prize, Miguel." She tossed an olive at him. "When their backs are turned and their eyes blinded by their precious fire, our blades will be ready."

CHAPTER
44

IT had been days and King Ferdinand was still thinking.

About war—it was certainly coming.

The caracaras—winged messengers—from the watchers in the Warlord's ring were definitive. Queen Inés had murdered nearly everyone in sight at her wedding. Although she had captured three crowns, her first order of business was to collect a fourth.

In less than a day, her armada would arrive in the port carrying her combined armies whose manpower, if not skill, eclipsed that of Ardenia's famed army. Which was currently spread thin across three borders. Well, two—the soldiers keeping watch over Myrcell had arrived at the castle. And though these soldiers were of the caliber only Sendoa and Koldo could have created, they weren't enough.

Not to fortify the port. Not to fortify the castle. And definitely not both at once.

No matter how superior, how well trained, there was no way for the Ardenian army to win against an opponent at least three times its size, if not more.

Ferdinand had laid the whole scenario out on a large table in the king's sitting room with his father's maps and figurines—Bear, Mountain Lion, Shark, Tiger—and guessed at the numbers. He had his father's estimates of the other kingdoms' resources in the records he found in the library, but Ferdinand did not know how many enemy soldiers sat at the borders, staring down Koldo's regiments. Or how many had been present at the wedding of Domingu and Inés. Defection was possible, too—these men had offered their lives to fight for King Domingu and King Akil, not the woman who had poisoned their wine and slit the throat of anyone who did not bend the knee.

Ferdinand knew that life. He did not want it back.

If only Koldo were here. She would know what to do. For twenty years, she had been at Sendoa's side as they built one of the most dominant military forces ever raised on the continent of Sand and

Sky. He was a fifteen-year-old boy pushing figurines about a map in the chambers of the father he never knew between sparring sessions with a mother who'd spent the majority of his life ruling through fear and intimidation—even though she called it love.

Ferdinand shot to his feet. Leaving the maps and strategies and unanswered questions in his sitting room, he struck out for his balcony. The sun had nearly set over the mountains, bathing their peaks in a rich, honeyed afterglow.

It would've been beautiful if it didn't feel like the cusp of the world's end.

Only days ago, Ferdinand had believed all these new, uncovered truths about his parentage would help bring safety and stability to this dazzling place. But that scenario had bobbled and crashed the moment Amarande returned and the lies began.

A king in name but nothing else. A figurehead whose only role was to legitimize orders filtered through Geneva's ambitions and his council's goals.

He literally didn't have the keys to his own kingdom.

And for that Osana suffered—he'd already tried more than once to order her release, but Geneva blocked his every attempt. The Queen Mother clearly suspected that the relationship they'd forged in the caravan was more than just friendship. The woman knew everything—it was easy to assume she knew that, too. The assignment of Osana to watcher and spy—posing as a hostage—had occurred only a week after Ferdinand worked up the courage to hold her hand one night after supper.

Ferdinand leaned heavily on the parapet of his balcony, willing a savior to come. Koldo, with her measured confidence and experience. Or perhaps the ghost of King Sendoa—the great Warrior King, eager to defend his people, castle, and legacy from even the star-bound afterlife. Or Amarande—she'd gleaned wisdom from both of them and she loved Ardenia more than anyone he knew. If only—

A sound came from his chambers beyond, wrenching him from spiraling thoughts.

"Ferdi!" Geneva called, the massive doors to his quarters crashing closed. She was the only one who would enter the king's quarters in that way or call him that. "Are you outside? Come in here!"

And her tone was absolutely *joyous*. That did not bode well in his experience.

Ferdinand reluctantly reentered the sitting room to find the Queen Mother sprawled on the divan, awaiting him as if she were the host and he the visitor. For once, she did not complain about King Sendoa's vintage furnishings. She was too busy positively grinning.

The Queen Mother held out a slip of parchment, as if it were the most delicious morsel. "My love! Such good news."

She'd always been this way with political snippets sent from watchers in various kingdoms. A spectator as if in sport, devouring each morsel of information from them all—Ardenia, Basilica, Pyrenee, and Myrcell.

Marriages. Deaths. Raids. Failed crops. Pirates. New trade routes. She savored all these tidbits with equal epicurean delight.

When word had come of Amarande stealing Renard's own sword from his scabbard and threatening him with it while giving an impassioned speech about marriage and consent in front of the open casket of King Sendoa? Geneva had literally pantomimed the whole thing for anyone who visited the Warlord's tent over the next several hours.

Then word came of Amarande's disappearance, and suddenly he wasn't just privy to Geneva's political conjecture, he was a key player. With whispers only afforded in the Warlord's tent, she shared in exquisite detail the marrow-shaking truth of his father's name, her past life, and the unique position they could achieve through the right alliance with the woman who bore him.

Now she jiggled this fresh morsel of news in his direction, as if he wasn't accepting it fast enough. "Read it, come now, don't make me wait any longer."

"News from the caravan?" The absence of the councilors made it a decent guess.

He plucked it from her fingers, but before he even had a chance to unfold the message she was already divulging its contents.

"Celia is headed here. With Amarande."

Ferdinand's heart skid to a stop. He'd wanted a savior to arrive, and instead an added disaster was rumbling toward the castle. "What?"

"She captured both Amarande and Taillefer at the Hand. You'll see she is demanding I cede permanent power in exchange for your sister."

Ferdinand blinked at Geneva, trying to read into her thoughts and how she might respond. Though he knew her better than anyone else in the world, he was completely uncertain as to her next course of action. "What will you do?"

She examined her nails and sighed as if she hadn't already made up her mind. "If I don't, I'm sure she'll march down to the port to greet Inés with yet another weapon to add to her arsenal. And Inés will take it."

Ferdinand did not blink. His mother would not cede power. Ever.

Since the first whispers of Amarande's disappearance, Geneva's plan had remained the same: Stabilize and gain full control of Ardenia, then properly, publicly, claim the Torrent.

A wise set of ideas until Amarande arrived and the Otsakumea was confirmed to not only exist but also be activating his base.

"Don't look so distraught, Ferdinand; I won't waste time negotiating. I'll simply steal back Amarande and repay Celia's demands with a knife to the throat and a call to the caravan to help fortify the Itspi's walls."

That was not the decision he'd expected. It was too overt. "You . . . would kill Celia and admit to your role as the Warlord simply to add more numbers to our army?"

"Not 'simply.' I can't leave someone who would make such a bold and foolhardy move in power. She's not fit to be Warlord. Obviously, I misjudged my nieces. First Osana, running off with Amarande. And now Celia. The whole line is out for themselves. My elder brother failed to raise them properly, or perhaps it was the fault of that social-climbing wife of his. Who's to say?"

Ferdinand swallowed. "What if it is a trap? What if she's aiming to draw you out to kill you and claim power that way?" Then he added, "It is something you would do—and she learned from you."

Geneva smirked. "Of course she learned it from me and of course it's a trap. She knows I will agree to the covert exchange in order to keep my identity as Warlord a secret."

He nodded. "Then we must work with what she expects but not do what she wants."

The Queen Mother's eyes sparked with approval. She sat straighter on the divan and covered his hand with hers. "Go on. What do you have in mind, my king?"

His eyes settled on the figurine of a roaring tiger standing atop the Itspi drawn on his father's map, staring down the port. More tigers were deployed along Ardenia's borders, facing off against ranks and ranks of bears and sharks to the south and many more mountain lions to the north.

No, Geneva did not trust him to have the keys to the castle. But Ferdinand still had plenty to work with.

"I will ride out to meet Celia and her party, Mother." Her eyes lit up—as he knew they would. "She's expecting a covert exchange. But what if I arrive, a king with Ardenian soldiers at my sides and her sister Osana for trade?"

"Yes, yes, go on." Geneva got up from the divan and started pacing as Ferdinand continued, laying out his plan.

"Celia won't expect it, she'll be frazzled, and our men will do anything to retrieve the Warrior King's daughter, miraculously alive. We can announce that we've vanquished the Warlord and thus gained control of the Torrent and capture Taillefer, too, both of which will surprise and frustrate Inés. Not to mention provide cover for Amarande's reappearance from the seeming dead."

Geneva approached Ferdinand, threw her arms around his neck, and kissed him soundly on the cheek. "*And* both stories will be confirmed by long-serving Ardenian soldiers of the most unimpeachable honor."

She tousled his hair as if he were ten years younger and smiled in satisfaction. "I do not care whose son you are, you get your head for strategy from me."

❧

THE intimidation was working.

Amarande sat in her wooden cage, staring at the vast dregs of the fire pit.

A city had once stood here. And now it was nothing but a crater of charred bones and dreams. Everything gone black, decayed. Gone.

Tonight, it would feed on more lives. Send more souls to the stars.

How many lives would it ingest in a single night? A handful? A dozen?

All the prison carts were strung side by side along this face of the pit—the Warlord had confirmed this was a new setup. Inspired by Amarande's escape with Osana. No more wire and chains. Now carts with removable wheels and built-in dramatics.

Amarande couldn't watch the other captives, their faces and fears pressed to the bars. Their cries sounded in her ears, yet died in the pit before reaching the other side.

She'd tried to turn completely around, her back to the pit. But the opposite side held a different type of horror. Visitors peering around the guards who stood sentry, for a glimpse at the Princess of Ardenia. Lobbing insults at her, and questions about her relationship with "the wolf cub" and if she'd truly spent her entire life locked in a tower, imprisoned for the Runaway Queen's misdeeds.

Taillefer did not seem to be of much interest. Perhaps everyone but the Warlord really did think he was a castle guard.

And so Amarande turned her back to the insults and stared out at the pit.

It was indeed the location of her last stand with Luca before giving in to Renard's demands. Choosing surrender rather than a fight that might have killed them both, or at least her—Renard had made it clear he would let Luca live long enough to take the blame for her death as well as her disappearance.

Their horse's galloping steps were perfectly intact and visible across the bowl, a huge divot at the base of the fire pit where their horse had stumbled while trying to flee. A deep crescent faced opposite their hard landing, a remnant of Renard's party. If the angle were better, she might be able to count all seventeen sets of horse tracks, or however many there had been.

What would've happened if she'd fought then?

Would she be dead? Would she still have killed Renard? Taillefer? All of them? And have been locked in a tower at the Itspi by someone whom she had always loved like a mother, a brother whose existence she had never even suspected, and her real mother, returned from the dead.

Her father and his tenets appeared to her then, dormant for so long.

Always forward, never back.

Did he truly always look forward and never back? Even when her mother left them? Surely he had a pile of mistakes as large as his victories. Mistakes were the seeds of regrets. Weren't they?

How could one truly live and not wish for some things to go differently?

Wasn't that how you became a better leader? A better person? By learning from your mistakes and the residue they left on your soul in the form of regret?

But just as with her father's plans for her future, for Luca's future, for all her father had taught her, she was simply left with questions. Questions, piled so high now, they towered over her, closer to her father in the stars than her world on the continent.

The Warlord's bell clanged across the camp.

The fire drums began.

The princess opened her eyes.

CHAPTER
46

Aᴛ the sound of the drums, Luca peered out into the falling night.

He wore the filthy, wide-brimmed hat he'd donned that morning. New tunic and pants, though—all the same sandblasted fabric. Ula's kerchief was gone, and her usual braids were in place. She'd switched to a different tunic from the one she'd worn while picking up food and surveying the camp. Again, she wore his dagger and he carried her sword. This was necessary to avoid attention, but that didn't mean Ula appreciated it much. "You are the only man I would let touch that sword without first feeling the power of its blade across your skin."

"You forget that I've had it pointed straight at my heart."

"Didn't draw blood."

"I will treat it kindly," he assured her, stepping out of the carriage.

"You better, *Miguel*."

The drumbeat fell in a relaxed rhythm, a heartbeat to the teeming masses traveling as one under the Warlord's flag. A city had once stood here of stone and memories, but in only a few hours a fresh one had risen, thousands strong. The sheer vastness of it all was just as impressive as the surprise of a city's worth of rebels living underground.

It might be that optimism that he wore with his heart on his sleeve, but not-so-deep down, Luca hoped these people would be spared. They'd already given so much to fear, fighting for the person who wielded it against them felt like the cruelest way to die.

No, more cruel still, they would die enveloped in a lie.

The Warlord was a symbol, no more than the one on his chest. But where his tattoo told a long-lost truth, this Warlord would stand in front of the crowd tonight, elevated by power she did not actually possess. This Warlord lied to her people as much as the one who sat beside Ardenia's throne, pulling strings.

The drumbeat seemed to come faster with each step, the musicians signaling the time was close. Luca and Ula were careful to walk shoulder to shoulder, but as they passed the intersection of each row more bodies flooded into their path, bumping, jostling.

Ula lunged a full stride in front of Luca. Physically blocking his body, fingers hovering above the sheath that held Luca's dagger. The flow bobbed along, the stench of the day heavy. The sword at his back made for natural space, but Luca hooked a thumb under the leather strap crisscrossing the front of his body, as the most casual measure of security he could offer.

Luca's heart beat faster in time with the quickening drums. But the pace slowed as the fire pit and the Warlord's tent beyond it neared— rows upon rows emptying into one of the throughways to the pit.

Within minutes, the crowd's clip was an excruciating crawl.

Half step at a time, heart pumping as if he were running for his life.

Sweat crowding his temples, Luca searched his periphery for other members of the resistance. But instead he found nothing but a wall of bodies. Men, women, children. Some armed, some not. Most were of Torrent, with the same dark hair and burnished skin he carried, golden eyes common, varying shades of brown, too.

He saw himself in every one of them.

Even if in mere moments any one of them might try to kill him.

Luca's height gave him little advantage here, so many of these men grown like the trees of the Oiartzun Forest, bone thin and always reaching toward the sky. Every bit of energy diverted toward the sun, rather than toward filling out. Yet he could see more than Ula, who plowed forward, eye level with the diaper end of a toddler, strapped carefully to his mother's back. The golden spire of the Warlord's tent was ahead and to the extreme right.

"Sera," he said, tugging Ula's tunic for her attention, the drums loud enough this close that it felt as if they'd originated within his person. "Head right at the next opportunity, would you?"

For several minutes, one staccato step at a time, they inched closer to the fire pit. When the path opened to a large ring around the pit, it felt as if they'd left behind a creek for a delta, plunging into the open ocean, room to breathe, yet the quarters still close.

They wound around, the drums not pausing between strikes now. Fevered, frenzied. The last warning before the lighting ceremony began.

Ahead, the blue-and-gold promise of the Warlord's tent. A fire burned from within, smoke exiting the vent at the top. And beside it . . . Amarande.

She was pressed against the bars on the pit side, her face catching the last strains of the sun's descent. In that moment, time stopped and Luca did, too. His feet no longer moved; he could not turn away. His heart lurched as if it would plow through Ula's stitches and sprint straight for Amarande, its owner.

She was beautiful of course—anyone could see that.

But he ran for the girl of his heart. Fierce and loving, and so determined. Her bravery etched in every inch of her body. Hard edges and lemon cake and kisses as soft as rain. Wind-whipped cheeks, and whispered secrets, and the breath knocked from him on the meadow floor, her body pinning him there, her dagger pressed to his throat.

Ula yanked his arm nearly out of its socket in an effort to get his attention. "Even the pretty ones burn all the same. Stop looking at her like that, Miguel; it's *embarrassing*."

He laughed, and flashed his dimples, and did everything else onlookers would expect from a boy caught looking at a beautiful girl. But he couldn't tear himself away from stealing glances as they moved into position, his body feeling as if it were blowing to ashes, littering the sandy russet earth with each step.

Always, Princess. I love you always. I will come for you always.

I am here for you.

Ula yanked his arm again, this time enough to bend his body to her whispering lips. "You are still looking."

"I've never seen a real-life princess before." His voice was appropriately strangled, no acting needed.

Ula pointedly rolled her eyes. "Obviously."

They settled in right where Ula had marked on the hand-drawn map distributed among the resistance members in camp. It put them in close proximity to Amarande's cart, the Warlord's tent—should she pull the princess away—and was on slightly higher ground. Plus, they were equidistant between both the lip of the pit and the cart set up outside the Warlord's aegis as a huge, rolling dais.

Guards lined the dais, all women with swords not unlike Ula's. They were young, too, probably no older than the Warlord herself. Fierce girls, grown into the role, goaded by equal parts honor and fear, most likely. Luca swallowed—not much unlike the conscripts in Ardenia's great army.

Then, with a chiming bell, the drums came to an abrupt halt.

The hum and crackle of the crowd, too. A breeze swept through, dormant ash swooping and settling from the sides of the pit, as if the gaping maw were blinking itself out of slumber.

At just the prescribed moment, the Warlord emerged from her tent. She was in yet another shade of electric blue, the crisp waters of the Divide poured into human form in the middle of the desert.

It was striking. And it was meant to be.

The sunset had faded, the stars still shy. The silken fabric pooled and shimmered with the last light before the camp made its own.

The Warlord absorbed that waning light and the silence with her shoulders back and chin jutted out to her people. "Tonight, we—"

"Burn the princess!" a few men shouted.

Laughter erupted. Luca turned away, as if coughing, head over his shoulder. Ula, meanwhile, froze. The joyous noise spread through the crowd, at Amarande's expense. Until, finally, the Warlord laughed, too—likely a sign she'd spared their lives despite the interruption.

"No, no! Tonight we *show* Princess Amarande of Ardenia the awesome power of our flames." The Warlord waved her hands over her head, from her place on the dais, tamping down the tittering wave rolling through the crowd. "Tomorrow, we dangle her life on the doorstep of the Itspi! And if Ardenia cannot comply with our demands?"

"We burn the princess!"

Again, laughter. "No, we burn it *all*. The Itspi will be the same ash as the Otxazulo. The mountain winds will spread what we've done far and wide, and Ardenia will be another piece of the people's vast empire."

Laughter gave way to applause. And then chanting. Thousands of voices, clapping and cheering, all within the Warlord's palm.

"*Burn it down! Burn it down! Burn it down!*"

Luca's stomach roiled.

"We have this. Dark. All we need is dark." Ula's voice was barely anything at all. But he held on to it, finding Amarande again in her confines. She gripped the bars with both hands, staring daggers at the dais. All her energy and fury targeted at this girl in exactly the

way that gave her the power she siphoned. Taillefer sat with his back
to the flames. Perhaps he'd hoped he'd been forgotten or was of disinterest.

The Warlord swung her arms above her head again, all her gestures grand for those craning to see. "Tonight, we honor the stars
with the lighting of this pit. Our kindling, members of the Serene
Caravan, who arrived *late* to our gathering. When the Warlord issues
a decree, I expect full compliance. It endangers all of us when we do
not follow the laws of freedom."

At this, five carts on the end of the row of prisoners were emptied.
Members of the caravan were tossed out, into soft ash at the side of
the pit. Luca was relieved to see that no children were included. Only
adults. It was difficult to gain purchase, and most slid or rolled or
were simply pushed down the side to the bottom. They emerged blanketed in ash and pieces of bone.

Ash swirled within the air, wafting up to the crowd before settling
back down on the victims. A brave few tried to climb the sides, but
most sat in the middle, resigned or too proud to make a show of it.

"Now, I am a woman who does not wish to lose well-meaning people.
And so, because I am benevolent, and we have guests to entertain—
yes, Prince Taillefer of Pyrenee, I have not forgotten you! Yes, that
boy believed to be the princess's guard was actually the young prince
in disguise! Curious, no, as last I heard, the princess *murdered* his
brother, the Crown Prince Renard!" The crowd roared—clearly they'd
not been privy to that piece of gossip. "Perhaps these two know a
good show when they see one, no? And people say politics is boring!"

The Warlord clapped her hands. "Tributes!" She waved to the
people below, who peered up at her, weary. "I will spare one of you!
To keep your life, all you have to do is survive. Fight to the death—
disfigurement, loss of consciousness, and general injury do not count.
You have to be the last living, breathing person standing. Go!"

Ula's breath caught. "Caravans are families. These people are related or know each other well enough that they might as well be. She's
asking them to eat their own."

Luca swallowed. "And they are."

Right before their eyes, neighbors turned upon each other. Stealing breath with faces smothered into ash, punches to the gut, kicks to
the head, eyes and ears torn at behind furious cries.

Luca's heart told him he could not look. His head told him he had to. This was what he was trying to stop. This was why he was fighting. So that no ruler could do this nightly, a game, for guests.

Amarande had pulled away from the bars, but her hands still gripped them. Facing forward. Forcing herself to watch, too. To feel the anger well within her, fueling every ounce of desire she had to end it. Or at least that was what he felt. And he knew her well enough to know she felt it, too. Yes, he had to watch.

Five minutes into the horror, the Warlord clapped her hands again. "You're too slow yet again, Serene Caravan. I rescind my offer."

Stars, no.

Panic began to rise in Luca as the crowd began to laugh. The Warlord nodded to a soldier to the left of her dais, one of a dozen placed at the intervals of a sundial.

Each man held a jug four hands high. As one, they poured the contents into the pit. Though the liquid appeared as clear as water, the air filled with the sharp scent of something not unlike the sagardon Osana and Urtzi had smartly sprayed at the torch-wielding bandits. This was where Osana had gotten the idea—she'd seen it performed nightly.

Ula smashed her face into his side, as if snuggling up, but the extra fabric of his tunic obscured her view. He put a hand on her shoulder, hoping it would appear loving. Hoping that no one who cared was watching close enough to know their internal terror rather than enjoyment.

The jugs were tossed aside, torches raised in their places.

There was no count. There was no bell or whistle or sign. These men did this every night, a service to their leader.

As one, they thrust the torches into the ashen maw.

The victims who were still able to move ran for it.

But it was no use.

In the space of a so many dying screams, the entire pit was engulfed in flame.

CHAPTER
47

IT was worse than the princess could have ever imagined.

Human kindling. Hopes and dreams consumed nightly, reduced to flesh, fat, skin, and sinew, until there was nothing left to burn.

The flames flew through the base of the pit, one hot spot human after another until they were one long, writhing asp, twisted in on itself. The screams left with each new curl and dip in the blaze. They seemed to last longer than the bodies themselves. The shrieking still coming long after each victim was unable to rise from the smoldering ash.

The stench was as unbearable as the heat. The stars and their infernal gases seemingly swooping close enough to skim the contents, water off the top of the stream, solar flare billowing back into the cooling desert night.

Tears flushed Amarande's eyes as she watched the horror below, the ashen lip of the pit so close she could reach out and touch its crumbling banks. The whoops and cheers of the crowd flooded in as the wailing finally began to cease, the humans below either dead or so close they could not go on. The stars receiving new souls.

Her eyes flashed to the crowd. Their faces backlit by the nearly lost sun. This squirming, serpentine mass, of cheers and sound. So fed by fear and the relief that tonight it wasn't them that they cheered these deaths as if watching a jousting match or other sport.

Bile clawed at her throat, as she allowed the anger within her to spread.

Her mother had sanctioned this exact horrific display every night for ten years. Presiding over the festivities. Living off the fear. No—thriving on it.

And yet her father did nothing.

"Why, Father. Why?" she whispered. Perhaps not even Taillefer, as close as he was—and silent . . . perhaps he was enjoying it—could not hear.

And yet a sound answered.

The unmistakable sigh of a blade carving the breath from a man's throat. One. Two.

Two bodies draped gently on the ground. One. Two.

Amarande tensed, her chin creeping toward her shoulder to look out the opposite bars. But then a whisper.

"Do not look my way, Ama. Do not let on."

Koldo.

Amarande froze. Every cord in her neck tensed. She pushed out a breath and slowly brought her face back forward. Her mind screamed as loudly as any of the bodies in the pit.

The general needed to leave. Now. The dead guards outside Amarande's cage would be bad enough. And if Taillefer noticed? Called attention? Koldo would be dead for an outcome that would be the same.

Behind her, Koldo was clearly checking the men's pockets. Foraging for keys on a ring. Finding nothing. Amarande felt the cart shift on its soft bed of sandy ash as the general's weight went into standing on the cart edge and leaning into the forged steel locks the Warlord had clearly made from the discarded metal wire pen.

Her dagger picked at the lock. Nothing. She would need the keys or something heavy enough to smash the metal in one go. Even her Basilican steel would take several noisy blows.

Amarande took a chance to implore her to go. "I am already to be delivered to my mother's feet as blackmail. Having you do it yourself will only be more painful. The result will be the same. Leave."

The general stepped down from the cart edge and sighed, strained. "I did not come here to hurt you. And I will not leave here without you."

Koldo was generally one of few words. Economy and efficiency were her hallmarks on every level. And yet she sucked in a breath and cracked open Amarande's heart with the next whispered blow.

"If we survive, I will explain. If I die in the process, please forgive me without my answers. I have made mistakes, but I have always loved you."

And then she was gone.

CHAPTER
48

❧

THE Warlord's horror show was just beginning.

Once the pit was fully lit, it was as if the sun blew out as easily as a candle, the last rays gone over the edge of the Earth's turn and the far western mountains beyond.

Though they echoed within Luca's mind, the screams were technically gone—everyone in the pit kindling, their souls lost to the stars, which were revealed with every coming breath. Millions of lives, sprayed into the inky blue above, the moon shy on the horizon.

His eyes found Amarande again.

She hadn't ever looked away. Only once did she turn her head, briefly. Spit and fury rolling across her features as the flames grew. They were far too close to her wooden box and metal bars than he would prefer.

Taillefer had finally turned around, watching, too. Luca would have expected that sly grin to mount itself on the prince's face and never leave, but his expression was blank.

Again, the Warlord clapped her hands.

"Now, we have a few questions, for some of our own." As she paced the dais, two of the women in her cadre of guards opened the cage next to Amarande's. On each short end, the guard had to climb atop the wheel-less base, and lean into the keyhole of a giant lock. It was difficult to see from their current angle, but Luca took it all in, knowing Amarande's cage had the same or worse.

The wood-paneled side popped open and swung down into a ramp. On either side, a woman walked down and into the firelight. The guards ran the women right up to the edge, the ground sloughing off the side under their weight, more ashen sand into the pit. The women tried to inch their way back, balance starting to go, but the guards held fast, not letting them move anywhere.

The flames danced before them, and Luca's heart plummeted to his boots.

"That's Naiara." His eyes shifted to the victim on the other side. "And her apprentice—Señe."

In her cage, Amarande seemed to realize it, too, one hand to her mouth now, as if stifling a scream. Any action would condemn the woman at a swifter pace. Nothing could save her.

"This can't happen," Luca whispered to himself more than Ula.

She answered anyway. "It's going to. The Warlord does not deal in mercy."

He shook his head, though he knew Ula was right.

Naiara had saved his life. And countless others, to be sure.

He could not let this happen.

He would not let this happen.

Stableboys could be chosen ones. Heroes, even. But what kind of hero did not try to save a good person's life?

On the dais, the Warlord leaned against the railing. She smiled at the healers, who did not look at her. They did not even look in the pit. Naiara watched the stars with determination. Señe's eyes, though, were tightly closed, her shoulders quaking.

"Where is Luca?" The Warlord's first question seemed to echo off the distant mountains, irritation already in her tone. "Where is the Otsakumea?"

A sob escaped Señe's lips, but no more. Naiara did not even flinch—silently, she watched the stars. Praying, perhaps, her lips moving in the leaping flames' illumination.

The Warlord did not appreciate the silence. "Old woman, you called his name. You referenced the princess in our company, who is known to be his companion. Where is he?"

When they did not answer, the guard behind Señe shoved the girl. The apprentice's eyes shot open as she lunged forward, bare foot suspended over the pit for one sick moment as she cried out. The guard at her back grabbed her arm to keep her from falling in, but the torque of it all meant both feet lost purchase and she was left dangling against the soft bank of the pit. Flames licked at her feet and trousers, the ash clearly hot as she tried to pull her way up the guard's grip.

The guard let her dangle. The Warlord tilted her head and stared at Naiara. "Tell me, old woman, or she will be lost to the flames."

The healer watched the stars. "The Luca I know was just an injured boy. He's not the Otsakumea. Just a child who sought my care."

The Warlord gripped the dais railing, leaning farther forward over her own flames. Señe's pleas came harder now, her body flailing. "He did not have ink on his chest?"

"I did not see."

"But you did see that he was with the princess?"

"He was with a girl—I never learned her name."

This was a lie. The healers could not have missed her name in conversation—he'd called her Ama at least twice, while she'd only called him Luca in their presence once. That he was conscious for, anyway.

"Yet you call her 'Little Queen'? Do not deny it. Fifty people here can attest to that truth, including two of my guards."

The Warlord did not give her time to answer, raising a hand. In coordinated movements, Señe was pitched over the side and Naiara was wrenched farther forward, her guard's dagger at her throat.

Luca panicked, watching the healer sway against the blade as the sandy footing beneath her crumbled with her weight and movement. Her apprentice was clinging to soft ash, trying to climb. Trying not to slide. The flames were so close to her he could not see her legs below the knees, the inferno blinding any view.

"Where are they?" he whispered to Ula.

Her eyes roved the crowd. "They're here. They're ready."

"Are you sure?" His heart pounded in his ears, his jaw set.

"Yes. But it's not—"

"I can't let her burn."

He did not come here to hide. He'd been hidden away his entire life. By those who loved him. And he would no longer stay in the shadows.

Luca found Amarande across the way, hand still pressed tightly over her mouth, eyes glistening. Naiara struggled against the guard's grip, and a line of blood oozed from the kiss of the blade.

Luca removed his hat and pressed it to Ula's hand.

"No, wait, don't—" Ula clutched for his arm, but even her strength was not enough to stop him.

He lunged forward, shouldering people out of the way, trying to get closer, into the light. The Warlord leaned forward, next question on her lips, or perhaps an order, as no answer appeared to be coming from Naiara. It was now or never—the Warlord expected him to be here. This was for show. She never actually needed the answers.

"I am Luca!" he yelled, raising his arms above his head, signaling as best he could as he pushed toward the firelight. "I am the Otsa-kumea!"

The crowd gasped, and those closest to him parted as if he'd waved a torch at them. Suddenly he was completely illuminated by the flames, the bright and open space enough clearance that he cast a long shadow.

His head was bare. His face was bare. There could be no question that he was the voice in the crowd.

The Warlord twisted his way, and for just that moment he thought she might be unsure. "Boy, do you think this is a joke?"

Luca aimed his words straight at the Warlord. He knew Amarande could see him now—Taillefer and Naiara, too. "Do not burn her. I am Luca!"

"Well, healer?" the Warlord asked. "Is he?"

Naiara did not answer.

The fire crackled and spit.

Amarande, bless her, had not moved an inch. Hand pressed to her mouth. Eyes reading his face. The Warlord surveyed the princess, surveyed Taillefer, Naiara, too.

Her disbelief was not something he'd anticipated. "Into the fire with you, simply for this stunt."

The Warlord motioned to the closest guards, but before they could even take a step Luca took a deep breath and tore aside the collar of his tunic.

Those same terrible, tortuous leaping flames illuminated his tattoo.

Five points. The black wolf. Right over his heart.

Unmistakable.

The crowd gasped.

"I am Luca!" he yelled again.

His periphery picked up Amarande as a blur of movement—lunging and shaking the bars of her cage—but he did not dare move his attention from the Warlord, pacing like a tiger across the fiery chasm. "I am the Otsakumea. The last of the Otxoa. I am Luca!"

More guards fell in, pushing forward as the crowd rolled with the buzz and snap of surprise.

Ula stepped in front of Luca. But her dagger stayed in her sheath. Instead, she fed a hand through the tunic ties across her sternum. "I am Luca!" she screamed. "I am the Otsakumea. The last of the Otxoa. I am Luca!"

There, over her paw print, was carefully finished ink, exactly in the same shape and location as Luca's own.

The Warlord laughed. "Do not play, girl—"

"I am Luca!" A man's voice.

"I am Luca! I am the Otsakumea!" Another.

"I am Luca! The last of the Otxoa!" A girl's voice.

"I am Luca!" A collective voice.

From all around the fire, men and women, boys and girls, stepped forward, announcing themselves as the wolf cub and producing an identical tattoo.

Five points. The black wolf. Right over their hearts.

Unmistakable.

Everywhere the Warlord turned, there was another call. Another flash of skin and ink. From her dais, her head spun. The caravan crowd buzzed, louder than the flames and Señe's dying wails.

Hundreds of people suddenly appearing with the same tattoo. The same call. Thousands, really, but the Warlord didn't need to know that.

And when screamed decrees and flashes of skin melded into a crescendo of voices and movement and shirking caravan members, making room, elbowing away, trying not to be muddled together with those who would dare be part of this coordinated trickery, the Warlord finally realized that this was not a stunt.

It was an attack.

"Don't stand there! Get them!" she yelled to no one and yet everyone all at once.

And that's when all hell broke loose.

CHAPTER 49

HEART in her windpipe, Amarande could not recall her last breath.

The complete disbelief of Luca calling out to the Warlord—revealing himself, revealing the tattoo—had flamed out, replaced by the complete disbelief that he'd done such a thing and was *still breathing*.

At the Warlord's order, the entire churning mass moved to chaos, but the dictator's followers were already a step too slow. Her voice still echoing against the distant mountains, sleeping darts shot through the air.

Not from her side, but the resistance.

Lodging themselves into soft spots of anyone drawing a blade or cuffing their own dart pipe to their lips. Men and women dropped as smoothly as the one Koldo had killed at her back, but no blood shed.

This was exactly how she went down for the man with the black wolf—so very quick. The opposition immediately nulled the Warlord's swiftest power, simply by having the distraction and wherewithal to strike first.

Make the first mark.

Indeed they did.

Amarande pressed herself against the fireside cell bars, searching for Luca. Where he'd been standing was now a swarm of bodies, churning and moving. It was the chaos of the wedding after she'd killed Renard, but literally a thousand times more frantic. Families raced for the paths leading away from the fire pit, spokes on a wheel, and suddenly just as clogged as they were in the minutes before the lighting ceremony began.

When she'd met her first set of bandits in the Torrent, Amarande had walked away with her life and a sense that she'd finally tasted battle.

That wasn't battle—this was.

Blood spray, bodies tumbling into the pit, the fire roaring and coughing smoke with each addition. Daggers and swords met in violent, reverberating clangs. Boots crunched bones, and live bodies, shrieking to the stars.

But she needed him.

"Luca!" Amarande screamed his name with all the love she had, knowing that he would hear that note, along with the anguish and fear that thrust it into the air.

The world seemed to yell back.

He's coming. He knows I'm here.

Survive the battle, see the war, her father had said, but which was she?

Across the way, the Warlord roared into the air in every direction as the resistance closed in. Five of her guards covered her in round-robin style, the dais creaking under their collective weight. These women had their backs to her directive spew, their swords out front, aimed at anyone who would dare rush at her with a blade.

They dared, of course.

The Warlord's guards circled her, a moving target aboard the dais, as rebels with blades closed in on the raised platform.

It was protection, yes. But it was also a mistake.

They should have sheltered her on a retreat the moment the fighting started, not let her launch orders into the night. Now they were sitting ducks.

And the rebels knew exactly how to attack.

With practiced precision, members of the resistance turned their sleeping darts on the Warlord's dais. Aiming for the guards closest to the railing that hung over the lip of the fire pit.

One. Two. Three. Three women dropped like flies.

The first, straight on the railing where the Warlord had leaned, splitting it in two with her weight as her crumpled body lost the balance it could not control and tipped over the edge and tumbled into the inferno below.

The other two fell right on the edge. The weight of the blow and the guard going over, in combination with these two dropped bodies, tipped the dais. It was still up on cartwheels, at a higher center of gravity than the princess's wheel-less cage. Just an extra couple of feet, but enough that the whole thing teetered.

The Warlord and remaining guards stumbled backward, toward the bodies and the fire pit. Their presence only served to make the dais heavier, and suddenly there was a great crack as the wheels far-thest from the fire pit inched off the ground while the piece of the dais with the new weight splintered.

Crack. Crack. Crack.

Boards began to split as the Warlord and the three remaining guards tried to gain purchase. One tripped over a dropped guard, her boot catching on her fallen form. That sent her flailing back. Her arms windmilled, one catching the Warlord's own outstretched arms.

A bolt of blue, she lost her center, wheeling around at the sudden blow.

The sand beneath one of the pit-facing wheels gave out then, the whole dais-cart lurched, and the Warlord was sent headfirst into her own flames.

Amarande's breath caught.

The Warlord was gone.

Dead.

Screamed the whole way down.

"That's a rather apropos way for a Warlord to go out."

Those were the first words she'd heard Taillefer say in quite some time, and she actually agreed with him.

"Taillefer, time to use your fire swamp. Let's go."

"I'm saving it. And besides, this is probably the safest place to be at the moment. It's nearly impossible to tell one side from the other unless it's your love facing you down."

The tattoos were all obscured now, it was true. But that was a stu-pid argument.

"Yes, but out there we can *help*."

Amarande rushed the bars facing away from the pit. No sign of the general and the keys she was hunting, but the princess screamed for her anyway. "Koldo!"

"You seriously think your general can hear you over this ruckus?"

"Why don't you help me? Use your voice. She'll help you, too."

"Or she will kill me for kidnapping you or rescuing you or what-ever crime she prefers to prosecute."

Stars, why did Taillefer choose to revert to the most infinitely ir-ritating version of himself in *this* moment? Frustration zapping any kindness from her voice, she played to his stated aim. "You have my word that I will protect you and help defeat Inés."

She could almost hear the fox smile cross his regal face. "We both know the word of another noble in the Sand and Sky is worth less than shared blood, and that's barely worth anything at all."

The cart shook as yet another pack of terrified people barreled past, the corner of the princess's side edging closer to the fire pit lip. It was the side where her door was, opposite where the wooden divider separated them. If she was headed out the door, it would need to be soon—too late and there would be no safe exit.

Amarande searched the non-pit side for signs of Koldo but found none. Still, she stayed on that side, trying to keep as much weight as possible away from the inferno. Though, it wasn't much help with the press of bodies. Something hard crashed against the cart and tossed her back. Then another slam. And another. Despite her weight on solid ground, the cart inched closer to the edge, an entire corner of her cell now hanging over the flames, nothing but air and death below it.

"Taillefer—the fire swamp! Burn a hole through the divider." The cart shook more from Taillefer's side, as if a pair of fighters had taken up residence on his door side. "I can crawl through, and we'll have more weight on that side—my cell is creeping over the edge. It's going to be a massive problem if we don't—"

Her voice died at another hard thud. A rattling cough and a spit of something wet—more blood. "Taillefer?"

There was the rattle of chains, the squeak of hinges, and for a moment the whole cart seemed on solid ground, anchored on Taillefer's side. She craned against the bars, angling for some way to see what was going on.

The sound of knuckles pounding flesh came next. A cry. A sword flew in her direction from the exterior. Men rushed past, no one lunging for the abandoned weapon—though Amarande did, striking her fingers through the bars. The bars squeezed her elbow less than a hand's length from where the Basilican sword lay dormant on the ground.

It wasn't Koldo's weapon—and she didn't think it would be. Koldo would come for her before Taillefer. Even though she'd told her she didn't want her to.

"Taillefer! Can you grab the sword? We can get out of here if you can—"

"I have my own problems, Princess." Face smashed against the bars, as she leaned for the weapon, Amarande wrenched around at the sound of his voice. Strangled. Hurt. Stressed. Yet she could see nothing.

Just when she returned her attention to the weapon, two bodies tumbled past. Blond hair, the same prisoners' garb as hers. The other was another light-haired boy, wrapped in a cloak much like the one they'd stolen, but underneath was a flash of the darkest aubergine.

Pyrenee. They'd truly come for him.

Taillefer struggled, hands in a fury, going for all the soft spots on the soldier's face—ears, eyes, lips. The prince's forearm caught the boy's windpipe, and his head flew back with a crack, sucking cry escaping from his lips.

Taillefer used that opportunity to wedge his knee against his chest and kick the soldier as hard as possible with almost no room. It gave him enough space that he dove for his sword.

As he wrenched it away from Amarande's outstretched fingers, she felt her chances evaporate, the sword his for his survival alone.

But.

In one quick aside, Taillefer shoved the sword between the bars, straight into her hands.

For a moment their eyes met. "The sword? As you wish."

Then a huge, hulking arm in aubergine jerked him away. Taillefer spun, ducking, grabbing a dagger straight out of the chest of a fallen man, and, as he was angling for the Pyrenee soldier, was devoured by the retreating crowd.

Amarande blinked as if he'd been swallowed yet again by quicksand, shocked that in that moment he'd helped her. She stared at the sword, almost believing it was a trick. But no, it was true Basilican steel.

A soldier's sword. *That* soldier's sword. The mountain lion crest of Pyrenee stamped at the hilt.

Another blow to the cart knocked the inaction straight out of her. The cart leaned.

She had to get out.

Putting as much of her weight toward the front as possible, Amarande began hacking away at the divider panel. It was thinner than the bars. If she could just bust a hole, she could break open this thin board. She could do it.

She could get out of here. To Luca, somewhere out there, fighting.

A couple of pointed swings of the blade and a narrow hole appeared, Taillefer's cell and the gaping door free.

"Ama!" Koldo's voice. She had an entire key ring now, but Amarande's locked door was now three feet over the edge of the pit. All her weight was in the remaining four feet of her side.

"I changed my mind. Please get me out of here." She held up her sword. "Help me hack away at the partition."

Without a word, Koldo sprinted to the opposite side of the cart and began to hack away at the partition with both her dagger and sword. Amarande worked from the corner out toward the center, where the general stabbed the wood with everything she had.

Within a minute, they had two good-sized holes there, but they needed to come together.

"Stand back! I've got it," Amarande announced, lining her blade up with the thin bit of remaining wood. One targeted strike would do it.

The princess wrenched back the sword. On impact, a chunk of wood flew away, creating just enough of an opening that Amarande was sure she could squeeze through.

At once, Koldo came into view. She was bloodstained, wounded in the shoulder and thigh, but standing there, a rare smile on her face. Koldo leaned forward, gloved hand out. "Ama, I am here for you. Not for her. I promise. I will explain—"

The ground shook and the general was tossed to the side. Amarande, too—hard enough that the sword tagged the bars and fell from her grip. It slid to the dangling locked-door side, the blade roasting over the fire.

Amarande tried to gather herself, her footing slipping, and suddenly she had one hand hooked on the bars and her injured hand, linen wrapping and all, clutching the rough edges of the newly splintered hole.

But instead she just hung.

At the top of her lungs she called to her love one final time.

"Luca!"

CHAPTER 50

AMARANDE'S call hit Luca in the gut like a cannon blast.

He withdrew Ula's blade from the man nearest to him. His opponent fell with a moist thud as Luca's whole body wrenched toward the sound of his name.

Across the full blaring roar of the fire, farther away from him than she'd been before, the chaos of battle moving him along the diameter of the pit. The cage was there—and honestly he'd thought her to be as safe as could be until he made it there, the reinforced cell keeping others out as well as it kept her in.

But now the whole thing had been shoved aside on its axis. Amarande's cell angling over the fire, more than half its length balanced precariously in the air, flames licking at the cart as the ashen ground disintegrated under the box's swinging weight.

Ula thundered in, blood smeared across her brow. "Did you hear it? We need to get there now. If it goes over, there's no way we can get her out."

He was already running, sword leading. "Move! Move!" he yelled, though it was no use. Hurtling over bodies, and people. Dodging blades of every shape and stripe as they aimed for others and sliced into the path.

"On your right!" Ula grabbed the empty scabbard that crossed his spine, wrenching him back just in time as a trio of fighters rolled through in a scrum of daggers and fists, all of them barreling straight toward the fire. "Oh stars, the cart's going. Run, run, run!"

She might have said more, but all Luca could hear was Amarande's voice. His name. Over and over. It thumped in with each breath as he ran, willing his snakebit leg not to stumble in the stride, the numbness a disadvantage.

Faster now, they edged past where the Warlord's dais had been, tiptoeing around the bodies, and the cries of those still kneeling at the flames for some sign she might rise from the ashes.

With everything he had, he sprinted toward his love—she could not have the same fate as the Warlord. She could not.

And, as they closed in, he finally knew she would hear him. "Amarande!"

CHAPTER
51

Amarande!" Luca's voice.

She tried to see him through the hole. He rushed in, the weight redistributing in the cart as he joined Koldo. Another shaking belch and suddenly the whole thing tipped.

"Out here!" Ula's voice. "Stand on the ramp. Weigh it down!"

The box shifted again, and suddenly Amarande knew all that was keeping her on solid ground was the weight and leverage of the three of them on Taillefer's cell door, the hinges at the bottom straining against the base of the cart.

More voices. More people. More weight.

A metallic sound. The hinges going, the door pinned down, but the whole cart coming apart at the seams. Pulled in one direction and the other.

"Rope! We need rope!" Luca called. "Now!"

More noise. Voices. Amarande held fast to the bars. Trying to ball all her weight as high up in the cart as possible. She glanced down at the sword. Out at the rapidly disappearing lip, sand and ash spilling into the fire as the stress of the cart pressed its full weight and tipping point leverage into the soft and heated earth.

"I am the rope! Use me as the rope!" Ula cried, kicking her boot out toward Luca. Glancing at Koldo. "Lower me. *Now.*"

Luca and Koldo barely exchanged a glance before Ula was already on her hands, holding her legs out like she were playing wheelbarrow. Koldo and Luca latched onto the pirate's boot and she crawled into Taillefer's abandoned compartment. She lowered the hip belt of her dagger.

Amarande's fingers scraped at the leather, scrabbling until they gained hold. Ula grunted, trying to reach farther, as Amarande wound the belt around her wrist. Then she slid the linen that bandaged her knife wound around the leather at her wrist and grabbed on to it all as tight as she could with her injured hand, trading the extra protection of the bandage reinforcement for the temporary pain shooting through her hand.

"Good." Ula's eyes glittered like stars, all the blood rushing to her determined face, veins and tendons on end. Her hair fell forward in braids, which only served to frame the strain. "Grab hold of my wrist. On three. One, two, th—"

The cart shifted again and the toe of Amarande's boot dug into the tipping wooden edge. The momentum sent her upward, but the cage shuddered violently as the final push decimated the sand-ash beneath, and a massive chunk of the fire pit lip dislodged and crumbled into the inferno.

"Pull!" Ula shouted.

Amarande was aware of Luca and Koldo clearly yanking them back, but as the cart fell away, the narrow opening caught on her shoulder.

For one sick moment, the weight of Amarande and Ula plus the cart was dragging against Luca and Koldo. Ula's whole body was stretched past discomfort into agony, her fingers slipping, teeth gritting.

"Ula, tell Luca I love him. Tell him I tried. I was coming for him. I didn't mean for him to do this without me. I'm sorry—"

With a belch, fire tore into the bottom of the cage, eating straight through the door and lock that had trapped her. Amarande screamed and lost hold of one of Ula's hands, the leather strap protecting the grip on the remaining one beginning to fray.

"You will tell him yourself. Close your eyes!"

With a grunt, Ula unsheathed the dagger pressed against her skin and began driving the blade into the splintering wood next to the hole just small enough to make it impossible to pull Amarande through.

She only got in four whacks before there was another screeching lurch and the entire bottom of the cart peeled away. Flames licked at Amarande's dangling boots as the cart listed, up and then flat back down, rocking like it was taking on water.

With an earsplitting shake, the whole thing began to slide.

Ula's dagger skittered away and she grabbed Amarande's single clinging hand with both of hers. The princess curled her useless arm into her body as tightly as she could . . . and with a splintering shake the prison cart fell away. Amarande and Ula slipped out of the wooden box as it plummeted, the momentum slapping them against the lip of the pit.

With one terrific heave, Luca and Koldo yanked them back and up until Ula's belly hit solid ground. So many hands, too many hands, reaching and bracing as Amarande came up over the edge, hot ash in her face and hair, free hand scrambling for the earth.

Her arm was bleeding from her shoulder through the length of her forearm, the wood of the fractured cart taking a sliding bite on the way down. The soles of her boots were melting as she dug them into the dirt, crawling onto her hands and knees before flipping on her back.

Vaguely, she heard a crash—the cart tumbling into the flames.

Father, I almost saw you.

Her body wracked with a cough from the smoke, eyes squeezed shut and watering. And when she opened them, Luca loomed above her.

Dimples and shining golden eyes and sand grit sticking to sweat and blood.

"Luca! You came, you're here, you're mine. Luca, Luca, Luca."

She pressed herself to her hands and knees and then in one great lunge tackled him.

In battle, even like this, every moment felt like an eternity. Action slowing to give every grain of sand in the hourglass its time to shine.

And in that sand grain of time, Amarande was back in the meadow with him. Moments before learning her father had died, she'd outfoxed Luca, trapping him with knees and elbows and practiced skill until his throat sat softly beneath the tip of her blade. She'd wondered then if he would say it. Now she knew not only that he would but also that he'd been saying it all along.

"Always, Princess."

Luca held Amarande as they fell back to the sand in a rush. Her body, bloody and covered in ash and shaking with the shock of what had just happened, pressed into his. Her boots knocked his shins, her arms propped against his collarbones, her face cupped in his palm.

Luca was here. He was truly here and hers and alive.

Amarande kissed him then. Eyes closed, mouth hungry, her whole mess of a body folded into Luca's warmth. His arms tightened around her, a hand snaking through her hair and to her neck.

It felt like an eternity but was simply the space of a few breaths, a forest of people around them instead of their junipers in the meadow—Koldo, Ula, others Amarande didn't know. Beyond them, the battle was still raging, less of a writhing mass and more hot spots in a forest fire that had spread, taking over the entire encampment and not simply the area by the fire pit.

"Let's move. We need to move." Ula's voice.

Then Koldo's gloved hand wrapped around the princess's uninjured arm and began to pull. "Ama, later. Not in the open. Let us regroup. To safety with you. Please, now."

Amarande nodded and let Koldo pull her up, her own hand out to Luca. He took it but did not put his weight into it, her blood sliding down the injured length of it and onto his fingers. He stood on his own, but as they were ushered away she did not let go.

CHAPTER
52

AMARANDE clung to Luca's hand as the four of them—the princess, the Otsakumea, the general, and the pirate—ran away from the fire pit and the battle that raged around it. His palm was warm with both life and the thrill of battle and held hers carefully, her blood snaking between them.

They dashed up a row of abandoned tents, the ground clearing of the debris of battle with every step away from the fire. Ula charged ahead, dagger out, Koldo bringing up the rear. The others who'd seemed to surround them when they'd been on the ground fell away.

"Luca, when you revealed yourself I thought it was the end." Amarande's voice was too loud for her ears, her breathing heavy with the run and rush of survival. Of seeing him. She squeezed his hand, daring to glance down at it in the jumbling rush of their tandem run, just to confirm her touch hadn't deceived her.

Luca was here. Koldo was here. Ula was here.

"I thought you'd sacrificed yourself for Naiara," Amarande tried to whisper, but the healer's name came out in a sob—she didn't know if she'd survived. "I thought it was the stars giving me one last look at my love before stealing him away."

"I did not mean to shock you, Ama, only the Warlord and her cronies," Luca answered. It was just then that she realized he'd stowed a sword at his back—one just like Ula's, slick with lifeblood that caught the firelight and moonlight as they ran. "I would never hurt you."

"But you would sacrifice yourself for another—"

"The timing even had me guessing, and I knew the plan!" Ula called from up ahead. She dodged down a different row. "Over here. There's water and cover. Princess, sit."

Amarande wanted to do nothing of the sort, looking over her shoulder to the battling bodies in the firelight, but both Koldo and Luca forced her down. Her back to the cartwheel, as Ula gathered water in clay cups from a covered tanker cart with a spigot, stacked to the side.

Amarande drank deeply, clutching Luca's hand. "I have so much to tell you."

"I know, and I have so much to tell you, but I must finish what I've started. My people need me." He cradled the sides of her face, then leaned in and planted a kiss to her brow.

Wait. She pressed her palms to those hands that held her, fingers curling tightly over his. He came away smiling, pried one of her hands away, and kissed the sand-crusted knuckles. His lips were warm.

"I do not want to go, but I must lead. I cannot be away until it is through." Amarande's heart caught as he read her face, golden eyes light. "It's what you would do in the same situation."

Pride and loss flooded into Amarande's chest, as equal as they were heavy. Suddenly she couldn't breathe, yet her grip loosened on his hand, still gently cradling one side of her face.

"I would. But . . ."

"Amarande, I will come back to you. You know this. I will always come for you. Always, Princess." He looked to Ula and Koldo. "Stay with her."

"On my honor." Ula.

"Of course." Koldo.

Luca pressed another fevered kiss to Amarande's lips, the princess shutting her eyes and drinking it in until, with one last gentle sweep of a thumb against her cheek, he drew away. She opened her eyes, willing the warmth of his touch not to fade as he charged back in the direction of battle, the curved sword drawn and out front.

Tears snaked rivulets down her ash-flecked cheeks. "No, no, he can't go back there. He made it out safe. He can't go back in. What if . . ."

Amarande was already struggling to get to her feet, but Koldo held her down. "Ama, he's won. I've seen enough war in my lifetime to guarantee it."

Ula nodded, pressure on Amarande's blood-soaked arm. "The moment the Warlord went into the pit, all the fight fled the people who feared her."

Amarande fought against Koldo enough to sling her clay cup toward the fire and fight, letting it smash against some unseen patch of desert dirt. "But that wasn't the *real* Warlord—" Amarande squinted through the night for Luca, but at that distance, all bodies were a smudge of movement. "My mother never relinquished. They're going to regroup. He's not safe; he's not—"

"Amarande, we heard it all—Luca and I," Ula insisted. "What the Warlord told you. About your mother and the puppet this one was. He knows, but the Warlord's people don't."

"Geneva didn't relinquish power? Are you certain?" This from Koldo.

Amarande shook her head but then thought better of it as a wave of nausea passed over. "She didn't. This Warlord planned to march me to the Itspi and bargain for her power."

Ula squinted at the princess. "Why were you with Taillefer? You should be with Osana and Urtzi. Who is Ferdinand?" She spun to Koldo. "And who is *this*?"

Where to begin? The princess had so many questions for Koldo herself. About her motivations. Her relationship with Amarande's father. Her relationship with Amarande's brother. *Stars*, her relationship with Amarande herself. She had all those questions, but she had the most basic answers to share in this context. None of that had changed.

"It's a mess of complication, Ula, but in short, this is General Koldo. My father's best friend, my surrogate mother, and the actual mother of my half brother, Ferdinand, who is sitting on the Ardenian throne."

Ula drew her knife. "Can we trust her?" She addressed Amarande but thrust her dagger across the princess's body, holding it a whisper from Koldo's throat. "Why are you here?"

"I am here because I love the princess and I was concerned for her safety."

Ula's eyes cut as deeply as that blade could. "But if your *son* is sitting on Amarande's throne, your loyalty is suspect."

"Ula, I trust her," the princess insisted. She didn't know where Koldo's heart sat, but she knew she was here and, even if it was simply powered by memories and what they'd just been through, that she still had faith in her. "I trust Koldo now because of where we've been, same as you."

The pirate removed the dagger from the general's throat. "Fine. But you have not earned my trust yet. Princess, let me inspect your arm."

"My arm is a mess, but it can wait—Ula, can you find Taillefer? A Pyrenee soldier stole him away. We need to find him."

"He needs to find his head on a pike for what he did to Luca," Ula seethed.

"I do not disagree, but we need him if we are to confront Inés."

"Inés?" Koldo asked.

Amarande nodded at her but addressed Ula. "Please, I'm safe with Koldo. See if you can find him. If you can't, or if you find his body, we'll come up with another plan."

"You want him alive? I can't guarantee it."

"If I managed not to kill him during our time together, I believe you can resist."

Ula gave a final warning glare to the general, reached into her boot, and pulled out a second dagger. "If I am to leave you with your trust and a trained soldier, I'm at least arming you." She handed the knife to Amarande without dropping her steeled stare from Koldo's face. "I will come for *you* if anything happens to her."

In a flash, Ula was gone, jogging back toward where the prison cart had been, prepared to retrace Taillefer's steps.

"Where did Luca find her?" Koldo asked, her general's mind admiring the soldier running away, even as her skin blushed red from Ula's blade.

"He didn't. She found him—one of his kidnappers. The story is long but not nearly as important as the rest I must tell you." Amarande clutched Koldo's arm. "Inés and Domingu conspired to marry and join their kingdoms—with Renard dead and Taillefer disowned, Inés now rules Pyrenee."

"Can't say that I am surprised. They were brewing up something at the funeral."

"Yes, but there's more—somehow Inés slaughtered not only Domingu but Akil, the heirs that were at the wedding, and all of the sycophants who wouldn't switch allegiance."

"*What?*"

"Inés has declared herself Queen of Pyrenee, Basilica, and Myrcell, and has an armada headed for Ardenia." She snatched Koldo's hand. "Straight for Ferdinand. And with three kings fallen, I highly doubt she's looking to acquire rights to Ardenia through another marriage."

Shock did not sit well on the general's features. It typically had no home there, and even now it was subtle. "But we have no soldiers there. Only castle guards who still wet the bed. They're sitting ducks."

"Inés knows that. She knows our soldiers are at the borders. What she doesn't know is that if she storms the Itspi, she might have what she needs to declare the continent hers." Amarande drew a steadying breath—it didn't do much.

"She can't, though. We know Ferdinand is illegitimate. Stars, you heard him; he abhors the lie. He will tell anyone who will listen, including her."

"Koldo, she won't care either way. She will kill him. She will kill Geneva, and then she'll kill me, and Luca, too. It does not matter who she thinks has the power; she will strike out all the possibilities and take it for herself. The covenants of the Sand and Sky are broken, and no longer matter. All we can do is oppose her."

The general shook her head. "Or Geneva will take a run at her, using Ferdinand as a shield. Geneva will assume she still has her puppet here—there will be no one to send a caracara with news of this battle. Secure in her power through Ferdinand, Geneva will challenge Inés. She likely has more claim to Basilica than Inés does through paperwork."

This was true. Amarande herself likely had a better claim than Inés to the right ears within Basilica, and that was through Geneva's Basilican blood.

"And," the general continued, the uneasy shock on Koldo's face giving way to battle-worn sight for the lay of the land, political and otherwise, "if Geneva somehow gets her hands on Taillefer, she could use him to put Inés's claim of Pyrenee on shaky ground. Conquest steals crowns, but blood is often hard to challenge."

"Unless you're a woman. Then a bastard boy is easier to install."

Amarande did not state it in a cutting manner, just as the truth. But tears formed in Koldo's eyes. "Yes."

Amarande watched as this woman, whom she'd never seen shed a tear until her father's death, began to shake, wetness growing along her eyelashes as she dropped her chin to her chest. Koldo drew in a steadying breath, and when she spoke it was with the precision of the soldier who had been the princess's surrogate mother. Always so strong, sturdy, direct. Even, it seemed, when she was falling apart.

"Princess, your father always had a plan."

All the air left Amarande's lungs.

Her injured hand scrabbled to her waistband. "Before Father's death, was he planning to go to war with the Warlord?" She pulled the map free, unfolding it. "See this? It's clear Father knew who Luca was. He knew Geneva was the Warlord. If he knew Geneva was here, he had to know about Ferdinand. What did he want? Why didn't I—"

Koldo cut her off with a gentle press of a finger to Amarande's lips. "Princess, your father always had a plan," she repeated, tears falling now. "For you. For Luca—for me, even. The only time his plans ever failed was when they were not followed."

Amarande tore herself away from the general's touch. "I would've followed! I would have done what he wanted. Luca would have, too, if we had only known. I knew he had to have a plan, but he never told me." Her voice shook. "How am I supposed to follow it if I don't know?"

The general took a deep breath and slipped a hand into her tunic. In one smooth motion, she revealed her own square of parchment. Not a map. Something else.

"Your father always had a plan for succession. I've had it with me since I left the Itspi in the days after your father died. I've been quite concerned someone—specifically Satordi, but now Geneva—might burn it."

She unfolded the parchment, the last bits of a wax seal crumbling off the tip of the paper with the movement, and offered it to Amarande.

"Princess, your father saw greatness in you every day. He protected you in so many ways I cannot begin to count." She nodded to the paper. "He always intended you to rule. He knew the complications that wish would create. The plan was never Ferdinand; it was always you. Of all his plans, you were his best one, and I failed you both by thinking I could repair it myself."

The Day of King Sendoa's Death

❧❀❧

LESS than an hour after the lifeless body of King Sendoa arrived at the Itspi, the Royal Council of Ardenia convened within the castle's north tower. Councilors Satordi, Garbine, and Joseba seated themselves in their usual spots, right in a row.

The king's roaring tiger chair at the head of the table gravely empty.

And, standing stiffly at attention at the room's entrance, General Koldo. Not changed from her dusty uniform. Eyes red and swollen from a deluge of tears unlike any she had experienced in the past fifteen years.

The general approached the table, which held a single guest chair. Tiger's head carved into the back, but a world less ornate than Sendoa's former seat. "You did not invite the princess?"

Satordi straightened. No eye contact. "It is not appropriate for her to be here. Not yet. This is no place for a child."

Though he was too cowardly to look at her, Koldo bared her teeth. This man would fear her frustration with a turn of tension he could not mute. "She is the last blood of Ardenia; she should have at least been invited."

Satordi shuffled the papers in front of him. Slim neck trembling over the bob of his throat. "If you would like to drag her crying from her quarters to the next meeting, you are welcome to do so. I have no time for such hysterics. We must get to the bottom of this."

Koldo stared back at the man with as much vitriol as she had left. "Then let's. We should read the will."

The general took the single seat across the table.

Now that they were on the same level, Satordi hazarded a look at her. Setting the tone, running the meeting, that was all this man knew in Koldo's estimation. He believed he had power, but he only sat in close proximity. "First, I have a few questions for you, General

Koldo, who was within three feet of our king as he died of seemingly nothing at all."

Koldo simply stared back at him. Waiting.

The other councilors remained silent and still. "General," Satordi said, "did the king share any information with you that you believe could have led to regicide?"

Koldo said nothing.

"General?"

"I do not believe so. No."

"It is your opinion that King Sendoa died of natural causes?"

Again, Koldo said nothing.

Satordi inhaled thinly. The afternoon light shifted, wind and shadow playing beyond the heaviness within the Itspi. "I shall take that answer as a yes."

"No," the general corrected, curtly. "It appeared to be, but I do not believe it was."

The councilor pursed his thin lips. "Fine. If you would like me to understand you the first time, please answer my next question to the fullest of your ability. General, I realize you've had a shock, but unless you answer me with words, there is very little I can do to amend this situation."

Sendoa was dead. There was no amendment to that. Just stars and rot.

"General, is there anyone who would wish to see our king dead?"

There was no shortage. Not really. So many of those who owed their crowns to the Warrior King had obvious motivations if exposed to the right light.

Bear. Shark. Mountain Lion. And the monster in the desert most of all.

"Yes."

Satordi's brows arched to the remains of his hair. "Would you care to elaborate?"

"He is—*was*—the protector of the Sand and Sky. Every king on this continent owes his neck and crown to Sendoa—"

"That should prevent—"

"I was not finished, Councilor." Koldo stared daggers at Satordi. When his thin lips snapped shut, she continued. "After years of this protection, it is likely that some may have believed he could steal their crowns as easily as he could save them."

Garbine was aghast. "Our king never seriously looked at seizing the whole continent. There are some who might angle for that"—*some*, meaning Domingu—"but Sendoa would have never, and unless you have knowledge otherwise, General, I take that as an offense to my king, whose body is not yet cold."

Koldo held up a hand, glove shedding fine windblown mountain grit. "King Sendoa would not have done such a thing and I was not suggesting he would. I was suggesting others thought he *would* because he *could*. His reputation itself was a constant, pressing threat to his very life."

Silence fell over the room.

In answer, Satordi gestured to the youngest councilor. "Joseba, read the will."

Doing as he was tasked, the young councilor took a letter opener to the seal, the king's garnet wax—tiger's head inlay, naturally—flaking to the table. Joseba unfurled the parchment, short as it was, and read the entirety of the page aloud, in a clear, crisp voice.

"I, Sendoa, Warrior King of the Sovereign Kingdom of Ardenia, claim the following to be my last will and testament. I decree that, upon my untimely death, my daughter, Princess Amarande of the Sovereign Kingdom of Ardenia, is until her marriage named regent of the kingdom in my stead.

"If Princess Amarande should be incapacitated, pass to the stars along with me or before her marriage and the end of regency, I decree that my right hand, General Koldo, should be named regent and protector of the Sovereign Kingdom of Ardenia.

"These wishes are unusual, of that I am aware, though I make them of sound mind and body and with the best interests of Ardenia at heart. I believe any other route would result in the end of our beloved kingdom. If the climate on the continent were something other than its current state, I would wish that my daughter rule without marriage as a prerequisite. I have long thought to garner support to change this unfortunate law, but believe perhaps even making such a simple request of the current ruling body would leave me ripe for assassination."

Joseba paused for a moment and then said, in a much more timid tone, "That is it. Simply a signature and a date—summer, nine years ago."

The young councilor flipped the page around as if to prove it— and Koldo's attention settled on the king's signature and the numbers comprising the date.

Almost exactly a week after Sendoa's meeting with the Warlord.

The king had asked Koldo to marry him yet again that week. And, still raw from seeing her son in the flesh, and in the Warlord's possession, she'd said no. Again. As always.

"Let me see that!" Satordi spit. He plucked it from Joseba's hands. The lead councilor devoured the page for a long moment as he reread every word more than once, eyes combing the knife-slash script.

Satordi dropped the parchment as if it were hot—and Garbine slid it her way with a gloved hand as the lead councilor sputtered. "Sendoa may have aimed to prevent war with this declaration, but it will start one. No one will allow it. No one."

Koldo leaned forward, that anger within her rising again. "Why *must* we let them allow it? It was his wish and it contradicts no Sand and Sky legislation, or decree. He meant to go around the bureaucracy and he did."

Satordi shook his head. "Regency by definition is not permanent."

"It is permanent if we state it is permanent." Koldo stood and snatched the paper from Garbine's hands, dangling in front of the council. "Sendoa declared it is permanent and so it is permanent. Do you dare defy our king?"

Satordi flung a frustrated gesture in Koldo's direction. "I will defy him if it means *war*. Something you should care very much about, General. Do you have the soldiers to protect our borders in a long, protracted attack from three sides, the Torrent—because someone will use it—and the sea?"

"No."

"That is what I thought." Satordi took back the paper. "Our king meant well, but the best thing we can do is to do as is customary. Marry off our princess so that she may access her power and hope for the best."

"There is nothing *customary* about a kingdom with a sole female heir." Koldo flung a hand right back at the man. "There has not been a situation like this in a thousand years. You are putting our princess to the gallows. War may begin simply with her choice."

Satordi was unmoved.

"We will make the choice for her. Weigh the options. Do what is best for the kingdom. Stave off war."

Koldo shook her head. "And what if one of our union kingdoms murdered our king to set this into motion? What then? Sendoa claimed it in his own words—he believed it to be a very good possibility or he would have asked for a change in law. He knew his situation could mean his death. Just as I suspected."

"You are right, General Koldo. But it cannot be undone. All we can do is mitigate it." Now Satordi made eye contact. "And you must prepare in case we don't. Conscription at a faster rate. Promotions. Reinforcements."

After a long pause, Koldo nodded. As much as she did not like any of this, he was right.

But that was not all that must be mitigated. "And what do we do until she's wed? She will not accept any of this. She will want an investigation. To challenge the law. She will challenge any regent you choose—"

"Would she challenge you?" Garbine asked. Koldo's attention snapped to the old woman, completely taken off guard by her question. The councilor continued. "If we made you regent, until she's married, would she object, General?"

"Over any of you? No. But how would that be better? How would that protect Ardenia from what our king feared? Or the princess?"

"It wouldn't," Joseba answered. "But given the circumstances, you must concur this is our best hope."

Koldo laid eyes on the young councilor, not much older than the princess in question. He could barely look her in the eye in return. "Hope is not a plan."

"General, I agree," Satordi said, smoothing Sendoa's last will and testament against the heavy polished wood of the table, "but in this case, hope may be all we've got."

Sendoa had a plan.

He always had a plan.

And though General Koldo hated to go against his wishes with every fiber of her being, she knew deep down they were right.

The status quo, no matter how unusual it was on their end, would be the best scenario to avoid the end of Ardenia.

But the general knew how to make a plan, too.

CHAPTER 53

AMARANDE sat with her father's last will and testament in her shaking fingers for several minutes. Koldo did not prod. Instead, she kept her attention on their surroundings, tracking movement. Looking for trouble. All the things she was trained to do.

After a long moment, Amarande finally spoke. "Father wanted me to be queen, but knew it could not happen peacefully."

Koldo shook her head. "Not with the makeup of the continent, no."

"And so he made me regent of my own kingdom? But the council did not believe that wise?" Of course they wouldn't—this was the most easy-to-understand piece of it all. Satordi should rot. "And you agreed?"

The general shifted, setting her own back against the wheel of the cart. Ula had not yet returned, nor had Luca, and though the night had become much quieter, Koldo's eyes roved the darkness once more before she leaned in, voice low.

"I agreed because I knew bucking the laws as written would mean war. What I didn't know was that it would happen anyway. Like this—three kings dead, two queens standing. And make no mistake, Geneva considers herself queen. She is Queen Mother only in name. She defies Ferdinand's suggestions at every turn."

"You did not account for that."

"No."

It was equally likely that much of Geneva's confidence came from the power she had tangentially in the Torrent. She would have reacted poorly to her puppet announcing her intentions for power so publicly at the door of what Geneva was attempting to make a legitimate seat of power.

Amarande did not agree with the council on many things, but she did wonder perhaps if knowing what Geneva had been up to all these years would have an effect on the amount of contact they gave her with their new king.

"No," Koldo repeated. "I did not account for that or for other surprises that came later. I did not account for the kidnapping of Luca to sway your hand. I did not account for your disappearance. I did not account for Geneva's announcement that she was bringing Ferdinand home. I did not account for the council actually moving forward with her plan." The general drew in a shaky breath. "I spent my life winning battles on my brawn, and avoiding them altogether as much as possible with my brain, and I'm afraid I have let you down. I have let my son down. And I have let Sendoa down."

Amarande's head spun with the facets here—all the sides of the diamond, just as her father had explained with so much relish. Every side reflected something new—a new motivation, point of view, decision, lie, truth.

"You did not answer my questions earlier," Amarande said, finally, quietly. "Did Father know about Ferdinand?" She gestured to her father's map. "Even though he knew Geneva was Warlord and planned to overtake her? With Luca. Yes? Why?"

Koldo smiled sadly. "Your father did not know about Ferdinand. If he knew I was pregnant, he never let on. When it became something I could no longer disguise, I feigned injury during the Divide Conflict, and returned to the Itspi to hide."

"Why didn't you tell him? Then? Or after? He loved you. He could not help without knowing."

"I was too afraid of what would happen. To Sendoa. To you. And so I never said anything. Not when my son was stolen away the night your mother disappeared. Not when the first letter from her arrived." Letters, of course. Blackmail. "I was in such disbelief that he was still alive, it felt like a reward for my silence. If I spoke it into the air, it felt as if he'd be taken from me again. I couldn't let that happen."

"When did you find out she was here? If you knew she'd become the Warlord, couldn't you have rescued him as you rescued me?"

"I didn't know where she'd gone, not until we visited the Warlord's camp." She nodded at the will. "The week that will was written, I was with your father when he met with the Warlord. As I waited for him, I saw a boy who had to be my son running the grounds and trying to push into the Warlord's tent. It was obvious that she was hiding in the caravan. And when Sendoa left his meeting with slashes across his cheeks and news that we would no longer pursue relations with the Torrent, I knew she was not simply the Warlord's guest; she was the Warlord herself. The title had passed."

Amarande could not picture any of this. "And he just let her go? Why? People accused him of her murder . . . she was already doing terrible things to maintain and grow her power. And yet he walked away? Let her cut him? I just . . . why did it take him so long to mount a war? He had Luca; he knew her identity; he had his army, you . . ."

Koldo sighed, heavily. "It's hard to believe now, but this road started when Geneva acted to save your father's life."

Amarande pressed the heels of her hands into her eyes. "You have to be kidding me."

"Your mother has done many terrible things in her life, but your father lived and so did you because of a brave choice she made."

"And just when I was beginning to wish she were dead."

Koldo placed a hand on Amarande's cheek. "The story is this. King Domingu had long had designs to make all of the Sand and Sky his. He'd tried many times, in various ways." The princess lifted her head. "This is part of the reason your father decided to build such an army. The goal was to protect the continent in general, but behind closed doors it was to protect it from Domingu."

This did not surprise the princess. It probably wouldn't surprise anyone on the continent old enough to name their kingdoms.

"And so the old king found a way—using his extensive web of family connections." Koldo took a deep breath. She was never one for lengthy speeches, in any capacity. "The plan was to install a family member in each castle. And, when everyone was in place, commit coordinated regicide in every palace but the Aragonesti. Every king, queen, child—gone. No one left standing except Domingu and his family."

"Wait. My mother—?"

"Yes. She was assigned to kill your father."

Amarande's mouth opened. Closed. Opened again. "And he still married her?"

"He did not know until the wedding night. He thought choosing a bride from Basilica would provide cover for Ardenia from Domingu's clear greed. He was wrong—and lucky Geneva still felt guilt and shame at sixteen. She told him the whole plan—who had been assigned to what castle, the timeline, the endgame."

This plan was indeed pure Domingu—more diplomatic than stabbing your brother in the back, but no less diabolical. "Inés, too?"

Koldo nodded. "Yes. She is a very distant cousin, and was part of the plot, too. Your father was sure she went through with it years later when King Louis-David fell ill and lingered in poor health for so long. She always had the means, and a decade after the plan was foiled she went through with it anyway."

Inés's words in the bath chamber in the hours before the wedding hammered through Amarande's brain. *So many opportunities to push a new regime into motion with one forgettable, yet fatal, interaction.* Inés had been speaking of her father's death, but perhaps that thought had driven everything she'd done for nearly twenty years.

Amarande's mind pulled back to her father's actions. "What does that have to do with the Torrent?"

Koldo nodded. "When his efforts to warn the other monarchs did not work, and no one warmed to the idea of starting a war with Basilica, King Sendoa determined a more radical approach: revolution."

"But . . . why Torrence? Why not Basilica itself? Cut off at the head?"

"The Kingdom of Torrence had been suffering of late, drought and tariffs destroying the economy. The people were not pleased, and the king was distracted by his new wife and a baby on the way. In a word, it was weak. Something that could be made an example without much effort."

"Sendoa set up the revolution." They both looked up to find Ula. The pirate was empty-handed save for her dagger. No Taillefer then. "The resistance told us that your king started it. Supported the leader, and then let him reign. It is true, then?"

Koldo nodded. "Yes. He sent me to find the right leader to support, someone who could make all the right noises, instigate enough instability to create a template for all rebels in each kingdom, to both freeze Domingu's plan and also develop enough natural fissures that it would be impossible for one ruler to take hold. I found him a man named Jericho Talmage."

Amarande squeezed her eyes closed. "The first Warlord."

"There have been four if you count the one who is ash," Ula said, jerking a thumb over her shoulder to the pit.

"Yes. But several things went wrong." Koldo's voice was strong but low. "Talmage was only supposed to create opposition; instead, he built a coup. He was never supposed to kill the royal family, burn the castle, install his own government. We gave him power and he went too far. This is what I mean about not following Sendoa's plans."

Amarande's breath caught—of all her father's tenets, there was none that fit this. All the pithy quotes of striking first, and preparing, and not underestimating your opponent did not matter at all if those who stood with you had their own agenda.

Ula made to move. "Perhaps we should retire from the open for this discussion? They've got an officers' tent set up; I am supposed to take you there and work on your arm. Luca will meet us."

CHAPTER
54

❧⚭❧

NEARLY seventeen years of planning and the first major battle in the effort to restore the Kingdom of Torrence was over within a handful of hours. A combination of events had gone in favor of the rebels.

The element of surprise.

The Warlord's very public death.

And the fact that so many of her followers did not want to be with her at all. They knew exactly why they had been called in by the newly installed Warlord: their bodies a buffer between her and whatever the resistance had planned. They knew the rebels had their champion. They knew an attack was coming. And they knew their role: shields.

Well before midnight, Luca stood among his men, Tala by his side. The fire pit had not been fed in hours, and yet it still burned, lighting up the trampled remains of the encampment. Healers were out, doing what they could, and a second wave of resistance members combed through the tents now, providing food and water to anyone in need. They were all one now. At daylight, they would see just what that looked like.

"Those who ran will not be hunted," Luca announced, as loudly as possible. His voice had started to go, water and rest needed. Beltza the black wolf nuzzled his side. "We will not begin this campaign with fear."

In a perfect world, this would be the only true battle on the journey to reinstate the Kingdom of Torrence. The rest of the fight coming with words—changing minds, sharing plans, gaining support.

Luca knew he could not control what others would do. Just that moment someone might be watching the stars with the seeds of prolonged resistance on their mind. But if he had his druthers, this would be the only blood shed.

"To your assignments, and your rest. Good night, my friends. Hitz ematen dizut."

The men responded in kind, and Luca turned away, Tala by his side, Beltza leading the way toward the camp tent the resistance had procured and guarded for Luca. Amarande waited for him there, and he'd been informed she'd tried to push past the guards at least once—they were there to protect her as much as keep her from joining the fray, injured and unarmed.

"My Otsakumea, by morning, we must tell the entire group of the Warlord's deception," Tala said with a long sigh. This man was not one to enjoy his victory with so much to be done. The information they'd learned about the faux transfer of power had rattled him, to be sure. "Those who toiled in the shadow of the Warlord for so long deserve to know that the snake has not been cut off at the head."

Luca touched the man's shoulder. The battle was catching up with him now—he could no longer hide his limp, his stitches were stiff and inflamed, and everything from his skin to the hair atop his head ached. "Yes, and by morning we will have a plan. For Geneva, for Inés and her army. For all of it. Rest, Tala. You need it and deserve it. Your plan worked better than we could have imagined."

The old man ran a hand through his salt-and-pepper hair. At his side, the black wolf sat back on her haunches. Waiting.

"How can I rest when my mind churns with the start of a new plan? Our people are tired; they may not be ready yet to face down the Itspi. It worries me so that we must do this again. And at the home that raised you—I know you care for Ardenia. It will be—"

"It will be fine." Luca squeezed the man's shoulder and then removed his hand. "I know you do not trust Ardenia and this new information does not help. But I need you to trust my princess—"

"My Otsakumea, I feel badly about your princess. I must apologize."

"Tell her tomorrow, Tala. After we're successful." Spent, the leader nodded, relenting. Luca smiled. "She will find a way for us. I will find a way for us."

CHAPTER
55

THE princess, the Otsakumea, the general, and the pirate convened in the officers' tent set up on the outskirts of the encampment. Eight pro-Otxoa soldiers manned the exterior perimeter. Inside, the world as they knew it lay in pieces atop blankets and flickering under candle lamps.

The fingerprints of dead kings littered it all.

Domingu's greedy attempt at mass regicide leading to a false revolution that became a real one.

A prince, orphaned by said revolution, being hidden in plain sight in Sendoa's kingdom, the best he could do for the family he helped murder.

Then, in a second act, a queen stealing the king's bastard son, abandoning her family, and raising him for her own and becoming the leader of the revolution her abandoned husband started after she refused to kill him.

And now, after more calculated deaths, they were left with two women on thrones they'd stolen via conquest rather than blood, facing off against each other for the continent.

Unless they were able to stop it.

"I do not pretend to understand the whims of royals, but *what in the stars is wrong with you people?*" Ula asked after a quiet moment, brows tucked together, as she rethreaded a needle to address the princess's wounds. She'd already cleaned and repaired some of Luca's stitches, gone ragged in the fighting. "Someone should've sunk a dagger in Domingu's heart twenty years ago and circumvented this mess."

"If not Domingu, it would be someone else. In fact, it *is* someone else," Amarande answered through clenched teeth.

Amarande was balled up on the tent rugs, held still by Luca's embrace. Her prisoner's tunic was sliced open, half her arm stitched as Ula again sterilized the needle over the flame. The wound from the prison cart cut her open from the bone tip of her shoulder down to the top of her wrist. The upper part was a violent wreck, and they'd agreed to attempt to keep the stitches above the elbow. Amarande swallowed and rushed out the words while she could. "It just took twenty years for the chips to fall and it happens to be two women vying for the end of the patriarchy."

Luca dropped a kiss on Amarande's shoulder and tightened his grip as Ula prepared to dive again into the princess's arm. "It would be poetic if not for the fact that unless these two powerful women kill each other, they're coming for us next."

He was not wrong.

Koldo stood and began a measured pace about one side of the tent, her soldier's mind silently churning.

"Hold still," Ula commanded Amarande. "I can't with this shaking."

"I'm not trying to," she insisted, grabbing a fistful of the rug that had been laid out for them. Ula had offered a stick, but she'd not taken it, wanting the chance to participate in the conversation. "One would think the amount of alcohol in my bloodstream from the disinfecting portion of this would make this easier."

"If you're asking to be knocked out, it's too late."

Luca leaned in farther, his whole body a vise, the strength he'd earned in the Itspi's stables doing what it could to keep Amarande still. "You are really terrible at being injured, Ama. It doesn't suit you."

His thumb brushed the ragged linen on her injured hand. "What happened here?"

Luca was trying to distract her. Despite the pain, Amarande forced out the words, "My. Brother."

Luca smoothed the gauze back down. "He must be a little like you, then."

"A. Little."

When the last stitch was finally tied off, Amarande forced her jaws apart. "I am no good at being injured mostly because I am terrible at being still. I cannot be stationary when a woman mad with power is bearing down on Ardenia with a threefold army. I may not be queen, but I must protect my people."

Koldo shook her head. "The timing is disastrous. Our regiments at the borders will not make it to Ardenia fast enough to beat the ships. And those border regiments are likely engaged with the soldiers who have been stationed there since the funeral."

Stars, yes. War may already have begun. Two-against-one at the crossroads between Ardenia, Basilica, Myrcell. Bile licked at Amarande's throat.

Koldo continued to lay out Ardenia's weaknesses with her usual military precision. "Based on when Inés left, she will likely arrive at the Port of Ardenia before sundown tomorrow, even with all those ships and unfavorable winds."

"And if the winds are favorable?" Amarande asked.

"Dawn. Ships can march all night."

A few hours from then.

Amarande chewed her lip, feeling just a twinge of guilt about what she was about to say next. "If only we had Taillefer as bait."

"That is the only way I'd put up with him," Ula spit, shoving her medical implements a little too hard into her kit. "Looked everywhere for that blasted blond creep. No sign of that psychopathic scoundrel or the man in Pyrenee purple who retrieved him from the prison cart."

The princess sighed. "We know where he is. Either the guard is delivering him to Inés's feet or he is going on his own accord to fight for the power he feels she's stolen from him."

Koldo did not lose a hitch in her renewed steps. "If he's truly disowned, the second son has no power, no matter the tantrum he throws."

Amarande shook her head. "One would assume. But with Taillefer assume nothing." She waved her good arm and stood, feeling better on her feet than she had in hours. "Let us forget him. He is the key to Inés, but we cannot even think of confronting her without first confronting my mother." Amarande caught eyes with the general. "And Ferdinand."

"I will handle Ferdinand," Koldo insisted, as smoothly as she would take an order. No one dared object. "The princess is right. Ardenia must come first. It will be much easier to defend from the inside."

"Yes, except my mother and brother have told the entire Sand and Sky I am dead to pave the way for his coronation—"

"Princess, to be fair, your brother wanted no part in that. He wished to tell the people the truth, as he told you." Koldo was not one to interrupt. Here, she did so with unwavering attention, nearly pleading for Amarande to understand her son was not part of the lie.

Amarande accepted Koldo's defense of Ferdinand with a nod. "I believe that, but his affection for the truth will not protect me any more than it will protect you, General. If Geneva finds it most convenient that either of us are dead, every blade but Ferdinand's will be drawn in an attempt to make it so."

"She wanted me to return you alive."

"She's my mother; she's supposed to say that," Amarande answered, blood hot in her cheeks. "But we all know it is clearly a much larger task to properly hide me away alive than it would be trotting out my body and blaming the madwoman who has come to conquer." Amarande laced Luca's fingers within hers. "Not to mention what she would do to Luca once she is finished with me."

Koldo rolled her shoulders. "I could return you alone, as ordered. She will not know we are on the same side. We gain entry, seek audience, and then—Princess, I do not mean to disregard your very complicated feelings for her—dispose of the Queen Mother."

The heaviness in Koldo's clinical delivery was the only indication that the general had been mulling *disposing* of the woman for years. It was the cleanest thing to do, and yet even the idea of it triggered the image of Renard in Amarande's mind. Decisions like that could not be undone.

Luca gently kissed the back of Amarande's entwined hand. "General, with all due respect, I'm not sitting this one out. If Amarande is going to Ardenia, I am going by her side."

"Then we fight." Ula drew in a deep breath. "This woman is not just your mother. She is the Warlord. We have the army we need to topple the castle."

Yes. Of course.

Luca and his people had won the battle, but they had not won the war. Not yet.

Luca nodded. "I planned to tell the resistance fighters in the morning. They will know, and they will want to confront her."

"They *need* to confront her. *You need* to confront her, Luca." Ula jabbed Luca straight in the shoulder. "The Otxoa cannot be restored if the Warlord's power is still viable in any way."

Luca jabbed her right back. "Then we storm the castle."

But Koldo wasn't convinced. The general halted her pacing and turned to them, every inch the woman who had been by the Warrior King's side for more than half her life.

"It is incredible what the rebels did last night, Luca. I do not want to diminish that success."

He drew in a deep breath. "But?"

"But they are not professional soldiers. They benefited from long-term planning and the element of surprise. We don't have either advantage here."

"What if we arrive at dark?"

Koldo shook her head. "Even if we gathered them to march right at this moment, we'd be approaching in complete daylight, as slow as they are. And if we put it off for a nighttime arrival, we might be too late and meet *both* Geneva and Inés."

Right. The general's experience was invaluable here. She understood not only the timing but also the psychology. Koldo was, as always, the best possible person to have at one's back.

Amarande's attention pooled on the parchment at the center of the tent. Her father, so wise, had to have the answer here. Somewhere. Yet after several minutes, his tenets stayed silent in her brain, exhaustion worming its way into her second wind.

But then instead of her father's voice came his actions.

"We stay the course."

The moment the words were out of her mouth, a new energy ignited within her belly.

Yes. This was right.

"The Warlord sent a letter via caracara to Geneva telling her she was coming with me in tow. She wanted to beat Inés there, which means she planned to arrive to Ardenia by midday tomorrow at the latest. So, we stay the course—and have *the Warlord* deliver me to my mother."

Amarande caught eyes with everyone in the room. She squatted to Ula and tipped the girl's chin up to hers. Reading her face shape. Her height. Osana would've been better, but yes, this might work.

"Ula, how would you feel about donning a tyrant's clothes?"

Amarande expected the girl to balk. Sigh. Or put up some other form of a fight. Instead, she simply asked, "Do I get to keep my sword?"

"I don't see why not."

Koldo's face puckered. "It is a good idea, Princess; it is. But Geneva handpicked this Warlord. Even if the rest of us manage to disguise ourselves well enough to appear as guards, which is doubtful at best, *she* will know Ula is an imposter the instant she opens her mouth."

Now came the Warrior King's advice, perfect and true—straight from her own line of thoughts rather than a menu of tenets.

Amarande grinned. "Which is why we must make the first mark."

CHAPTER
56

❦

TAILLEFER had not imagined the end would be like this. Covered in blood that might be his. Might be Captain Nikola's. Might be someone else's.

It didn't matter, of course.

He was still alive and mostly upright, lashed to Nikola's torso and manning the reins from behind, adding blood he knew was his to the mess that was both his shirt and the captain's uniform with each sputtering cough. That was the blood he should be concerned about—the kind that signaled a festering problem from within and grew darker with each new wheeze and hack.

But no. He had much larger things on his mind.

As the sun peeked over the eastern horizon of the Port of Ardenia, the stolen horse they were riding was pulled to a pause. Taillefer read the scene below like a memory because it was exactly as he'd pictured it.

At least fifty warships crowded the mouth of the harbor. It wasn't a full armada—too many soldiers were inland, protecting the borders—but it was still impressive and was designed to be. Just the size alone was meant to be a warning shot in intimidation.

A single ship among them had docked, flying a triptych flag—Mountain Lion, Bear, Shark. But the body of the ship was pure Pyrenee. His mother, awaiting entree from Ardenia. The gangplank was lowered, guards with their eyes on the ribbon of road that ran down from the Itspi.

She'd likely sent her demands already, hoping to win this war on intimidation alone, accept a quick surrender, and move on.

Taillefer drew in as deep a breath as his damaged lung would allow.

It would not be that easy.

"Up there with you." It could've been a question, but the captain was bleeding from too many places to add the extra uptick in his voice.

"Yes, yes, up there," Taillefer answered, dismissively. To his mother. Yes.

The pair picked their way down the swinging switchbacks to the harbor, the horse moving fast despite the long ride through the night from the Torrent to the eastern edge of Ardenia. Taillefer hung on to the reins as Nikola listed with each turn, the captain's massive body barely anchored in the stirrups.

"You're almost to your queen. Straighten up, man. I will not be delivered by a captain who is looking less than professional."

He jabbed the captain in the side and Nikola's chin shot up, his back wrenching from a concave slump to a rigid shoulders-back arc of pain. The soldier grunted.

"There. Was that so hard? Easier to make your announcements without your voice projecting at our ankles."

The soldiers atop the gangplank tensed at the advance of a rider. Expecting Ardenia, of course, but then, upon closer inspection, receiving the shock of familiar faces aboard a pilfered pony, black in color rather than the typical Pyrenee white. When escaping a massive battle, one must take the horse one can get.

"Captain Nikola?" one asked, squinting and leaning forward, the dawn light winking off the gold pieces on his aubergine uniform. Of course Taillefer's mother would only trust Pyrenee men in these early hours. "Is that you?"

"Aye." Taillefer jabbed him in the side again, and the captain straightened further, planned words on his lips. "Queen Inés ordered me to deliver Taillefer, disowned prince of the Kingdom of Pyrenee, to her, and I have done so. I must have an audience with her at once. Permission to board?"

"Yes, Captain," the men answered, making way.

The horse was nudged up the gangplank. The captain and his captive dismounted in a tangle together, Taillefer's arms wrapped about Nikola's torso, in a way that meant they moved as one, their weight oddly distributed in a shuffle and slide across the deck planks, toward the queen's quarters.

"Shall I fetch Medikua Aritza?" one of the soldiers asked the captain, concerned.

"Can she embalm a body? That is the real question," Taillefer answered, though the inquiry was not meant for him. He accentuated it with a shuddered cough, splattering the shiny deck with spots of his royal blood. The soldier took a full step back in mild horror—clearly this one had yet to see a battlefield. "Leave us be. The medikua will have much to do in time."

The soldiers gave them a wide berth after that, wrenching open the doors to the royal quarters. "My queen, Captain Nikola has arrived with the former prince."

From within, his mother's voice, laced with delight: "Oh, you're kidding!? What a surprise!"

Nikola and Taillefer entered as one, the prince hooked under the soldier's arms, grasping tightly to his body. The queen stood from where she'd been alone at a desk, discarding the parchments she'd been shuffling, and bustled over to shut the double doors herself. "Leave us, boys; we have much to talk about! Knock only if word arrives from the Itspi." She smiled back at the pair, her glacier-blue eyes cold with light. "Though this should not take long."

The doors clicked and Inés arced around the captain and his captive, who had not moved far from the threshold. "Captain, I will admit I thought you'd been unsuccessful. I'd resigned myself to it, and yet here you are, with my treasonous traitor of a son in your grasp. Obviously, having the princess, too, would have been preferable given the lever we're trying to pull, but when one expects nothing she cannot be disappointed with something." She set her eyes upon Taillefer. "And this one is certainly something."

"Hello, Mother. I've missed your backhanded compliments."

A smile flickered across her face. "I am glad you have, Taillefer, but I was engaged in conversation with Nikola."

"I know." With that answer, Taillefer straightened, all his weight on his own—and in moving his hand from where it had been hooked around Nikola's torso, twisted and removed a dagger from where it had been lodged in the soldier's liver for hours on end.

No longer held upright and lifeblood gushing from the punctured organ, the captain lurched and staggered. In one terrific sway, he crumpled to a heap. The candles stationed around the room sputtered and nearly extinguished at the gust of air generated by the falling body.

Taillefer tested the point of the blood-soaked blade on his finger, his eyes never leaving his mother. "It is truly a marvel of precision in weaponry that he did not bleed out hours ago. This blade was the perfect blockage."

The prince reached behind him, barring the doors with the pull of the crossbar lock.

The queen began to back away, toward her desk. She likely had a weapon in there—perhaps a letter opener or possibly an actual dagger—but Taillefer had eyes only for the chemical warfare lined up in neat rows of vials in open-top wooden crates behind her.

"If you've come here to kill me, it won't work. One scream, and a hundred men will rush those doors. They'll come down the flue if they have to. They will come and you'll be dead."

"What does it matter if I've already succeeded in killing you?"

He advanced with the knife, and she skated two steps back—knocking into her desk, the candles there wobbling in their glass cages. Still, her chin remained impossibly high, and Inés looked down her nose at him, though she stood a head shorter than her son.

"Taillefer, I don't know what you think you're getting at, but no matter the end game, you have no claim to Pyrenee—not upon my death, not upon your blood, not upon anything." She leaned on the edge of the desk now, as if she'd meant to bump it. "You are no longer an heir. No longer a prince. No longer anyone of consequence. Simply put, my boy, you, like the Sand and Sky, are mine."

His favorite sly grin slipped across his face. "You have named me disowned, but the only way that works for treason is with a trial. Believe me, I read up on the laws before I fled the Bellringe."

"Anything can happen with the right people in the room." Inés tossed her arms about, showing off the space. "It happened right here, you know. The councilors and I, the paperwork, the proof—technically it was simply the contract we pulled from the captured pirate, rotting away in our dungeons. But I knew when none of the rest of them did that we were actually surrounded by hundreds more pieces of evidence." She did not need to nod or wave or gesture in any way to the vials. "Did you think I would be so stupid or so blind by ambition that I wouldn't question *why* Domingu requested the contents of your workshop as dowry?"

Taillefer smiled. Held off the cough rising in his blood-addled lung. "Mother, of course I knew you would question it. I just did not know how you would use that information. I am often called clever, but *you*, letting Domingu's own plan play out and twisting it your way? That was a stroke of genius."

She held up parchment pieces from her desk. None of it signed, the top note was the last one.

The tiger has fled, the mountain lion is dead, the wolf has found his head.

"I'll admit I did not expect compliments on the murder of your *advisor*." Inés waved it in front of him. "I'm willing to bet you sent this to the Warlord, too. Playing all sides. No matter how much you admired Domingu, you knew he was using you to get what he wanted. Poison in his hands. Poison in Sendoa's drink. Poison in mine. Poison, poison, poison, from a boy who was more than pleased to do anything the old king said." She lifted a brow. "Though I'm assuming having Amarande kill Renard was your idea, not his—more creative and painful. That is your hallmark, is it not?"

Taillefer didn't answer. He didn't need to.

Inés dropped the paper along with the rest in a cascade of proof of his relationship with Domingu, dating to his father's funeral. When one ambitious younger brother took aside a devastated child and told him about all the things a younger brother could be. What he could do.

Far from his thoughts, Inés laughed. "Did you think I would not recognize the penmanship I'd paid for with that trollop of a governess?"

"Do not speak ill of Alisea; she did more to raise me than you ever did."

"She raised something, all right. I believe it is my right as a scorned wife to use that term when discussing the woman who slept with my husband," Inés answered as if Taillefer did not wield a knife.

"That was no reason to kill him."

His mother smiled tightly. Changed the subject. "Nevertheless, compliments will not make an ally of me this late in the game." She arched a brow. "Did it work on Amarande? That's where you were, wasn't it? When Nikola found you? Trying to pull off the marriage your brother could not and steal the throne from under my nose."

"The throne you *stole* from Father," Taillefer spit. "You poisoned him daily."

"You have no proof."

"Ah, but I do have an encyclopedic knowledge of what every plant and potion on this damn continent will do to a body. Sanded brimstone in tea, was it? Daily for two years? That would do it."

Her smile widened. "You're very lucky I waited so long to murder him. You wouldn't be here if I'd followed *your mentor's* plan." She let that hang, relishing the flicker of surprise across his face. "But keep at it, boy. Though, just like everything else here, you won't win."

Taillefer lunged at her then, dagger charging for any piece of exposed skin.

But that cough he'd suppressed could no longer wait. His blade bobbled, and his step faltered, his entire body shuddering uncontrollably. She spun out of his trajectory, and Taillefer and his dagger caromed into the desk. The blade skittered away, onto the floor, bouncing off built-in bookshelves and angling toward the queen.

Taillefer gripped the desk, blood dribbling heavily down his chin, clotting on the papers, and drew a deep, wheezing breath. And when he saw his mother again, she held aloft the dagger.

His eyes followed as Inés and the weapon crossed to the crates of vials, which were neatly stacked and so high they brushed the bodice of her dress. Domingu didn't need much to poison the wine at the wedding—three vials at most. More than a hundred sat there calmly, his fire swamp and concentration of hemlock both. There was enough there to kill every last soul on this continent with the right mechanism. A good amount in a popular water source. Wine casks. Sagardoa. Any number of sauces popular throughout the region. The vehicles were as endless as they were unobtrusive.

"There are only two ways this ends for you, my traitorous, treasonous, disowned-but-clever scion. You die, or you wish you were dead."

Taillefer swallowed and righted himself. There was no letter opener on the desk. No seal stamp or anything else heavy he could use against that dagger.

"If you survive me now, if you survive whatever internal damage you've clearly acquired, I will lock you away in one of my castles—honestly, whichever I have to visit the least, because I'm sure your suffering will be quite distracting—and you will make more of this. You make the antidotes, too," she announced. "You will churn out vials until you keel over or ingest one of your concoctions yourself simply because you want out."

Taillefer wheezed.

Satisfaction sparked in his mother's eyes. "I do see myself in you. And for that, I cannot let you succeed. You are less experienced, yes, but still very, very dangerous."

A grin slipped across her face, and for once Taillefer saw himself staring back—fox-like, ambitious, unforgiving. Standing in front of his hard work, toiled upon in the shadow of his grief for his father.

Knuckles blanching, Taillefer gripped the sturdy scrolls and swoops of the solid wooden desk and pulled himself to standing, careful to avoid elbowing her candles off the top. He brushed the blood from his mouth but only served to smear it.

He was dying, yes. But he'd come too far for this to be the end.

"One thing about being the creator of the fabulous tinctures at your back, Mother, is that I know more about what is in those vials than anyone else." His eyes were as cold as hers. "And one thing I know about the liquid is that it is highly flammable."

With all the strength he had left, Taillefer tossed both the desk candles at the vials.

The glass surrounding the candles shattered in a hail of shards, hitting the corners of the wooden crates SMASH SMASH—the sound shoving Inés out of frozen disbelief and into action.

As the fire caught, she and the dagger spun away from the crates, hands thrust up to protect her regal head as she dashed for the door.

But to get there, she had to pass the desk—and Taillefer was ready.

He popped the cork of a vial hidden in his tunic. It was half-used, and his hands were unprotected. But he didn't care.

And, as he splashed the remaining vial of fire swamp on the woman who bore him, he thought of Amarande's horror in her prison cell. *You would purposefully use that on a human?*

The right one. Yes. He regretted Luca—a little. But he would never regret this.

The bright green liquid caught Inés mid-turn, droplets hitting her from the point of her chin, down the side of her neck, her chest, all the way to her kneecap. It burned straight through the silken aubergine gown she wore, through her skin, through her capacity to scream.

She fell almost as hard as Nikola had, dissolving with a thump and gag as the tincture went to work on her windpipe.

Taillefer furiously rubbed at his hand, spotting with smoking holes from the tiny droplets that had sprayed back upon him with the thrust of the vial. He gathered himself as her movements began to slow, crossing to the crates and stamping out the flames, the damage minimal.

When he turned back to her, she was only shivering now. Not really breathing.

The tincture had dissolved the skin at her throat, the meat of her exposed, veins and capillaries burned back like parchment blackening and curling in flame before vanishing altogether.

It was a mishmash of exposure, the very inner workings of this woman who called herself queen, revealed for all the stars to see, her beautiful exterior gone. The blackness within bare in the light.

Taillefer bent and peered into the single eye facing him, the other swallowed under hair and pinned to the floor. It watched him, unblinking, but still full of life.

"Mother, you should know by now that I lie as easily as I tell the truth."

She couldn't answer, of course. Her voice taken along with the air from her windpipe, all exposed. If he'd had the time, it would make fascinating research.

But he did not have the time or the tools.

As the light faded in that one brilliant eye, Taillefer saw her out with an exact replica of the smile she'd given him. Clever, confident, malicious. It was fitting that this was the last thing she would ever see.

"I only wish your death had been as slow and painful as what you did to Father. Rot in the stars, Queen."

CHAPTER
57

❧

THEY looked the part.

An efficient little group of the Warlord, her captive, and two scarf-swaddled guards. The kind of party that could travel swiftly, boldly. An entire army plausibly following in their wake.

Much of this was because of Koldo, who had two decades of experience in the art of this. Sweeping in under the cover of darkness. Navigating hairpin turns. Traveling like a grain of sand in the wind—quiet, nearly invisible, blink-and-miss-it kind of movement.

But, as the sun shimmered over the horizon and the spires of the Itspi were somewhere straight ahead, their clothing became just as crucial as their on-a-mission, breakneck pace.

Koldo, in the suntan-brown tunic and tights, cuffs at the wrists in leather matching the waist scabbard for her sword and dagger. Ula, swathed in the Warlord's silken clothes and head covering—chin high, determined, obviously important, even when seen through the haze of dark before dawn. And Luca, dressed in the brimmed hat and sun-bleached canvas of all the Warlord's bandits, a handkerchief around his neck. He transported the prisoner, strapped to him with rope in much the same way he'd been transported by Ula not long ago.

To play her part, they'd given Amarande clean prisoner garb to go along with the deceptively secure knots of rope at her wrists. She clung more tightly to Luca's back—mindful of the wound he had there—than any of the rope clung to her. A quick twist of the wrists, and they would fall away. Better still, a dagger sat in her boot, an easy draw for her practiced fingers. Despite appearances, Amarande felt more in control and more certain than she had during any other time in this long and winding journey.

The plan wasn't perfect, of course. Not like something her father would conceive, but it cleverly deployed their resources and an element of surprise, and it was what they had. That was not nothing.

What they did not have was rest. But that would come soon. In victory or in death.

There really wasn't much in between.

As the narrow road wound before them, shifting from sleepy gray to a russet-pocked beige, Amarande snuggled into the warmth of Luca's back, lifting her chin just enough to drop a kiss behind his ear. "There were times over the past few days when I was sure I'd reneged on my promise. That I wouldn't see you again soon. Not ever . . ."

Her words trailed off.

"I knew I would see you. You never abandon your promises, Ama. To me, to your people, to the stars. You will find a way."

Something heavy stuck in her throat. This—exactly this—was the manifestation of love Ula described in the Pyrenee tent that night, when Amarande's despair squatted on her chest as she stared down the turn her life had taken with surrender to Renard.

Do you know how many times he told us you'd come for him? How much faith he had—has—in you? I could nearly pluck his love for you out of the air and slice it up for dinner, it was so solid. He loves you and you love him—true love, simple as that.

Amarande's arms tightened around Luca's body, her cheek nuzzled to the broad warmth of his back. His heartbeat thrummed against her ear, a torch carried not only for her but now for an entire people. He'd always had to share her with the people of Ardenia, and now she would share him with the people of Torrence. He was no longer hers alone.

Destinies mirrored—hers needed saving; his needed building.

And though she wished to somehow untwine her heart's desires for him and her heart's desires for her people, it would not be possible to tease them apart.

Not now. Not ever. Not with who they were.

Perhaps that was why love so often did not fit into the royal equation. But if they succeeded, they could change that.

Once it was full light, she couldn't snuggle in like this. And so Amarande used the last moments she had. In subtle rotation, she pressed kisses anywhere she could reach. To his spine. His shoulder blade—one, and then the other. Up his neck. Again, behind the ear—one, two. She settled the curve of her throat over his shoulder, her chin coming to rest on his collarbone, parched lips at his ear.

"Luca, no matter what happens with my mother, with Inés, I love you. Please hear me when I say that if I fail, it wasn't that I did not love you enough. I love you more than anything in this world, even if I didn't say it until it was almost too late."

He reached up and cupped her head with his hand, fingers laced in the fall of her hair. Her cheek pressed against the side of his neck, the brim of his hat shrugged away—stupid thing. Her lips met his jawbone, her chest pressed against his spine, her own heart pounding against the double layers of fabric wedged between their skin.

"You didn't have to say it, Ama. I always knew. Even when I never thought I had a chance to say it back. I love you."

"Masks up. The castle looms." Koldo's voice was low and direct and sent Amarande jerking back and away from Luca, as if they'd already been spotted.

Ula and Koldo pulled the linen tighter to their faces, obscuring their eyes, which had been left bare for faster negotiation of the rocks and roots along the hairpin trails. Luca shrugged up the handkerchief at his neck, covering his nose and mouth—his eyes his only discernible feature.

Amarande bent forward and pressed one more kiss to the nape of his neck and then set herself back, so that only the insides of her bound arms touched him, a manufactured sliver of space between her torso and the swoop-and-curve of his back.

Dawn had spread into true morning now, the sky a vibrant blue canvas for the red spires of the Itspi. Amarande craned her neck to peer over Luca's shoulder at the first glimpse of her home. "It will be crawling with guards—new recruits for the king."

"The princess is correct," Koldo intoned. "The guards are novices, yes, but they have eyes. We will be spotted long before we reach the gates. I suspect Geneva has a rider prepared to greet us. From this moment forward, we must assume we are being watched."

The hourglass was now turned, sand pouring through, marking the time between this moment and when that first mark must be made. Luca had worked with resistance leaders to create waves of fighters, who would follow them. But even the first wave would not arrive until at least two hours after they did.

Thus, they had to assume they were facing this alone. Any aid would come late or not at all. At best, it would be to a triumphant victory. At worst, it would be a funeral march.

It was too much to ask, Amarande knew, for all of this to be hammered out in parley and negotiations. In verbal promises and then decrees, and the trial and imprisonment of her mother for the atrocities she'd committed as Warlord.

No. It started with blood. It would end with blood.

On the next hill, it became so much worse.

"Hold." Koldo's voice came crisply, sharply against the wind.

The party fell into line at the crest of an overlook, detailing not just the spires but the entirety of the rolling grounds of the Itspi. They were bathed in the unflinching sun of a new day, parched grasses and rocky grades stamped down with summer—and hundreds, perhaps thousands, of men and women in full garnet-and-gold regalia.

They stomped across the yard, grounds, arena. A cluster of them even ran drills in the meadow Luca and Amarande had long called theirs. These men and women lined the parapet of the wall ringing the Itspi, arrow quivers glittering in the sun. Pockets of them stood outside the entrance, far more in number and far more menacing than the green guards and closed gate Amarande met in the day before her brother's introduction and coronation.

Stars.

"That . . . is a much larger number of guards than we encountered days ago." Ula adjusted the linen about her face for a better look.

"Those aren't guards; those are soldiers." Amarande wished she were wrong.

"*A lot* of soldiers," Luca amended, glancing to Koldo for confirmation. "At least a regiment's worth."

Anger flashed about Koldo's stern features, jaw muscles flickering as she ground her teeth, her stare boring down the hill. "I told them not to recall my soldiers from the borders. Clearly they did anyway."

They meant Amarande's mother. Or Ferdinand acting on her behalf.

The Warlord always had her most trained soldiers surrounding her at all times, the strongest ring of protection a halo of her person, her tent, her carriage. Thus, this adjustment was in line with what Geneva would have been accustomed to in that role. And it was lucky, given Inés's approach by sea instead of land.

But from their point of view, this added protection presented a significant problem.

"I am suddenly feeling far less confident about our plan," Ula announced.

"Perhaps we wait until the resistance arrives," Luca offered. "All of it. Not simply the first wave."

Koldo shook her head. "No. They're on alert for Inés. See those clusters? They're forming parties to send into the countryside, on the lookout for any signs of movement from Inés."

Amarande swallowed. "They aren't just going to wait for her in the harbor?"

"Not when they know she can dock ships nearby and send a whole regiment on foot to create a helpful obstruction between the port and her arrival at the castle."

The small amount of time Amarande had spent in the council room over the last year had yielded some insight into her father's strategic mind, but not this. "What shall we do, Koldo?"

"What we don't do is our plan," Ula answered, out of turn. "See those archers? Ten arrows in my back the second I identify myself. Geneva didn't intend to negotiate; she intended to kill her puppet and gain her prize."

Ula was correct. Arrows would be coming for Koldo and Luca, too. The princess put the possibility of her being left standing at one-to-one. It depended greatly on the narrative Geneva and Ferdinand planned to deploy against Inés. Though Amarande very much doubted Inés would back off an invasion simply because Ardenia offered to extradite its fugitive princess.

Amarande bit her lip. "Okay, new plan. Koldo, these men and women would know you on sight, wouldn't they? They would listen to you, let us through, obey if you gave them a command?"

The wind kicked up as the general worked through the scenarios, her dark eyes searching the grounds. "Perhaps, but we have no way of knowing how they've been instructed by the Queen Mother, who recalled them. I do not put it past Geneva to name me a threat as easily as she might name you, Princess, if it is to her advantage and the king is not within earshot." She inhaled deeply. "I think perhaps our best course of action is through you, Princess. If you speak, they will listen."

"Koldo, they think I'm *dead*."

"Exactly." Koldo's tone remained even and direct, but now contained the power of confidence she'd clearly lacked during their earlier planning. "These are my soldiers. They attended the king's funeral before striking out for the borders. They know your face, your voice, your reputation. They will believe you when you confirm your identity, and know they've been lied to. It's imperfect, but if I can shelter Ferdinand from any ill will to come from this—"

"Shelter me from what, Mother?"

All eyes snapped to the sound of a new voice. And there, rounding the bend at the bottom of the hill, was the king himself.

CHAPTER
58

❧

STARS, he's a ghost.

For the second time on this journey, Luca had nearly the same thought. This time, seeing someone whose life he knew rather than someone whose end he'd given.

Luca stared down the hill at the boy on the horse, his lips falling open, no sound coming out. Amarande stiffened against him, the space between them erased. Her heart rattled against her rib cage in a fluttering cadence against his spine. The rhythm repetitive, and nearly words themselves. *Friend or foe? Friend or foe?*

Luca's own heart lurched simply in making eye contact with this boy. The spitting image of King Sendoa, twenty years younger. At first, Luca hadn't understood how Geneva had strode into the Itspi with this boy and managed to claim the kingdom and dispossess Amarande at the same time.

Now it was clear.

Luca knew what the councilors saw. What the people saw from the stands still warm from Sendoa's funeral. Who those soldiers saw when they'd been called to defend the Itspi.

Their king. Back. Anew. Here and safe, and protective, against all of the fear and uncertainty and change that Amarande's ascension to the throne might have wrought.

Luca's attention slid to Koldo. The boy's true mother. And before the stars and strangers, he'd called her that in the open.

"My king, as commanded, I have retrieved the princess," the general announced almost mechanically, as if an archer would strike her dead if she didn't follow the script.

They'd agreed that Koldo would deal with Ferdinand, but staring him down, this ghost of the tiger who prowled the grounds of his childhood, keeping him safe, planning his destiny, all the while bearing the guilt for destroying his family—it was much for Luca to take in.

The strap of linen covering Amarande's injured hand fluttered in the breeze. A reminder of what Ferdinand could do, even to someone as strong as her.

Luca's palm flattened across the hilt of his sword.

"I—Mother, please stop. It is unnecessary." Ferdinand's eyes swept about the group. "As an effort of good faith, please see who I've brought with me."

The boy king advanced, straight-backed and regal on a black stallion—Marcel, sibling to Amarande's beloved Mira. It was possible the boy knew this, and if not, the coincidence was stark. No cadre of guards flanked him. Rather, a thin rope ran around the bend, and within a few breaths another horse made the turn—Ana, the gray mare, with two riders smashed together atop a single saddle.

One, a head taller, all dark curls and burnished brown skin. The other, dark haired and petite.

Urtzi. Osana.

Both gagged, bound, and summarily led.

Luca's pounding heart plummeted to his boots. On his order, they'd gone to the castle. And, even though he was not yet sure of Osana's loyalties, they'd paid the price.

Ula drew her sword with a deadly clang and a whisper of Urtzi's name. The king threw up his hands, the sword and dagger about his hip scabbard untouched. "Understand they are not my captives. They only appear to be."

To punctuate the point, Osana reached for her gag and pulled it down easily. Either it had been poorly tied or it was just as much for show as Amarande's own ropes. "We're better than we've been in days. Please, listen to Ferdinand."

The pronouncement of his given name from Osana was a surprise and a confirmation.

Osana. The watcher. Sister of the regent Warlord. Of course she knew Ferdinand. Luca was still not sure of her loyalties, and yet here she was, begging.

Next, Urtzi shrugged out of his gag. "Ula. Listen, please."

That was . . . unusual coming from him.

"My king," Koldo said, "we are listening."

His green gaze swept the four of them, clearly picking up much from their glances beyond him, to the bend, and through the junipers pressing in along the road.

"First and foremost, I am alone. We can speak freely. And to prove it, I will start." Ferdinand took a deep breath. "I was sent by Geneva to meet the Warlord. A fact I assume by how you are dressed you already know, along with the fact that Geneva was and still is the Warlord. The one with the caravan, Celia, is a mere puppet."

No one answered him.

"I was to negotiate with her for Amarande, dangling her sister's life before her. As, again, I assume you can guess by Osana's presence."

Osana and Urtzi meant nothing to Koldo, but everything to the rest of them. At Luca's back, Amarande swallowed, her arms squeezing his sides, as if shielding him.

"Geneva had no real intention of negotiation. I was to come with soldiers at my side, and slay Celia and her guards for her insolence in believing she could siphon power with blackmail." He caught Amarande's eyes over Luca's shoulder. "And then I was to march my sister back to the Itspi, to be dealt with after the coming attack from Queen Inés, who is hovering like a storm cloud in our port, shuttling demands in a way that makes it clear she believes Ardenia is already hers."

All the air left Luca's lungs.

They were too late. The resistance would be too late, as well. War was at Ardenia's shores.

"She's here?" Amarande asked.

"Yes, Sister. But the good news is you are, too." He looked to Koldo. "And you, Mother. I cannot emphasize how much we need you." Ferdinand caught eyes with each of them. "We need all of you." Now he looked to the girl holding the single drawn weapon. "I can only assume by that sword and palpable vengeance that you are Ula."

Ula's blade did not waver.

"A handy double for Celia, for sure," he continued. Osana read Ula's hands. "And if Celia is not here, and her clothing is available, am I correct in guessing you, my good sir, are none other than Luca, the Otsakumea?"

In answer, Luca drew his own sword.

A smile tugged at the king's pursed lips. "My sister hugging you as tightly as life itself is a dead giveaway."

Ferdinand knew everything. How did he know everything?

"My king," Koldo started, her voice more unsure than Luca had ever heard it, "what is your intention for us?"

"Mother, you know I have a preference for honesty, and understand that what I am about to say is the truth." Koldo nodded. "My plan was this: Remove Osana from our dungeons—and her friend, Urtzi, as well—rescue Amarande from a tyrant, and confront Geneva with an ultimatum that would put my sister in power."

"What?" Amarande's voice was breathless. "You would cede to me?"

Luca knew nothing of Ferdinand, but anyone with royal blood lacking ambition on this continent was certainly someone to be suspicious of.

"Sister, Ardenia needs you. I need you. I hate the lie I've been told to live, and Ardenia wilts under the weight of it. Queen Inés is in our harbor, preparing her attack, and if Ardenia is going to fight, I want you by my side."

Amarande hesitated, and Ferdinand held up a hand.

"I trust you, Sister. If you do not trust me, that is a danger I am willing to live with to help Ardenia survive this."

CHAPTER
59

***

KING Sendoa always had a plan.

That knowledge had both comforted and vexed Amarande since his death.

She tried to live in his image as he made it—to be strong, thoughtful, confident—and though Ferdinand knew nothing of the man, it was clear he was the type to make plans, too.

Previously: to kill the false Warlord and her seconds and arrive with Amarande in hand and demand changes, leveraging their father's blood to both the Royal Council and Geneva.

Now: to arrive with Koldo at his side, triumphant in her *rescue* of Amarande from the Warlord, and leverage their blood just the same but with the general in the room and on their side.

However, neither plan worked for Amarande, or Luca.

"We must be together," the princess announced, as all of them stood in a circle, their conversation and horses moved into the juniper groves that crawled up the mountains lining the final stretch to the Itspi. "That is how it is."

"I will not leave her side," Luca added, gripping her uninjured hand firmly.

Amarande returned a squeeze to his fingers in equal measure. Together forever now, never to be apart again. That's what they'd agreed at the start of all this—and the next move they made certainly could be *the* end.

And, if the stars agreed, maybe a beginning, too.

"You can't blame them," Ula said, extra fabric yanked away from her face. She herself had not moved away from Urtzi's side.

The king and his mother chewed on this—their faces pulling taut in the same thoughtful way. Osana stood at Ferdinand's other side, hugging herself tightly.

In turns, Luca and Ferdinand had explained the story of Osana and Urtzi—sent by Luca to collect Amarande but tossed in the dungeons by Geneva. It was a wonder she didn't kill them on the spot. Perhaps the way Osana leaned her shoulder against Ferdinand had something to do with it. Or perhaps it was her blood and previous occupation. Amarande still wasn't sure.

They didn't have much time to rework the plan—the soldiers would be leaving the gates soon, if they hadn't already—eyes out for signs of Inés as diplomacy churned but ears to the ground for anything unusual, including the king by the side of the road. It was a wonder Ferdinand had gotten out of the castle at all.

Koldo spun the possibilities round and made her choice. "My king, perhaps the best course of action here is twofold. You can parade Amarande and Luca through the grounds of the Itspi as hostages you saved from the Warlord—the castle inhabitants will rejoice in this—and then present them behind closed doors to the Queen Mother as hostages you collected for *her*. Geneva will be delighted to lay eyes on the two people threatening her immediate power, rather than simply one."

Amarande's heart leapt.

Yes. This was the plan. Just as her father would devise. Playing the angles, all the facets covered, as best they could be, using the advantages they had.

She caught eyes with Koldo and her brother. "Perfect. Let's go. Before Inés complicates matters."

Ferdinand frowned, still tossing about Koldo's spin—not perfect in his mind, no. "It would help both Amarande and me to have you in the room as we negotiate with Geneva and the council. This group does not much like the opinions of those they consider both figureheads and children."

Amarande almost grinned—perhaps gender couldn't protect even a boy with the shoulders of a man from the council's opinions of participation from children.

Koldo put up a hand.

"I will be there. As will the others. Listen close; this is what we will do."

CHAPTER
60

THE Itspi was completely different from when Luca had last laid eyes on it.

Then: open gates, commoners and highborn alike in mourning, the grounds sunny despite the heaviness of King Sendoa's funeral.

Now: closed gates, soldiers marching in military precision, every square inch of the grounds flooded with a bloodred mass of bodies, sprawled across the rock-bitten hills and summer dry grass.

One last breath from Sendoa and truly everything had changed. A thousand years of peace bought with brutal patriarchy, and in the scheme of a fortnight all pieces shifted.

For the better, Luca hoped.

Koldo's plan was a solid one. All the tactical brilliance he'd only witnessed tangentially on display. It was exactly the best course of action to negate the threat of Geneva so that they might focus upon the threat of Inés and her new power, churning in the harbor.

What she was waiting for, Luca didn't know. Inés was simply a named storm, power gathering on the horizon.

Hand looped in hers, Luca held tight to Amarande as they wound through the grounds, trailing her brother's lifted chin, sunset hair, oxen shoulders. Luca wondered how Amarande could set her eyes upon Ferdinand—even from his position adjacent to the family, it was unsettling to be within the king's orbit.

So familiar yet so much not. Not Sendoa. Not someone either of them really knew at all.

Amarande had made it clear that she'd literally spent about ten minutes with her brother, only a few tense sentences between them. Luca knew he'd trusted many—most recently Tala—with less than that because it was his nature. The fact that Amarande, always so suspicious, *was not* made him apprehensive, to say the least.

"Ama," he whispered, as Ferdinand greeted the guards stationed at the entrance to the inner walls of the Itspi, the winding sandstone and marble halls beyond, "I know it is not usually my role to be wary, but do you trust him? Really?"

Amarande licked her lips, not meeting Luca's eyes, only watching her brother ahead, saying all the prepared things to the castle guards carefully eyeing the pair of them. "I have you. If he breaks our trust, we will fight our way out together. Yes?"

His thumb swept across the top of the hand that twined with his. "Always, Princess."

The king signaled them to follow. "The Queen Mother will receive us in the council room."

That was not the plan.

It had been to meet in the throne room. Or the red hall. Somewhere with space to fight and more than one exit for escape if things went south.

Uncertainty clawed at Luca. The dagger in his boot pressed against the tendons at his ankle as he took step after step toward a swiftly pivoting plan. They would not receive the Queen Mother alone. The Royal Council and their opinions would be there. Along with the external threat of Inés, the internal threat of Geneva's status as Warlord, and whatever secrets hid within the king.

It was impossible to say if he truly was more loyal to his natural mother or the one who'd raised him. If Ferdinand were actually his father, this conundrum would be much easier to parse. If the king turned out to be as greedy and backstabbing and brutal as every other royal in the Sand and Sky, Amarande would likely be the one to take him out herself.

The party wound through the castle, past guards running this way and that. As they passed the red hall, the great tiger's head doors swung open, revealing officers bent over lines of tables, carved wooden figurines of the sigils of each of the kingdoms of Sand and Sky.

Geneva first.

Inés second.

That was the plan, though it was difficult not to be distracted by the buzz of unease and anticipation wafting from the red hall and into the stones at their feet. Luca hoped this would be quick. And if not, that it could be effectively tabled as they united for a common enemy, the subject of which crown sat on whose head saved for later.

They moved swiftly up the stairs of the north tower. Luca's heart thumped wildly as they pushed into the council room, four guards stationed at the entrance. He'd never been allowed within before. Yet here it was, all regal tapestries and dark window light, the Royal Council positioned as a tribunal at a highly polished table. The doors swung shut.

"I have returned with Princess Amarande," Ferdinand announced. The line was what had been rehearsed and seemed a little stilted and obvious, but he delivered it, shoulders back as he stood tall before them—the three council members and the Queen Mother, who resembled Amarande so much, Luca's breath caught.

"Our princess, returned to us. What a surprise. And Luca by her side," Garbine cooed. The older councilor's voice was one of show. As if everyone in the room did not know what they'd done to Amarande when she'd last appeared in this place.

Amarande cleared her throat. "Before you lock me away, we have much to discuss. No, not *discuss*. You have much to hear from us, if you can bother to listen."

Satordi tented his fingers, elbows smashing down the parchment he'd been reading.

"Welcome back, Princess; I did miss your gift of conversation." Satordi's dry admonishment of Amarande earned him a wry smile from Garbine. Joseba wilted farther into his robes, appearing as if he wanted to melt into the marble floor.

The princess bared her teeth.

"If you'd like a conversation, then you must consider me a participant, even if you do not like what I'm about to say," she shot back. "Hear me now, or stave me off with your put-downs until Inés's arrows fly through the window. I do not care. You may consider me a danger, but in truth I am far less of one now than what will be at your doorstep once Inés steps off that ship."

"With all due respect, Princess Amarande, this is not your council room. It is King Ferdinand's—"

"And it is my wish that she continues," the king announced placidly from his position next to Amarande. Geneva stood from the great chair at the head of the table—one that only could have belonged to King Sendoa in life—and offered it to the current king with a wave of her hand. He did not take it.

Amarande swiftly produced a slip of parchment, the king's knife-slash signature unmistakable at the bottom. "My father's will was that I be made regent of my own kingdom until I desired to marry."

Satordi squinted across the distance. "Where did you get that?"

"It does not matter. All that matters is that the Royal Council who served my father so closely for years did not serve him in the end. Amending his wishes as it best suited them."

Satordi held up a hand. "That is not what happened, Your Highness. We simply didn't believe it was prudent—"

"To listen to my father? This man who inspected every facet. Sought every angle. Only flexed his muscle when he needed to, avoiding blood whenever possible. He always had a plan. A *good* plan. Instead, you carved it to pieces, and then tossed more bad decisions into the stew."

"Princess, we worked with what we had."

"What you *had* was his plan and me until a woman you hadn't seen in fifteen years conveniently appeared with a male bastard and a plan of her own in your time of need."

"Princess, the general confirmed—"

"I am not finished." Amarande dared Satordi to continue, but his thin lips sealed shut. "You were so enamored with your luck, you didn't even bother to ask the right questions."

"Princess, look at the bigger picture. I implore you." Amarande tensed against Luca's hand—Satordi had tried this before on her, the well of his experience being flaunted about in the same breath that firmly shut her out and away.

"You are always *imploring* me, but you do not listen."

Luca gripped her hand tighter, palm pressed against the linen about her wound, his upper arm touching her now, too—his strength was her strength and he wanted her to use it. "If this council had abided by my father's last wishes rather than conveniently ignoring the majority of his last will and testament while strong-arming Koldo into regency, there likely would not have been war at our doorstep now."

"No, it would've happened anyway," Geneva disagreed, dismissive. "Bear, Mountain Lion, Shark, Tiger"—her eyes slid to Luca's—"Black Wolf. All sigils in the Sand and Sky are predators by design. Trade one for the other and you still get the teeth."

Though Geneva had been subtle in her open threat to Luca, the passage of his identity and hers ships in the night, Amarande aimed her next question at the council while having eyes only for her mother. "You didn't ask the Runaway Queen where she'd been, did you?"

The council was silent.

"Now is the time for answers, not silence. That question was not rhetorical—answer me. I want to know." Amarande met each one in the eye, left to right—Joseba, Satordi, Garbine.

Satordi drew in a thin breath. "We cannot properly deal with caveats to succession, not with war nearly at our door. We need to be united, and the cleanest way to do that is to unite under our king, not squabble over the particulars of previous actions—mine, yours, hers, King Sendoa's. The answer does not matter with an armada making demands in our harbor."

He thrust a hand out to gesture to the polished table before him, littered with maps, yellowed directives to the kingdoms of the Sand and Sky, and a fresh slip of parchment, stamped with three seals—Mountain Lion, Bear, Shark. Inés's opening parry, to be sure.

"The answer does matter. Here, I'll give it for you," Ferdinand replied, arms wide. "You did not."

Sunlight danced across the shoulders of the council's ivory robes, their lack of defense an answer in itself.

Amarande turned to Geneva. "Would you like me to tell them or will you? Or perhaps our king will do it—he's partial to the truth."

Their mother smiled at first, as if to mock her children. One for her brashness, the other for his perceived weaknesses. Neither of them grinned back, twin frowns in return. Finally, Ferdinand said to Geneva, "You tell them or I will."

The councilors' attention was fixed on her now. Geneva sat up, spine straight. Then, with a heavy sigh, the Queen Mother stood and yanked down her lace sleeve, revealing a tattoo on the underside of her wrist. The leaping bouquet of flames—the fire pit in distinct, satiny relief, the same kind of ink that sat upon his chest.

"For the past ten years, I hid in plain sight, as the third ruler to carry the name the Warlord."

The distinct flush fled Joseba's cheeks. Garbine shrunk away. Satordi, to his credit, leaned in for a closer look. Luca held his breath. Here was the moment of truth. Only this blow could come from Ferdinand if it was to land properly.

"*Are*, Mother," Ferdinand corrected. "You *are* the Warlord. I was there—for the negotiation, the orders, the plan. Council, my mother never intended to cede her power."

"Ferdinand, you misunderstood—"

"I did not and do not. The Warlord's power did not change hands. And the person handpicked to wield power in your stead is dead. You are still the Warlord as much as I am king."

"My king,"—Geneva's teeth flashed—"you twist my words."

"I do not."

Geneva scoffed. "Shall I retrieve the letter and detail the plan *you* devised in the study within your chambers?"

Satordi bit. "What letter?"

"This one." The king pulled a slip of parchment from his pocket, as smoothly as Amarande had. "It is in cipher, but what it is, is an attempt at extortion—the princess for permanent power transferred to the temporary Warlord. Exactly what happens when loyalties are divided."

The king let that accusation hang, and it sucked nearly all the air out of the room. Was this what it had been like when Amarande had stood with Koldo by her side, demanding these same people change the laws so she could access her own power and not be beholden to laws that served only the vipers surrounding her?

Luca had never known his mother—the queen or his surrogate mother, Lygia—but he did know the chiding look Geneva gave the boy she raised as her son. It said he was silly, a child, one who did not understand the weight of what his words meant. "You killed her. To obtain the princess and her stableboy for the good of Ardenia. Is that what all this is about, Ferdinand? Did you want credit for your bravery in saving your sister? Rather than to keep it just between us? Well, now everyone knows how loyal you are to the sister who sees you as a threat."

Amarande took a step forward and Ferdinand thrust out a hand to hold her back.

"Mother." Even with Ferdinand's Koldo-like calm, frustration bit at the word. "I did not kill her, but she is dead."

"The semantics of this person's life do not matter," Satordi announced.

"Geneva's loyalties are divided, yes, and the semantics of this person's life *do* matter," Amarande assured him, the pressure of her shoulder against Luca's body increasing. Now she was supporting him—and Luca's heartbeat sped up accordingly. "Because the person believed to be the Warlord by her own people was killed when the Warlord's camp was ambushed and claimed by the rightful leader of the Kingdom of Torrence."

Geneva did not betray a hint of surprise, other than to coolly set her attention on Luca. He swallowed but gave it to her right back, staring down the Warlord now, free of her secrets and masks, everything now in the open.

Joseba's erudite voice entered the fray. "The Otxoa were the rightful leaders of the Kingdom of Torrence—and they are extinct."

"I assure you they are not."

Satordi squinted at Amarande. "How—"

"As a prisoner in the Warlord's camp, I saw the whole thing with my own eyes," Amarande answered. "The ambush, the attack, the symbolic Warlord plummeting to her death in her own fire pit. And then, her people's retreat and surrender, to the rightful king."

Here, Luca's love turned to him, looked him straight in the eye, and made sure none of these people would call him stableboy again. "Luca, the rightful heir of the Otxoa, sheltered here at the Itspi by King Sendoa, all these years."

Amarande smiled at him then, and he shared it as the weight of every eye in the room pressed in upon him. "And before you ask, Satordi, we have proof. Proof that Luca is heir, proof that King Sendoa knew. And proof that he'd planned to not only alert Luca to his destiny but help him fulfill it, by attacking the Warlord, whom he knew to be his Runaway Queen."

Each accusation hit like a cannonball, breaking apart the bow, the hull, the mast of this ship they were on, sending it splintered into the forever sea of time, intention, work.

Though they had it at the ready—the tattoo, the map with Sendoa's plans upon it, and Koldo's direct knowledge, if she ever arrived—neither Satordi nor any of the other councilors requested that proof. Instead, the lead councilor tented his fingers and looked to Ferdinand.

"My king, I think perhaps, given this new information shared by both yourself and the Princess, it would be best if the Queen Mother be relieved of further discussions of King Sendoa's plans for Ardenia, and the Torrent—her loyalties as stated are murky indeed and a danger to Ardenia, in my estimation. If you believe that prudent, I will call a guard to remove her."

"That won't be necessary," Geneva insisted.

"It *is* necessary." Ferdinand squared his shoulders. "I appreciate your concern, Satordi, but that decision is not mine to make. My sister, as rightful heir and queen, what is your wish?"

The mouths of each of the councilors fell open while Geneva's jaw tightened, betrayal and anger fierce upon her cheeks. Amarande did not budge. "Guards shall escort the Queen Mother to her chambers and remain outside her door."

In a show of support, the king called to the hall, "Guards, please remove the Queen Mother to her chambers and keep watch there!"

Movement came from beyond the door, and as the men and women sorted their new orders Satordi's voice rang low, livid, across the length of the room. "My king, with war on our doorstep am I understanding that you are . . . ceding power?"

"Yes. A lie made me king. It is one all of you participated in, and I as well. I am not the rightful heir and my decisions are secondary to my sister, who is the rightful queen."

"But the union of kingdoms of the Sand and Sky must approve—"

"Must approve what?" Ferdinand asked, still calm. He did not care that the guards had entered and that they could not ignore what he was saying. "That I plan to cede the crown to my sister, who should by any measure be queen? A crown, I recall, that was given to me without consultation from the rulers of the continent. As it stands, we have two-thirds of the rulers of the Sand and Sky standing right here." Ferdinand looked to Luca. "Will you vote with me to allow female heirs to rule outright in your Sand and Sky?"

Luca smiled. "Gladly."

The guards appeared at the Queen Mother's side and she shrugged away from them, opting to remove herself from King Sendoa's large chair herself. "Perhaps I should have you vote to grant me Basilica. I have the blood for it—my cousin can barely compete."

"That is not how any of this works," Satordi sputtered, not to Geneva as much as to the whole idea of this casual transfer of power. "A king cannot name a queen and step aside; a single battle does not reinstall the Otxoa."

"Satordi, do you hear yourself?" Amarande exclaimed. "Inés just murdered two kings and claimed three-fifths of the continent over spilled wine. In this room lies her path to the other two kingdoms. It does not matter what the laws say; none of it stands. The Sand and Sky that wrote those stupid, ancient rules is no more. The future of this continent—"

With a crash, one guard and then another fell to the floor, assassin's smiles carved across their throats, blood gushing onto the collars of their regal Ardenian uniforms. Geneva stood over them with twin daggers in her hands, both of them stained crimson with arterial blood.

Nearest to her, Joseba shot to his feet, his chair falling over in his haste. It was unclear if he meant to disarm her or escape. It didn't matter. One quick thrust and he was down, blood blooming across the chest of his ivory robes.

Amarande and Luca both dove for their boots, knives out and ready quick as a flash. Ferdinand was even quicker, shielding them with his sword as they armed themselves, prepared to block an attack.

All could see that the two daggers that Geneva had been holding were now protruding from Satordi and Garbine. Geneva had stabbed the old woman in the heart, and she was slumped over the table, bleeding all over the papers strewn on it. Satordi she had caught in the side, missing vital organs but incapacitating him. The lead councilor struggled to stand, gasping for air like a hooked fish, before finally falling behind the table.

Completely ignoring their dying moments, Geneva bent to retrieve the swords from the dead guards and raised the twin Basilican blades with a shrug.

"They were getting in the way of our discussions. Rules and regulations and knickers in a twist over the minutiae of power transfer. You should thank me for removing that obstacle for you simply out of my own annoyance." Geneva smiled, both King Sendoa's scions now in her sights. "Now, children, your only obstacle is me."

Yes, the Warlord would go out fighting. Not flee like the Runaway Queen she once had been.

"Guards!" Ferdinand called, his voice even louder than before.

This was a relief, too. Despite the show he'd put on, Luca hadn't been fully sure Ferdinand would not turn on them.

Geneva took a step toward him, sword at a deadly angle. Luca's eyes fell to her shoes—boots, not slippers. A dagger could be in them, or two. Perhaps even hidden in her bodice. A woman like her could easily have many more weapons hidden away.

"You would have them cut me down, Ferdinand?" The Queen Mother took another step, brow steeply arched. "After all I've done for you?"

Ferdinand did not relent. "You used me. Every inch of the way."

"No, I stood with you. *For* you. And you repay my love by staring me down with a sword."

From the hall there was a commotion, and Luca's heart fluttered with relief.

Koldo. Ula. Urtzi. Osana. Right on time, despite the unplanned location.

"Mother, in here!" Ferdinand called again, and Geneva visibly flinched.

It was clear now that he did not want to kill Geneva, only remove her influence. Let them deal with war on their own—become triumphant or lose everything to Inés and let her deal with her contemporary, should she survive.

Geneva's smile widened in a way that caused Luca's heart to shrink back. "They're not coming, my boy."

Bile rose within Luca as his grip tightened on the knife. Next to him, Amarande was already scanning her periphery for movement beyond the heavy double doors.

But then, despite that announcement, a noise came from behind her. Footsteps and then the clanging of a lock and latch releasing. And there, entering the room from a door hidden beyond the council table, was an opponent Luca did not expect.

Taillefer.

CHAPTER
61

❦

AMARANDE'S blade stiffened in her hand.

Taillefer.

It couldn't be. But it was. He'd changed into the unmistakable aubergine and gold of Pyrenee. Washed his face, too, blood and grime gone. But still he sported the fox-like smile the princess had seen so much of during their journey.

"How did you . . . why did you . . ." Amarande's voice died out and that smile increased. So pleased he'd made her stumble.

His eyes glittered, landing on her brother. "Won't you introduce us, Princess?"

"*Queen*, we just made her queen," Ferdinand corrected, eyes tracking this new threat while still angling toward Geneva and her double swords. "And you will refer to her as such."

As always, Taillefer found humor in something that wasn't funny. He let out an audible laugh as he stepped over Satordi's dying body. He didn't explain what humor he saw, and he also didn't come farther into the room, both his dagger and sword still stowed in their scabbards at his waist.

As it was, that put him in literal alignment with Geneva and her weapons—facing the rest of the room from either end of the oval-shaped council table.

Amarande stared at her mother and the prince.

Were they a team? Some sort of loose alliance? Or was this another of Taillefer's clever tricks? Whose side was he really on? Her mother's? Hers? Or simply his own?

"What are you doing here?" This from Luca. Amarande hadn't believed Luca had the capacity to hate Taillefer as much as he *should*, but the harshness in his tone said otherwise.

Where was Koldo? Ula, Urtzi, Osana? It was too much to hope for the resistance fighters. Not yet. But they needed reinforcements. With Luca and Ferdinand and herself facing Geneva and Taillefer, their odds looked good. But someone had clearly taken care of the guards and it was impossible to tell who else was in the hall. Worse, Taillefer had arrived from the antechamber behind the council room, outside the cell in which she'd been imprisoned. What else was back there? Who else? And how had Taillefer arrived inside the Itspi wearing the uniform of Pyrenee without being stopped by their soldiers down below?

"I am here to attend this delightful reunion, same as you, wolf cub. I do apologize for my tardiness, and the regret is my own as I see I've missed the portion of the programming where you try to put aside your differences long enough to unite to face a common enemy." Taillefer made it a point to examine the mess of the room. Plans discarded, bodies strewn on the floor, lifeblood in various stages of release. Lines drawn in marble rather than sand. He inspected it the same way a governess would look down upon a particularly messy child's room. "Couldn't find it within you to join forces against my mother?"

"Negotiations are still in progress," Geneva answered, her swords unwavering.

"Well, the good news is that she and I also could not rally together to beat you. So, I took care of her."

Silence smothered the room at the implication. Amusement twinkled in his eyes, and Amarande's teeth ground together. Never plain-spoken, this boy.

"Taillefer," Amarande spit, "did you kill your mother?"

"King Taillefer, and yes. There will be no clash of the queens." He bowed in a deep, mocking way. "You're welcome."

Luca's eyes narrowed. "How can we believe you?"

Taillefer took another step closer. "Oh, wolf cub," he answered, almost lovingly, "you of all these people should believe me. I spared you when I said I would. You're welcome for that, too."

Amarande addressed Taillefer again, almost hopeful. "Are you here for a truce?"

"He is here for me," Geneva replied. She'd been standing back, watching with her blades, but now she took another step forward, so that again she and Taillefer were aligned. "His Highness and I have been allies for quite some time."

Amarande's mouth went dry. "That can't be."

"Can't it? Is it really easier for you to believe that a boy you attempted to murder would stand with you and not against you, darling daughter?" The skylight blue of her mother's eyes flashed. "Tell me, again—how did your daring escape come to pass?"

A weight settled in Amarande's stomach as she ran through that night's events again. The timing. The location. All the intangibles. Finally, she swallowed, watching a smile creep across her mother's face. Amarande's voice rang hollow in her ears. "You knew where I was being kept—not because you're so clever but because my mother told you."

In confirmation, Taillefer arched a brow. "It is quite possible that I do not know everything, Queen."

"You are playing us both," Ferdinand accused.

"Yes, that is what smart players do—you've done that yourself somewhat. Applause to you, little Sendoa. There is always more than one side of play, and I have played them all. Your mother. Your sister. The Torrent. Ardenia. Myrcell. I have alliances with every player, my finger in every pot. There is nothing particularly special about either of yours—" Taillefer turned to Geneva. "Though I daresay alignment with the Warlord's cause is a much less enticing proposition than previously, given the Otsakumea has risen and is standing in our midst, and your supporters are fleeing with the wind or rotting into the sand."

Geneva wheeled upon him. *"Excuse me?"*

Taillefer ignored her and sent a questioning glance in Luca's direction. "I assume you were successful, if you're standing here." He winked and gave a thumbs-up. "A stableboy as the long-lost heir to an extinct throne certainly is one for the songbooks."

Geneva's whole body pivoted toward Taillefer now—her blades and fire and spite. "As long as I stand, the wolf cub has won nothing. And you stand with me, boy."

"No, I think not." Taillefer turned to Amarande. "My mother is dead. I now rule Pyrenee. Arm-wrestle your mother for Basilica and Myrcell for all I care. I only want what is mine.

"My offer is this: Recognize me now as king and my ships will disperse. No war at your door." Taillefer glanced from Amarande to her mother and back, his lips curling. "Well, unless you consider this *negotiation* of yours to be civil war, in which case you work it out and just send me a scrap of parchment with the winner's name when it's over, will you?"

"That . . . actually sounds reasonable," Luca whispered from Amarande's side.

And it was.

No Inés? No war for the whole of the Sand and Sky? Just a simple agreement, a handshake, and a parting of ways? No. It couldn't be.

"Taillefer," Amarande called, "I will recognize you as King of Pyrenee if you will honor my claim as Queen of Ardenia and the Otsakumea's birthright to the newly reformed Kingdom of Torrence."

That fox smile flashed. "As you wish, Your Highness."

"No! I think not!" Geneva shouted, twin swords clanging as she crashed them together for emphasis. "The continent will not be decided this way! By the fickle wishes of children with no basis in fact. These words mean nothing."

Just that moment, the doors burst open and General Koldo, Ula, Urtzi, and Osana came in, breathing hard and worse for wear. Their weapons had been used, but they'd made it despite whatever obstacle Geneva had clearly created for them.

"Ah, look at that," Taillefer observed, gleefully. "They were coming after all."

The Warlord's eyes narrowed upon the general, yet another assumed ally who became a traitor.

Koldo stepped in line with her son, shoulders back and sword out. "This is the end, Geneva. You are defeated. As the Warlord, as the Runaway Queen, as the Queen Mother. You hold no titles now. No land. No army. Nothing. The Sand and Sky has been forever changed but you will no longer play a part in it."

"What I did, I did for Ardenia." Geneva's furious blue eyes found Amarande's face. "I protected my daughter's legacy from the threat of Koldo's child."

She wheeled on Ferdinand. "I protected *you* from death. You could've been my first kill, and instead you became my son."

Ferdinand shook his head. "You stole me from my rightful mother and then dangled me as blackmail for the entirety of my life, right up until the moment you regained Ardenia's throne by using me."

"I did it for you. I did it for both of you. I did it to stave off war. I did not know what Inés would do." Geneva pointed a sword at Taillefer. "Or her psychopathic children."

"Hey there, that is a *king* you are talking about," Taillefer cut in. "At least call me a genius instead of a child—psychopathic genius. Yes, the *king* will take it."

Everyone in the room ignored him.

"You did not do it for *us*," Ferdinand said, his fury evident even if his voice stayed restrained. "*You* stole Amarande's chance to grow up with her mother, and at the same time you stole *my* chance to grow up with my mother and father. Think of what we've lost."

"No! I did what was best for both of you when *she*," Geneva gestured to the general, "attacked my daughter's legacy."

Again, Ferdinand shook his head. Lowered his sword and tried to touch her heart—the only mother he had known for fifteen years, no matter how twisted that love turned out to be, letting his words be both his offense and defense. "You cannot blame Koldo for what *you* did."

"No—I gave you so much. I didn't *steal* anything!" This time her voice shook. "From you, from Amarande, from anyone else. I—"

"*Stars,*" Ferdinand swore, "you even stole *Luca's* chance to grow up with his mother."

"What . . . ?" Luca's voice was tight. "What do you mean?"

Koldo answered, gently. "Your mother did not die of lung disease, Luca. She witnessed Geneva running away with Ferdinand. Geneva admitted to strangling her. I'm so sorry to tell you this now, this way—"

A moment of thunderstruck silence.

Then Ula let out a cry of rage. "You *what?*" The pirate lunged forward, curved sword at a deadly angle. "You killed Lygia? Strangled her?"

Luca caught her arm as she passed but Ula furiously shook him away, advancing on the Warlord, step by step. For the first time, Geneva inched backward, retreating from the fury in Ula's eyes, covering that involuntary weakness with a scoffing laugh.

"Who *the stars* are you and why do you care? Lygia wasn't *actually* Queen Elixane, I killed some lowly nursemaid." Her voice was all taunting bravado, and Taillefer actually had the gall to chuckle, thoroughly entertained from his corner. "You have summarily ruined my son's glorious speech vilifying everything I've done for the past fifteen years. Stop ruining the flow—I'm sure he's about to move on to the way I ruled with fear and an iron fist in the Torrent, even though he *gladly* stood by my side and watched each victim burn."

Ula lifted her chin. Sword out straight. Shoulders back. Luca moved closer, but did not attempt to restrain her again. "My name is Ulara Vidal. You killed my mother. You made my homeland a wasteland of fear. And—"

"And what?" Geneva narrowed her gaze. "I'm going to die at your hand? Get in line, girl."

With a cry, Ula lunged, her curved sword held high in both hands. With deadly force, she sent it arcing downward—only for the blow to be parried aside by the crossing thrust of Geneva's twin blades. The momentum sent Ula in a spin that turned her around, back to Geneva, vulnerable to the next slash of the Warlord's sword. One quick shove and Luca pushed Ula out of the way.

Leaving himself exposed.

In a flash, Geneva lunged and with her nearer blade—three feet of true Basilican steel—thrust straight for the vulnerable flesh of Luca's unprotected torso.

"No!" Amarande leapt for Geneva's sword arm. She got both hands on the outside of her mother's arm, and yanked, spinning her around. Her own dagger fell, skittering across the marble floor.

The whole motion sent them both stumbling unsteadily toward the tapestry-covered wall. Amarande careened into it first, the woven depiction of some dead Ardenian king doing absolutely nothing to cushion the blow to the back of her head and upper back. Breath knocked out of her, Amarande held fast to her mother's arm, bashing her wrist over and over into the stone wall in an effort to release the sword from her grip.

Blood.

There was blood on her mother's sword. Luca's blood.

"Luca?" Even in her own ears, Amarande's voice was strangled. "Luca, are you—"

Geneva smashed her body backward, driving Amarande even harder against the wall, so hard that her skull thudded off the unforgiving stone with a terrific crack. The world immediately became slow and muffled, her perception blurred by tears and a sudden pounding in her head.

Amarande tried to focus her addled vision, barely able to make out

Luca in the chaos before her. Ula and Urtzi were pressing in, Osana dashing after them. Ferdinand shielding them all from Geneva's second blade, still lashing out as Amarande maintained her grip on the sword arm that had struck Luca. It was futile, of course, because Geneva couldn't truly reach.

And so, with one great swing, Geneva arced her second blade toward her daughter, pressed against the stone.

In a flash of steel and bootstrikes, Koldo attacked.

The general rushed Geneva's flailing sword with her own, smashing it flat against the stone wall behind her. For a split second, Geneva's body was stretched in a cross—Amarande still pinning one side with both hands, Koldo going for the other with her sword.

But then, just as Koldo reached maximum pressure, Geneva dropped that sword. Koldo's own sword lost its leverage, and she went stumbling away.

With a great crash, the general careened into the heavy wooden council table, papers and figurines scattering. And as Koldo's body hit, Amarande's attention caught on another movement from that side of the room—Taillefer slowly backing away toward the door from where he'd come, apparently no longer entertained.

But Amarande was not yet done with him.

"Taillefer! Someone stop Taillefer!"

To Amarande's surprise, it was Luca who heeded her call. In a blink, he scooped up her fallen dagger and slung it end over end toward the new King of Pyrenee. Amarande did not see the blade make contact, as Geneva spun to face her daughter and punched the tapestry in what at first seemed to be a missed strike to Amarande's kidney.

But then the stone at Amarande's back rumbled to life. The entire length of the wall behind the tapestry rotated, the princess and her mother with it. Geneva's face broke into a calculating smile.

"Before this castle was yours, it was mine."

And, as they were plunged into utter darkness, Amarande's mother laughed.

CHAPTER 62

THE panel was stone again. The entire party save for Taillefer rushed it, prodded at it. The tapestry was gone and the wall completely solid.

A secret passageway.

Luca had lived at the Itspi his entire life, had combed every corner with Amarande—every stairwell, every floor, every nook and cranny. They'd even spent years using the library dumbwaiter as their own personal secret entrance into the yard.

But he'd never seen a wall *move*.

He stabbed at the stones the same height as the one Geneva had struck, Ferdinand and Urtzi punching ones farther up, Ula and Osana jabbing balled fists and braced shoulders into ones farther down.

General Koldo hauled herself up from where she'd landed on the table. She was bleeding from the head, a huge gash over her eye from where she'd made contact with the massive piece of scrolled furniture.

"Koldo," Luca called to her, "do you know—"

"The library." As she said it, she collected Geneva's discarded sword, caught eyes with Luca, and tossed it his way.

"Is that the only place?" Ferdinand was already pivoting for the double doors, not waiting for his mother's answer.

"Yes."

"You don't need to tell me twice." Ula raced after Ferdinand, Koldo, and Osana. "We're coming, Amarande!"

Taillefer hissed out something of a laugh. "I *knew* that library had a hidden passageway—Amarande denied it. But I knew. Go on; I can certainly entertain myself while you settle this family feud." His voice was weak—Luca's dagger had speared his fine aubergine collar against the door from which he'd appeared. Taillefer didn't reach for the latch, but he would the moment they disappeared; that much was guaranteed. "I'll wait."

"You had to tempt me." Ula wheeled on him, sword out and Urtzi at her back. "I have much to say to you after your treatment of Luca, Taillefer."

Luca waved her off. "I will say it. Go, Ula. Your sword is meant for Geneva if Amarande doesn't get her first. Go, for Ama and for Lygia."

"I'm not leaving you," Ula replied, firmly.

Taillefer sighed. "I have what I want. I have no quarrel with you, wolf cub."

"We have all the quarrel. You don't get the quarrel," Urtzi spit. Apparently, he wasn't leaving either.

Luca needed to be quick. Amarande could not wait, even with the others' help. She needed him. And them. But they also could not let this evil boy out of their sight and near the ships still lingering in the harbor.

"If you think we will let you leave with your word and a handshake, you're wrong." Luca lunged for Taillefer's weapons, drawing his sword and dagger from their sheaths. Taillefer did not fight, hands limp at his sides—Luca did not trust that. A bluff. "How are we to know you won't leave here and order your mother's troops to attack Ardenia?"

"You don't." That same wheeze they'd heard through the fabric of the Warlord's tent chased the words out of his mouth, along with a cough that racked his entire body. If it had happened during his earlier performance, Luca'd missed it. "But it won't be a problem."

Taillefer grinned, but it was not a healthy thing. Blood framed each of his teeth in stark red, as if he'd sunk them into a still-beating heart.

It was then that Luca realized that he hadn't just caught the fabric of Taillefer's collar while pinning him; he'd caught his neck.

A weak slice to the jugular.

Not an assassin's smile, but also not easily fixed. Blood bloomed around the blade, thickly seeping into the fabric. The cold blue of Taillefer's eyes sought Luca's. "You've killed me. Fitting, after what I did to you."

Ula placed a hand on Luca's forearm. "Come, Luca, we don't need to watch this. You didn't mean to do it."

"Wait. Please." Taillefer's voice was weaker here, and Luca did not have it in him to leave. "I need you to tell Amarande something."

As much as he hated this boy, Luca had to give him this. Taillefer was one to have the last word. He already may have been at death's door, but Luca had slammed it in his face. Taillefer's trip to the stars was on him.

"The poison at the watering hole. That was me. It's the worst thing I ever did."

Luca swallowed, breathing hard though the action was over. "Don't say that. Don't lie with your last breath. You killed Sendoa with poison in his water, the same way. I know it. Don't deny it."

Air wasn't filling Taillefer's lungs. No inhale. No exhale. Nothing. Luca could not look away as Taillefer's face paled.

"I didn't kill Sendoa. My poison did—Renard did." Taillefer's voice was failing now, but he kept talking. Kept explaining. "I cataloged every vial. Knew what I'd sent to Domingu as a sample. One additional vial of hemlock was missing and so was my brother the day King Sendoa died."

Taillefer coughed again, so hard his body slumped afterward, the knife blade all that was keeping him upright. With his final breath, the brief King of Pyrenee showed remorse for his part in the act that started it all.

"Tell Amarande I'm sorry I didn't stop him."

CHAPTER
63

HER mother had the single sword.

A head start.

The advantage of knowing where she was going.

Amarande was sprawled face-first on the floor—the same rough sandstones as the walls, not the smooth, showy parquet marble. Painfully, she pulled herself out from beneath the ornate tapestry, its weight falling upon them as they spun into this space.

A hallway.

Amarande blinked. Torches lined the walls in an alternating pattern, vast shadowy voids clouding the narrow, downward-sloping floor before her. The darkness was such that at first she couldn't see her mother, only hear her sprinting footsteps in the distance. Then, as her eyes adjusted, Amarande caught a glimpse of a figure, dressed in a ball gown, barreling forward, sword held out in front of her, and clearly limping as she craned back over her shoulder to check her lead.

The Runaway Queen was fleeing, yet again.

Oh no you don't.

Amarande spun into action, boots churning beneath her. She had no weapon. Her arm smarted. Her legs burned, as she went from stationary to all-out sprint.

Amarande's heart lurched at the idea that after all these years *she* was the one chasing after the Runaway Queen.

Geneva flashed in the distant light again. Amarande was gaining on her—the yards of lace and silk and all the underpinnings easily weighed double the sword she carried. And though her mother was indeed strong and trained, she'd likely spent very little time working agility drills in a ball gown during her reign as the Warlord.

Amarande gained on her with every passing moment. Fifty feet behind. To twenty. To ten.

Her mother came to a halt at a dead end. Geneva dropped her skirts and began punching various stones on the wall.

How many hidden doors were there?

Amarande now understood exactly how Geneva had managed to move about the castle with a stolen infant and escape into the night. She knew the Itspi's veins as well as its bones.

That knowledge didn't matter. Neither did the fact that Amarande had no weapon. She and her mother would go through that wall together or they would end it here, in this hallway, alone. "I won't let you run away again. Surrender or fight. There is nothing else."

Geneva turned around to face Amarande. "There's winning. I want to win."

"Win *what*? Ardenia? Not going to happen. The Torrent? You've already lost."

"As long as I live, I can gather opposition. So can the previous Warlords. They're alive, you know. And they are not the sort to let their legacy go quietly."

"Do not threaten me, Mother."

"It's not a threat to you; it's a threat to your boy up there."

"A threat to him is a threat to me."

"Fine; then I'll beat you both." Fury seethed about her fine features. "I have a great interest in keeping the Torrent safe from *patriarchal imperialism*. You know, the exact kind of thing that has left my own daughter powerless."

"I am not powerless." Amarande was unarmed, yes, but she always had the power she needed. "And if I'm not mistaken, you used that patriarchal imperialism to worm your way back into this castle and steal my crown."

"I believed you were *dead*. I believed I would save Ardenia."

"No." Amarande shook her head, eyes not wavering. She reached for the nearest torch, not as a weapon, but to hold between them, so that she could read every inch of her mother's face. "You believed you'd gain control over Ardenia, and add to your domain, *Warlord*. You swear up and down that you love Ferdinand. No. You loved what he could *do* for you."

"That is not our relationship."

"Is it not?"

Geneva's hands still scrabbled about the stones behind her. Sword hand and free hand pushing anything beneath her fingertips, looking for just the right pressure point. Her sword was in striking distance.

Amarande did not retreat—the torch, her fists, her wits. There was much she could use. But if Geneva got that panel open and she was left in this hallway, she would lose her chance entirely. And so she stayed less than an arm's length away.

Geneva tried out a smile. "I wanted a relationship with you, you know."

"You voided that possibility the second you ran away."

"I came back."

"And locked me in a tower! Keeping me prisoner isn't a relationship; it's manipulation. It's not love. You do not love me, no matter what you say. And I could never love you."

Those eyes, so much like her own, narrowed, her mother's upper lip snarling.

"Is that supposed to cut me, Princess? Is that supposed to hurt me down deep?" Though smiling, Geneva's expression was as cold as the worst of a Pyrenee winter. "It may have in the past. The woman I was when I kissed your forehead good-bye? Sure. The woman I was when I stole into Koldo's midnight quarters and snatched her sleeping babe? Possibly. The woman I was when I lashed that baby to my chest and ran for the stable, only to find Lygia awake, nursing her cough with boiled water and honey? Maybe."

She paused here, taking joy in watching Amarande's heart drop. The princess's breath went shallow.

Geneva continued, voice hard as the Basilican steel still in her grip. "The woman I was when I crushed Lygia's throat as she made to sound the alarm? No. The woman I was as Warlord and the woman I am now? Never."

Amarande's heart was in her boots, but she held fast. Did not wrench her eyes from her mother's still-girlish face.

"The person I became the night I left this castle no longer feels pain. You cannot cut me, Amarande. You cannot hurt me. And you and your love will not defeat me."

"I will. I _have_. If you would just surrender—"

"I am not surrendering. I've said as much." Geneva's teeth flashed. There was truth to what she had said—_All sigils in the Sand and Sky are predators by design. Trade one for the other and you still get the teeth._ And now her eyes narrowed. "Why haven't you cut me down? Lit my hair and dress on fire with that torch? Relieved me of my sword and stabbed me through as I frantically searched for my way out?"

"I—"

"Why, darling daughter? Why?"

The threat of tears pressed against Amarande's eyes as her heart climbed out of her boots, pounding with what she must do. She set her grip on the torch. "I don't want it to end this way."

Her mother's lips curled. "Not all princesses get a happy ending. Queens don't either."

Amarande swung the torch then, the flame aimed straight for Geneva's head.

As Amarande ran through the motion, tears crawling into her eyes, her mother ducked, the torch connecting with bare stone of the wall behind.

There was a groaning shudder. The wall finally moved—revealing the concealed exit. Amarande lurched forward to brace herself as the floor spun, too. Arms up, torso exposed. Weapon neutralized.

And that's when the distinct sting of a blade entered Amarande's thigh.

Not the sword. A dagger. Geneva crouched over an exposed boot as they spun. Amarande registered the boot, then the blade. Not so different from the one she'd grown up with.

"A gift from your father."

Amarande swayed, her hands wrapping around the dagger hilt as they completed the turn.

The walls shuddered to a halt. Amarande slumped all the way to the floor as Geneva got to her feet, not retrieving the knife. Knowing exactly where she was and where she'd be running.

Amarande blinked.

The library. The turntable had yawned open: A massive bookcase spun into the passageway, covering the hidden doorway.

Stars, Taillefer's hopes were true.

More heavy tapestries bled from the walls, stained windows rinsed with noon light, her ancestors peering down in stony silence. And, as the last queen of the Ardenian line pulled the knife from her own leg, her mother met her eyes.

"I did love you, Amarande."

Although her mother's sleeves were charred from the torch, Geneva was not gravely injured. She could walk away. Run away. Again.

Without another word, Geneva turned away, leaving it at that after all those years.

Her mother may have been finished, but Amarande was not.

Just like that day in the meadow, her body knew exactly what to do.

Amarande swung her good leg out as hard as she could, knocking her mother off her feet in an instant. Then Amarande crawled atop her mother, pinning Geneva's arms between her knees, her weight on the woman's belly, her elbow thrust across her windpipe.

The knife a whisper from her neck.

Amarande's leg wound was weeping at a terrible rate. Fueled by adrenaline, her strength was both false and fleeting. Blood bloomed across her trousers.

The doors plowed open, Koldo leading the way as her ragtag soldiers followed. They'd wormed their way through the hallways and down a flight—the only direct line from the north tower to the library the one they'd taken, apparently.

"Ama!"

Koldo's call was not much different from that awful day. When she'd thundered toward the meadow, alone and crying. This time, Ferdinand and Osana were at her flanks. Then Luca appeared, sprinting from behind, Ula and Urtzi on his heels.

Amarande caught eyes with Luca.

That was all the opening her mother needed.

Geneva thrust a thumb straight into Amarande's leg wound, and the princess's body seized as she cried out, vision fading to white. Her mother shoved Amarande and her blade aside, and scrambled free.

The princess clawed blindly toward where her mother's body had been. As the white in her vision began edging black, Geneva crashed against the revolving stone door, hitting it hard enough that the whole mechanism began to slide shut—Amarande's body positioned between the concealed door and the jamb as they hurtled toward each other.

Amarande tried to pull herself away from the colliding walls of stone, but her limbs didn't listen, all her adrenaline tapped, blood pooling under her body from her leg, arm, somewhere else.

Still, she scrabbled for her fallen dagger and aimed for her mother. First looking to the hidden passageway, but then tracking movement not there but across the library—atop the gold-upholstered banquette. The five-sigil tapestry peeled aside, dumbwaiter shaft visible.

Then came movement but no clean edges.

And, just as all her senses died out, Amarande wasn't sure if she'd won or lost. Only that the stars would choose.

EPILOGUE

A WISE pirate once said true love was the most powerful force on earth. Yet that power had been traded for fear at every turn—simpler to wield, to dole out in equal measure. To quantify in grand gestures of gross, undeniable terror.

But in the foothills of Ardenia, fear had no place. The stars had sorted things out.

And at sunset the day after the royal bloodshed in the Itspi, Amarande awoke to streaming mountain light, and the smile of a boy she'd loved since she could form the word.

"Luca?"

"Ama." His fingers splayed across her cheeks and into her hair. An embrace. He pressed a kiss her to forehead, her nose, her lips. "Thank the stars you're awake."

Strong enough to kiss him back, she did so, moving her hands to his hair, keeping Luca where she wanted him until she realized they weren't alone.

Knowing what Amarande was thinking, Luca pulled away, his weight shifting on the bed—her bed, her chambers, her western sun. She tried to sit up, of course.

"Whoa there, the medikua might have something to say about that."

Ferdinand. Amarande blinked up at her brother, as he didn't try to stop her and ended up helping her, moving pillows about for support before bumping into the nightstand while hovering near the headboard.

Beyond where Luca sat, the warmth of his frame crowding her body, were the others.

Koldo, coming to her other side, no uniform on today—simply dressed, her hand pressed to Amarande's leg. Here, she wasn't the general. She was the only mother Amarande had known, really.

At the foot of the bed, the others. Ula. Urtzi. Osana. Amarande's misfits—pirates and orphans and spies turned to their side. They were cleaner than she'd ever seen them, rested, too, moved to standing from furniture pulled to her bedside from all corners of her chambers.

Amarande gathered herself for the answer she needed most. "Did we win?"

"We're still alive." Ula grinned and nodded. "That might be the definition at this point."

The raw throb in Amarande's thigh confirmed that. No pain without life. No life without pain. Such as it was. She read their faces, pausing on Ferdinand. "My mother?"

He swallowed and shook his head.

Gone, then. Again.

Amarande wet her cracking lips. "Taillefer—the ships? The soldiers?"

At this, Luca squeezed her hand, careful of the knife wound, still healing. "His army did not attack." Something flickered across his handsome face. "Taillefer did not make it, but I do have news from him—for later."

The princess nodded. With Taillefer there was always more. Until there wasn't. She didn't know how to feel about that. "And the Sand and Sky?"

Koldo leaned in and grabbed her other hand. "It is what we make of it, now, my queen."

The title dropped from Koldo's lips in such a way that stole the breath from Amarande's lungs. "Ardenia, Torrence"—Koldo nudged Luca with her elbow across Amarande's body—"all of the Sand and Sky. But that is for later, too."

And with that, the general stood, the salmon light of dusk catching the wisps in her dark braid. "Let us leave her to rest and have a go at a meal. The medikua will want to see her before nightfall."

The rest did as they were told, Koldo's direction as good as an order. "Medikua Aritza?" Amarande asked. "She's returned?"

"A gift from Taillefer, if you can believe it," Ula explained, adding, "though I stitched you up first."

"Stop bragging," Urtzi chided, snagging her hand. "It's time for food."

Osana laughed. "Your priorities are always intact, Urtzi." She hung on the doorframe that led from the bedchamber to the parlor,

Ferdinand hulking over her shoulder. It seemed he'd grown another inch since she'd first met him. "Rest well, Amarande."

A thread of panic caught Amarande as they filed out. Luca still sat on the bed, and she scrabbled to trap his hand between both of hers. "Wait, you're not leaving me, Luca? Are you? Take dinner with me. Rest with me. Stay with me. Please." Then she added with a hint of a smile, "My king."

Luca grinned, those eyes of his the color of sunrise on snow, as warm as the summer sunset behind. "Of course I'll stay. I'll stay until the end of time. As long as you need me, I'm here. Always, my queen."

As the Sand and Sky found new footing, midnight came quietly to the Bellringe.

The moon was high and no longer weak, the clouds gone, the night ripe with silver energy. A platinum light slithered across the summer-dry landscape of King's Crest and the Pyrenee mountains beyond, bathing everything it touched in glitter beneath a million stars.

Those stars had power too, as all in the Sand and Sky knew—the night sky marked by departed souls, looking down, watching over those below. As designed, the Bellringe's chapel's windows were especially good at capturing the glow from above, being so much closer to the sky than any other kingdom—even Ardenia.

Tonight, the windows shimmered a little more than usual.

For on the table beneath those great starborn windows lay the body of Crown Prince Renard.

Stinking of herbs and tinctures, shirtless, the gaping wound under his ribs sewn closed, skin puckering under the pull of sutures, Renard appeared just the same as when the medikua had left him days before, taking her bags and talents with her for the royal ship in the Port of Pyrenee.

Yet, in that gleaming moonlight, things were not the same at all.

No, that silver light beamed across his unshaven face . . . and the air charged, suddenly full with all the power of the stars and their peculiar magic.

And there, alone in the silence, the mostly-dead would-be king opened his eyes.

ACKNOWLEDGMENTS

This book, like so many others, was lovingly shaped during the illness, upheaval, and general chaos that defined the United States in the year 2020. I think that truth must be acknowledged first and foremost, because books aren't created in a vacuum. Just like people and places can be shaped by time and events, so can art.

Producing a book during the COVID-19 pandemic was creatively jarring, to say the least. A time of quarantine, doom-scrolling, bleeding personal and professional boundaries, and uncertainty on literally every level of life, did a major number on my work process—and I admit that as someone who is usually highly regimented in my time management and always relentlessly moving forward. Thus, this book would literally not exist without the vast help of my support network, both in publishing and at home.

Usually, when writing my acknowledgments, I thank my family last because they're my anchor, and I like the poetics of it (as a writer, I'm allowed to think like that!). But this time, they're front and center. They are always so supportive of me in all of my endeavors, but the truth is that without their help this time, whether it be by providing child care, space to work, mental breaks, or simply an ear as I talked through this very complicated tale and all my hopes for it, this book wouldn't exist. And so, I'd first love to acknowledge my parents, Craig and Mary Warren, and my husband, Justin Henning, who collectively made writing and editing a book during the hellscape of 2020 possible. And to Nate, Amalia, and Emmie, for being the cutest distractions ever. Dash, Pearl, and Camo, you too.

Next, to my team at Tor Teen, who were so gracious with my princess and her love. To my editor, Susan Chang, for your enthusiasm and patience as I tried to get this book right—your kindness, understanding, and quick turnaround (every single time!), made everything fall into place, and I'm in your debt. To Melissa Frain, for loving it first. To Patrick Canfield, super assistant, for your careful work behind the scenes. To the fantastic publicity and marketing team, including Giselle Gonzalez, Saraciea Fennell, Isa Caban, Anthony Parisi, the social team, for your guidance and help in shepherding these books into the hands of readers. To Lesley Worrell, for her gorgeous cover design and Charlie Bowater, for the fantastic cover art. To production, including Nathan Weaver, Katherine Minerva, Jessica Katz, Steven Bucsok, and Rafal Gibek. And to everyone else at Tor Teen—thank you so much!

To my agent, Whitney Ross, who is always my first and best cheerleader. Your spirit and dedication to both my work and me were a light through the storm and swagger of 2020. I'm so very lucky that you opted to come along on this ride with me.

To my strong, local YA writers group—our Whine and Wine Zoom evenings were such a bright spot in this long slog. I miss seeing your shiny faces in person. Maybe, by the time this book is out, that will be a thing again. Or not. (Sigh.)

To my oldest friend, Cory "Cass Anaya" Johnson, whose life was cut short by COVID-19 in January 2021—you shaped this story and all my others just by being your wonderful self. I miss you.

And, finally, to my readers. Thank you for coming with me—and my characters—on yet another bloody jaunt into the Torrent. I hope that this story helped you get away from it all for more than a little while.